Casey's Warriors

Ann Mayburn

"You know you're in love when you don't want to fall asleep because reality is finally better than your dreams." - Dr. Seuss

Acknowledgements

I would like to thank, as always, my readers for giving me a chance to entertain you. Without you I'd just be a dirty old woman day dreaming about men with vibrating penises. ;) I would also like to thank Kitty Kelly and Knotty Kitty from 'The Smutty Kitty' for always having my back, and my front. To my personal assistants Annette Romaine Stone and Leagh Christiansen thank you ever so much for helping me organize the chaos that is me. I hope that you enjoyed Kadothia and I would LOVE it if you left me a review and included who you would like to see the next book in the series be about; Paige or Roxy?

Casy's Warriors

Lorn Adar has searched more than a lifetime to find his bondmate—the one woman he was born to love and the only woman who can save him from the approaching madness that threatens all unbonded males of his race. When a wormhole opens from his galaxy to Earth and the women who could hold their future, Lorn will do all in his power to not only find his mate, but show her a Universe she never knew existed.

Casey Westfall's normal life changed forever when she finds the sexy leather clad man on her doorstep. One innocent kiss leads to an adventure that will span worlds and Casey will have to choose between the man who is the other half of her soul and never seeing her family or her world again. To complicate matters Kadothians live in polyamerous family units and Lorn will have to convince his Earth bride to accept not only his love, but the love of his best friend and brothers in arms or risk the chance of losing them to either the madness or the Hive—the race of sociopathic women bent on destroying and enslaving everything in their path, but Casey can't see loving more than one man as being anything other than a sin. Lorn will have to teach his bride that she was created for both of them just as they were created only for her.

In a Universe where all is possible, the battle to protect not only his people, but his heart rests on the soul of a human woman who must face the unknown and take a leap of faith that could save or destroy them all.

Chapter One

Earth

Deep in the clutches of the mid-nineteenth century poem she had to memorize for an English class, Casey absently scratched the back of her leg with her foot and tried to focus on the words before her. Unfortunately, the large quantities of spiced rum she'd consumed with her roommates last night had turned her brain into mush. It was finals week and tomorrow she'd take the last test she needed to before she went back home for the summer. She was mad at herself for getting drunk, but her roommates had all taken their last finals yesterday and celebrated the end of their sophomore year by getting wasted. In a way, it wasn't even her fault. They had guys from the frat next door physically pick her up from her porch and carry her across the street to the party.

If anything, she was a victim....ish.

Sort of.

The guys from the football team and swim team had been doing a wet sausage contest for charity. How in the world could she not want to watch a wet underwear contest? She'd been so good all semester, studying diligently instead of trying to date. She deserved a little sexy time, even if it was spent staring at drunk guys in their underwear doing the bump and grind. At the very least she'd gotten a good laugh out of it. Most of the guys were average, but there was one tall, skinny kid on the swim team who packed some serious dick. When the girls at the party saw him they went wild. Poor guy was blushing hard enough that she worried about him having a stroke.

Not wanting to think about last night anymore, she sipped the triple espresso her awesome roommate, Kimber, grabbed for her during her morning run. Unlike Kimber, Casey couldn't imagine doing anything more than stumbling around for a couple hours, in her pajamas, feeling like crap. The bitter taste of the rich coffee filled her mouth and reminded her she hadn't even bothered to brush her teeth. When she realized she'd slept until nine o'clock that morning immediate panic set in, and she stumbled to the bathroom before diving into all the crap she had to try to memorize. Her eyes were still gummy with sleep, but she forced her wandering attention on the book.

She could do this. Life was going well, but she was really focused

2

on her goal of someday managing a five-star resort in some exotic location. She sighed with longing at the thought of living somewhere other than Michigan, somewhere it didn't snow. Someplace exotic, where she could do new things, taste new foods, and give other people the kind of vacation experience they deserved. If she did well on her tests, she'd have a better chance of earning a recommendation from one of her professors that would get her into a kick-ass internship in Bali. The image of her lying on the beach was so clear for a moment she swore she felt the sun on her back.

No more shoveling snow nearly every day from December until April. No more freezing her ass off while digging her car out of the snow.

No more fish-belly pale skin nine months of the year.

Ahhhh, bliss.

But all the wishing in the world wouldn't help her pass this class, so she lightly smacked her cheeks in an effort to wake up. She was still in her pink jammies and an old sports bra, her long black hair up in a messy bun, downing the espresso as fast as she could while praying to the gods of caffeine to wake up her hung over brain. Finally, her gaze focused and stayed on the poem, her lips moving as she read it to herself.

She closed her eyes and whispered the last stanzas of the poem while chewing on her pen, striving to give the words depth and meaning; according to her professor, 'depth and meaning' were forty percent of the grade.

> *This is the way the world ends*
> *This is the way the world ends*
> *This is the way the world ends*
> *Not with a bang but a whimper.*

A chill raced down her spine; she wrinkled her nose at the odd sensation then groaned as a headache began to throb behind her eyes.

Being hung over sucked and drinking coffee certainly wasn't helping her dehydration.

She barely heard the shrill ringing of the old-fashioned, rotary dial house phone and almost got up to answer it before Kimber's voice came faintly from downstairs. Ignoring her friend, Casey tried to figure out how to put more feeling in the words and kept saying the last part over and over, unable to strike the right depth of tone she wanted. It was a rather eerie poem, and she sighed in desperation at ever getting the right tone; she thumped her head against her pillow and swore profusely.

"This is the way the world ends, not with a bang but a fucking

3

whimper."

"Casey, phone," yelled Kimber. "It's your sister."

Normally, she would have ignored the phone call—she had her cell phone turned off for a reason—but at the mention of her sister, Casey reluctantly stood with a sigh. She left her small room in the massive old home she shared with her three other roommates, deep in the student-dominated section of Ann Arbor. There were frat houses and sororities all around them, but Casey and her friends were just a group of girls who'd known each other since elementary school sharing a house. With a sigh she stretched, tugging at her top when it tried to dip down too low. While she knew she'd been blessed by the titty fairy, it still sucked that, even with a bra on, she had to cross her arms over her chest to run down the steps. The battered, sturdy stairs creaked beneath her weight as she raced through the small foyer, decorated with paintings by some of her roommate Dawn's artistic friends, to the expansive kitchen area. Kimber stood holding the phone and chatting with Roxy, Casey's sister who was home on a rare leave from the Army for the next two weeks.

Casey would start packing up the last of her stuff tomorrow, and she couldn't wait to go spend time with Roxy. Her older sister was her hero in many ways, a woman who'd managed to fight her way up in the military ranks and not let anyone stop her. Where Casey was short and pudgy, Roxy was long and lean, taking after their father more than their petite mother. Unfortunately, her sister was going through a rough patch after her divorce. The cheating fuck her sister had married in a moment of weakness got another girl pregnant while Roxy was deployed overseas. Casey had always hated his douchebag ass anyway and was glad to see him go, but his betrayal really hurt Roxy.

A sharp, almost terrified gasp pulled Casey from her dark thoughts and she looked up, surprised to see Kimber nervously pacing, holding the phone to her ear so hard her knuckles were turning white. The tall, slender half-Dominican half-Polish woman, who was on a track scholarship at the University of Michigan, always moved with a grace that reminded Casey of a cheetah. Bubbles from washing plates in the sink stood out on her honey brown skin, and one popped in the bright morning light coming in through the kitchen windows.

Without relinquishing the phone Kimber turned to Casey. Her friend's hazel eyes were wide in her pale face. "Okay, I'll pack as quickly as possible. Here's Casey."

Casey held the phone to her ear as she watched Kimber dashing

4

for the stairs, her ponytailed corkscrew black curls bouncing with her movements, before she screamed for Paige and Dawn as she raced up the steps, her long legs taking them two, sometimes three at a time.

Shaken up by Kimber's weird behavior, Casey said, "Hey, Roxy, it's me. What's going on? Are Mom and Dad okay?"

"Listen up, kiddo," her sister said in a tense voice. "You need to get home as soon as possible."

"Why? What..."

"We don't have time!" Roxy roared loud enough that Casey had to take the phone away from her ear. "Mom and Dad will explain, but you need to get yourself and your friends' asses into your car ASAP. Don't bother packing; just get in the fucking car and go! Once you're back in Chelsea, stop and get some gasoline at the gas station closest to the house. Buy and fill up as many of those emergency gas cans as you can fit in your trunk. Dad has enough bottled water in the garage to last a month, he's out at the gun shop right now getting bullets, and hopefully everything will be back to normal in a couple weeks. World's about to go to hell, little sister."

Fear made sweat break out in a harsh sting over Casey's skin as she fiddled with the long, curled cord of the old phone. "Roxy, what is going on?"

Her parents' voices rose in the background, but Roxy's clear, controlled words blotted them out. "Shit's hit the fan. I don't know who, what, or why, but I've been called up. Something about martial law being instituted."

"Should you be telling us this?" Casey whispered. "I don't want you to get in trouble."

Roxy's laugh made the hair stand up on Casey's arms. "Fuck that, you're my family and I have a feeling warning my family won't even make anyone bat an eye in twenty-four hours. Look, I have more calls to make. Just get your ass home before martial law goes public and you're stuck in Ann Arbor with a bunch of fucking hippies who suddenly can't get their non-fat, half-caf, mocha java chino, made from beans dried in the sun on the thighs of beautiful young island women. They're gonna be scared, and they're gonna get stupid. Think Lord of the Flies with Deadheads and geeks. I don't want you there when it happens. I want you home with Mom and Dad, now. I love you."

A loud click came from the line as Roxy hung up on her, and Casey stared at the wall, not really seeing the large dry-erase board filled with messages from her housemates, or the battered old fridge covered in cheesy magnets holding up pictures of friends and family.

Her mind was going so fast that her body had stalled, only her autonomic nervous system keeping her breathing.

Roxy was scared—and that terrified Casey.

Her older sister was fearless, never showing any signs of stress even when under enemy gunfire, and she had a drawer full of medals to prove it. Ten years ago, when Casey was just turning nine, she had wiped out on her bike and scraped a layer of skin from her right side. It was a bloody, disgusting mess, really nasty, so Casey didn't blame her mother for fainting when she opened the door and saw her daughter crying and looking like she'd had the skin on the side of her right arm and leg erased. Her sixteen-year-old sister had been the one who not only got Casey into the car after giving her basic first aid, but also revived their mother with smelling salts. Even when faced with an unconscious mother and a screaming, bloody little sister Roxy hadn't appeared the least bit ruffled, more annoyed with their mom fainting than anything else.

If Roxy was scared that meant shit was really, *really* bad.

"Casey!" Kimber yelled from right next to her, startling Casey into dropping the phone, now buzzing with a busy signal.

She turned and found Kimber, still in her silky pink running shorts and black tank top, standing with Dawn and Paige. Dawn, a slender, pretty redhead with a mass of freckles, stood there with her backpack and bag stuffed to overflowing with clothes and books, while Paige, a plump, cute, blue-eyed brunette, nervously chewed on her thumbnail, her bags stuffed full, but not overflowing.

Paige and Dawn were still in their pajamas, and Kimber grabbed Casey's purse off the counter then shoved it at her. "We gotta go, now."

"Yes," she whispered. "We have to go."

Dawn strode over to her and lightly smacked the side of her face. "Wake up, Casey. We need you to drive us home. You're the only one with a car."

"Right...home."

Her roommates dragged her out the front door, and as they got to the big porch with its old couch and tables still littered with the red cups from last night's drinking, she tried to turn back. "Wait! My homework."

"Fuck your homework," Kimber snarled in a low voice as she looked up and down the quiet street with its big old homes now used mostly by students. Lots of porches still bore the remains of a night spent drinking, showing that Casey wasn't the only one stressed out about finals. How many of their friends were going to be trapped here? She should run up and down the street and try to warn them,

6

but she couldn't. She promised Roxy she would get herself and her friends out.

Kimber said in a low voice, "Roxy said school was probably going to be canceled."

"What?"

By this point, they'd reached Casey's reliable old car, and her friends piled in while she went through the motions of getting in and starting the car more out of habit than rational thought. Trying to clear her head, Casey took a shuddering breath. "What did my sister tell you?"

Kimber snapped on her seat belt and ran a shaky hand over her hair. "Just that shit had hit the fan and we needed to get home."

"Do you think it's terrorists?" Paige asked in a low voice from the backseat.

They all remembered 9/11, even if they were young when it happened. Terrorists had become the ultimate boogeyman of US culture, malevolent creatures seemingly bent on destroying the American way of life. Her heart sank as she tried to imagine what would happen if they went to war again. Shit, if that happened it might be a long time before she saw Roxy.

Dawn leaned forward and growled out, "Drive."

Giving herself a mental shake, Casey returned her focus to the present. Okay, she needed to get her head on straight. She'd had her time to freak out, now she needed to get her shit in gear. She wasn't just responsible for herself, but also for the friends she loved like family.

"Right, drive. Do me a favor and call a couple of our friends. Don't waste time trying to win them over, just tell them to get the fuck out as quickly as they can and hope that someone listens. Same with your families though I'm sure my mom and dad have already contacted your parents. Maybe if they get a phone call from both of you they'll take...whatever it is seriously."

It didn't take them long to get out of Ann Arbor and head west, and they were soon on the freeway speeding past corn and soybean fields to the nearby small town of Chelsea where they'd all grown up. Thank goodness no cops were around, because Casey was doing ninety-five down the clear stretch of road in her junky old car. They all looked around as she drove, trying to find something unusual, something to tip them off to some imminent, terrible disaster. Casey had gotten over her shock, and she listened to her friends talking to their loved ones on the phone, each passing along the warning that something bad, really bad, either had happened or was about to happen. As soon as they mentioned Roxy's name whoever they were talking to would stop arguing and they would move onto the next person on their list. Evidently Casey wasn't the only one who thought Roxy was a badass.

Paige didn't have very many people to call; her only living family was her abusive, drunk father, but she'd called him anyway, for all the good it would do, then called their friends and the people she babysat for.

Casey glanced into her rearview mirror then looked over at Kimber. "Turn on the radio, see if they know anything."

While Kimber flipped through the stations with a shaking hand, finding only music, morning talk shows, or commercials, Casey took the turn into her small town and a little bit of her tension drained away. Surrounded by miles of farmland and fields, Chelsea was a very pretty place, the kind of small town that hadn't changed much in the last hundred years. Outside of town the homes were spread out, and there was a good-sized state park with a lake where she swam when she was growing up. The main street was filled with quaint shops and well-maintained buildings that the Chelsea Historical Society kept watch over, making sure the current owners didn't do anything to take away from the 'character' of the town.

As she drove down the street, she once again searched for signs of trouble among the cute shops and bright pots of blooming crocuses, but everything looked normal. If anything, Casey and her friends driving down the street in their pajamas staring at everyone was the most abnormal part of this idyllic scene. Casey's back itched, like someone was watching her, and she had to resist the urge to keep checking her rearview mirror, as though one of the Four Horsemen of the Apocalypse was trotting behind her rear bumper. That long-buried fight-or-flight instinct was kicking in, and she swore her vision had somehow sharpened.

She quickly pulled into the gas station and ran inside with her friends hot on her heels.

"Hey, Casey," Merl, the old man behind the counter she'd known since birth, said with a smile. "What's the rush?"

For a moment, she debated telling him anything, but as she paid for the gas cans she leaned forward and said in a low voice, "Merl, something bad has happened. I don't know what but Roxy told me that she's been called off of leave because the government is about to declare martial law."

He gaped at her for a moment, then began to laugh, his wrinkles bunching together as he smiled. "Good one, you almost had me going for a minute there."

Grabbing the cans she gave him one last look as she ran out the door. "Merl, I'm serious. Get your son here with your gun. If shit really has hit the fan, you're going to be mobbed with people soon."

With his admonishments about a young lady not using that kind of language ringing in her ears, Casey hurried to her car and began to fill up the gas cans, leaving the other girls behind in the store while they bought up all the bottled water and non-perishable foods that the small store had. Casey was a little over halfway done when a high-pitched, deafening squall of static came from the station's overhead speakers. The sound startled Casey so badly she almost sprayed herself with gasoline before she released the trigger on the nozzle. The fumes from the spilled fuel burned her eyes as she put the nozzle into the gas can with a shaking hand and nausea gripped her in a stomach-clenching cramp.

Dogs in the surrounding neighborhood began to bark and howl, and Casey watched in stunned horror as birds began to fall from the sky. A sparrow landed nearby, fluttering its wings weakly, tiny black eyes still focused on the sky that had just rejected it.

Three loud bursts, like gigantic flamethrowers going off all around the world at once, rent the air, and Casey screamed.

A moment later, an extremely deep, terrible noise vibrated through her forcing the breath from her body and almost knocking her to the ground. She had no idea that sound could have weight, but this did, and she would later swear the atoms in her body shook around like dry beans in a can. The sound was brief, no more than half a heartbeat, but it felt like a century. Her body rang with an echo of the tone and she dragged in first one harsh breath, then another.

The digital readout on the gas pump went wonky, the numbers racing before it blanked out completely.

Off in the distance tires screeched and the unmistakable crunch of metal hitting metal echoed in the air followed by blaring horns. She took the now useless nozzle out of the can and hung it up, then fastened the cap onto the can while trying to keep her fear from turning into blind panic. She was overcome with the need to see her parents and feel the safety of their embrace. Her heart sank as she realized she'd only managed to get twenty gallons of gas, but the urge to get home immediately filled her. As she was putting the cans into her trunk her friends ran out, their arms loaded down with plastic bags.

"What happened?" Dawn asked as she shoved the bags into the car. She was crying; her freckles stood out from her pale skin like blood on a snow bank.

"I don't know," Casey said in a thick voice, fighting the urge to just break down into hysterics. "If that was a terrorist attack I have no idea what the fuck just happened."

Paige went to jump in the car, then paused and looked around. "Looks like the power is out everywhere."

"Holy fuck," Kimber whispered and they all looked over to her, only to find her staring slack-jawed at the sky.

Following Kimber's line of sight, Casey looked out into the clear, sunny sky and gasped. Instead of the usual faultless blue, the sky was now filled with undulating waves of color. Ribbons of apple green, lemon yellow, crimson, and various shades of purple danced in the sky. It was the most eerily beautiful thing she'd ever seen.

"It's like the northern lights, during the daytime," Paige whispered. "But that's impossible."

Merl came out the front door of his store, the jingling bells drawing Casey's attention away from the sky. It wasn't like the northern lights she'd seen on TV. Those were wispy, almost ethereal-looking. These streaks of light were more like bright, sustained fireworks.

"Solar flare," Merl said in a choked voice while wiping his face with a faded blue handkerchief. "Must be a huge solar flare that knocked the power out."

From nearby came the sound of car alarms going off and she shook her head, trying to block out the background noises.

"Get in the car," Casey said in a low, choked voice. When none of her friends moved she screamed, "Get in the car!"

The four-block drive back to her house, normally less than five minutes, took ten as she drove around people who had abandoned their cars in the middle of the street to stare at the sky, forcing her to drive up on lawns and sidewalks in places. Police sirens sounded from all around town and the noise was driving her crazy. An image of what must be happening in Ann Arbor filled her mind and she wondered how bad the streets were leading in and out of the city as desperate students and commuters tried to leave. Then her imagination took a dark turn, and her stomach clenched as she wondered what was happening in the major cities. She'd learned in her sociology class that humans were, at the best of times, one step away from reverting to their primitive self, that in times of crisis a herd mentality tended to kick in; if the herd freaked out, the world would go down the shitter real quick in a stampede of fear and stupidity.

When they pulled onto her street she let Kimber off first, then Dawn, not stopping to talk to the frantic parents who cried tears of relief at the sight of their daughters.

Paige climbed into the front seat next to Casey and gripped her hand while still staring at the sky. "Do you think it's a solar flare like Merl said?"

"I don't know, honey." Some of her anxiety eased as she pulled into her driveway, the familiar flower beds and white painted porch with its terra-cotta pots filled with tulips soothing her heart. "Thank fuck we're home."

As soon as Casey got out of her car her mother burst out of the front door of their two story Craftsman home, her dark brown eyes wide as she ran down the steps. Dressed in a pair of tan capris and a cute pale yellow sweater, she looked like she was on her way to a garden club meeting rather than experiencing some kind of crazy terrorist attack.

The relief on her mother's face made Casey's nose burn. "Thank God you made it!"

Letting her mother sweep her up into her arms, Casey hugged her back. "Mom, what's happening?"

Her father came out of the house a moment later carrying his rifle, wearing his grey business suit and no-nonsense brown tie. While her mother was short and round with dark hair and eyes, her father was tall and blond, kind of like a Viking, if Vikings had been rather nerdy accountants. "Satellites are down," he said in a gruff voice. "Cable hasn't been affected but all the news stations are chasing the holes in their asses. No one knows what's going on."

"I thought the power was out?" Casey glanced up and down the still empty street.

"It's going in and out," her mother replied. "But we've got the generator. The phone lines are down, or overwhelmed, and we can't get a signal on our cell phones."

"I've got gas in my trunk," she said quickly, and Paige added, "I have food and medicine."

Casey's dad gave Paige a pleased smile that made the other girl light up. He looked at Casey. "Smart to stop for gas."

"Roxy told me to," she said in a low voice, wincing when her mother made a pained sound while her father audibly swallowed.

Gathering himself, he stood taller and lifted his chin in a defiant gesture that Casey could remember Roxy doing. "Well, we're not doing any good standing out here, and I don't know about you, but I'd feel better if we got off the street."

Neighbors were coming out of their homes here and there, yelling information to each other. More than one person yelled thanks to Casey's parents for their warning, and her father gave them a quick pep talk about keeping their family safe and coming over if they needed a place to stay.

He gave Paige a hug. "You *are* staying with us, understood? You will always have a room at our home, whenever you need it."

Paige nodded, and for once, didn't give any protests about not wanting to be a burden. "Okay."

Chapter Two

Sixteen hours later, Casey stared at the unsteady picture on the television, trying to absorb as much information as she could during one of the brief periods when they had power. A fire crackled in the marble-framed fireplace and her dad snored lightly on the couch. Her mother occasionally glared at his sleeping form when his snores drowned out the newscaster speaking with a never-ending parade of experts who didn't have a fucking clue. Paige was beside Casey on the oriental rug next to the couch, both of them lying on their backs against huge floor pillows and covered up with blankets. Thank goodness it was springtime and not the dead of winter, or they would have been in some serious trouble with the cold.

The newscaster, a pretty middle-aged woman with unstyled light brown hair and nowhere near the usual amount of makeup, visibly gathered herself. Out of all the talking heads on TV right now Casey and Paige agreed that she was the only one who hadn't given into hysterics. A few hours ago, they'd been watching one of the well-known night anchors until he'd taken a bottle of whisky from beneath his desk and began doing shots in between each clip. He'd apparently been hustled off camera during a commercial, and the weatherman took over as lead anchor.

After swallowing hard, the female news anchor said, "Though we don't have any confirmed data at the moment due to the nature of the event, it is estimated that over two thousand planes in the United States alone went down, with an unconfirmed death toll of approximately just under two hundred and ten thousand passengers and as yet unknown numbers of dead and injured on the ground at the crash sites when the burst of intense magnetic radiation came through the atmosphere and disrupted their electrical systems. Some of them crashed into populated cities, causing more havoc as the local fire departments struggled to get to the scene, blocked by people trying to flee the city."

Casey's mother let out a soft sound of dismay. "God bless the innocent and keep them safe."

"With our satellite system down," the anchor continued, "we are having to rely on old fashioned reporting. This video that we just got into the studio is graphic and unsuitable for children. I cannot emphasize enough that this is not for the eyes of our more sensitive viewers. Please have them leave the room now."

Both Casey and Paige sat up as the newscaster stared into the camera with tear-filled eyes.

A moment later the anchor was replaced by a scene that Casey had trouble understanding at first. It appeared to be the inside of a church with hundreds and hundreds of people slumped over in the pews—men, women, children, all dressed in their Sunday best. As the camera swept over the congregation Casey realized that she was looking at dead bodies, not people. Paige must have figured it out at the same time because she gasped and reached out blindly, gripping Casey's hand as the anchor explained that this was the scene of a mass suicide among a fundamental sect of Christians who believed it was Armageddon. The anchor mentioned that scenes like this were playing out all over the world and she begged those watching to not let their fear overwhelm them, that while the situation was confusing and they were facing an unknown and unprecedented event, that there was absolutely no reason to believe that it was the end of the world.

The screen abruptly went blank and Casey blinked, wondering if they'd lost power again during the rolling black outs that had been instituted to conserve energy. The government had been able to somewhat predict when the event was going to happen due to the disruption of their deep space exploratory satellites that detected the initial formation of the disturbance. Roughly two hours after the first small waves had been detected, a massive eruption of magnetic radiation had hurtled through space. Earth would have been fried, but by the grace of god her tiny little planet had been on the other side of the sun, which absorbed a great deal of the impact. Only minor damage was done to the electrical systems and soon things would be running like normal, or at least the government said it would.

Noticing that the light beside the couch where her dad snored was still on, Casey looked over to find her mother setting down the remote control with a grim look.

"Why did you turn it off?" Casey said, her voice coming out rough with lack of use.

"Because," her mother said standing, "we've been sitting here watching the idiot box for far too long without learning much of anything. It's four in the morning, Casey. The sun will be up soon and we'll get a better grasp of what's going on then. You two girls need to sleep and I'll feel better knowing you're in the same room just in case...well, just in case. I can set up beds down here for you, or you can both bunk down in Casey's room if you like, but you are going to bed."

"But what if something happens while we're sleeping?"

"Then I'll wake you up. I would prefer it if you slept together tonight like you did when you were little. It would do my heart good to know my girls are in the same place." She gave a weary sigh and helped Casey and Paige stand up. Pins and needles prickled Casey's feet and she shifted while watching her mother. "Girls, we can stand around for the next twenty years asking 'what if'. While our imagination is one of our greatest gifts, it also gets us into trouble sometimes if we don't reel it back in. I don't know what the future holds, but I refuse to believe that this is the end. Now, the only thing I do know for sure is that if you don't get some sleep you'll get sick. So, off to bed with you."

Casey and Paige exchanged a look, then shrugged. Part of Casey wanted to protest that they were both almost twenty-one and they weren't kids to be sent to bed, but her mother was right and she felt beat up from the inside out. Other than scrounging up food and using the bathroom neither of them had moved from the living room. While Paige yawned and stretched, Casey grabbed her mom's hand.

"You sure you don't need me to stay up with you?"

The lines around her mom's eyes deepened as she smiled. "And do what?"

"I don't know. I mean there are all those riots going on and stuff."

"That's happening in the big cities. You saw Mr. Hadley earlier with his posse, and Officer Jones and Officer Douglas, they're patrolling our neighborhood. After 9/11 a lot of communities started taking their disaster preparation seriously and have plans in place for how to deal with situations like this. Well, maybe not exactly like this, but you get my point. Don't worry, the National Guard is already restoring order in the big US cities where the real danger...." Her mother swallowed hard and looked away for a moment, no doubt thinking about Roxy in the middle of all that peril down in Detroit and its surrounding, heavily populated suburbs.

"She's fine, Mom," Casey said.

Paige nodded then said in her gentle voice, "Roxy is the toughest person I know, man or woman. All she has to do is glare at a looter and they would not only return what they stole, they'd clean up the mess they made as well."

"I know you girls are right, I just worry." She briskly clapped her hands, startling Casey's father mid-snore. "Now, enough dilly-dallying. Off to bed with you. The world is going to keep right on spinning through this, and no matter what tomorrow brings you'll face it better after some shut-eye."

They said goodnight and Casey went up the stairs, pausing for a moment at the top step to look back into the living room; her father was now awake and talking quietly with her mom before placing a gentle kiss on her mother's lips. She followed Paige into the bedroom where Paige had spent the night at least three times a week when they were kids, and took a moment to brush her teeth before flopping into bed. Paige appeared from her room across the hall a few minutes later, wearing a clean pair of pajamas. Casey wondered if she should do the same, but her bed felt so safe and comfortable. This house had been built by her great-great grandfather and she'd lived here her whole life. This was home.

Paige slid beneath the covers of Casey's queen sized bed then whispered, "Night, Casey."

Glad that her friend didn't want to talk about 'The Event', as Casey was beginning to think of it, she turned on her side and pulled the covers up tight.

As she drifted off to sleep the last part of T.S. Eliot's poem kept repeating in her head.

> This is the way the world ends
> This is the way the world ends
> This is the way the world ends
> Not with a bang but a whimper.

****

Casey stood beneath a stormy sky at the edge of a massive cliff of dark stone, looking out over a gray desert. Her black dress fluttered around her in the faint breeze; the only spot of color surrounding her was her hair and skin. The air tasted dusty against her tongue, and as she looked down into the sand, it shifted to form words that she couldn't quite read. A strange apathy filled her and she continued to stare at the sand, the words coming so fast they looked like meaningless squiggles all writhing together until it was as if she was looking into a pit filled with snakes squirming together in a big ball.

The desolation of this place made her soul shrink and goose bumps rise up along her skin. This was an alien world, somewhere she had no place being, a land where nothing lived on the surface. But beneath, down deep in the sand, she sensed a malevolent presence. Her mind urged her body to step back from the ledge, but her feet remained stuck to the stone like she was merely an observer in her dream. The sand moved faster now, the obscene shapes that defied logic tearing at her mind, creating pain like being stabbed in the spine.

A little whimper escaped her as tears fell down her cheeks and she prayed to God to rescue her from this horror.

The sand below began to flow upwards like a bowl filling in reverse, and she knew if that sand touched her she would die. Before it reached her, a warm wind began to blow from behind her, pushing the sand away as if it had no more weight than talcum powder. The breeze brought the scent of green things, of life, joy, and happiness. Control of her body suddenly returned to her and she managed to turn around, to be greeted by the sight of two of the most amazing men she'd ever seen.

Both wore a pair of black pants that reminded her of something a martial artist would wear, and their long, beautiful hair was loose around them.

The man on the left had silver hair that had an almost metallic sheen, silky and falling to his mid back. The deep bronze tone of his skin also shone like burnished metal, and when she looked up into his bright blue eyes her heart swelled with a sense of...completion, of finally finding something she didn't know she'd been looking for. His features were solid, almost aristocratic. There was an aura of control and power around him, an intangible sense of command combined with Alpha male dominance. In an effort to free herself from his intense gaze, she looked down, only to be distracted by the sectioned ridges of his abdominal muscles. He had the faintest trail of platinum blond hair leading down from below his naval, drawing her gaze down the sweet V-shape of his groin and ending on his very, very thick erection pressing against his pants.

Casey drew in a startled gasp. *Oh, fucking my.*

Movement came from the right and her attention turned to a man with amazing long, blood-red hair streaked with thick highlights of honey blond. It reached almost to his waist, and she bit her lower lip as she examined his stockier frame, her fingers twitching with the need to touch him, taste him, find out if his chest was really as firm as it looked, or if she would break her teeth biting the chorded side of his neck. There was a faint pelt of red hair on his chest and she had an overwhelming urge to lick him. He had fuller lips than the silver-haired man, but the rest of his features were rougher from his prominent nose to his heavy brow. Masculinity poured off of him and when she met his glowing green eyes, a full-body shiver raced over her as her nipples hardened so quickly the sensation almost stung.

For a long moment, they all stood frozen, studying each other before the men took a step closer to her almost as one. Startled, because these guys looked like football players on dinosaur-strength steroids, she took a step back only to find her heel meeting empty air. A scream escaped her as she almost fell off the cliff, reaching out blindly to be grasped by two pairs of very large, rough hands that pulled her back to safety. Pressed between them, inhaling their combined scent, her mind turned off and her body turned on. Her skin abruptly sensitized, and when the red-haired man skimmed his hands over her throat, saying something in a language she didn't understand, all she could do was sigh in delight. With the blond at her back she studied the other man, the look of arousal on his face as he stared down at her cleavage making her feel unexpectedly bold and powerful. This wasn't some dumb college guy still figuring out how to be a man; this male specimen before her was in his prime and it showed.

A rush of hormones filled her and she sighed when the man holding her against his hard chest began to run his fingers through her hair, whispering to her in a melodic language that was an aphrodisiac in itself. Tears stung her eyes as she relaxed into them, a feeling of anticipation and satisfaction tickling at her mind along with a raw, intense hunger. She tried to reach out to those feelings, to identify why they were so odd, but the more she concentrated on them the more insubstantial they became. Desperate for more, struggling to not lose this amazing connection with these unbelievably sexy men, she tried to reach out to touch them but everything was fading around her.

As the dream vanished along with her connection to the men she began to cry, screaming that they come back, that they not leave her, not now, not when she'd finally met the men she was supposed to be with. The unfairness of it caused her to break down in sobs that shook her from the inside out. Someone shook her and she tried to bat them away, wanting to be alone with her grief and the rapidly dissolving memory of her dream. It all melted away, leaving her with only a feeling of loss.

"Casey, wake up!"

With a groan, Casey opened her eyes, then touched her wet face. "Paige?"

"Oh, thank God."

She looked over and found a sleep-rumpled Paige chewing her thumbnail in the bright morning light. "You were having a nightmare, and I couldn't wake you up."

Rubbing at her face, Casey then stared at her wet hands. "Was I crying?"

"Yeah. And you kept begging someone not to leave you."

Sitting up with a groan Casey rubbed her face dry on the edge of her t-shirt. "Wow, that's weird. I don't remember what I was dreaming about."

Giving a rough laugh, Paige got out of bed and began to sort through her backpack. "Well, with all the shit that went down yesterday I'm not surprised that we both had nightmares."

Casey took in Paige's pale cheeks and the dark circles beneath her eyes. "Are you okay?"

"Yeah. I don't really remember what I was dreaming about but when I woke up I was crying. You probably heard me in your sleep and that's why you were crying as well."

The digital clock next to the bed showed that it was just after nine in the morning. Casey's mind spun as she realized that at this time yesterday her biggest fear was reading a poem aloud with feeling. She stood and went over to her window, pulling back the curtain and cautiously looking up at the sky. The ribbons of light were still there, but they weren't moving as fast and their color had faded a great deal. Among the dew-covered lawns and bushes, some of her neighbors were out on the street, drinking their morning coffee and talking in small groups. On her front concrete walkway, her mother was talking with Kimber's mom and Dawn's dad, their expressions subdued, but not as tense as yesterday.

There was a knock at the door, and a moment later, her dad popped his head in. "You two awake?"

Searching his face for some kind of indication as to what had happened while she slept she noticed that he seemed more relaxed. "Dad, is everything okay?"

"Yeah. The government has been on the news all morning. The Event was caused by something happening in the far outer reaches of space, out by Jupiter."

Paige gasped softly. "Do they have any idea what it is?"

"Oh they're spouting a lot of hot air, but what it boils down to is something happened out there, it slammed into earth and caused all kinds of trouble, and now the world is dealing with all the crazies this thing has stirred up." He looked over at Casey. "We saw Roxy on the news somewhere in the outskirts of Detroit. She looked tired, but good."

A weight eased off of Casey's mind and she let out a deep breath. "That's great, dad."

He briskly clapped his hands together. "Okay, you two, get dressed. We need to head out with some folks to Main Street to help clean up the mess. Some assholes tried to loot the liquor store and they left broken glass all over the place. Then we need to head over to the high school. Some strangers got trapped on the freeway and we need to bring them clothes and food, and see what we can do to help them out. Remember, in times of need the best way to help yourself is to help others."

With that he left Casey and Paige alone, staring at each other. Finally Page sighed and looked away before tugging one of her schoolbooks from her backpack. "Is it weird that I'm sad we're going to miss finals?"

"Yes, very weird. I think The Event might have given you brain damage."

Laughter bubbled up from deep inside Casey, pushing away the remnants of her fear as her friend started to snicker, then laugh until they were both wiping away tears. She felt much better after the laughing bout, and Paige was still snickering while she went across the hall to her room. As Casey began to get ready for the day she couldn't help but wonder if the changes to her world were finally over, or if they had only just begun.

Chapter Three

Kadothia

Enough!"

Lady Elsin Adar's shout and accompanying psychic blast of anger had its intended effect, silencing the bickering among the members of the High Congress. She smoothed her hands over the pristine white robe that almost matched her platinum blonde hair and glared around the massive chamber, making more than one Warrior look away from her ice-blue gaze. At her side, her husband, Malin Adar, stared down the few who dared to look back, his fingers caressing the hilt of the sheathed plasma sword resting beside his chair.

With a soft hiss of displeasure Lady Elsin placed her palms on the shimmering surface of the massive silver stone table that seated the three hundred delegates of the High Congress. As ruler of the richest and largest territory, the Northern Continent, Lady Elsin's political power was rivaled only by the representative from the almost as influential Southern Continent, Lady Yanush. The women were not only political opposites, they were physical opposites as well. Both women were past their prime, but where Lady Elsin was tall and pale, Lady Yanush was short and dark.

Lady Elsin stared directly at Lady Yanush and said in a voice that chilled the room, "I will not let this meeting dissolve into anarchy. There is too much at stake."

From the other side of the table, Lady Yanush stood and lifted her chin, refusing to cower before the other woman. "Then you need to open your ears and your heart to our words. To do otherwise is not only childish and dangerous, but arrogant as well."

Lorn Adar let out a silent whistle from his seat at the back of the Congressional Chambers. Sounded like the ladies were spoiling for a fight today. He, along with six of the highest ranking unbonded Warriors from his legion, were permitted to attend this meeting. They all exchanged worried looks as the two women squared off; a psychic storm building between them could lead to real trouble. His father, looking more like Lorn's brother than his sire with his deeply tanned skin and silver hair, stood and placed a hand on Lady Elsin's shoulder. While Lorn had his father's bronze skin and silver hair, he had his mother's blue eyes, but thankfully, not her temper.

"My Matriarch," his father said in a soothing tone as he discreetly stroked her back. Of Lorn's three sires, Malin was the only one who held a High Congress seat, so he alone had the unenviable task of tempering his wife's anger while Lorn's other fathers watched from nearby in the gallery. "Ladies, I would beg you to remember there are a great many unbonded Warriors in attendance."

Each woman stiffened and, on the other side of the table, Lady Yanush's husband appeared to be trying to calm her as well. Despite their fearsome reputation, the Warriors of Kadothia knew all too well it was their women who were the most deadly. Men might fight each other until they were beaten and bloody, but women went straight for the kill. The last thing they needed were two powerful houses engaging in a power struggle. There were already enough of those going on, and throughout the domed room whispers rose as alliances were formed and destroyed based on the mood of the High Congress.

Lady Yanush took a deep breath and let it out slowly, her multitude of dark braids falling over her shoulders as she bent her head in Lady Elsin's direction. Lorn actually liked her, despite the fact she was often his mother's greatest opposition. Or maybe he liked her *because* of that. "Forgive me for my outburst. It was uncalled for."

Though he could see it pained his proud mother, she nodded in return. "Apology accepted. However, that does not change the fact that the wormhole is too unstable to send our unbonded men through. They are spread thin throughout the galaxy as it is, guarding us from the Hive."

At the mention of the sociopathic race of women every man in the audience, Lorn included, made a warding gesture with their right hand, asking for the protection of the Lord of Life from their greatest enemy.

"That is exactly my point." Lady Yanush gave Lorn's mother a pleading look. "We have taken our quota of Matriarchs from all available known worlds. It will be another fifty cycles before we can once again allow our Warriors to find their mates. Fifty cycles. You and I both know if we wait that long we will lose untold men to the madness, including my sons and yours."

Lorn could feel the gaze of everyone in the room settle on him but he gave no outward indication of discomfort under their scrutiny. What Lady Yanush said was true; he was nearing the point where the madness would begin to overtake him if he didn't find his *alyah* to bond with. While he had a partial bond with a Matriarch, his soul could no longer be held together by her will alone. His impending madness was one of the only reasons he'd left the men he commanded on the battlefront and traveled to Kadothia in order to attend this meeting. As if that wasn't bad enough, his blood brother, Nast, was also slowly beginning to lose himself. Watching the man he loved degenerate into an unthinking animal would kill Lorn as surely as a blade through his heart.

Lady Elsin's sharp voice interrupted his thoughts. To most people she would sound biting, but he could hear her fear beneath her strong words. Contrary what many people thought, his mother actually did have a heart. "But if the wormhole closes..."

Giving Lorn's mother an exasperated look, Lady Yanush said, "Then at least they're stranded on a world where they have a chance to find their soul mate."

"A barbaric world," Lady Elsin sneered in disdain.

Lady Yanush smirked. "Some would consider your birth world barbaric as well, Lady Elsin, while others would find it to be the height of civilization."

His mother tensed at the veiled insult, but before she could go respond his father stood and gestured to an elderly Scout waiting in the shadows. "Why don't we give our advanced guard a chance to tell us about this planet and the potential Matriarchs it contains."

Dressed in battered tan armor, the Master of the Scout Division of Kadothia's army moved forward and carefully placed a small crystal disk on the center of the table. A moment later an enormous image of a world with blue oceans and brown and green continents cloaked in white clouds appeared before the assembly. Lorn leaned closer, hungry for a look at the world that might save his soul and that of his blood brother. Lorn and Nast shared the unique chemical combination that would allow them both to become husbands to the same Matriarch, but Nast's chances for finding a bondmate had been destroyed when his mother attempted to assassinate Lorn's mother.

Usually Warriors tried to keep the identity of their blood brothers secret until they were about to bond their Matriarch, but under threat of execution, Lorn had been forced to reveal that he and Nast were blood brothers, making it impossible for Nast to have betrayed Lorn and, subsequently, his family. They were joined together on a soul-deep level; Nast would have been unable to hide his betrayal from Lorn, and there was no way Nast could have hidden any deception from Lorn's mother. Lady Elsin could rip down almost anyone's mental walls and read their souls. Not that she needed to. They'd told her about becoming blood brothers as soon as it happened, needing not only her support, but also her formidable political protection.

It was only because of Nast's proven loyalty to the House Adar that he'd only been demoted, not executed. Either way it cost him the opportunity to seek a bride until he could earn enough points in battle again and he was even closer to the madness than Lorn. They'd fought through countless conflicts together, had been each other's sole source of affection and love in a world where nothing was guaranteed and every day was a gift that could be snatched away at any moment. For years they'd worked to build the manor that would someday house their *alyah,* and when Lorn had been injured during a fight or when it seemed like he'd never make it out of a battle alive, he would hold on to the dream of someday sleeping in safety with their beloved nestled between them, the final link that would draw them together as a true family.

He glanced over at Nast, sitting next to him, and studied the other man. His blood brother was dressed in his black officer's armor that set off his long, blood-red hair streaked with blond and his deep green eyes. Nast met his gaze and the excitement and worry he saw in his friend's eyes made him want to reassure him, to reach out through their psychic bond and send his love. In this viper's pit of politics, however, he didn't dare to do anything that might give their enemies ammunition against them. Their shielding was formidable, forged over hundreds of cycles spent together, but even the best shielding in the world couldn't protect them from the powerful minds of the Congress. So he had to settle for giving his blood brother a small nod, moving his head only a fraction while still letting Nast know it would be all right because he would make it all right.

Lorn's attention was drawn back to the center of the room when the Master Scout with his dark, weathered skin cleared his throat. "I present to you, Earth. A planet smaller than our tiniest moon with a populace of a little over seven billion."

Doing a quick calculation Lorn surmised that in accordance with the ancient Treaty of the Matriarchs, they would be allowed to take seven thousand women from the planet. His heart sank as he realized how many of his friends and fellow Warriors would lose out on the opportunity to search for a Matriarch. Thankfully he'd been a Warrior for over six hundred cycles and through his military efforts had enough points to be at the very top of the list of those approved to seek their soul mate. But even that wouldn't help if the diminutive planet didn't contain a woman who could be both his physical and spiritual mate. After all, he'd gone through three Reapings already and hadn't been able to find a suitable woman on planets twenty times the size of this place called Earth.

Drawing in a deep breath, the Master Scout said, "The people of Earth are a very young race, but they possess the characteristics of what we recognize as a civilized society. They are a mainly monogamous culture, and though there are polygamous households, they tend to remain hidden for fear of discovery and retribution from their government. Like all children of the Lord of Life they bear the physical characteristics of our race. The humans, as they like to call themselves, have a reproductive system similar enough to ours to birth our children; they are intelligent, and for the most part, honorable people." He stopped and looked around the room slowly before returning his attention to the High Congress. "Our scientists agree, these beings are a biologically compatible race to seek brides from."

A burst of conversation came from the assembled Warriors, and Nast leaned over and whispered in his ear, "If you find a bride and she doesn't want to bond more than one husband, promise me you will not jeopardize your own happiness for mine."

Nast knew him far too well and Lorn didn't even try to lie as he whispered back, "The Lord of Life created us all with more than enough love for the entire universe. I refuse to believe He did not gift the women of Earth with His greatest blessing. Have faith."

The Master Scout reached out to the crystal and adjusted it. "High Congress, I present to you the females of Earth."

Whistles and cheers rose from the audience of men and they returned their attention to the holograph as it switched to an image of around two dozen nude women. They had skin colors ranging from the deep brown to pale cream, and hair in shades of blonde, brown, and red to the rare black. Some had slanted eyes like the people of the Middle Continent of Kadothia and the highly prized dark brown eyes seemed to be common. Ranging from slim to deliciously plump, Lorn said a silent prayer of thanks that the women of this distant world were not only compatible with the Kadothian males but, even by Kadothian standards, beautiful. Their sex was shaped to be receptive to his cock, even if they were smaller than most females of the Bel'Tan galaxy. Leaning slightly forward he examined the images closely, noting the women appeared to have extra skin on the exterior of their sex, folds that looked incredibly soft and his cock stirred as he imagined taking all that tender flesh into his mouth and tonguing it. Staring at the exotic petals of the Earth woman's sex, he imagined how good it would feel to have that extra skin caress his cock as he took his female.

The Scout raised his voice above the multitude of the excited whispers, "They have the ability to form psychic bonds with their mates, but for some reason, the power remains dormant in them."

At that the crowd hushed and Lady Elsin gave the Scout a narrow eyed look. "How do we know this?"

The Scout bowed his head in her direction. "Lady Adar, with your permission, I would like to allow one of my men to testify about his experience bonding to an Earth woman."

His mother managed to hide her reaction quite well, only a slight lift in her delicately arched brow betraying her surprise. "Proceed."

The attention of the room focused on a young male of the Scout class as he made his way down from the viewing stands to the elderly Scout's side. "High Congress, my name is Nilin of House Brusk."

Lady Yanush spoke first. "Did you manage a full bonding with an Earth woman? Blessed by the Lord of Life?"

"I did, Lady Yanush."

Suddenly Lorn's father growled and the Scout paled as Lorn's mother glared at him; her displeasure spread through the air like a firestorm and sizzled along Lorn's skin in painful sparks. "How dare you shield yourself before the High Congress."

Nilin dropped to his knees while the elderly Scout stepped forward, physically putting himself between the young man and Lady Elsin's displeasure. "He is not shielding, Lady Elsin. It is a side effect of his bond with the Earth woman. It appears that bonding with her shields him from all other minds. Even the High Priestess of the Lord of Life could not reach his mind after the bonding ceremony was complete."

A shocked silence fell over the entire room and Lorn exchanged a startled glance with Nast.

Lady Yanush was the first to speak, her voice tremulous. "He is right, I cannot access his mind."

Cendor, the High Congressman representing the Islands of Tranquility stood, his green armor denoting him as a Healer gleamed in the bright lights. "You said the High Priestess blessed their union. Was she able to read this Earth woman through Nilin before she performed the ceremony?"

Nilin stood, and after the elder Scout nodded, he approached the High Congress once again. "The High Priestess was able to read my Matriarch through me, and she said that Mary, my wife, had a pure and good soul."

Lady Elsin relaxed slightly, her expression pensive. "Was your bonding different in any other ways?"

"The full bonding will not take place unless the Earth female is in love with her bondmate."

Lady Yanush blinked in surprise. "What do you mean?"

Nilin gave her a wry smile. "It means that only after Mary began to fall in love with me could I penetrate her shields. Without her trust, without her true love I would never have been able to touch her soul."

"Unheard of," Lady Elsin said in an incredulous whisper. "You mean to say you could not project your feelings to her at all?"

"Not at first. The more she trusted me and the more she allowed herself to care for me, the more I could begin to sense her." A rather ribald smile filled the Scout's face. "Earth females are very physically receptive and passionate. I found that the more I bonded with her sexually the more willing she was to allow my soul to touch hers, though she had no control of her shielding and wasn't even aware of its existence. In addition, she reacted to our sacred first kiss differently. Once the enzymes in my blood began to work on her hormones, she went into...well, a kind of rut."

One of the elder Warriors on the High Congress barked out a laugh while the Ladies of the High Congress looked appalled. "Do you mean like a Warrior's rut? Is that even possible?"

The elder Scout gave an exasperated sigh while Nilin grinned even wider. "Close to it. While she didn't go into a breeding frenzy, it did make her very, very receptive to my touch, to the point where she craved it." The Scout flushed. "While our rut is caused by our male's fertile time once a cycle, women on Earth are fertile multiple times in each Earth cycle and are not dependent on the men. They even go into heat with no males around. And they always produce nectar to ease the way if they are aroused, not just during their breeding period. Her need lessened after our first time mating, but she remains more highly sexual than most women of our galaxy. The longer we're together the deeper our bond grows and the better the sex becomes. Once you get them past their initial resistance, Earth women love pleasure and will demand their lovers take care of her needs."

It took a great deal of effort for Lorn to keep his shields in place as lust surged through him, hard and hot, swelling his cock enough that the pleasure ridges threatened to extend. He took in a deep breath, trying to distract his body from the idea of having a Matriarch's nectar available to him at all times. Just the thought feasting on his female had his libido going into overdrive. He wasn't the only one because the vast hall of the High Congress was soon flooded with a psychic ocean of lust. Next to him Nast groaned and he echoed the sentiment. He could all too easily picture one of the deliciously curvy Earth women pressed between them, muffling her cries while Nast licked her delicate sex as she sucked on Lorn's cock. Another hot rush of desire filled him through their psychic link, adding to his until he was about two heartbeats away from dragging Nast from the room and fucking him up against the wall. He glared at his blood brother; Nast merely grinned back.

With an audible sigh Lady Yanush and Lady Elsin exchanged an exasperated look and stood. Working together, they soon cleared the air of the intense emotions and the audience settled down.

"Did anyone else bond with you?" Lady Yanush asked with a hopeful expression on her dark face.

Nilin shook his head. "No, my Lady. Mary was raised to believe it is immoral and wrong to love more than one man. I tried to introduce her to other Warriors but she was very resistant. However, I will say she is slowly easing into the idea of having more than one husband. She is developing feelings for another Warrior, my blood brother, who I have brought to our bed for her pleasure. It was disturbing for her at first to know my blood brother and I shared sexual relations, but soon through our bond she grew to realize he wasn't a threat to our own love. Once she got over her misconceptions, she's grown to love my blood brother and I hope soon we will form an everlasting bond with him as well."

Lady Yanush gave a confused frown. "Why did she find your physical affection disturbing? All Kadothian men are trained to please their mates. Did you not complete your sensual training?"

Lorn had to hold back a laugh at Nilin's offended expression before the other man cleared his throat. "My Lady, I did complete my training and have never had any complaints about my bedroom skills. On their planet they are taught men or women loving those of the same gender is evil." He paused to let the shocked laughter and whispers die out in the audience before continuing. "I know it sounds absurd, but without a psychic bond she would have had no way of knowing the love I have for my blood brother doesn't make me love her any less. Imagine how hard it is to just accept that someone feels the way they do because they say it? In the Earth culture a great many men betray their woman in many ways. They lie, cheat, steal, and beat their females all while claiming they love them. They even make laws to keep their females subservient and claim their God demands this from them. It is very hard for an Earth woman to even begin to understand the concept of true love because I think very few have ever experienced it."

Lady Yanush shook her head slowly with a disbelieving expression. "How would our Warriors even begin to win their hearts if they are so guarded?"

"It is was not easy, but it is worth it." His gaze grew distant and a fond smile curved his lips. "My wife is strong, brave, intelligent, beautiful, and very loving. She is everything I ever wanted in a bondmate and a Matriarch."

The Master Scout gave the young man a nudge and Nilin's expression sobered. "Yes, right. I would caution you against sending men in teams for the initial seduction. If you approach an Earth woman as a unit she will ultimately reject one, if not both males in most cases because her upbringing insists only morally corrupt women, they call them sluts on her planet, take more than one mate. Earth women are also very jealous, so I would also advise any Warrior who mates them to cancel his contracts with his pleasure servants and remove them from his home."

Lorn and Nast exchanged a startled glance. All Kadothian homes had at least one pleasure servant per household for the Kadothian males in residence. In fact, Lorn and Nast had contracts with six different pleasure servants to service them when they were home.

One of the Lords out of Lorn's line of sight at the end of the table spoke up. "They would have jealousy issues with a pleasure servant? But why? Those women provide a valuable service that our Matriarchs appreciate almost as much as our males."

"Earth women do not understand the concept of a relationship between a man and a woman being purely sexual. They view any type of physical interaction between their bondmate and another woman to be a betrayal of the deepest kind on the male's part. Pleasure servants are considered tainted; on Earth they aren't treated with respect or dignity. When my Mary found out I had a pleasure servant at my home she almost broke our bond. It never occurred to me she would see my pleasure servant as competition for my affection, but she did, and it hurt her badly."

The same Lord made a shocked sound. "But what about when a Warrior goes into rut? I can see using a pleasure 'bot or relieving oneself with another husband when necessary, but in rut a Warrior needs a woman at least three times a day. Your Matriarch's body will break if she tries to accommodate the need. Does she not understand the death sentence she is committing herself to? We cannot control our lust while in the rut and you could very well kill her."

"Not true. Unlike the females of our galaxy the Earth woman's sheath will not swell shut after intercourse. I've had relations with my Matriarch as many as seven times in one day." He grinned. "My Mary has more than enough passion to leave me satisfied in ways I never imagined and still enough energy to pleasure my blood brother as well. There has been many a night where we make love until the sun rises. They are a lusty race, thank the Lord of Life."

Lady Elsin took a seat and shook her head while the assembled male crowd chuckled and whispered. "This is all wonderful, but we've been informed by our best scientists that the wormhole will be open for one Kadothian cycle, at most. That is not enough time to follow the sacred courting rights, especially if the brides are resistant to our ways."

Gripping her hands into fists, Lady Yanush stood fairly shook with anger. "We must at least try!"

"Try to do what? Break our sacred oath, our covenant with the planets of our galaxy? How dare you even to suggest it."

"How dare you-"

A harsh male voice rang out from the crowd. "My Ladies, if I may?"

The audience turned as one to look at Commander Trenzent as he stood outside the circle of the High Congress. While most men would have never dared to interrupt the High Congress, Commander Trenzent had both the political clout and the experience to back him up. Dressed in the form-fitting black armor of the Warrior class, he exuded danger even standing still. Unlike most Kadothian males, Commander Trenzent kept his silver-streaked black hair short, making his already scarred face even more foreboding. Lorn had fought beside him many times and considered the man a good friend and a deadly foe.

He really hoped his mother didn't do anything to piss him off.

"Proceed," Lady Elsin said with a sour twist to her lips.

Commander Trenzent made his way to stand next to the Scouts, the lights gleaming over the metallic prostheses, the result of his capture and subsequent torture by the Hive. While he could have undergone surgery to make cyborg elements blend seamlessly with his skin, he chose instead to keep the damage as a visible reminder of the very real threat the Hive posed against all living creatures. Many of the people on Kadothia who moved here from different home planets that never experienced the Hive tended to dismiss them as a threat used by the High Congress to keep itself in power. But there was no denying the prosthetic left arm and the metallic glint of the portion of his left lower jaw that had been crushed beyond repair. The fact that he remained sane and survived the torture he'd been put through long enough to be rescued made him a living legend among the Kadothian Warriors—someone not even the High Congress could ignore.

He was a big man, imposing, and when he faced off against the High Congress it was without an ounce of fear.

"I have a proposal for the High Congress regarding the females of Earth," he said with absolutely no expression showing on his scarred face, and determination radiating from his soul.

"And when did you have time to formulate a proposal, Commander Trenzent?" Lady Yanush asked in a dry voice. "As far as I was aware all information about Earth is strictly classified."

"I've learned to think on my feet," he answered, a thread of amusement mingling with the determination.

Lorn knew for a fact Commander Trenzent had spies pretty much everywhere. The Commander trusted no one and liked to keep himself aware of the myriad political and personal conflicts within the Kadothian Empire. It was, however, surprising to see him speak so boldly about such classified information, even in a roundabout way. Then again, Commander Trenzent was two hundred cycles older than Lorn and not fully bonded as well. No matter how strong a man was, the madness was inevitable, and he wondered if the Commander would try to find a Matriarch among the Earth women. Lorn couldn't imagine what kind of bride would be the general's soul mate. A rather hideous image of a beast of a female with the psychic signature of an angry *venan* bull came to mind.

Lorn's sire barely hid a smirk. "What is it that you propose, Commander?"

The mockery left the Commander's face as he grew serious. "We all know the sacred courting rights were mandated to help our Matriarchs become accustomed to their mates, but the rights were made for the women of our galaxy who were aware of both their own psychic powers and of the history of our race. They know becoming the wife of a Kadothian male means unwavering love and pleasure from their husband, along with security. It is considered an honor to become a Matriarch and it is a position that is highly coveted. With Earth women, I believe we must go a slightly different route."

"Are you saying we should abolish the Sacred Rights?" Lady Elsin hissed, her displeasure sparking through the room causing Lorn to jerk at the sensation of knives slicing at his skin. The pain faded quickly when Lorn's father soothed his mother.

"Absolutely not. I am merely saying we make some adjustments taking into consideration the stunted psychic potential of Earth females and the limited timeframe due to the instability of the wormhole. This would not be unprecedented. For the Matriarchs of Bintaina we adjusted the rights to take into account their hibernation cycle and for the Matriarchs from Nolun we altered the rights to include their twin." He met Lady Elsin's gaze head on. "My proposal is this. At their very basic level the rights of courtship were instituted so no Matriarch would be forced into a bond against her will. We use the courting rights as a way to ensure all parties are willing participants because without true love the bond is weak and will quickly fail during the trial period. From what we've learned from our Scouts we know that once the enzyme from our kiss begins to affect them, the women of Earth become much more receptive to our efforts to win their heart. While it is nice that the women of our galaxy know from the start what our intent and emotions are, Earth women do not have the same advantage. I believe in order to give them the free will we all hold so sacred, we make it mandatory the first kiss has to come willingly from the woman. The men can try to seduce it from them, but the woman must be the one to initiate the kiss."

Lady Yanush and Lady Elsin stared at each other and Lorn wondered what they were saying on their private mental link. After a few moments Lady Yanush nodded. "Agreed. Continue."

"After the first kiss, if the chemical reaction happens as it should, the Warrior will then need to give his intended bride a climax at least once before he brings her back to the Reaping ship. There the Warrior can attempt a full courting and be close enough to the wormhole that if it begins to close he will be able to make it back home, hopefully with his Matriarch."

He paused and slowly looked around the room. Lorn could see Trenzent's despair, his desperation, and he echoed the Commander's strong emotions. They'd lost far too many males with weak partial bonds to the Hive because there were not enough Matriarchs, and each death weighed on the Commander. Lesser men would have broken beneath the strain, but he remained strong. One night after a particularly bloody battle, Lorn and Trenzent had gotten drunk and the Commander revealed to Lorn the only thing that helped resolve the guilt and pain over losing one of his men was helping another man live long enough to find his Matriarch.

Finally returning the gaze to the High Congress, his silver eyes hardened. "The bitter truth is we are losing to the Hive, and without more well-bonded Warriors we stand no chance. I know every member of the High Congress is sick of having to attend the funerals of our fallen Warriors, dead because of a lack of Matriarchs. With this in mind I would also suggest we triple the number of potential brides. Because the Reaping of planet Earth will more than likely be a one-time event, as we've never recorded a wormhole opening in the same place once it closes, there is no threat of taking more women than the planet can afford to give and still remain stable. Not only do the women of Earth possess a natural psychic barrier that would protect them and potentially their offspring from the Hive, but on a more basic level our Matriarchs give our Warriors something to live for, something to fight for. Without the bond, we are all one step from madness."

Complete silence ruled the hall as every male in attendance gave the Commander their support, knowing he spoke the absolute truth.

Leaving his hands open at his side, Commander Trenzent took a step forward. Beneath his resolve was a hint of desperation. "The Hive doesn't care about treaties, or rights, or disturbing a planet's population balance. They exist to destroy, to feed, to consume. If you do not give our men the chance to find a Matriarch to either bond with or serve under, I'm afraid for not only our people, but the entire galaxy that looks to us to protect them from our greatest enemy. High Congress, I am begging you, please give our people a fighting chance."

Lady Yanush bowed her head in the Commander's direction, a sign of great respect. "We will meditate on your proposal, Commander."

For long, tension-laden minutes the assembled High Congress sat in silence, debating with each other through their private mind link. Small shifts in expression would indicate subtle emotion, but nothing obvious enough for Lorn to interpret. Instead of looking at the other members of the High Congress he focused on his mother because he knew her best. Her expression went from outraged, to contemplative, and finally resigned along with a hint of fear.

After exchanging a look with Lorn's sire that he couldn't decipher, she finally stood. "Though I am not originally of this world, I consider Kadothia my home. Like every Matriarch before me for the last ten thousand years I was brought here willingly by my husbands not only out of love for them, but also out of the need to prevent my birth planet from falling to the Hive. These human women are different. They do not know our history, our traditions, or face a threat like ours. We will need them to love our Warriors in a way none of us have ever experienced, without the truth of emotions that comes with a psychic bond."

Her gaze traveled over the audience until it fell on Lorn. A brief mental touch full of love and worry caressed his mind before she returned her attention to the High Congress. "Here is our mandate: For the women of the Earth only we will allow an accelerated version of the courting rights. Once the first, willing kiss has been achieved and the woman proves able to convert her hormones enough to bear our Kadothian children, and only after the woman has had a consensual climax with her potential bondmate, will we allow her to be taken to one of our ships. The Warrior must then win her heart through his own devotion and cunning. If he has not managed to do that in the span of sixty Earth days, her memory will be erased and she will be returned to the surface, unharmed and ignorant of our existence."

Lady Yanush stood and let her gaze travel over the audience. "We could take the entire female population of Earth and it still would not be enough to bond all eleven billion Kadothian males who are still seeking their Matriarchs. As such, we will allow three million of our highest ranking Warriors to search for their Matriarchs. Warriors, it will be your duty to try and convince your bride to bond not only you, but other Kadothian males as well if at all possible. They will of course be men of the husband's choice, but it must be done. If what the Scouts report is correct you are going to be dealing with women who will see bonding with more than one man as a sin. You *must* convince them otherwise if at all possible. If she refuses, you may of course still bond her but I do not need to remind you of the danger to yourself and your Matriarch if she heads an empty House."

A stunned whisper went through the crowd and Lorn looked over to Nast, silently promising him he would find their bride.

Nilin stepped up next to Commander Trenzent with a nervous look on his face. "High Congress, I would like to add something."

"What is it?" Lady Elsin said, an impatient expression thinning her lips.

"We aren't sure, but the High Priestess believes Earth women may be able to easily bond hundreds of our Warriors."

Lady Elsin sat with a hard thump and Lorn's shock mirrored hers. "Hundreds?"

"Yes, hundreds due to their psychic differences. One of the other Scouts bonded to a less sexually repressed Matriarch who has partially bonded forty-two other males so far with no stress on her own shields."

A stunned silence filled the hall before Lady Yanush blew out a low breath. "You say your Matriarch has only partially bonded one male, correct?"

He squared his shoulders. "I'm hoping my Mary will partially bond more men in the future, but I cannot and will not rush her. You cannot force someone to love, especially a woman."

A faint smile curved Lady Yanush's lips. "Indeed. Do not worry, Nilin, no one will try to force your Matriarch to bond any male against her will. We trust that because you love her you will work on explaining to her the necessity of bonding other males not only for her safety, but for theirs as well."

Nilin bowed low. "Thank you, Lady Yanush."

Lorn's sire stood as Nilin returned to the Master Scout's side, turning to address the audience full of Warriors. "We will release the list of those qualified to seek their Matriarch in one day's time along with information regarding the customs of Earth. The Galactic Laws of Exploration still apply. You will do nothing to draw attention to yourselves as anything other than Earth natives and will introduce no new technology or information to their world while you are there."

Anticipation filled the air and Lorn shifted in his seat, trying to contain his own growing excitement. This was the first time in over three thousand years a new source for Matriarchs had been found, and from the sound of it these brides were like none they'd ever encountered. If half of what the Scouts reported was true there would be fierce competition for their favor. While he'd never actually been in love or tried to make a woman love him, it would be cruel to allow a woman he could never love in return to care for him deeply, having a Matriarch to call his own was the dream of every Kadothian male.

He'd resigned himself to at least another fifty cycles of loneliness, to the slow, excruciating death of emotion that was the hallmark of the madness until he was nothing but a primal beast that killed without thought and had to be exiled one of the prison moons. But now, he had hope that something other than that grim fate might await him, and the men he considered brothers. He put his hand on Nast's forearm and gave it a squeeze, silently urging the other male to hold onto his sanity for just a little bit longer.

Lady Elsin stood and her troubled gaze again found Lorn's. His sire placed a comforting arm around her as she said in a slightly shaky voice, "I beg you to bear in mind the instability of the wormhole. We will be able to give you four Earth days at best to make it back to the ship once the wormhole begins to degenerate. That gives you very little time to make an Earth woman fall in love with you, but if anyone can do this it is the men of Kadothia. You have one week to learn all you can of Earth culture before the Reaping ship will depart. May the Lord of Life guide you in your quest."

Chapter Four

Nast let out a long sigh and looked out over the vast orchard that spread all the way to the river. Far beyond the border of their land, the gleaming spires of the northern capital city of Harsk rose into the sky, reflecting the brilliant oranges and greens of the sunset against the backdrop of the massive desert cliffs far beyond the city. His muscles ached and he'd long ago shed his shirt, leaving him covered in a layer of rich dust and dirt from hauling rocks out of the ground he hoped his *alyah* would someday use as a garden.

Over two hundred years ago, soon after Nast's mother attempted to assassinate Lady Elsin, he and Lorn had won this land from the former owner, a Warrior slowly slipping away to the madness. While outright war was forbidden on Kadothia, territory skirmishes were allowed when the current owner and protector of a region wasn't living up to his duties. The land that was now an orchard had been a battlefield all those years ago and the beautiful trees that bore such delicious fruit were nourished with the blood of the dead. Kadothia was a sometimes cruel and often harsh world, but it was also so beautiful it made his heart ache. He hoped Lorn's bride would like it and could learn to love both the land and the people she would rule. And he could only pray she would love him as well.

He brushed off the encroaching despair and returned to clearing the ground near the western wall of the manor he shared with Lorn. In the distance, he heard the laughter of the female servants harvesting fruit from the orchard for the evening meal, and pride filled him that he and Lorn provided a good home not only for themselves, but for the people they governed. They'd spent over two hundred cycles together building their home room by room, working hard towards making their manor a place where their Matriarch would be proud to live and giving the people of their village a place to come when they needed help. It was now large enough to comfortably house over a hundred Warriors and servants in addition to the opulent personal space for the hoped-for Matriarch and her husbands.

"What the hell are you doing?"

Nast turned to find Lorn staring at him. "What does it look like I'm doing? I'm clearing some land so your *alyah* will have a proper space for her personal gardens."

Hurt filled the fragile psychic bond they'd managed to establish between each other and Lorn shook his head. "Our *alyah*, Nast. Always ours."

Clenching his teeth he began to ease a boulder out of the dark soil. "I told you, you stubborn bastard, if you mess up your chance for a bondmate by pushing her to accept me as a husband before she's ready I'll slit your fool throat myself. And that would really piss me off considering how much time I've invested in keeping you alive. Now are you going to stand there like the spoiled ass you are or do you think you can get your hands dirty with me?"

Stripping off his shirt Lorn growled at him. "You know we have machines and servants that will do this."

"Right, but I want the land to know our touch."

"Ignorant farmer," Lorn muttered and Nast grinned at the familiar insult.

"Pampered city boy," he shot back.

Lorn shook his head, his silver hair gleaming in the setting sun. They managed to rock the boulder out of place and roll it off to the side where it would later be crushed up to make gravel for the flower beds. Lorn leaned against the stone and crossed his arms over his broad chest, drawing Nast's gaze to the sweat trickling down the chiseled sections of his abdominal muscles to the tight fit of his blood brother's pants. With so few women available, the men of Kadothia often turned to each other for release, but his feelings for Lorn had gone beyond physical long ago. They'd formed as close a bond as two men could without their Matriarch to complete them. Lorn was not only his lover, he was also his best friend—the one man in the Universe Nast could trust without any doubts.

"Come here," Lorn said in a gruff voice and held out his arms.

Normally, Nast would give Lorn shit about such a public display of affection; they had their reputations as fierce Warriors to maintain, but his blood brother would be leaving tomorrow for Earth and Nast missed him already. Though they'd been separated many times they'd always come home to each other. Now he might lose Lorn forever, yet he couldn't resent the other man for leaving. If their situations had been reversed, or if his blasted birth mother hadn't been such a greedy, envious bitch he would be the one going to Earth on what might be their last chance to find their bondmate— the one woman in the universe meant only for them.

He turned and leaned back against Lorn, the other man slightly taller than him, and inhaled his rich scent. His blood brother wrapped his arms around Nast and together they looked at the home they'd built from the ground up. In traditional northern Kadothian fashion it was four levels with graceful spires and balconies that were situated to enjoy the warm breezes blowing off the distant thermal river. Made of shimmering white stone, it was strong enough to withstand the fiercest of winter storms yet open to allow the natural light in. Their blood and sweat had gone into its construction all with the hope of someday gifting it to their bride.

"I dreamed of her last night," Lorn said against his cheek as he stroked Nast's chest.

"What?"

"Our Matriarch. I dreamed of her."

Excitement lit through Nast's blood. "A true dream?"

"Yes." Lorn sighed. "I couldn't really see her but she had beautiful dark hair and generous breasts. I think she was also small. In my dream I had to pick her up to kiss her and she was so soft."

Chuckling, Nast turned his head and gave Lorn's neck a gentle nip. Their physical love had always been rough—that is how it was between Warriors—but Nast hungered for the time when he could be gentle as well. Having a Matriarch would allow him that, a soft body to hold against him, a woman's tender heart and love filling their home with life. "And what made you think it was a true dream?"

Lorn moved and pulled something out of his pocket. Nast looked at what appeared to be a torn piece of gold cloth. "What is that?"

"Smell it."

Curious, Nast took it from him and brought it to his nose, inhaling deeply. Instantly the delicate aroma of a woman filled him, but not just any woman. The most delicious female he'd ever smelled. Her scent was reminded him of the essence of life, of warm sunshine and the air after a cleansing spring rain, mixed with hot passion. He greedily pulled in one lungful, then another, his heart racing as her fragrance roared through him. "Where did you get this?"

"Her fragrance was on my hands when I woke up after my dream as if I'd been holding her in truth. I wiped it off quickly on the sheets so I could preserve it." He closed Nast's hand gently around the silken scrap. "The Lord of Life sent this dream to me for a purpose, Nast. Keep her scent with you when I'm gone and know I will bring her home for us."

He wanted to fight, to argue, to do the noble thing and demand Lorn bond her no matter what, but with her natural perfume still filling his nose he couldn't protest. His soul cried out for the mysterious woman who carried this scent and he drew in a shuddering breath, holding the cloth to his face. She smelled sweet, and soft, and there was a hint of arousal beneath her natural fragrance. His cock hardened and Lorn's dick began to swell against his back.

"Smells good, doesn't she?"

"Like everything pure and beautiful."

Lorn began to kiss and lick the side of Nast's neck and he groaned deep in his throat, the scent of their bondmate lingering in his nose and starting a fire in his gut not even his blood brother could quench.

Though Nast was more than eager for him to try.

Twisting in Lorn's arms, he attempted to pin the other man to the stone, the savage need that ripped through him urging him to play the dominance games they both enjoyed so much. The urge to make the other man submit wasn't as much a matter of true dominance and submission, but more like a game that catered to a Kadothian male's instinct to conquer. They were almost equally matched in terms of strength so it made the struggle between them all the better.

Nast went to grab the cloth back but Lorn growled against his lips and he snarled, crushing his mouth to Lorn's and reveling in the taste of his blood brother. If their *alyah* tasted like life, Nast's blood brother tasted like fire and heat, the energy that powered the universe. With a quick move Lorn managed to flip Nast over onto the stone, his back rubbing against the rough surface but his tough skin kept him from getting scratched.

The scent of male sweat filled his nose, and as he struggled to push Lorn off, he shoved the scrap of silk into his pocket, wanting to protect her scent to keep him company during the long days that Lorn would be gone. Nast would have to return to the battlefield, and for the first time he feared for himself, for his safety rather than the lives of his men. He and Lorn were so close to the moment they'd been born for, the woman they'd been made to love beyond all reason. The Lord of Life wouldn't be cruel enough to kill him now, but if it was his time to move onto his next life he would go knowing Lorn would be happy. There wasn't a doubt in his mind Lorn would bond the little Earth woman who haunted his dreams.

Leaning up he savagely bit Lorn's neck, hard enough to draw blood.

With a roar, Lorn threw him off and Nast twisted midair, landing on his feet and snarling. The taste of Lorn's blood filled him and his body gave an answering surge of arousal. With his cock aching he deliberately licked his lips and a rough surge of lust came through their bond. It reminded him of the first time he'd tasted Lorn's blood during the ceremony that bound them together as blood brothers. Even then the wild taste had driven him insane and they'd barely made it back to their barracks before falling on each other in a fury of need. Time hadn't tempered their desire, only deepened it.

Lorn made a beckoning motion. "Is that the best you can do?"

Growling, letting the beast that lived deep in his soul slip its leash, he leapt at Lorn and the other man grabbed him about the waist before slamming him to the soft earth. His breath escaped him in a harsh grunt and he arched as Lorn pinned him then ground their cocks together; Nast's bollocks drew up tight as their lust twined together, two fires feeding each other until it was a burn threatening to consume them both. He met Lorn in a kiss full of teeth and tongue, rolling as they grappled together.

With the snarl of fabric parting, he tore at Lorn's pants, eager to get to his bloodmate's hard body. Lorn tried to buck him off, but he clung tight, managing to slide one finger between the tight crease of his blood brother's buttocks. For a moment Lorn arched against him, a small shiver working through his body, before he began to struggle again. Though they switched up who gave and who received, the need to fill Lorn with his seed consumed Nast. He wanted to know the embrace of Lorn's body, needed to lose himself in their love.

"No," Lorn ground out and he groaned when Nast managed to free one of his hands to rip the front of Lorn's pants open, exposing his cock.

"Yes." He rubbed his hard abdominals against Lorn's dick and gave the other man a savage snarl as Lorn's precum wet his skin.

To his surprise Lorn managed to twist out of his hold and straddled Nast's shoulders, reaching back with one hand to rip open his pants while shoving his cock in Nast's face. Lorn rubbed the wet tip against Nast's lips and he tried to buck the other man off. Grabbing Nast's ridged shaft, Lorn gave it a good squeeze.

"Suck me or I'll tear your dick off."

"No, you will not," Nast panted as he continued to struggle. "You like it too..."

Before he could finish the sentence Lorn shoved his dick into Nast's open mouth and he eagerly swallowed the other man's hard length, sucking at the thick mushroom head before running his tongue over the pleasure ridges lining the shaft. Those quarter inch ridges remained dormant until a Kadothian male was near his orgasm, then they would vibrate as they filled with his seed. The sensation of Lorn's vibrating shaft in his ass was one of Nast's favorite things, but he was determined to have the other man. So he sucked at Lorn with long, greedy pulls until Lorn's attention began to waver. The lust coming from his blood brother had Nast thrusting up into the other man's hand, straining for a tighter grip, a harder stroke.

Groaning deep in his throat, Lorn fucked Nast's mouth and when Nast felt the first quiver of the pleasure ridges filling he moved lightning quick, knowing Lorn would feel his intent through their bond. With a shout he managed to roll Lorn over and he placed his hands between the other man's shoulders, effectively pinning him as he rubbed his dripping cock over the tight crack of Lorn's ass.

"I suggest you settle down," he growled while Lorn bucked beneath him, "Or I am going to take you hard and rough without opening you first."

The blast of desire had Nast shuddering even as Lorn attempted to unseat him. "Fuck you."

Grinning, Nast slid one thigh between Lorn's, spreading the man enough that he could fit the head of his shaft over the sensitive entrance to Lorn's body. "No, fuck you."

They both cried out as Nast began to work his way into Lorn's ass, the abundant precum lubricating enough that he wasn't tearing Lorn, but he was making the other man hurt. Pleasure and pain became almost the same thing when they were this aroused, and Nast opened their bond as much as he could, pouring his love and devotion into Lorn even as he savagely entered his body.

Lorn stilled beneath him and relaxed slightly, tilting his ass up for better penetration while he sent his love and devotion back. A sense of determination filled the other man and Nast let out a low groan, sinking all the way in until his balls rubbed against Lorn's. Lord of Life, the tight clasp of his blood brother's body felt good. He couldn't even imagine the ecstasy that would come from mounting their bondmate together. The thought of her sweet, delicious scent had him lifting one hand to grab the scrap of cloth from his pocket while Lorn shoved his ass back at him, demanding more, harder.

He leaned forward and covered Lorn with his body, moving so their faces almost touched then placing the scrap of cloth between them. They groaned as one when the feminine perfume filled their senses, each of them jerking and straining against each other. Nast's desire doubled, tripled, as he took in her scent mixed with their own combined musk.

"When we bond her I will take you like this while she watches, tied to our bed and unable to touch us, making her come from our bond alone. I'll tie her legs spread wide as well, keeping her slick, sweet flesh open to us but not letting you lick her while I fuck you."

Lorn groaned and clawed at the ground while Nast took him harder, their flesh slapping together. "I'll make her ride your face while I fuck you, make you shove your tongue into her sweet pussy while she covers your face in her nectar. Imagine it, blood brother, how good it will feel when she completes our family, how perfect it will be."

No longer able to speak past his lust Nast savagely ground himself into Lorn's willing body, loving the strength, the honor and trust coming from the man taking him so perfectly. They worked together for their release, each man now growling in a long, continuous stream that blended together until it felt as if the earth was shaking around them. The fucking amazing vibrations started along his cock and Nast pushed himself up, the scent of their *alyah* lingering against his nose while he hauled Lorn's ass up and battered his blood mate with his cock. Everything inside of him tightened, hardened and yet relaxed as his orgasm approached. With their bond fully open he could feel Lorn's body readying for his release as his lover ground his shaft against the soft grass of what would someday be their Matriarch's garden.

He couldn't think of a more perfect way to bless the ground than with their release. Pulling out he quickly rolled Lorn over and grabbed his blood brother's throbbing erection before fisting his own aching cock. Looking into Lorn's brilliant blue eyes he jerked them off together until the pleasure became too much and he threw his head back, roaring out his pleasure while Lorn did the same, their combined seed splashing over Lorn's stomach as wave after wave of pleasure crashed into him and tore him apart.

Collapsing onto Lorn he rolled over onto his side and with a shaking hand scooped off their pale lilac seed and spread it on the grass between them.

Lorn smiled at him, his voice shaky as he said, "Blessing the garden? You can take the boy off the farm but you can't take the farm out of the boy."

Chuckling, Nast continued to anoint the earth with their combined passion. "Yeah yeah. Just because you city dwellers have forgotten how to thank the Lord of Life for his gifts doesn't mean all of us have. I want this to be her place of refuge, Lorn. I want her to be able to come here when the stress of the world becomes too great, so she can lose herself in the peace and beauty we'll make for her here. I know you think my western continent traditions are foolish, but I know how hard it is for the brides of our galaxy to leave their homes, let alone one that has no idea we even exist. I want her to love Kadothia as much as we do, to find comfort in it because she's going to be so far from her home world."

Lorn blinked at him for a moment before clasping him tight. He pressed the scrap of cloth into Nast's hand. "We will be her comfort, Nast. We will love her so often and so well that she will never know a moment of loneliness. And we will never have to leave her, never have to return to the battlefront because keeping her safe will become our world. You just need to keep your foolish ass alive long enough for me to win her heart."

"Don't worry. I'll be deep in the safe zone babysitting new Warriors."

"It would be just my luck that you would be killed by some stupid child dropping his weapon and discharging it at your head."

They chuckled together and Nast stared at Lorn, committing his blood brother's face to his mind. Born of the elite ruling class of Kadothia, Lorn had the refined features of his ancestors, a square jaw and high cheekbones along with full, sensual lips. His dark skin set off his brilliant silver hair, and the shifting blues of his eyes always entranced Nast. He was beyond lucky the Lord of Life had seen fit to gift him with such a good man as a blood brother. He considered the rumors the Earth women, who had been bonded by the advance Scouts so far, reacted very negatively to taking on a second husband. Scout Nilin's bond had almost been broken because of his bondmate's horror at the thought of taking a second husband, and even worse, another Scout had lost his bride before a bond could be formed because she couldn't accept two men loving each other as anything other than a sin. That Scout had taken his own life as result and his blood brother followed him soon after.

He would not let that happen to Lorn.

Nast closed his eyes and rubbed his cheek against Lorn's head, their silver and blood red hair blending together in the soft breeze. Lowering his voice even though no one was anywhere near close enough to hear them he said, "I'm afraid, Lorn. I've waited so long, wanted and dreamed of her for so long, but what if she can't accept more than one husband? It would hurt but it would flat out kill me if you let that come between the two of you. You must promise me you won't push her into anything she doesn't want to do."

Fierce determination with a hint of apprehension came from Lorn through their still wide open bond. "Don't be afraid, because she will love us, both of us."

"How do you know?"

Pulling back enough so he could look Nast in the eye he brushed his thumb over Nast's cheek. "I know because the Lord of Life created us all with an endless capacity for love. She's just been raised on lies. Once she sees the truth, once she feels how right it is, she will love you as well."

"But..."

"No, no buts. I will go slowly; I will take my time with her and I will win her heart for both of us. You were created to be my blood brother and she was created to be our *alyah*. It will work."

The faintest hint of worry and doubt came from Lorn and Nast closed down his side of the bond to hide his shock. Lorn was the most confident man he knew, and rightly so. His blood brother led the 98th Legion to victory after victory, getting them out of situations that would have led to their slaughter under a lesser man. Shit, they'd faced down an army of Hive mercenaries, with no more than two dozen men and a damaged gunship, and come out alive. To feel his lover doubt himself gave Nast the strength to let go of his own worries.

"I know you will. You're right. The Lord of Life created her for us and us for her. One cannot argue with the will of the Creator."

Lorn closed his eyes and pressed their foreheads together as the sun slowly set over the distant horizon. "I will miss you."

Swallowing back a lump of emotion Nast hugged him closer until no room was left between them. They held each other like that, the songs of the night birds filling the air while the darkness overtook the horizon. He drew in Lorn's scent and smiled when his blood brother brought that tiny, insignificant bit of fabric between them that held the very real scent of the other half of their souls.

Their Matriarch, their bondmate, their *alyah*, a simple word of affection that meant their eternal beloved.

Chapter Five

Casey Westfall tried to keep from staring at the huge, scary, unbelievably hot guy who walked through the automatic front doors of the small grocery store on the outskirts of Chelsea, Michigan. The night was exceptionally warm for late May, bringing to mind going to the beach and summer barbecues. So when an enormous man with hair so blond it was almost white hanging past his shoulders, dressed in a full length black leather trench coat, black leather pants and a black shirt came striding into the store all of Casey's internal alarms went off.

While life had returned to what passed for normal, and they didn't have to worry about gangs of looters trying to rob the place, she couldn't help a little shiver of fear. There was something so...commanding about this man. Totally intimidating and not just because he was über hot in an unusual way. With his deep tan and startlingly blue eyes, he was at once the sexiest and scariest man she'd ever seen. He moved with a startling grace despite his large size, and she had to stop her gaze from drifting down to see what he was packing behind those tight leather pants. As he got closer she returned her attention to his face and met his electric blue eyes. Danger seemed to radiate from him, and when their gazes met, she stepped back with enough momentum to bump her hip on her register.

It looked for a moment as if he was coming right for her, and her heart slammed against her ribs as she wondered if she could make it to the hidden alarm before he pulled a gun out of his long trench coat. He stared into her eyes and she swore something close to elation lit his face, turning him from handsome to a downright sex god. Even in the crappy florescent lighting his hair gleamed with hints of the purest silver and she found herself drowning in his bluer than blue eyes. They were so neon bright, so perfect that they had to be contacts. Then he licked his lower lip and her body gave an answering surge of raw lust, which knocked her out of her stupor.

She looked around for her useless night manager, Jerry, but only saw her friend Kimber over at the next register looking equally dazed. When Casey turned back she found the stranger had moved off into the produce section and out of sight. Disappointment surged through her even as she let out a sigh of relief the night hadn't started off with a robbery. Working the late shift at the grocery store sucked ass, but it was better than being unemployed. It gave her the money she needed to live on when she returned to college full-time in the fall.

At the next register, Kimber fluffed her soft black curls, a blush warming her light brown skin, and stared at Casey, her eyes as wide as Casey had ever seen. "Holy. Fucking. Shit. Did Thor just walk into our grocery store?"

"I have no idea." Casey tried to stand on her tiptoes to see if she could find Mr. Sex-on-a-Stick, but at five foot three she didn't see much of anything other than the endless rows of shelves.

"Do you know him? You must know him because he looked like he was about to jump in your panties."

"No...not at all. Trust me, I'd remember someone like him. Holy fucking shit, indeed."

Casey rubbed her face and wished she'd done something with her hair other than tie it back in a dark, lumpy bun. Then again, she wasn't exactly the kind of girl men lost their shit over. Short, chubby, with baby cheeks that never seemed to go away no matter how much she dieted and exercised. Yeah she had a nice rack, but that guy had been supermodel material.

Kimber leaned over the empty conveyer belt between them with a grin. "Do you think he's a movie star? Maybe I should get my phone out and take pictures. We could sell them to some gossip rag and have enough money to go on vacation. You know, a real vacation. Where we have to pack a bag for more than one day. Hell, with everyone still afraid to fly and tickets being super cheap we could probably go to Australia for three hundred bucks."

After The Event, many airlines went out of business as people swore never to fly again. As a result, more and more people were taking mass transit to go places. And the cruise ship industry was seeing a huge surge in business. The memory of all those planes falling from the sky still haunted the public's mind. Casey figured if she was going to die it was just as likely to happen on the ground as in the air so her family had taken advantage of the cheap flights to fly down to Texas to visit relatives. One positive side effect of the natural disaster was that people seemed to spend more time with their families now and Casey made it a point every chance she got to tell her friends and family how much she loved them.

Too bad she didn't have anyone to share her love with. Someone who would be there when she went to sleep at night, someone who would hold her tight and murmur sweet nothings in her ears. A man who smelled as good as he looked and had the most amazing eyes.

Still disconcerted by the memory of the man's shimmering blue eyes and the raw lust she must have mistakenly read in them, Casey shrugged, then squatted down and pretended to rearrange the plastic bags beneath the counter. "With our luck he'll turn out to be some wanted criminal who will stalk and kill us for your camera phone then make a dress out of our skin." She giggled and said in a terrible accent, *"It puts the lotion on its skin or it gets the hose again."*

When Kimber didn't respond and the conveyer belt of Casey's register started up she closed her eyes and prayed to the gods of nerdy girls everywhere that fate wasn't taking a crap on her yet again. Dread filled her stomach as she slowly stood and when she turned and found Mr. Sex-on-a-Stick staring at her intently she cringed. Hoping he didn't know they were talking about him, and that he didn't hear her terrible impression, she pasted a big, fake, and she was sure was a somewhat creepy smile on her face and tried to still the trembling in her hands. He was at least a foot taller than she and big enough to make a pro-football player look like a wimp.

And so unbelievably hot it made her mouth dry and her panties wet.

"Good evening, Casey," he said in an accented voice that moved through her like a caress.

Dumbfounded, she stared up at him while randomly grabbing whatever the hell he'd put down on the conveyer and scanning it. "What?"

For a moment he frowned and she swallowed hard. "Is that not how you greet each other? Good evening?"

Movement behind Mr. Sex-on-a-Stick caught Casey's attention and she flushed in mortification as she caught Kimber taking pictures of them with her cell phone. The embarrassment helped clear her head enough to realize she'd scanned the same item four times.

"Oh, crap," she muttered, then blushed even harder. "I'm sorry. I'll fix that right away, Sir."

"Lorn."

"What?"

"My name is Lorn, and your name is Casey."

"How did you know that?"

With an amused smile he slowly reached over the counter and gently lifted the ugly green vest all the employees had to wear. Though his fingers never actually touched her skin she swore his body heat burned through her clothes. "Your identification tag. Casey Westfall."

Her brain refused to work until he withdrew his touch, and once

47

he did, she was pretty sure her panties were soaked. God, the way he said her name, it was like he was slipping his hands down her pants and stroking her pussy. "Oh, yeah. Uh, nice to meet you, Lorn."

He smiled at her and his nostrils flared. The blue of his eyes darkened and he abruptly shoved his hands into the pockets of his trench coat. "You honor me."

Utterly thrown for a loop by this blond sex god she forced her gaze off of him and managed to focus on the cash register. To her utter embarrassment she noticed she'd fucked up his order so bad that she'd have to call her manager. Great, having Jerry, the sexist asshole, cut her down in front of a customer always made a great impression. Wishing the floor would just open up and swallow her whole she closed her eyes and took a deep breath before facing Lorn.

"I'm sorry, I've made a mistake on your order. If you'll give me a moment I'll have my manager come fix it."

"There is no need to alert your superior."

His odd speech reminded her of the way her German grandfather spoke; it suddenly dawned on her that all of his peculiar mannerisms must be because he was foreign. "You're not from around here, are you?"

He tensed for a moment, then slowly nodded. "That is correct. I am from Europe."

Poor guy, no wonder he looked and acted so out of place. People came from all over the world to attend the University of Michigan or work in Ann Arbor so she was used to getting all kinds of people renting homes in her small town. Empathy for him made her relax and she picked up the phone to call her manager. "I'm so sorry about this, Lorn. Just give me one second and I'll fix it for you."

The bemused smile he gave her made her want to giggle like an idiot. He really was too good looking to be real. She had no idea what part of Europe he was from, but holy moly, did they grow 'em hot over there. After a brief conversation with Jerry, the douchebag night manager, she hung up the phone and smiled at Lorn. Not even the thought of Jerry trying to rub his dick against her ass while he fixed her order could dampen her sudden happiness.

"So what do you think of the States?"

"It is very...different."

"I bet."

His gaze turned intense again and her conversation skills ran away with her mind when he leaned over and brushed a stray strand of her hair back from her face. "You have the most beautiful eyes, they remind me of *benali*."

"What's that?"

He stroked her cheek and she had to lean against the counter as her knees went weak from desire. Looking into her eyes, he continued to trail his big fingers lightly down her jawline, and the scent of leather from his coat and whatever awesome cologne he wore overwhelmed her with the need to tear his clothes off. His voice lowered further until he was practically purring his words. "It is a rare gem in my...country. Very expensive and sought after for its exquisite brown color. Your eyes are like it...shades of brown and gold swirling together. Stunning."

"Casey, what's going on here?"

She jerked away from Lorn's touch and turned to face her irate manager. Jerry was the youngest son of the family that owned the grocery store and an all-around prick. He'd been a few years ahead of Casey in high school and had been a spoiled asshole even back then. After failing out of three colleges his family finally gave him a job at the grocery store where he lorded over everyone like he owned the place.

For the last three years, Casey had worked here during her summers off from the University of Michigan and got along well with the owners of the store, but Jerry seemed to have it out for her. It probably didn't help she'd turned him down repeatedly for dates. As if she'd ever go out with a guy she'd once overheard saying he dated fat chicks because they were easy.

Now his mean little face was flushed red enough that his spiked, gelled, and bleached blond hair stood out in an almost comical manner. While the rest of the employees wore the store uniform, Jerry always dressed like he was going out clubbing. Tonight his ensemble included a shiny blue shirt that stretched too tight over his steroid-built muscles and enough gold chains to make Mr. T jealous.

"I'm sorry, Jerry..."

He narrowed his eyes at her. "I told you to call me Mr. Hebbles. God, can't you do anything right? I have better things to do than come over and fix your screw ups."

"Sorry, Mr. Hebbles, I mis-scanned some of this customer's items. I need you to clear them off the bill please."

Jerry smirked at her then turned to look at Lorn and he suddenly blanched. Alarmed he was going to pass out, she moved to steady him but a low growl stopped her. Her jaw dropped open as she realized the almost subsonic rumbling noise was coming from Lorn. When she turned to face him she found the big man glaring at Jerry hard enough to make the other man shake.

"You are disrespectful to Casey. That is unacceptable. Apologize." His lips curled back from his teeth and she swore his canines were longer than usual. "Now."

"Sorry!" Jerry squeaked. He jerked the manager's key off his hand so hard it left scrapes on his knuckles and practically flung it at her. "Here."

With that, he fled, leaving her with a man who watched Jerry's back with murder in his eyes. When he turned his attention back to her his gaze softened and he made a soft, almost pained noise. "I scared you. I am sorry."

She shoved the key into the register with trembling fingers and cleared his order as quickly as possible, too shaken to even look at him. "No, no, it's okay."

Bagging his items as quickly as she could she said, "Your total is thirty eight dollars and ninety-five cents."

He used the credit card machine to pay for his items and when she finally looked at him he appeared so sorrowful that some of her fear seeped away. "I am sorry for frightening you, Casey. You must understand that among my people we hold Matri...women in the highest regard. To see him so blatantly disrespectful to you is unacceptable."

She let out a shaky laugh as his receipt printed out along with some coupons. "It's okay. I mean he isn't that bad, kind of a jerk, but I've dealt with worse."

Anger flared in his expressive glowing blue eyes again but he took a deep breath and visibly calmed. "I suppose you will not tell me the names of the men who have offended you, will you?"

"Why?"

"So I may defend your honor." Her jaw dropped slightly and he chuckled. "I take it that is not custom here."

"Uh...no. I mean not for a long time. I guess guys in the old days used to do it but not so much anymore. Chivalry is dead and all that."

He looked confused as she handed him his bags with the receipt inside. "What is chivalry?"

"It was like a code of honor knights used to live by. You must know what it is, but they probably use a different word in your language."

"I will research it when I return to our base, I mean, my home." He ducked his head the slightest bit so he was looking at her through his dark gold lashes. "May I call on you?"

"What?"

A line formed between his eyes, then cleared. "Dinner, may I escort you to dinner?"

"You want to take me to dinner?"

"Yes."

He grinned at her and she couldn't help but smile back, then sobered as reality intruded. Sex gods did not ask geek girls out. "Why would you want to take me to dinner?"

"Why would I not? I am new to the area and would enjoy the company of a local woman so I may learn about this place."

Whatever silly hopes she'd had that this would be some kind of romantic dinner were quickly dashed as she realized he was just a lonely guy looking for a friend. Casey didn't know what it was about her, but she'd had more than her fair share of guys wanting to 'just be friends'. Trying to hide her disappointment she nodded. "Sure, sounds great."

"Thank you, Casey." He leaned forward and looked directly into her eyes. "Tell Jerry that if he ever disrespects you again I will find him and make him pay."

"Uh, okay."

This close she could smell his breath and its scent was unlike anything she'd ever experienced. Wild, rough, spicy, and utterly delicious. It was as if everything masculine had been distilled into one arousing aroma. She wanted to bite him, lick him, and kiss him until they passed out.

Before she could do anything stupid, Kimber walked up next to her with a too bright smile on her face. "Hey, Casey, Jerry called to say he needs you back in receiving to help the stock boys with an incoming shipment. And he needs his key back."

Casey jerked back from Lorn like she'd been stung and nodded so rapidly she probably looked like a bobble head doll. "Okay, right. Um...nice meeting you, Lorn."

Before he could speak she took off at a pace just under a run, her heart hammering in her chest while her body screamed at her to go back to that big hunk of man meat and climb him like a tree.

Five hours later at a little past one in the morning, stinking like the spoiled shrimp she'd spent the last two hours clearing out of a broken down freezer in the back of the grocery store, Casey dug through the plastic bag where she'd put her purse looking for her keys. Her clothes were stained with rotten shrimp guts and she had a bunch of empty plastic grocery bags to put over the seat of her car so she didn't ruin the upholstery.

Her back ached, her stomach kept threatening to empty itself, and she was pretty sure Jerry was going to make every moment of her life at the store as shitty as possible before she returned to school in the fall.

The lights near the back of the lot flickered weakly as she neared her elderly sedan that had seen better days but still chugged along. Despite the late hour she was keyed up over her earlier encounter with Lorn and the memory of his—well, shit—everything. Kimber had come back a couple times to show her pictures she'd snapped of Lorn and Casey talking, much to her dismay. Seeing an image of them together, with Casey staring up at him like some love struck idiot, only pointed out how very far out of her league he was.

He was perfect. Absolutely perfect. From the top of his white-blond head to the bottoms of his ass-kicking black motorcycle boots, the man was a walking advertisement for everything hot and virile. Well other than his overly long canine teeth, but it was better than him missing teeth, as some of the people of her small town did. And his breath...she wondered if he tasted as good as he smelled.

While enjoying a rather vivid daydream of licking her way along Lorn's body and finding out if his carpet matched his drapes, her gaze wandered to the anomaly in the night sky. Deep in the far reaches of space a brilliant point of light flared in blues, greens, purples and touches of magenta. It had appeared in the sky after the aurora from The Event faded, and for a brief time, everyone had thought the world was coming to an end. For two weeks things had been a little hairy but order had soon been restored. Everyone kept waking up with the world still spinning around as it had for the last four billion years with the same bills, the same politics, the same bullshit, and humanity had pretty much gotten over it.

Oh, there were theories aplenty about what the light was, everything from God getting ready to bring the end of times, to the ancient Atlanteans returning to earth. Casey, being a sci-fi fan, liked to imagine it was some kind of communications beacon from an alien race. Her idea wasn't any more farfetched than the most, but for right now the only thing everyone could agree upon was that it was very pretty.

The lights in the parking lot began to go dim and flicker, plunging her section into semi-darkness. She could still see enough by the streetlights to make out her car near the tree line, but apprehension skittered up her spine. Trying to tell herself these shitty ass lights were always going out, that this wasn't like a scene out of a horror movie where the dumb co-ed got chopped to bits by the serial killer clown, she walked faster. She swore she heard the sound of heavy footsteps behind her, but when she looked over her shoulder she couldn't see anyone among the few vehicles still in the lot.

Putting some pep in her step, she hurried to her car and gripped the small canister of pepper spray on her keychain. She'd laughed at her dad when he got it for her, but as she flipped the safety off, she was grateful for the protection it offered. Another glance over her shoulder revealed a dark, vaguely man-like shape, around six parking spots away, heading toward her and she debated if she should scream for help or just make a run for her car. Then the shape began to quickly advance and she decided to say fuck it and do both.

With a loud, blood curdling scream she dashed for her car, hitting the locks so she'd be able to jerk the door open and slide inside. Just as she was about to reach the handle an impossibly large hand gripped her arm and she spun, spraying her attacker full in the face with her pepper spray. His startled yell cut off her scream when the figure's long, pale hair flew back as he bellowed and rubbed at his face. She stood dumfounded when Lorn said something in a foreign language that didn't sound very complimentary.

The sight of tears running down his face snapped her out of her daze. "Oh shit! Lorn, I'm so sorry! Wait, stop rubbing your face!"

"Woman, what vile weapon did you assault me with? I cannot see!"

He went to rub his face again and she gripped his arm, trying to pull his hand back before he touched himself. "No, wait, I'm so sorry I maced you. I thought you were attacking me. Don't touch your face with your hands, use your shirt but blot, don't rub. Oh shit, I'm so sorry. I thought you were a clown, I mean, not a clown, a psycho, but you're not and I'm *so* sorry!"

Crouching down on the pavement he ripped off his trench coat, then his shirt. She shamelessly ogled his half naked body and creamed her jeans at the sight of his perfect six, no eight pack. The man had an honest-to-god eight-pack that was as smooth as a baby's butt. His broad chest was equally built, and the way his massive arms flexed as he tried to remove the pepper spray from his skin, made her want to rub herself against him in the worst way even as guilt pierced her over hurting him.

He made a pained noise and she shook her head, scolding herself for standing back and getting an eyeful when she should be helping him.

"Hold on, I have emergency water in my trunk. Let me get it and we'll try to rinse some of it off."

She took his grunt as approval and quickly opened her trunk, pulling out the two gallons of water her father insisted she carry everywhere with her. "Move your hands, I need to pour this over your face."

She handed him the water and stepped back as he lifted his face and poured it over his skin. When she caught sight of his reddened cheeks and swollen eyes guilt panged through her and she started babbling again. "What were you doing? Why didn't you say something? I thought you were some kind of psycho that wanted to hurt me."

"Number," he growled out as he shook his head, water flying through the air and splattering her. "Can you please pour the water on me?"

She did as he asked, trying to get as much of the pepper spray off his eyelids as possible. "Number?"

"I wanted to attain your number. Without it we would not have dinner."

"Oh..." she was so shocked that she kept pouring the jug over his face, half drowning him before it emptied. "Shit, I'm sorry."

He shook his head again and she tried to resist the urge to run her fingers along his slick chest, to trace each perfectly cut muscle beneath his tanned skin. "It is my fault. I should have realized you would not see me in this light."

"Are you okay?"

He gave her a bleary blink. "I am fine."

Dropping the jug she went to touch his face but he grasped her hand. "Do not. You will injure yourself."

Her guilt tripled and she had to blink back tears. "I'm so, so sorry, Lorn."

"It is all right, Casey. I have suffered worse."

Poor guy, his eyes were practically swollen shut and he was trying to comfort her. "You can't drive home like this. Is there someone I can call to come pick you up?"

He hesitated, then shook his head. "I am alone here."

"Where's your car?"

"I ride a motorcycle."

"There is no way in hell you're driving home on a bike tonight." Casey's mother was an ER nurse and she shuddered at all the stories her mom had told her about treating motorcycle accidents. "If it's okay with you, I can call a cab or you can come back to my place and take a shower."

The last part slipped out without her even being aware she meant to say the words. Her treacherous libido must have hijacked her mouth. To her surprise Lorn smiled and quickly stood. He looked down at his soaking pants and shirt wadded in his hand. She hoped the water didn't ruin the leather of his pants and her inner slut whispered he should probably take them off just to be safe.

"I am afraid I am not fit to ride in your vehicle."

"Don't worry about that. I have a bunch of spare grocery bags I can put over the seats."

After covering the seats with the bags and an emergency blanket she kept in her trunk she gently took his hand, unsure of how well he could see. Just the bit of backdraft she'd gotten from the pepper spray made her own eyes burn like a mother so she couldn't imagine how painful it was for him. The warmth of his much bigger hand wrapping around hers sent a pleasant rush of sensation bubbling through her, reminding her in the most carnal way possible that it had been far too long since she'd been intimate with a man.

"You have the softest skin," he said in a rumbling voice her libido loved. "Like the finest *ushan*."

Flushing, and wondering what the hell *ushan* was, she helped him into his seat before going and retrieving his trench coat, along with her purse and his shirt, before tossing them in the backseat and sliding into the driver's side. Hopefully the few bags she put down on her seat would keep her from stinking everything up. With an inward groan she realized she must smell hideous to Lorn.

"Sorry about the smell," she muttered as she turned her car on and pulled out of the lot.

He cleared his throat. "That is not a normal...scent for women here?"

"What? God no. I had to clean out a deep freezer that broke and it was full of rotten shrimp. Totally nasty."

That scary growl came from Lorn again and she gave him a quick glance before focusing on the road again. "Did you just growl?"

"Yes."

"Um...why?"

"You should not be doing such menial work. You are a woman."

She couldn't help but laugh. "You mean women in your country don't do menial work?"

"No. They are too precious."

"Are you for real?"

"I am very real. Why do you ask?"

"Sorry, language barrier. What I mean is I find that hard to believe."

"Why?"

"Because women have always been the ones to do the dirty work. At least in my house that was true. My dad and brother would make the mess while me, my mom, and sister cleaned it up."

"Does your father not love your mother?"

"Of course he does. It's just that over here in the States women are the ones who usually take care of the family. Don't get me wrong, I know a lot more families where the guy stays home to take care of the kids while the woman works, but for the most part, it's the woman who changes the diapers, cooks the food, cleans the house, all that stuff."

"I find that very strange. Is it something you want to do? Something that you find pleasurable?"

"Well, no, but it has to be done." She tapped her fingers on the steering wheel as she turned down the gravel road to the small house she was renting from her uncle. "Actually in a way I kind of do. I can take care of myself, clean up after myself, and don't have to rely on someone else to do it."

"You enjoy being independent."

Since he said it like it was a fact, not a question, she nodded. "Immensely. The best day of my life was the day I moved out of my parents' house and got my own place. God love them, but they are overprotective to the extreme."

Pulling up to her small two bedroom house with its cheap, white vinyl siding, chipped concrete front porch and window air conditioning units, she was a little apprehensive about him being in her home. It was clean, but the furniture was all second hand and her plates didn't match. As she turned off the car, she had to laugh at herself for worrying about matching plates, but suddenly, she wanted very badly to make a good impression on Lorn.

Especially after macing him.

Pasting on a bright smile she inwardly winced as she examined his still swollen face. "We're here."

Chapter Six

When Casey reappeared after cleansing herself, Lorn let out a silent breath of relief that she no longer smelled like that hideous rotting odor which had covered her natural sweet scent earlier. Dressed now in a pair of soft blue pants and loose white top he sucked in an involuntary breath at the sight of her beautiful, still damp, dark hair falling loose around her shoulders. When she spotted him by the sink a beguiling mixture of happiness and uncertainty filled her expressive face. Then her brows drew down over her *benali* eyes and his heart lurched at her beauty.

Nast was going to love her.

Lorn had traveled through the wormhole earlier in the day and spoke briefly with his blood brother, but Nast was in the middle of getting a new Legion ready for battle which left them precious little time to talk. When he showed him an image of Casey he thought Nast was going to burst with pride and satisfaction. They were too far apart for Lorn to feel his emotions, but Nast's joy was easy to see in his huge smile. It probably looked identical to Lorn's. They'd talked briefly about Casey before Nast had to leave, once again making Lorn promise he wouldn't do anything to jeopardize his own bond with Casey. Nast had a sense of honor so deep that it was reflected in every facet of his life, even to the point of ripping his own heart out so Lorn could be happy.

As he eyed his little bride and took in her soft beauty and warm scent, he had to choke back a growl. She carried the same natural perfume as in his true dream, and her home was saturated with the aroma of young, healthy female. It was all he could do to keep from grabbing her and burying his face against her soft little belly and rubbing his cheek against her to mark himself as hers. The shadows of the dark hall caressed her full cheeks, and he ached as he examined her lush, petite body. The women of Earth had larger breasts and hips than most women of his galaxy, and he thanked the Lord of Life for his luck. If she had been born in the Bel'Tan galaxy she would have been much sought after by every male that saw her. But she was theirs, made by the Lord of Life to be their mate, and when Lorn met her gaze he caught her confused yet aroused look and noted how her nipples peaked behind the thin fabric of her shirt. How he wanted to take those hard little berries between his lips and suckle her until she was dripping wet for him. He couldn't wait to see what her sex looked like, to lick her until she was so sensitive that she would climax with one thrust of his cock.

She took another step toward him from the corridor that he assumed led to her sleeping quarters. "Wow, I guess the old wives' tale about pouring milk over yourself to get rid of pepper spray really works."

It took him a moment to drag his thoughts from her body and realize that she was talking about his appearance. He'd actually used a chemical neutralizer, but she couldn't know about any of those things. Not until he had his first kiss and buried himself up to his balls in her hot body. More than a little eager to get on with things so he could claim his bride he gave her his best charming smile, the one that made the pleasure servants sigh with delight.

"Yes, thank you."

She moved across the room toward him, and he was mesmerized by the sensual rhythm of her walk, how it made her breasts sway slightly. When she was almost to him she paused and looked up at him with an apprehensive expression. There was a fragility about her he wasn't used to, and he worried for a moment about injuring her during their coupling. She was so petite she barely came up to his chest while standing before him barefoot, but the teasing scent of her juices dampening the intriguing folds of her sex had his cock rapidly filling with blood. With a hesitant hand she reached towards his face then paused. Realizing their height difference he lowered his head so she could touch him.

Her fingertips trembled slightly as she stroked his cheek and his soul rejoiced when her energy washed over him. Without a doubt, she was the one meant to be their Matriarch. He wanted to howl with victory, take her repeatedly until his seed took root in her womb, and bound her to him forever. Immense relief filled him that he wouldn't have to watch his friends fall to the madness, that he and Nast could finally fill their home with the light and love of their *alyah*.

Casey was worthy of every bit of pain and sacrifice it had taken to give her a home worthy of her. This beautiful female was the one he'd been searching for, the only woman in the universe the Lord of Life had created for him and Nast. If they'd been a normal bonding couple they would be celebrating finding each other and by tonight he'd be enjoying the first stage of the courting rights with her, but because of her naturally impenetrable psychic shielding he couldn't get any read on her emotions other than what he could interpret from her body language and her scent.

Her delicious, mouthwatering scent and abundant nectar.

Nast, with his love of tasting a woman's need, was going to lose his mind when he met their Casey. A fierce arousal filled him as Lorn thought about all the ways they could pleasure her, of all the ways they would bind her to them with their love and give her a satisfaction so great she would never want to leave them.

But first he had to win her kiss.

Slow, he cautioned himself, *treat her like a skittish bufonti.*

In a way, she reminded him of the soft and timid little creature from his world with her petite stature and her shy, hesitant behavior. He certainly wanted to cuddle and pet her until she purred for him.

Lord of Life, she smelled so *good.*

She smelled like his.

The faint thump of her heartbeat increased as she examined his face, trying to keep her expression impassive, but failing miserably. He could easily read both her passion and her uncertainty. When her hand cupped his cheek he couldn't help a sigh of relief, her energy calming him as no other's could. This is what he had been searching for and not found in any of the potential brides he'd met during previous Reapings—the soul-deep recognition of his true mate.

"Well, you look like you've recovered," she murmured in a husky voice then cleared her throat. "I'm afraid I don't have any shirts that will fit you."

When her gaze strayed down his face to his exposed chest her arousal deepened, making him desperate to seduce her. Throttling back his lust was difficult, but he had to take things slowly with his little Earth woman. Mary, Matriarch of the Scout who had spoken before the council, had lectured the Warriors going to Earth on how to seduce human women. She'd urged them to take things as slow as they could, not to rush it for fear of scaring away their bride. If they proclaimed their undying love for a woman the moment they met her, an Earth female would consider them mentally deficient, no matter how true it was.

"You have the softest skin," he said in a voice barely above a growl.

She blinked up at him and her scent cooled a touch. "Um, thanks."

With that, she stepped away from him, and he tried to figure out why complimenting her would repulse rather than attract. Did the women of this planet not enjoy hearing how they affected a man? Did they not want their mate to appreciate them? He needed to get her mind back on her attraction to him.

Gently clasping her hand he pulled it down his cheek, over his neck, and to his chest, letting it rest over the heart that now belonged to her. "See, my skin is much tougher than yours."

She stared at where her small hand rested above his heart and he looked down as well, enjoying the contrast of her creamy skin against his own dark bronze tone. "Do you get spray tanned?"

The immediate flush that went from her neck to her hairline made him grin. "What is that?"

"I'm not sure what the word would be in your language. It's like a thing people do to make their skin darker." She glanced up into his eyes then back to her palm on his chest again. "Usually you only find your hair and eye color on really pale people."

His little bride was far too observant. "This is the way I was born, Casey. No artificial enhancements."

Well that wasn't entirely true. He had plenty of enhancements that heightened his sight, his hearing, his strength, and his endurance. All things a Warrior needed to survive. There were also small crystal chips embedded in his brain that allowed him to boost his psychic powers and connect with his men over long distances. Right now he was in contact with his friend Cormac who waited near Casey's house in case he was needed.

She bit her pretty pink lower lip when he began to gently caress her hand. "Wow, you sure lucked out in the genetic lottery."

It took him a moment to process her words and he smiled. "You find me attractive?"

Her response came out in a whisper. "Very."

Both his pride and his cock hardened further at her response, the ultra-sensitive nerves of the pleasure ridges swelling along his shaft. "I find you very attractive as well."

Once again she seemed to find his compliment offensive and tried to pull her hand away from his chest. "Don't bullshit me."

Utterly baffled he stared down at her. "Why would I make a bull shit on you?"

She gaped up at him, then giggled. "Sorry, it's a slang saying in America. It means don't lie to me."

He dropped to his knees, their height difference putting her only slightly taller than him. He wanted to look her in the eyes, begging her to see his sincerity even if she couldn't feel it. The darkness of her gaze grew and at this level the perfume of her nectar was even stronger, making him tremble slightly with the roaring need to bury his face between her thighs and tongue her to her release. The generous pillows of her breasts called to him and he marveled that someone so small had such abundance. Even though his conscious mind knew she wasn't in heat, his body demanded he take her, now, that he satisfy her every need.

"Casey, I will never lie to you." He inwardly flinched at the thought that he was lying to her right now about who he was, but he pressed on. "You are beautiful. Where I come from men would fight to the death for the honor of your smile."

She let out a slow breath, the scent of a healthy, fertile female filling him like the first rain over the desert of Valdoon. "Where the hell are you from?"

"Someplace far away."

"No shit. Wherever it is, I know about a million women that would like to go there for vacation."

The irony of her statement wasn't lost on him, and he smiled, enjoying the way her gaze kept straying to his mouth. Moving slowly, he placed his hands on her hips, resisting the urge to squeeze. Mary had said Earth women were self-conscious of their natural softness, that having body fat was considered unattractive and how they wouldn't understand a Kadothian male's intense pleasure at grasping them where they are the most feminine. Like Casey's beautiful rounded belly and generous thighs. Just the thought of her lying on his chest, nestling his cock against her giving flesh, had him fighting with everything he had not to rush her.

She tilted her head to the side and examined him. "You have the strangest eyes."

"What do you mean?"

"They...kind of change color. I mean, I know that eye color can change depending on the lighting and the clothes you wear, but yours..." She reached out and touched his face again, filling him with elation, "they go from aquamarine to an almost navy blue."

He turned his head slightly and brushed his lips over the tender skin of her forearm. Her response was an immediate and maddening rush of desire. For the briefest of moments the psychic shields around her softened and he read the desire, confusion, doubt, and hope spinning through her. Wanting to heighten her arousal, he removed one hand from her hip and grasped her arm, moving her hand so he could gently nibble on her inner wrist. While she was unaware of the significance of the act he rejoiced that his bride offered such a vulnerable part of her body to him so freely.

"What are you doing?" she asked in a whisper-soft voice.

"Tasting you."

"Why?"

"Because you are delicious."

"Oh."

After a few moments of caressing her skin with his tongue and teeth she made a soft moaning noise. Worried he'd hurt her, he looked up and found her watching him with half-closed eyes, giving him a look so damned arousing that he had to choke back a growl. Human males didn't growl and they certainly didn't howl their joy at claiming their bride.

Unable to fight off his primal urges any longer, he looked up at her. "Kiss me, Casey."

The dart of her tongue wetting her lips had his erection pressing against his pants. She began to lean down slowly and he bit the inside of his lip, allowing his blood to flow and fill his mouth. Only a drop or two was needed to start the hormonal chain reaction, but he wanted to do everything he could to connect Casey to him because his soul already belonged to her. Bonding ceremony or not, this young Earth female was his Matriarch.

She hesitated right before their lips met, close enough that they inhaled and exhaled each other's air.

Desperate at the thought she might reject him, he did the unthinkable for a Warrior. He begged her. "Please, Casey, please kiss me."

A moment later their lips met and elation filled him.

Soft, giving, gentle, her lips explored his as he kissed her back, not seeking entrance yet, determined to give her the kind of kiss that she deserved. Their noses rubbed together as she changed the angle of her mouth, the sweet scent of her desire enveloping him and making his whole body tense with need. He wanted to devour her, to taste every part of her flesh, to make her climax until she fell into an exhausted sleep, but those were later stages in the courting ritual. Right now he lost himself in the glory of her maddeningly hesitant touch.

With a soft moan she parted her lips for him and he took advantage of her surrender with a growl he couldn't stop. She tensed but before she could pull away he stroked his tongue against hers, sharing his blood with her, marking her as belonging to him. Soon her scent would change, merging with his so every male knew she had been claimed as his bride, his beautiful Casey Westfall, soon to be Matriarch of House Westfall and his *alyah*, his beloved and the future bride of his blood brother, the Lord of Life willing.

The sensation of her fingers stroking through his hair as they kissed sent pleasure spinning through his nervous system until he had her clasped against him as tightly as he could, her large and tempting breasts pressing into him and driving his desire higher until it was an inferno of need. She tasted so damn good, like the essence of joy, and he finally understood why Kadothian males considered finding their bondmate life's ultimate pleasure. He'd listened to their tales, had been taught what would happen, but nothing had prepared him for this. Soon she was tugging on his hair and kissing him harder, rubbing her body against his in a silent plea for him to ease her need as her nectar spilled from her sweet body.

He wanted to take her, over and over again, but if he did he would lose his chance to bring her back with him, to have a full bonding witnessed by his people. Once she fully transformed he could plunge his shaft into her willing body, but until then he would have to be satisfied with this one stolen moment.

Tongues stroking together, they kissed for what seemed like a lifetime, tasting each other and burning hotter until Lorn was desperate to mate her.

Tearing his mouth from hers, he leapt to his feet and tried to put some distance between them, afraid he would soon be unable to control the primal need to make her his in all ways.

Her shocked gasp alerted him to the fact that he'd moved faster than an Earthling could even as he struggled to keep from hauling her decadent body against his.

"Forgive me, Casey." He quickly sent a message to Cormac on a mental link to come get him, now. "If I keep kissing you, tasting your need, smelling your sweet pussy all wet and waiting for my mouth I will not be able to control myself. I will tear your clothes from your body like an animal and lick every drop of nectar from your body until you scream my name."

She crossed her arms over her chest as if she was cold, hugging herself as she stared at him with wide eyes. Her hard nipples pressed against the thin fabric and his cock ached like an open wound with the need to plunge into her willing heat. Casey wanted him, there was no doubt of that in his mind, but this was too important to rush her.

After licking her lips she whispered, "What if I don't want you to control yourself?"

The woman was temptation itself wrapped up in a stunningly feminine package. His gaze strayed down to her hard nipples again and his mouth watered. "I must, for both our sakes."

"I don't understand." She took a hesitant step closer then hurt filled her expression as he stepped back.

Trying to think of some way to soothe her without revealing too much, he took inspiration from the sound of Cormac approaching in an automobile. Earth's technology was so primitive that creating identities and securing wealth had been no issue. Lorn had enjoyed exploring this region called America on his motorcycle while Cormac had chosen an automobile made for going fast, or at least what passed for fast on this planet.

"My friend is coming to pick me up and will be here any second. I do not want to dishonor you by having you spread out on the table before him while I feast on your delicious cream."

"Oh." Her cheeks flushed bright red and he had to hide a smile at her adorable embarrassment.

Unable to resist the urge to soothe his bride he crossed the space between them and gently grasped her chin, tipping her face up so he could look her in the eye. "I wish I could stay the night with you, *alyah*, but I cannot."

Small lines formed around her kiss swollen lips. "What does that word mean?"

Conscious of Mary's advice to be gentle with their bride at first, he brushed his thumb over her lower lip, clearing away a trace of his glimmering, deep purple blood. The low rumble of the automobile pulling into her driveway made Casey take a step back, breaking his hold on her as her gaze darted to the door. "Is that your ride?"

He nodded and moved away to gather his trench coat from the couch. If, Lord of Life forbid, she did not transition it would be better to leave no trace of himself. The thought of having to leave Casey behind started a panic through him that he couldn't control. Before he could stop himself he went to Casey and gathered her in his arms, loving the gentle give of her body against his as he whispered a desperate prayer against her neck that she made the transformation. She would make a wonderful mother and fierce longing filled him as he pictured his and Nast's sons running around their home.

A knock came from the door and he released her to go answer it.

Cormac grinned under the porch lights and his nostrils flared as he took in Lorn's scent. Dressed in a white button-down shirt and jeans, his dark blonde hair streaked with brown was pulled back into a tight braid. His grin widened and he said in Kadothian, "Congratulations on finding your bride."

Lorn wanted to hug his friend but Mary had warned them that on Earth men touching and loving other men was considered taboo. Stupid savages, as if any form of love could ever be immoral. Still, he didn't want to give Casey the wrong impression. There was only one man he loved beyond friendship and it wasn't Cormac.

Moving to the side so his friend could see Casey, he smiled with pride. "Casey Westfall, I would like you to meet my friend, Cormac."

The other man knew better than to approach Lorn's bride so he raised a hand in greeting. "It's an honor to meet you, *alyah* of Lorn."

Silence met this statement and Lorn looked over at Casey. Surprise radiated from her and he couldn't help but revel in the fact he was able to read his bride's emotions, just the faintest bit. The Scout had been right, physical intimacy did allow him a way past her shielding. She blinked at them, opened her mouth, and blinked again before saying in a high-pitched voice, "Hello."

Concerned, Lorn moved quickly to her side. "Are you all right?" Surely it was too early for the DNA changes to take place. So far, the brides that had been found needed at least twelve hours to go through their transition, but who knew what kind of anomalies could happen.

She looked from him, to Cormac, and back to him again. "There's more of you?"

"What?"

Flushing, she looked down at his chest rather than in his eyes. "Never mind. It was nice meeting you, Cormac."

The sound of dismissal in her voice irritated him. "You will see me again, Casey."

She gave him a small smile and even without the slight foothold in her soul he could have read the doubt in every line of her body. "Sure. Give me a call next time you're in town."

"I live here now."

"You do?"

"Yes."

He debated telling her they'd bought the old farm down the road from her house once he'd identified her as his bride. Cormac now lived there along with a rotating crew of Kadothian males who had sensed their mates somewhere in the area. They could narrow the range to six hundred miles and this part of the planet known as Michigan made a good starting point for many of the men. Lorn had been unusually lucky to find Casey after only two days of searching. It took most of the other men who had found their brides much longer. The women's natural shielding made it hard to get a lock on them unless they were close enough to scent. However, once a Warrior locked onto a scent he would find his female quickly. Three days ago Lorn had found Casey then immediately researched her. He'd discovered the neighboring farm to her property, along with its bunkhouse that could sleep fifteen men and huge barn, was for sale and it was too good of an opportunity to mess up. It was a miracle she hadn't seen him before now but they'd been very careful not to draw attention to themselves. Still, it would break the growing trust between them if he did not mention it. Not wanting to lie to his bride, and unable to resist touching her, he smoothed a stray lock of her hair from her face, marveling at the smooth texture.

"We are your new neighbors."

"What?" Her jaw dropped, making him want to taste her again and slide his tongue against hers. "You're the one who bought Johnson's old farm?"

"Yes."

She glanced between him and Cormac. "Why?"

Cormac laughed, smoothly turning her attention to him. His friend had always been quick on his feet and his brain wasn't muddled by the huge surge of hormones filling Lorn's body. "We are models from Europe who are running a boot camp for other models to improve their skills and exercise in fresh air."

"You're running a European male model boot camp here? Chelsea, Michigan? Why in God's name would you do that?" She cleared her throat. "I mean, why not New York or something?"

Lorn answered her with the excuse Mary had given them to explain their presence. "We wanted to come to a place where we would not be hounded by fans and photographers. A place where we can exercise and improve our skills without constant public scrutiny. In a small town like this, we believe we will go unnoticed."

Her hysterical giggle made him worry about her sanity. "You think you're going to blend in here?"

When she began to laugh hard enough that she had to sit down on her worn green sofa he exchanged a confused look with Cormac. "Why do you find that humorous?"

"Oh God," she wiped away a tear and started to giggle again. "Look at you! Two of the hottest guys I've ever seen, anywhere. You're like sex on a stick."

Cormac gave her an unsure smile. "Being sex on a stick is bad?"

Embarrassment heated her cheeks, but she still giggled. "No, no, it's good. What I mean is you aren't exactly going to blend here. And once the women of this town find out there is a houseful of male models I wouldn't be surprised if you have to put up guards to keep them from sneaking onto your property to ogle you."

Lorn frowned at her, not liking the thought of other women coveting him. "You are the only one who is allowed to ogle me."

"What?"

Cormac cleared his throat. "It is getting late and we need to be up early. Say goodnight to your *alyah* and let us return to our home."

Pulling Casey to her feet, Lorn picked her up and hugged her tight, smiling when she gave a surprised squeak then wrapped her legs around his waist. "Put me down, I must be breaking your back."

He snorted while Cormac laughed. "You weigh far less than my pack and I had to run the circumference of your pl-I mean Earth with it on my back."

"Model training," Cormac interjected even though Casey was staring up at Lorn.

"Your eyes are a different color again," she said in an absent voice as she examined his face.

"Time to go," Cormac urged and laid a hand on Lorn's arm.

Without thinking Lorn growled at the other man being so close to his bride and Casey gasped and pushed at his chest. He let her slide out of his arms as the need to keep her grew.

"What the hell was that?"

Giving a forced laugh, Cormac threw an arm around Lorn's shoulder and practically dragged him out the door. "Oh, that is just something us models do."

It was obvious Casey didn't believe him, but she nodded. "I guess I'll see you soon, neighbor."

Lorn took one last look at his bride, looking so beautiful his heart ached. "Soon, Casey, I will see you soon."

"Night," Cormac shouted as he shoved Lorn out the door and slammed it behind him.

"Way to blend in with the humans," he muttered in a voice too low for Casey to hear even if she was standing right next to them. "You need to watch more of those movies with me to learn how to act."

Lorn snorted. "Those, what do you call them-romantic comedies? Thank you, but I have no urge to act like a bumbling idiot around Casey."

"I'm telling you, Earth women must love those stories for some reason. I need to figure out why so I can use that knowledge to help seduce my bondmate."

"Any luck finding her yet?"

"No. She was here, then gone, then back in the area again briefly." Cormac snickered. "Your *alyah* is watching us from her window with a rather concerned look on her face. You sure you don't want to watch 'When Harry Met Sally' with me tonight? It might help you blend in, act more normal."

Opening the door of Cormac's red Corvette ZR1 and sliding in, Lorn snorted. "Sure, this car blends with the other automobiles I have seen in town."

Giving Lorn an unrepentant grin, Cormac drove out of Casey's driveway and took a right to go the short distance back to their base. Looking through the tinted window he detected the shadow of her figure in the living room, watching them pull away. Did she feel the same desperate need to be together that he did? Was she feeling that connection between them that urged him to come to her?

Cormac glanced over at him. "Will you be able to stay away from her for the required time? If you have need we can restrain you or send you back to the ship."

The thought of not being on the same planet as Casey was unacceptable. "No, I am strong enough. I will do nothing that could jeopardize my chances with her."

Already the urge to return to Casey gnawed at him and he closed his hands into fists hard enough to almost break the tough skin with his nails. He'd suffered through some of the worst fighting conditions in the Bel'Tan galaxy, endured merciless training that broke the minds of more than one Warrior, and survived the Hive for nearly four hundred cycles, yet his formidable self-control was about to shatter because of one tiny, beautiful Earth female.

His female.

With a sigh Cormac glanced at him then back at the road. "I envy you."

"How is your search going?"

"My *alyah* is here, somewhere, but she is hard to track down." He frowned. "She moves around a great deal, though I know not why."

"You will find her," Lorn said, trying to comfort his friend even as his mind kept returning to Casey. Lord of Life, she was as hot and tempting as a woman could get. So passionate, yet shy, a combination sure to drive any male insane.

"I will," Cormac said with determination filling his voice. "And when I do she will never disappear on me again."

Chapter Seven

C asey curled into a ball on her bed and clutched at her stomach. "I'm going to fucking kill Jerry for making me clean out that cooler."

Kimber made a noncommittal noise and Casey looked up, finding her friend staring out the window of her bedroom to the old Johnson farm. Dressed in a pair of jean shorts that showed off her long runner's legs and a loose black t-shirt, Kimber had quickly abandoned Casey for the view her window provided.

"Hey, I'm dying over here. A little sympathy would be nice."

Dragging her gaze to Casey, Kimber rolled her eyes. "For someone who's dying you're making an awful lot of noise. So you somehow got food poisoning; the doctor said you'll be fine, to just drink plenty of fluids, blah, blah, blah."

With that she turned back to the window.

Gritting her teeth as a cramp contracted through her lower abdomen, Casey glared at the back of Kimber's curly black head. "I didn't invite you here so you could drool over the neighbors."

Kimber, that bitch, just laughed at her. "Yeah, right. You have a house full of hot-as-shit supermodels living next door to you, outside, working out without their shirts on and I'm supposed to not look? Have you lost your damn mind? You could charge admission for women to come use your windows and make a fortune. By the way, Dawn and Paige are on their way over."

"I'm dying and you invited them over to stare at some guys?"

"Not just any guys, epically hot guys."

A shudder ran through Casey's muscles and she shut her eyes, wishing whatever the hell it was would work its way out of her system. She'd thrown up a couple times last night, but then the nausea had gone away leaving her with bone deep shivers. She didn't have a fever or any signs of an infection, so despite her pain and nausea, her family doctor sent her home with her mom and told her to rest. Her mom went back to work and Kimber came over to keep her company. Casey snorted at the advice from her doctor, as if she could rest when it felt like she had period cramps all through her body. And to make matters worse, as those cramps eased they were replaced by the unmistakable burn of arousal.

Then again, her horniness might have more to do with her obsession with Lorn than whatever whacked-out illness she'd managed to contract. When she did sleep she dreamed of him, kissing him, touching him, licking him, and doing things with him that were probably illegal in some states. The more she thought about him the more turned on she got until she'd had to change her panties three times because she'd soaked them with her arousal. Thankfully, Kimber thought the barely stifled moans of need were moans of pain. What Casey needed was Lorn, right here, right now. She didn't care if Kimber watched them and took pictures, she needed that man inside of her in the worst way.

The doorbell rang and Kimber sprinted from Casey's room, returning seconds later with an excited Paige and Dawn in tow. Paige, a plump and pretty girl in a wholesome way with her long chestnut brown hair and light blue eyes, had the good manners to stop by Casey's bed first with a sympathetic expression. Working as a nanny during the summer break, Paige had the mothering thing down pat even though she wasn't married and didn't have any kids of her own.

"How are you feeling, sweetie?"

Grateful someone gave a shit, she gave Paige a weak smile. "Not as bad as that night we stole a bottle of your dad's moonshine, but pretty close."

"Ugh, that's awful." Her gaze strayed to the window where Kimber and Dawn practically had their noses pressed to the glass. "Dawn, you could at least say hi to Casey."

The sun shining through the window turned Dawn's mass of red curls the burning orange of fall leaves, as her friend barely glanced over and grinned before returning her attention to the window. "Hi, Casey."

"Oh. My. God," Dawn whispered. "I have died and gone to washboard abs heaven."

Kimber moaned in agreement. "Look at the shoulders on that guy with the long brown hair wearing the dark blue pants."

"Niiiiice," Dawn purred.

Paige, appearing increasingly distressed, quickly tucked the covers around Casey. "Can I get you anything?"

The only thing Casey wanted right now was a vibrator and a pack of batteries. "No, go ahead and join the peeping thomasinas."

After Paige wiggled her way between Dawn and Kimber she made a little noise somewhere between a sigh and a whimper. "You weren't exaggerating. It's like a farm that only breeds incredibly sexy guys over there."

The sun was setting and Casey was feeling increasingly better and increasingly aroused. She couldn't seem to stay still, wanting to rub her body against the mattress, run her hands over her stiff nipples and change her wet panties...again. Having to listen to her friends talk about the hotties next door certainly wasn't helping.

As they gossiped about the men's bodies and good looks all she could imagine was Lorn over there, jumping, spinning, and turning so his hair flowed over his broad shoulders with every move. He had the most cut chest she'd ever seen and each solid square of his abdominals begged for her kiss. She savored the memory of his rough skin rubbing against her, the strength that flowed through him as he easily picked her up. And his eyes, goodness his eyes, she'd never seen anything as beautiful as those shifting blues. Her mind wandered to his lips and she touched her own, the skin tingling at the memory of his kiss. It had been, without a doubt, the best kiss of her life. He'd savored her instead of rushing, stroking her arousal high enough that she ended up nipping his lips, sucking on his tongue, and greedily devouring his mouth. While she enjoyed kissing, she'd never been so aggressive before, so confident that the man she kissed was enjoying it. He'd tasted so good, a flavor she couldn't describe other than fresh and pure. Like taking a breath of cold country air after a big snowfall.

Except his touch didn't make her cold; it made her almost unbearably hot.

Her pussy continued to throb with need and she wished her friends would get the hell out of here. It was hard enough to hold back her moans as it was and she distantly wondered what the heck was wrong with her. She'd never heard of food poisoning making someone desperate to be fucked. Craving the feeling of Lorn's large erection being driven into her hard enough that she had to brace her hands on the headboard consumed her. He had nice, thick thighs, as muscled as the rest of him, and she could only imagine how good it would feel to wrap her legs around his trim waist and surrender to him.

"Are they fighting or dancing?" Paige whispered in an awed voice.

Kimber shook her head. "I don't know."

Dawn abruptly stepped back from the window, a dangerous gleam in her hazel eyes that meant nothing but trouble as she slipped the strap of her thank top that had fallen off one freckled shoulder back in place. "Casey, you haven't met them yet, have you?"

Clearing her throat, she pulled her comforter up, trying to hide her obviously stiff nipples behind her t-shirt. Figures, she was actually feeling better but now the need for sex replaced the need to puke. "Just two of them. Lorn and Cormac."

"God, even their names are sexy," Kimber said with a pretend swoon.

Narrowing her eyes, she gave Dawn a look that let her know she wasn't screwing around. Everything inside of her demanded she stake a claim on Lorn that would let her friends know she'd kick any woman's ass that touched him. "Hands off the platinum blond hottie. His name is Lorn and he is mine."

Kimber giggled. "They kissed last night."

"What!" Dawn leapt on her bed. "Why didn't you tell me?"

"Oh, I'm sorry, I was too busy thinking I was going to die."

Paige tore herself from the window with obvious reluctance. "I don't see him out there."

Dawn looked up at Kimber and smiled. "You know, they must be worn out and hungry after all that exercising. It would be the neighborly thing to bring them over some cookies or something."

"Oh yeah," Kimber's eyes lit up and her full lips curved in a wicked grin. "It would be the polite thing to do."

Even Paige looked excited at the prospect and she usually found men too intimidating to even be around thanks to her abusive shithead father. "I'm sure we could find something in Casey's kitchen. She always has good snacks. Or we could make something. Guys like girls who can cook, right?"

Irritated, Casey glared at her friends. "Hey, I'm right here."

Paige smiled at her and felt her forehead. "You're looking much better."

"Yeah. Why don't you go take a shower and wash up? I bet you'll feel even better, and then you can come with us to deliver cookies to the sex gods."

"Yeah, come with us" Kimber grinned. "If we have you there we have an excuse for visiting."

"Thanks," Casey said and bit back a moan as she pushed herself up and her thighs pressed together over her swollen, wet sex. The thought of seeing Lorn again definitely interested her body. "Okay, okay, I'm getting up."

"Perfect!" Dawn leapt up and sped from the room with Kimber hot on her heels.

With a worried look Paige lingered by Casey's bed. "Are you sure you're okay? I don't want you making yourself worse by getting out of bed if you're still feeling crappy. I can stay here with you if you want."

The fact that Paige actually seemed interested in talking to the men was so unusual that Casey didn't want to do anything to discourage her. The poor girl was still a virgin and had only been on two dates her entire life. Forcing herself to try to look perky, Casey shook her head. "No, I'm just going to wash up and get changed. I think I have stuff to make chocolate chip cookies, and brownies. Go be domestic while I get ready."

Paige giggled, her pale blue eyes sparkling as deep dimples appeared in her cheeks. "Okay."

Once the door slammed shut and the voices of the women faded Casey let out a sigh that was part relief, part pain. She was hyper aware of the scent of the sweat from her illness covering her and it icked her out. Moving as quickly from the bed as her still weak body would allow, Casey lurched across the room to her bathroom, leaving a trail of clothes as she went. With the removal of each article of clothing her skin tingled and burned, more sensitive than she'd ever felt. Even the caress of her long hair falling down her back as she took out her braid sent shivers of arousal through her.

The sound of her friend's voices coming through the thin walls of the little house faded as Casey turned on the shower and waited until it was barely warm before jumping in. She sucked in a harsh breath of air as the cool water fell over her heated skin and quickly showered, replacing the smell of sick sweat with her peach body wash. While soaping up all she could think of was Lorn, his skin, his scent, his taste. The man was so fucking hot it should be illegal. After rinsing off she did a quick check of her legs and pussy to make sure they were still smooth from her last waxing. At the touch of her fingers on her slit she had to stifle a groan. God, she was so swollen down there it was embarrassing.

After blow-drying her hair until it was slightly damp she moved quickly into her bedroom, the smell of baking cookies and brownies filling the air. Her stomach growled as she jerked on a pair of jean shorts and a cute pink tank top with her best pushup bra. Looking at herself in the mirror above her dresser she had to admit she looked cute. After a quick application of light makeup she slipped on her sandals and went to the kitchen, following her friends' excited chatter.

Kimber spotted her first and her eyes went wide. "Wow, you look a lot better."

"You're all bright-eyed and bushy-tailed," Dawn added with a grin as she cut up a tray of brownies and put them in a travel container.

Paige shot her a quick glance then returned her attention to siding cookies off the baking sheet and onto a plate. "You look very pretty."

Trying to pretend she wasn't practically jumping out of her skin at the thought of seeing Lorn, she went to her fridge and pulled out a partially full case of beer from a bar/brewery in Ann Arbor where Dawn worked.

Kimber grinned when she spotted Casey with the beer in her arms. "Good idea."

Paige bit her lower lip with a worried look. "Is it really a good idea to bring them alcohol?"

With a soft smile Dawn gave Paige a quick hug. "Honey, I'm sure these guys will drink responsibly, and if you feel uncomfortable, we can leave right away. Besides, as big as they are they'd need a case a piece to even get a buzz."

Tears shimmered in Paige's faded blue eyes and instantly her friends surrounded her in a hug. The young woman's fear of men became almost a phobia around guys who were drinking, one reason she never went to a frat party or a bar. Casey hated Paige's dad with a passion for the way he'd abused her friend, but most of all she hated how it had warped Paige's way of looking at any man.

"Hey now," Casey pulled back and wiped away a tear from her friend's cheek. "We can leave the beer here. No biggie."

Paige shook her head and gently moved out of their arms, grabbing some cling wrap to put over the plate of cookies. "No, it's okay. My therapist and I think I need to start facing my fears."

"Just think of those killer abs," Kimber said with a forced smile.

"Or," Dawn added, "those amazing back muscles. Good lord I just want to rub myself all over them."

The tension broke as the women joked about the men's physical attributes while they made their way down the gravel road to Lorn's property. It was a beautiful, warm late spring evening in the country and Casey took a deep breath of the air, enjoying the scent of the grass and new growth in the forest off the road. Her friends were like a pack of excited puppies talking about the guys they were about to meet and despite her earlier sickness, Casey felt surprisingly good. She laughed at some outrageous thing Dawn said about calling dibs on three of the guys so she had a better chance of getting one with a big dick, while trying to spot Lorn among the throng of men around the big farmhouse. As they approached, their joking fell silent when at least a dozen half-naked men stopped their sparring and watched them approach. Even more unnerving, additional sex gods came out of the house until they faced a small army of yummy men as the sun set.

Kimber said in a low voice, "Why are they all staring at us?"

"Maybe they're really hungry?" Paige replied in a whisper.

"Yeah, hungry." Dawn swallowed hard. "Are you sure this is a good idea?"

Before Casey could suggest they turn tail and run, Lorn came out the front door and the smile on his handsome face as he spotted her made her heart do flip flops and butterflies filled her belly.

"Holy shit," Kimber whispered. "He's even hotter than last night."

Casey couldn't reply, her gaze devouring the handsome man coming down the front steps of the large farmhouse. Today he wore a pair of loose black pants and a black tank top that showed off his massive arms and chiseled chest. Almost against her will she followed the tight V of his waist down to his groin then jerked her gaze back to his face before she stumbled with the case of beer. Either he was really excited to see her or he had a water bottle in his pocket. His white-blond hair had been pulled back into a tight braid, and his teal blue eyes practically glowed as he quickly crossed the big grass-covered front yard.

By this point they'd made it to the walkway leading to his house but her friends moved closer together until they were practically touching as they approached the men.

When Lorn reached them he immediately took the beer from Casey and set it down, then knelt before her. "Hello, Casey."

Kimber actually sighed at the deep rumble of Lorn's voice and Casey wasn't faring much better. "Hi, Lorn."

He studied her from head to foot, then leaned forward and audibly took a deep breath of her skin before letting out what sounded a hell of a lot like a purr. "You smell delicious."

"Peaches," she blurted out.

His fair brows lowered as he gave her an odd look. "What?"

"Peaches," she repeated again, trying with all her might to resist the urge to grab him and kiss him senseless. "Peach body wash. I don't actually wash with peaches. That would kinda go against the point of getting clean. I mean then I'd be all covered in peach syrup and I'd taste good but I'd be really sticky. So. Yeah. Peach soap."

Thankfully, Dawn came to her rescue while Lorn stared at her like he wanted to lick her, right here and now. "We saw you, um, working out and thought you might be hungry."

"For food," Kimber added then giggled like an idiot. "Of course, I meant food. What else would I mean?"

"Brownies," Paige added in the shy whisper she used around men.

Dawn cleared her throat and her voice still came out high pitched as she said, "We have beer. It's really good. I helped make it. I mean brew it. I work at a brewery and make beer. Good beer. That I brew."

Casey wanted to groan at how dumb they all sounded, but she

was having too hard of a time not molesting Lorn. "Is there somewhere we can put this stuff?"

He stood with a small, amused smiling curving his lips. "Please come with me. It is a nice evening and the men would enjoy your company."

With her heart slamming in her throat and her nipples hard enough to cut glass, Casey had to remind herself to breathe as Lorn picked up the case of beer with one arm and held his hand out to her. She slipped her hand into his and barely held back a groan at the rough sensation of his skin against hers. The golden light of the setting sun deepened his already dark tan and when he smiled down at her she stumbled.

Right away he stopped and gave her a concerned look. "Are you all right?"

"Yeah," she replied while her cheeks heated up enough to fry an egg on.

"She was sick earlier," Kimber said as she trailed behind them when Lorn continued to move toward the back yard and the mass of silent men watching them intently.

Lorn stroked her hand with his large thumb, sending tingles of desire spilling through her blood and moving to her already needy sex. "But you feel better?"

"Yeah, I'm okay."

Behind the house there were two wooden picnic tables set up and Lorn placed the beer on one while Page and Kimber put the cookies and brownies on the other.

Glancing at the still silent men, Casey tugged at Lorn's hand until he leaned down so she could whisper in his ear. "Um, is it okay for you guys to have sweets? I mean I don't want to mess with any diet you're on or anything."

He took a seat on the bench of the picnic table and pulled her closer until she stood between his spread thighs. His muscular, warm, massive, spread thighs that she wanted to rub herself against like a cat in heat. When he pulled her closer so he could whisper back in her ear goose bumps raced through her body at the brush of his lips against her oh so sensitive skin.

"Do not worry, Casey, we are honored that you seek to care for us."

She turned and hoped he didn't notice how she inhaled the scent of him before replying, "Why aren't they saying anything?"

Lorn moved her so she at on his knee and had no choice but to cuddle up against him. "They are waiting for you to introduce yourselves. In our culture it is considered rude to speak to a woman before she permits it."

Tearing her gaze from Lorn, resisting the need to kiss him until she couldn't breathe, Casey looked at her friends. "Say hi."

Dawn was the first to raise a hand and smile. "Hi, my name is Dawn."

With an unusually shy grin Kimber waved as well. "Hi, I'm Kimber."

The gaze of all the men focused on Paige and her friend swallowed hard and moved slightly behind the other two women before saying in a barely audible voice, "Paige. I'm Paige."

Lorn gave Casey an odd look and she quickly whispered, "Paige is really shy around men."

"Shy or scared?" Lorn whispered back while her friends busied themselves unwrapping the sweets as the men approached.

Not wanting to reveal Paige's history, but needing Lorn to know so he could pass it along to his friends, she said, "Both."

With a nod Lorn gently moved her off his lap then stood and said something in a language she didn't understand. The men making their way to the table paused and she watched them all visibly relax and their looks went from hungry to friendly. One man with long whiskey brown hair said something and looked at Dawn, then back to Lorn.

While they conversed Casey made her way over to the other women and whispered, "It's okay. They're not going to bite you."

"I wish they would," Kimber whispered back and the women giggled.

One of the men came out of the house with a portable stereo and soon music filled the yard while another group of men started to build a bonfire. Dawn quickly opened the case of beer and began to hand them out with the practiced ease of a bartender. Casey was puzzled as she watched the men take a drink of the beer as if unfamiliar with it while others sniffed the cookies before eating them, then giving surprised but pleased smiles. Almost as if on cue the men began to approach her friends in sets of two and three. Soon the other women were surrounded by extremely hot guys who were showering them with attention. Even Paige was giving an older man with some visible scars on his face and body a shy smile while he made an obvious effort to put her at ease.

Lorn grabbed her hand again and pulled her to her feet. "Come with me."

She shot her friends a look over her shoulder but they were all too busy drooling over the beefcake buffet to notice.

Following Lorn into the house she smiled as memories of visiting this home when she was a little girl. Her grandmother had been good friends with the family who used to live here, but all traces of them, other than the fussy floral wallpaper in the kitchen, were now gone. Instead of country style, it was clearly a man's domain and as he continued through the living room to the broad front porch that faced the gravel road she caught glimpses of a massive TV and comfortable grey leather furniture along with a bunch of electronics she couldn't identify.

Once they were on the wraparound porch out front Lorn took a seat on the padded swing hanging from thick brass chains screwed into the wood beam ceiling of the covered porch. The chains creaked alarmingly but held as Lorn tugged her down until she was draped across his lap with her head resting on his bicep. The position was very intimate, yet she wasn't uncomfortable, at least not because of embarrassment. Now that they were alone—voices from the backyard faintly reaching them along with feminine laughter blending with the soft chirp of crickets—she could devour him with her gaze as much as she wanted.

The sun had dipped below the horizon, and as she stared up at Lorn, she couldn't help but compare his eyes to the color of twilight, a beautiful dark blue mixed with almost purple.

"Are you feeling better?" he asked in a low voice that made her nipples harden to an uncomfortable state where just the rasp of her lacy bra was erotic.

"Yes." Words failed her as she studied his lips and wondered if his kiss was as good as she remembered.

Adjusting her on his lap as if she weighed no more than a feather, she became of aware of his very hard, very thick cock pressing against her butt. Her pussy grew wet, well wetter, and she vaguely wondered if she'd managed to soak the crotch of her jeans yet. The temptation to touch him proved too great to resist and she reached up hesitantly, pausing before she actually touched his lips.

He let out a soft groan and kissed the tip of her finger before sucking it into his mouth. It felt so good, too good, almost as if her finger had a direct line to her clit. Then he released her finger and in a swift move had her straddling his lap with his cock pressing up against her in a breath stealing rush of hormones. He smelled so damned good that she just wanted to bury her face against his neck and breathe in his cologne. She'd never smelled anything like it before but it was lethal to a woman's sense of decorum.

Threading his long fingers through her hair he gently tugged her closer until their lips met in a whisper-soft kiss that tore through her. She grasped his thick shoulders and groaned against his lips at the feel of his warm, slightly rough skin. He continued to kiss her with a skill that made her wanton and left her squirming against him, her pussy pulsing to the beat of her heart. Frantic for more, she tried to reach between them to lift his shirt but he stopped her.

"Easy, *alyah*." He nipped at her lips with unexpectedly sharp teeth and she rocked her hips against his erection.

"I need you," she panted while kissing along his jaw down to his neck where he smelled so good and hot. "Let me touch you."

With a low growl he restrained her hands. "No."

Stung, she tried to move off his lap but he held her in place. "No, let me touch you. Let me bring you pleasure."

"But I want you to feel good, too."

He grasped her face between his large hands. "Touching you, tasting you, is the best thing I have ever felt. You have no idea what just being here with you does to me. Let me savor you, Casey."

The sincerity in his gaze tugged at her heart while the obvious heat tugged at her libido and she swallowed hard before nodding.

"Place your hands on my shoulders. The feel of your little nails digging into me drives me insane, but if you keep touching me I will not be able to resist taking you hard and fast, bent over the railing with your sweet ass in the air."

Her eyes almost closed as the carnality of his statement made her clit throb. Part of her was totally on board with that plan, but the more rational part of her mind protested that anyone could walk in on them. However, that rational part of her mind was getting weaker by the second as Lorn ran his hands down her neck, over the bare skin of her shoulders, to lightly skim her rock-hard nipples.

She cried out at the first brush of his touch over those aching nubs, arching into his hands even as he continued his caress until he gripped her waist.

"Lord of Life, you test my self-control," he murmured while kissing along her neck.

"Please, Lorn," she whimpered, drowning in a sea of sensations too intense to be real. "Touch me."

His voice took on a carnal tone that had her rubbing her hips against the hard bulge of his cock. "Oh, I plan on touching every inch of your luscious, soft body. I want to lick you, bite you, and feast on that delicious nectar I can smell spilling from your pussy."

A hard shudder worked through her as his lips lowered to her cleavage. He slipped one hand beneath her ass, and in an amazing show of strength, lifted her so he could bury his face between her breasts, growling hard enough that his mouth vibrated against her skin. Vaguely she realized she should be alarmed by his growling and disturbed by how easily he held her against him, but his lips were moving closer to her nipple and she wanted to scream with the tension filling her.

She felt the soft, wet rasp of his tongue as it slipped between her bra and the very edge of her areola, and she jerked her top down followed by the cups of her bra until her breasts spilled out.

He froze against her and trembled, then leaned back and let out something akin to a snarl. "So pretty, so large and soft. Look at your nipples, pink like flowers and begging for my touch."

"Please, Lorn," she begged, "suck them."

"Oh, Casey, I plan on doing much more than that."

He dipped his head down and when his mouth wrapped around her right nipple she let out a choked scream. So good. His mouth sucked at her hard and she grabbed his face, holding him to her breast as she rocked faster on his lap, hitting her clit in a muscle-clenching burst of sensation. The need to come overwhelmed her and she shouted when he bit down on her nipple before switching to her other breast.

The rough tip of his tongue teased the nub while he began to rock back against her, the chains of the swing creaking with his movements as the hard muscles of his body tightened even more until she felt as if she was being pleasured by a stone statue come to life. Pleasure built, exquisite sensations filling her until she jerked her hips against his lap, grinding herself against him. His hands convulsed on her, then helped her ride the cloth-covered mound of his very big dick. Everything inside of her tightened, drawn into an almost painful clench of muscles as Lorn continued to feast on her breasts, suckling her nipples hard enough to send electric bolts of lust from her nipples straight to her soaked pussy. Another hard moan was torn from her throat as Lorn raked his sharp teeth over her nipples while squeezing her swollen breasts.

A slight vibration came from the area of Lorn's lap and she vaguely wondered if he had a cell phone going off in his pocket, but she didn't really care. Her orgasm hovered just on the edge and when Lorn raked his big dick against her clit she came with a scream. The suction of his mouth on her breast, the vibration from his cock, his scent, his touch, his everything shoved her into an amazing orgasm that was filled with pleasure and an odd sense of pride.

Her body shook against his and he growled again before whispered against her breast, "Mine."

"Casey?" Dawn's voice hit her like a cold splash of water and she opened her eyes to see her friend rounding the side of the house. She took one look at Lorn with his mouth wrapped around Casey's breast and let out a yelp then spun around. "Oh, shit! I'm so sorry! Oh shit, I'm leaving. Fuck...sorry, sorry."

Mortified and feeling like a complete whore, Casey wrenched herself away from Lorn. "Let me go."

He released her nipple with obvious reluctance and gave her a hungry, but puzzled look as she jerked her bra back in place. "What is wrong?"

"What's wrong? I'm dry-fucking you on the front porch of your house! Your friends could have come around the side at any second and seen me." She tried to move off his lap but he wouldn't release her.

"They don't matter." He tried to tug her shirt back down but she smacked at his hands.

"They don't matter? Are you fucking kidding me? I'm not the kind of girl who will let some strange guy see my tits. Let me go!"

He released her and stared at her in confusion as she stumbled away from him, humiliation burning away her arousal. "Why are you so upset?"

"One of my best friends just saw me almost screwing you on the front porch. Fuck! I came on your lap!" He frowned and she trembled with desire, confusion mixing with her volatile emotions until she felt like crying. "I've gotta go."

He stood and came after her as she sprinted down the steps. "Where are you going?"

"Just-just leave me alone, Lorn."

"Casey, come back here." He started to move down the steps and she walked faster until she was practically running. "Casey!"

"Just leave me alone," she yelled back and to her horror found Dawn and Kimber staring at her as she bolted back to her house.

She'd barely made it in her front door before her friends came in after her. Kimber grabbed her shoulder and whipped her around to face her. "Did he hurt you? Are you okay?"

"Yes." Tears started to fall and she hid her face with her hands. "I'm so sorry you had to see that, Dawn."

"What did you see?" Kimber asked.

The familiar scent of Dawn's perfume filled Casey as her friend hugged her. "I'm the one who's sorry. I heard you scream and thought you were in trouble, not making out with that sex god."

Kimber laughed and Casey lowered her hands to glare at her friend. "This is not funny!"

"What's the big deal? If I had someone as hot as that to make out with I'd screw him on the roof of his house."

81

Groaning, Casey collapsed on her couch and wished her body would stop throbbing with need. "I feel like such a slut."

"You," Dawn sat down next to her, "are not a slut. So you were making out with a guy on the front porch. Big deal."

"But I don't do things like that. What is wrong with me? I hardly know him. Shit, I don't even know his last name and he was practically at third base with me."

Kimber snorted. "Who gives a shit? He's fucking hot and obviously way into you. I saw how he looked at you, that man wants you, bad. He can call himself Lorn King Kong Balls, for all I care."

"This is so messed up." Casey tried to take a deep breath to slow her racing heart but her body was way pissed off that she'd left Lorn's arms. The memory of his hot mouth sucking her nipple made her want to scream with longing. "He must think I'm a psycho."

"Don't worry," Dawn stood. "I'll just tell him you aren't feeling well."

Kimber patted her knee. "Yeah. It'll be fine."

With a sigh Casey clasped her hands together and looked at her fingers. "I'm such an idiot. He'll probably never want to speak to me again."

"Well, I think you scared him but he seemed more worried than anything else." She started towards the door. "Come on, Kimber, we can't leave Paige alone over there."

Casey felt like a total asshole for only thinking about herself. "Oh, shit, Paige. Is she okay?"

With an odd look on her face Kimber nodded. "Yeah, she's fine. When I left she was talking to some scary-looking dude over by the fire."

"Really?"

Dawn opened the door and nodded. "Yep. Don't worry, we'll take care of Lorn for you. We'll tell him you had to puke or something."

Feeling horny and miserable Casey nodded. "Thanks."

Kimber blew her a kiss as they left and she leaned back, thunking her head against the couch. Great, she finally meets a man who hits all of her buttons, and first she acts like a mega slut, then freaks out and runs away from him like a spazz. She'd be lucky if Lorn even acknowledged her if she ever saw him again. The thought of never feeling his touch, tasting his kiss made tears burn and she struggled to process the feeling of soul-killing loss. What the hell was wrong with her?

The more she thought about Lorn the more she wanted him until she was groaning on her couch and pressing her thighs together to try and relieve the ache. Damn, she was so fucking horny she could barely think straight. She needed to take a cold shower then go to bed and try to get some sleep. Maybe in the morning things would be clearer.

With that in mind she left the lights in the living room on just in case one of her friends wanted to crash here tonight and made her way to her bathroom, shedding her clothes as she walked through her small bedroom to her bathroom. The air seemed to caress her skin as she stripped down and a restless hunger moved through her. Her whole body buzzed and just the action of walking made her disturbingly close to having an orgasm.

Looking into the mirror over the chipped white porcelain sink she tried to see if she could spot a rash or something on her skin that could be the cause of her weird sensitivity. Maybe she was allergic to Lorn's cologne, or detergent, though she'd never heard of an allergic reaction that would make someone horny. As far as she could tell she looked pretty much the same, except her lips looked kiss-swollen and her nipples were harder and pinker than she'd ever seen them after the adoration of Lorn's talented mouth. A quick check between her legs confirmed that her pussy was indeed engorged and her inner thighs were slick with her arousal. Biting her lip, she slipped her fingers over her waxed mound and her knees almost gave out at the raw bolt of need coursing through her blood.

She jerked her hand back and staggered to the shower, hoping that somehow washing would soothe her skin, or at the very least, if she had to call an ambulance for fatal horniness she would be clean. Before the water was even warm she stepped beneath the icy spray and gasped as her nipples hurt from the direct contact of the cold water. The water quickly warmed as she took in deep breaths, trying to calm her body when all it wanted to do was fuck.

Now.

With trembling hands she poured out a palm-full of her shampoo and quickly washed her hair, moaning at the feeling of her fingers stroking her scalp. Hell, it felt better than sex. When it came time for the conditioner her whole body ached, and she wanted a man between her legs like an obsession. The urge to touch herself and attempt to regain some of her sanity was too great to resist, especially after she soaped her breasts then her pussy. The memory of Lorn's lips sucking at her had her moaning as her touch turned to a caress.

Leaning back against the blue tile wall she spread her legs and slid her fingers between them, crying out at the merest brush of her fingers over her clit. Okay, something was really, really wrong with her but it felt too good to stop. Unable to even touch her clit because it was so sensitive, she slid her fingers over her slick outer labia, massaging the flesh with a gentle touch producing a constant stream of moans and whimpers.

She stared with unseeing, pleasure-glazed eyes through the clear vinyl of her shower curtain, slowly learning her body like she'd never touched herself before. When she brushed the entrance to her sex with her fingertip she actually screamed, unable to help herself as the dangerously wonderful feeling combined with her ever-growing need for fulfillment. Her mind switched to Lorn and she imagined it was his finger touching her, his lips wrapping around her nipple.

Her orgasm crept closer, leaving her languid with bliss. Hell, she might never stop touching herself if it always felt like this. Tracing the fingertips of her other hand over her nipple she closed her eyes and leaned her head back against the shower wall, drowning in pleasure.

With a crash her bathroom door was thrown open so hard it came partially off the hinges and she screamed as a very scary Lorn stared at her with his lips curled back from his fangs.

Fangs?

What the fuck?

Before her mind could even process anything he'd crossed the room and tore the shower curtain aside, stepping into the bathtub with her and burying his face against her belly, crowding her into the corner of her small tub.

"Lorn? What the hell are you doing?"

He shuddered and continued to rub his face against her like a big cat. "I am sorry I scared you. Your friends said you were sick and...I had to come."

Embarrassment mixed with her arousal and she swayed at the sensation of his tongue licking around her belly button. "What are you doing?"

"You smell so good," he replied in a gruff voice. "So hot. You smell like mine."

She bit back a moan as she tried to tug his hair, all but melting against him. "This is crazy. You have fangs!"

"Only when I am angry. I was furious something might have happened to you. Do not worry *alyah*, I would never harm you."

Using every bit of strength she had, she tried to push his clever mouth away from her aching body, knowing that if he put his lips anywhere near her pussy she would utterly lose her mind. "Lorn, stop, please."

With obvious reluctance he did as she asked and stared up at her with eyes that had gone a dark, midnight blue. "Do you not wish for

84

me to bring you pleasure? To ease your need? I can smell it, Casey, like nectar from a ripe fruit waiting for my mouth to drink it down."

Her hand shook as she gently lifted his upper lip to reveal that he did indeed have fangs, though they seemed to be receding as she watched. "Are you a vampire?"

It would make sense, the inhumanly good looks, the delicious taste, how quickly he moved and the way he'd mesmerized her from the moment they met. He laughed and stood abruptly, flipping back his wet hair. "No, not quite."

Before she could protest he lifted her against his chest, smashing her sore breasts against him. She moaned and wrapped her arms around his neck. Looking concerned, he stepped out of the tub before gently setting her on her unsteady feet. "Casey, are you in pain?"

Embarrassed at her obvious out of control arousal, she shook her head. "No."

"Then why do you moan and cry out?"

She turned her back on him and grabbed a towel, wrapping it around herself before facing him again. Wet from the shower, with his shirt plastered to his body and his jeans looking like they were painted on he was everything she'd ever desired in a man. She momentarily lost her train of thought as she stared at the impressive bulge in his pants. A craving to have him inside of her gripped her like an addiction and she clutched at her towel.

"Who are you? I mean who are you *really*?"

He stood up taller and became more imposing. "I am Lorn Adar of the House Adar, eldest son of Lady Elsin Adar, Captain of the Ninety-Eighth Legion of Kadothian and Protector of the Bel'Tan galaxy."

It took a few moments for her stunned brain to kick into gear, but when it did she took a weary step back. "Okay..."

He frowned. "I displease you?"

"No, no you don't displease me." Her voice came out as faint as she felt and she sucked in a deep breath of air.

Her mind spun and she moved as quickly as she could for her closet, choosing to not even try and put pants on for fear of climaxing from the seam rubbing against her. The Bel'Tan Galaxy? House Adar? What the fuck. A different galaxy meant a different planet, which meant...

"Holy shit, you're an alien!"

When he didn't respond she turned to face him, finding him watching her all too intently. Like a predator ready to leap. There was that coiled tension in his limbs and the way he studied her body left her no doubt about his own sexual arousal. His gaze focused on her the space between her hips and he licked his lips.

"Mind closing your eyes while I get dressed?"

"Why?"

"Because I don't feel comfortable with you staring at my ass."

He grinned and nodded, then closed his eyes. "You are shy, I understand that. It is normal among brides but you will soon realize you have nothing to fear from me. When you see me looking at you with hunger you will know all I want to do is bring you pleasure in every way possible. Oh, Casey, the things I want to do to you..."

A fresh rush of cream wet her sex and she tried to still the shudder from the accompanying ache. Picking out a loose, pale yellow sundress she quickly slipped it on and grimaced at the sensation of the cloth teasing her nipples. In a weird way her freakish arousal was helping her deal with all the shit Lorn was throwing at her. It was hard to go into hysterics when her body was begging her to fuck the handsome man...alien...whatever until she couldn't walk. She glanced up at Lorn and caught him staring intently at her breasts. When she glared at him he had the balls to merely grin back.

With a sniff she went to walk past him to grab a rubber band for her hair, but he halted her in her tracks by wrapping his arm around her waist and pulling her tight to his body. His warmth seeped into her and she shivered as the water still dripping from him soaked her dress. God he felt so good, so hard and the warmth from his skin seemed to sink all the way to her soul.

"Let me go. You're getting me all wet."

His nostrils flared and his voice came out in a scary rumble as he said, "You are already wet, Casey. Let me ease you. Smelling your need is driving me insane. Help me find control; allow me to soothe you. I am trying to go slow for your sake, but it is so hard when you smell this good."

He didn't wait for her response, merely reaching beneath the edge of her dress like he had every right to touch her. Whatever protest she was going to form died a quick and brutal death when he rubbed one large finger against her aching slit, sliding through her juices. Surprise widened his eyes.

"You are dripping wet. I love it, so hot and soft for me. I cannot wait to get my tongue in your sweet sex."

"I need you," she moaned as he slowly explored the folds of her pussy, crying out when his finger found the bump of her clit.

"That is a pleasure center for you?" The strength went out of her legs as he pressed down hard on her sensitive nub, almost throwing

86

her straight into an orgasm. "I will take that as a yes. Interesting."

The more he explored the more she needed him until her womb felt as if it were cramping. "Lorn, please, it hurts. Make me come."

"Oh, my beautiful bride, all you have to do is ask."

"Bride? Wai..."

He captured her lips in a kiss that coincided perfectly with his finger breaching her.

"Lord of Life you are tight, hot, and so slick. You strain my self-control, *alyah*."

Too aroused to care about anything but getting off, she rocked herself against his hand, moaning with abandon as he kissed his way down her throat, pausing to nip at her pulse point. He would lick, then suck, then bite again all while teasing the entrance to her body. If he really was an alien they couldn't be that biologically different because he knew exactly how to work her into a frenzy. The sharp nip on the sensitive skin where her neck joined her shoulder froze her in his arms, and when he eased his finger deep inside of her sheath, she lost her mind.

The world exploded in a flash of light and pleasure that had her clutching onto Lorn, shaking apart while he finger fucked her ruthlessly, fighting the hard clench of her pussy as she tried to keep him inside of her, moving in perfect time to each blissful contraction. All through her climax he kept saying something to her in that deep, growling voice until she was a jerking, moaning, incoherent heap in his arms, totally destroyed by the orgasm to end all orgasms.

In her pleasure-drunk state she became dimly aware of his hunger, his pride filling her as if it were her own. Dazed, she looked up into his eyes and whimpered when he removed his finger from her and licked it clean with relish. The wonderful scent of him washed over her and she felt something...odd. The impression of a pure love so intense she had no name for it, a satisfaction so deep it redefined her sense of the word.

"There you are," he said with a satisfied smile, then threw his head back and gave this scary roaring howl loud enough to wake the dead.

She screamed and tried to scramble out of his arms, but he stopped howling and held her close, refusing to let her go. "You are fearful, why? Did I not please you?"

Staring up at him, shivering as the dampness of her dress tried to steal her warmth, she managed to say, "You roared!"

His white teeth flashed against the dark tan of his face. "Yes. I was announcing to the Universe that I have found my bride."

"Bride? Like *marriage* bride?"

"Yes." His smile slowly faded and hurt replaced his happiness. "You do not look happy about that."

"Lorn, I don't understand any of this. What is going on? Why are you here? And why do I suddenly feel like a nymphomaniac? I don't even really know if you're even a for real alien. I mean for all I know you could be some hot psycho."

His fair brows drew down. "What is a psycho?"

"It's a crazy person who harms others."

"I have not fallen to the madness," he suddenly growled, once again scaring the crap out of her.

"Stop that, okay? Stop that growling shit. It scares me and I can't think when I am scared."

He released her and dropped to one knee, bowing his head to her. "Forgive me. It is never my intent to scare you, *alyah*."

"Why do you keep calling me that?"

Standing quickly, he scooped her up into his arms and began to walk out of her room.

"Hey, wait, where are we going?"

"This is not the place for this conversation."

"Put me down. I can walk."

They passed through the living room in a blur and she clutched his shoulders once they stepped outside. Night had fallen and despite the quarter moon it was dark enough that she couldn't see far beyond her porch light. In the distance, a bonfire roared in the backyard of the house where Lorn was staying, and her mind immediately went to her girlfriends over there with Lorn's alien buddies. House full of male supermodels her ass. They really needed to work on a better cover story she thought as a hysterical giggle bubbled in her chest.

"Wait, Lorn, what about my friends? Are they okay? Your guys won't hurt them will they? They're aliens too, right?"

Lorn looked highly amused as he glanced down at her and walked out to the middle of her drive with her still in his arms. "Your friends are safe. A Kadothian male would slit his own throat before ever hurting a female."

She tried to twist in his arms to look in the direction of his house but his massive shoulders blocked her view. "Where are we going? I'm wet and it's cold out here. If we're going to the bonfire I'll need a jacket."

Looking down at her, he held her tight. "Hold on, Casey, and close your eyes."

"What?"

Chapter Eight

Lorn smiled down at his bride, finding her utterly adorable as she stared up at him, confusion and frustration along with arousal brushing against his soul like the softest of kisses. He was unsure how she would react to being fast tracked to the ship so he pressed her close to his chest so she couldn't look. While he was used to the disconcerting sensation of being returned to the ship via molecular transport, it was disconcerting to see your body dissolve and yet remain conscious. It happened so quickly that his Casey didn't even have time to blink, let alone breathe. One minute they were on the surface of her home world, the next aboard the massive Kadothian Reaping ship. It was specially designed for housing the brides during the beginning stages of the courting rights and the spacecraft boasted all the comforts a woman could desire.

They'd added some luxuries since the first wave of Earth brides arrived, including a large public market where the women could be introduced to some of the goods from the Bel'Tan universe and a huge information center where they'd brought some of the primitive computers from their planet and linked them up to the Kadothian network so the brides could do their own research on their new people. Earth females were particularly stubborn and liked to learn things on their own, so they'd also set up classes taught by both Earth Matriarchs further along in the bonding process and Kadothian Matriarchs here to help them adjust.

Grimnan, one of Lorn's men, let out a howl of victory as he spied Casey in Lorn's arms. "Congratulations on finding your bride, Captain."

Casey screamed and looked wildly around her, the panic racing through her strong enough to push his anger to the surface as she fought his hold. He tried to control his temper, knowing that Grimnan didn't meant to upset his bride, but he couldn't help the warning growl that rumbled through him. Casey must have felt it because she smacked his chest as he stepped off the platform and made his way to a quiet corner of the busy terminal.

"Stop that!"

She began to shudder and he rubbed her body as best he could, trying to soothe both her fear and her body. "Easy, *alyah*, soon I will have you in our quarters where I will care for you."

Her eyes met his and he read absolute terror in her expressive face. "Lorn?"

"Hello," a female voice came from his right and he looked up to find a pretty, dark skinned Earth-born Matriarch coming towards them.

By her scent she'd fully bonded with two men of the Healer class and she wore the green robes of a new Matriarch. They differed from the robes of a Matriarch past her childbearing years by displaying the top curves of her breasts where her bondmarks proclaimed her as married. His first instinct was to bow to her, but he held Casey in his arms and he would do nothing to risk his bride.

The woman gave him a dismissive snort and reached out to Casey, gently patting her shoulder. "Hey now, you're okay, sugar. I'm guessing by your freaked out expression this big lug didn't tell you anything about anything. Typical."

Casey unpeeled herself enough to look over at the other woman and her instant relief was obvious. "You're human."

"Yep. Some of the other brides and I have put together a kind of informal greeting committee. I passed out during my first trip to the Reaping ship. They didn't seem to consider we'd be terrified about being on a space ship, surrounded by hundreds of thousands of guys who look like extras from a Conan movie, and unable to understand what the hell anyone is saying." She looked over her shoulder and smiled at a Healer Lorn seemed unfamiliar with, a dark-haired man with pale skin who watched his Matriarch closely. "That big brooding hunk of man meat over there is my husband, Mavet. My other husband, Xentix, is nearby I'm sure."

He allowed Casey to wiggle out of his arms, trying to keep from holding her against him and not letting her move an inch. Remembering his manners he bowed his head to the Matriarch. "It is an honor to meet you..."

"Jazmin, um, I mean Jazmin, Matriarch of House Brooks." She smiled at Casey again. "But you can call me Jaz."

Casey glanced over at Mavet then back at Jaz. "You have two husbands?"

"Oh yeah, girl. It's the normal thing to do in their culture and not a hardship, at all. Hell, Mavet would have been happy if I bonded, their version of marriage, to two more guys." She chuckled and cast her bondmate a fond look. "But don't worry about that right now. First, let me hook you up with something to help translate."

Lorn tensed as Jaz took something from the pocket of her robe, then relaxed at the sight of the tiny crystal and mentally scolded himself for not thinking of it first. Jaz swept Casey's hair to the side and placed the crystal behind her ear.

"There, now you should be able to hear everyone. It's some kind of translator thingy. Damned if I know how it works, it just does. You can now speak and understand over eight hundred and fifty thousand languages. Big guy, talk to your bride in a couple languages and help me make sure it works."

Going to his knees, he grasped Casey's hips and pulled her close enough that he could rest his head against her soft, cold belly. A hint of her arousal flavored her body and he restrained himself from growling since it seemed to upset her. "Hello, beloved. I'm sorry you are chilled. Please forgive me for not thinking of your comforts and frightening you."

"Lorn?" she said in a soft voice and placed her small hand on his head. "What am I doing here?"

Before he could answer Jaz laughed. "That is a long, long explanation and if you're anything like the rest of us human brides you're already feeling the need to get your man back into the bedroom."

Irritation mixed with embarrassment flowed through his bride. "Is he responsible for this crazy arousal?"

Jaz's grin widened. "Yep. When you first kissed he gave you a little bit of his blood. It probably made you sick as hell as it changed your hormones and it acts like some kind of super strong aphrodisiac. Don't worry, it won't always be this bad. I know right now you feel like a nymphomaniac on Spanish Fly, but that will ease as your body adjusts. After the bonding you'll still be a nympho for your man—who the hell wouldn't—but it won't be quite so overwhelming. Let me tell you, the things these Kadothian men can do in bed that human men can't...wow."

"Son of a bitch." Casey yanked his hair, hard. "Get off of me."

Confusion filled him and he backed away then stood and examined his Casey. A light flush colored her cheeks and her dark eyes were filled with fire. Even in her anger she was so beautiful his heart ached. "You are angry with me?"

To his horror tears filled her eyes. "I'm cold, hungry, confused, on a fucking alien spaceship and...and I still want to throw you up against the wall and screw your brains out. This is bullshit!"

All around them people laughed and Casey covered her face with her hands, her shoulders slumping forward. He gathered her into his arms and glared at those who would dare laugh at his bride. More than one Warrior quickly left the area while Jaz watched with amusement. Her bondmate came up behind her and wrapped his arms around the dark skinned woman, dwarfing her with his size.

She stroked his arm and gave Casey an understanding look.

"It's not that bad. While it's Lorn's place to explain it all to you, I can tell you this. Kadothian men worship their women, and I'm not exaggerating. He will never, ever cheat on you, hurt you, or leave you. He will die before he lets anything happen to you and will..." Jaz paused and looked up at Mavet, "What did you say you would do to anyone that would harm me?"

His low growl vibrated through the air and when he spoke his lips lifted to reveal his extended canines. "I would eviscerate them, slowly, then remove their internal organs while keeping them alive, making sure I left their eyes and throat for last so they can see their destruction and scream-"

Jaz placed her hand over his lips with an amused look. "Yuck. So yeah, you will never find a man on Earth who will love you like they love you."

Casey shivered and Lorn gathered her into his arms again. "I am taking her to my quarters."

His bride looked over at Jaz. "I'm scared."

Irritation filled him that Casey was looking to another for comfort but Mavet met his gaze and shook his head ever so slightly.

Jaz gave Casey a sympathetic look. "I understand, I really do, but please believe me that you're safe here. Just give him a chance, okay? His life quite literally rests in your hands. If you liked him enough to kiss him try to hold onto that feeling."

"Okay." Casey hid her face against his chest.

Lorn nodded to the Matriarch and her husband. "My thanks."

"You're welcome, Warrior." Jaz grinned. "Now, go show her how much fun the courting ritual is."

He left them, walking quickly through the ship to his quarters and despair crushed his heart as he felt Casey's love for him fading. Misery filled him as he realized not only was he losing her, but he would have to tell Nast he'd failed. Darkness threatened to overwhelm him but he prayed to the Lord of Life as he carried his reluctant bride through the halls of the ship that he would find a way to make her understand that all he wanted to do was love her.

Casey took a deep breath of Lorn's scent, her mind so overwhelmed by the changes happening to her life that she couldn't do anything but exist. She caught glimpses of metal walls, more men like Lorn, and the occasional woman, but mostly she just hid against his body. That damned arousal was beginning to flood her again, making her aware of how good Lorn smelled, and how worried he was. In an odd way, she could feel his anxiety and she didn't like that either.

Finally he stopped moving and said, "Welcome to our temporary home, Casey."

Peeking over her shoulder she let out a soft gasp. It was beautiful and definitely not what she expected. The furniture was all sleek, smooth lines done in pastel gold tones mixed with different shades of brown. The floor was covered with what looked like cream carpet but it was smooth with no lines or imperfections anywhere. What she assumed was framed artwork adorned walls, images of fantastical forests where the trees hung heavy with jewel toned fruits and the grass was a deeper green than the kind on earth, almost a pine green color with hints of teal. Dragging her gaze from the pictures she took in an array of what appeared to be electronic equipment on the far wall and more curved furniture. He let her slide out of his arms and she shivered as soon as she was away from the heat of his body. Stepping away from her he placed his hand on her cheek, turning her gaze to him.

"You are cold. Let me get you something warm to wear."

She could only blink at him and he sighed then left her standing in the middle of the room. Taking a hesitant step forward she smiled as it felt almost like she was walking on wet sand. Either way it was very comfortable and gave her the courage to take another step to the nearest chair. After cautiously touching the surface, she gasped softly at the silken feel of the fabric or whatever it was covering the chair. While it was soft like satin her hand didn't slide over the surface and it had a slightly velvety rasp to it.

Lorn's scent filled her a moment before he stepped up behind her. "Please remove your wet garment, *alyah*."

For a moment she considered fighting him, but there really was no point. She was cold and bone-tired, yet still aroused. As she pulled her dress off the sensation of the fabric dragging over her skin tore a little moan out of her which brought a corresponding growl from Lorn. A moment later soft, fluffy fabric enveloped her when Lorn helped her into some kind of thick peach robe made of a shimmery material. It seemed to both warm her and dry her instantly.

"Thanks."

He moved into her line of sight and set his hand over hers as she continued to stroke the chair. "Casey, please look at me."

A childish impulse to ignore him raced through her, but she pushed it aside and gazed up at the man who made her feel such crazy things. His blue eyes were light, almost white and his handsome features were tense. Even if she didn't have the slight impression of worry coming from him she could easily read his fear in his face. It shouldn't matter to her that he was upset, but she couldn't help the urge to soothe him any more than she could fight the need to breathe. He'd removed his wet shirt and now wore a pair of loose black pants that showed the impressive bulge of his cock. Tearing her eyes away from his groin she clutched the robe about herself and returned her gaze to his face.

Tilting her head, she studied him. "Why are you afraid?"

"I fear your hatred for me will close your heart."

The raw honesty of his words moved her. "Lorn, I don't hate you. I just...this is a lot to take in okay. I know we're on a ship, but where are we?"

He held out his hand and when she slipped hers into his warmth flowed between them, chasing back her fear. "Come, I will show you."

Following him through the large room they went into a short hallway with a single door on one side and two doors on the other. He made a gesture with his free hand and the door slid open, revealing a room about half the size of what she assumed passed for the living room of his apartment. To her right a huge bed covered in shiny gold fabric butted up against the wall. Pillows done in brown and green tones softened the curved headboard and when she took another step forward, still holding Lorn's hand, she smiled at the sight of the soft cream walls and a table near the door constructed of a shimmery white material. On the table there was a vase that held what she assumed were flowers. They were pale pink in the center with elongated, curved creamy petals that stretched out in a frill almost like lace.

"What are these?"

"On my planet they are the first gift we give our bride. My blood brother grew these for you on our land." He smiled at her and urged her forward. "Touch them, smell them."

She hesitantly bent over the flower and gasped in surprise when the wonderful perfume enveloped her. It smelled like fresh baked cookies mixed with a floral perfume she couldn't identify. When she leaned back and touched a petal little glowing beads of pink and white light floated through the air before dissipating. She touched it again, amazed at the light coming off of the flowers.

"Wow."

"I want to show you something."

Curious, she followed him across the room with a little more confidence. They reached the bare wall on the far side of the bed and he stopped. Tugging at her gently, he pulled her into his arms. As soon as he held her the sense of comfort, of being loved intensified until if filled her soul, chasing away the last traces of fear. God, being held by him was like taking a sedative without getting fuzzyheaded.

He waved his hand and the wall began to dissolve; what it revealed on the other side left her speechless.

"Holy shit, is that...*Jupiter*?"

"Yes. We are on one of its moons. I believe it is called Callisto on your planet."

She tried to remember to breathe but it was an effort. A rocky lunar surface with jagged spires of dark stone stretched out before her, but beyond that outer space filled her vision. Stars, so many stars surrounded the huge planet in the distance with its never-ending storms. Unlike most images that she'd seen of Jupiter on Earth, from this perspective the world wasn't merely shades of tan, but brilliant swirls of green and gold with hints of blue swirling through the brown. Her heart sped as she eagerly took in the view, marveling at the beauty of space. But the stars...she'd never seen anything so beautiful and there were so many. In theory, she knew the universe was immense but it was one thing to imagine it, but to see it...she felt like she was looking at God.

"It's so beautiful."

Lorn rubbed her arms through the plush fabric of her robe, awakening sensitive nerves to his touch. "It is."

Unable to look away she nodded in the direction of Jupiter. "Is that where you're from?"

"No, we came through the wormhole from the Bel'Tan galaxy. It is the space anomaly that your scientists are studying that appeared a few Earth months ago causing what your people refer to as 'The Event'."

"Really?"

"Yes. The other side of the wormhole opens into my galaxy."

She contemplated the idea for a moment. "Why did your people come here? To explore?"

He stiffened slightly. "No, we came here seeking brides."

"Why? Don't you have women on your planet?"

"No."

Shocked, she managed to tear her gaze from the glory of space to look up at him over her shoulder. "None?"

"There has not been a female Kadothian born in over ten thousand years."

"What?" Now she turned so she could fully face him. His grave

95

expression told her that he wasn't joking. "How is that even possible?"

"May I close this?"

"Sure." Her curiosity about Lorn's planet eclipsed everything.

He waved his hand again then led her over to the bed. "Please sit."

She did, jumping slightly at the soft, warm feel of the bed. It was an odd sensation, but very comfortable as the mattress seemed to mold around her without her sinking into the surface. Lorn sat across from her, his eyes a shade of blue she'd only seen in pictures of the Caribbean Sea. The muscles of his chest, arms, and abdomen flexed as he adjusted himself, making her want to touch him. Looking away from the temptation of his exposed body was even harder than looking away from the window, but she managed.

To her surprise he smiled at her, some of the darkness fading from his expression. "I am pleased you find me attractive."

Refusing to be distracted by her hormones, she gathered the robe around her and got comfortable. "Talk."

He reached out and took her hand again, the sensation of comfort easing her tense muscles. "I come from a race of what your people would call empaths. While the word does not describe exactly what we are, it will work for this conversation. We can feel the emotions of others if they are not properly shielded and the strongest among us can talk to each other mind-to-mind as well as use that empathy as a weapon."

"How can they do that? What do you mean?"

"If one of our Matriarchs, the name we use for our bonded females, is very angry and strong enough her anger can translate into sensation that can hurt those not strong enough to shield themselves from her. A very strong Matriarch can cause a weakly bonded or shielded individual's body to shut down, their hearts to speed until they burst, and destroy their mind. And she can do all of this by merely looking at a person."

A shiver worked through her and she swallowed hard. "I thought you said there were no women on your planet."

"There are not. All brides, who become Matriarchs, come to us from other worlds. It is not only considered a great honor but a dream of many of the females in our galaxy to be a Kadothian Matriarch. They know if they bond a Kadothian male they will be taken care of and cherished for the rest of their lives."

"But, what happened to your females? I mean at some point you had to be a fledgling race, someone most have given birth somehow."

He looked down at their joined hands and rubbed his thumb over her skin, sending pleasant tingles through her blood. "Ten thousand, six hundred and seventy-two years ago, when your race was just beginning to establish its civilizations, my home world was embroiled in a six-thousand-year war among the different factions living on Kadothia. We were far more advanced than Earth, had already discovered space travel, and were slowly exploring the galaxy. Kadothia was on the brink of complete destruction when someone decided to use a virus to alter the neural pathways in our females' minds to make them the perfect weapon. Women have always been stronger than men in mental warfare and though we do not know who did it—both sides blamed each other—the end result was the same. The virus changed the women's DNA and spread across the planet, making them into the perfect weapon."

"How so?"

"The virus altered their DNA, destroying any possible mental capacity for compassion and empathy, leaving them as pure killing machines. They no longer loved, they no longer even understood love or had the ability to even imagine it. Our women—and every female born after the Great Sorrow, as it came to be known—were tainted. They could not care about anything other than their own personal survival and advancement. They did not feel emotion as we understand it; their only gratification seemed to come from inflicting physical and emotional pain on others. No matter what we our scientists tried, every female was born evil. Because of this, a Kadothian's DNA is altered at conception so that we cannot have any female children, only males."

"Holy shit." Casey tried to wrap her mind around the concept. "So they were sociopaths?"

His gaze grew distant for a moment and she swore his pupils dilated rapidly before refocusing on her. "It is as close to a direct translation as we can get, but still different. These women could think rationally enough that they banded together to work toward mutual goals."

"I thought you said they felt no compassion or emotion. Why would they work together?"

"They do not. Every action is based on their survival, and they survived longer working together. Their decisions are not founded on any form of emotion, only cold logic. In fact, they worked together so well, they almost exterminated the Kadothian race before my ancestors put aside their personal hatreds to band together, but our men were severely handicapped. Without a Kadothian female to bond with we had no mate, and without a mate our minds will slowly degenerate to a state similar to the females, but more animalistic. We do not know if it was by chance, or how exactly it happened, but our scientists managed to modify our glandular system enough that if we exposed a compatible female to our blood, one that our souls could bond with, we could mate them. Hence, the start of what came to be known as our Matriarchs."

He reclined on his side, a tempting visual treat of heavy muscles and powerful grace. Even resting he managed to look intimidating and delicious. His scent grew heavy in the small space between them and each lungful of air seemed to feed her runaway libido. Trying to get her mind off the need to lick him all over, she focused on his face. "So that's why you seek brides?"

"Yes. A group of the altered Kadothian females managed to make it off planet and formed their own society on a planet at the edge of our galaxy known as The Hive." His nostril's flared and a hint of his anger filled her. "Unlike the Kadothian system of seeking a mate which assures the bride is willing, the Hive began to plunder planets in the Bel'Tan galaxy to take males for breeding. It is...it is a mercy to kill any males we manage to rescue. Through drugs they are forced to perform sexually while being tortured for the Hive female's pleasure. The only blessing is their minds quickly break and that only a small percentage of the Hive females actually manage to conceive."

Her stomach roiled at the thought of anyone being subjected to the endless pain and terror.

"That is terrible." She lay down on her side, needing to be closer to Lorn. Never in her wildest imaginings did she think such pure evil could exist. "How come they haven't attacked Earth?"

"Your planet is too far away. It would take four generations of travel to reach you without the wormhole. There is no need for the Hive to do that when they have everything they need in the Bel'Tan galaxy."

"But what about now? I mean the wormhole is open and everything. Could they come here?"

He frowned. "In theory, yes, but the wormhole opened near Kadothia in heavily guarded space and they have no reason to take such a risk when they have outer planets that make easier targets."

"Good." She studied him, trying to imagine what his life had been like. "Are you one of the men that fight the Hive?"

"I am. While all Kadothian men are Warriors, I am a Warrior in truth. There are other subsets such as the Scouts, Healers, Assassins, and the Negotiators who also fall beneath the umbrella term of Warrior. I am a fighter and am partially bonded to a

Matriarch which gives me immunity from most of the mental attacks of a Hive female."

"What do you mean most?"

For the first time she saw a hint of fear on his face and that scared her more than anything he'd said. "There have been occasions where the Hive has managed to get past partial bonds. When they do they can temporarily use the Warrior's body to destroy his Legion from within. It has only happened a few times but the resulting carnage was...I was part of a Legion that had to retrieve the bodies from a battlefield where a Warrior had been compromised. As one of the highest-ranking officers it was my duty to bring the remains of my brothers in arms back to their families. It took me three months to visit them all, three months of funerals and mourning."

Compassion filled her and she had to blink back tears. Moving on instinct, overwhelmed by the need to take his mind off what was obviously a nightmare-inducing encounter, she closed the distance between them and held him close. He buried his face against her chest, taking in deep inhalations as he held her tight.

"I knew the Warrior who was compromised, Ulint. His mother was friends with my mother. He was a good man, a good warrior, but the Matriarch he was partially bonded to had bonded too many men and her protection was stretched thin, but Ulint was a good man and the women found him very charming, so even though his Matriarch knew her protection might not be enough she couldn't send him out with nothing."

"Why didn't he just stay home? And what is a partial bond?"

Lorn released her and rolled onto his back, his gaze on the ceiling and his expression tight with sorrow. "My people are the only thing that stands between the Hive and our galaxy, but we are stretched thin, especially our bonded males despite the other planet's willingness to allow us to seek brides. The mated males have the strongest shielding against the Hive but they must stay behind to protect their bondmate. If the Matriarch dies, all of the bonds dissolve instantly. Matriarchs will take on secondary males that they will form a weaker bond with, not a full loving partnership but more like..." he struggled before his gaze cleared. "The best way I can put it so you could understand is that our Matriarchs are like your queens and while she may have several kings, she has a legion of knights. They are not as powerful as the kings, but still deadly in their own right."

"If you have all those planets willing to donate brides, why do you need women from Earth?"

"There were safeguards put into place that only allows us to take so many females from each planet. We have exhausted the supply for another fifty cycles, the equivalent of over one hundred earth years. Our partially bonded men are dying quicker than we can replace them. In periods between Reapings all males nearing the time of madness have no hope of finding a bond mate to save them, to love them, and their minds degrade quicker from depression. I've had to accompany far too many of my friends to our prison planets over the last few years." His gaze grew bleak and he closed his eyes for a moment before opening them and staring at her with such hope, such affection, that her breath froze in her chest. "Then we found Earth and our prayers were answered. My prayers were answered. You have no idea how close I was to losing myself."

A hot blush heated her cheeks at the open love and reverence in his voice. Then his words registered. "You mean you almost went crazy?"

"I would have been safe for a few more cycles, but it was getting harder to temper my anger, to find forgiveness in my heart. That is why I insisted on staying on the battlefront for so long. There I could let loose my killer instincts against an enemy who constantly seeks to destroy everything and everyone I hold dear."

"And you think I'm your bond mate?"

"I know you are."

"How?"

He gave her an amused smile. "Casey, I could feel you before I even knew of your existence. You were a song in my heart, a calling that echoed in my soul the moment I made it through the wormhole. Then when I found you everything in my life clicked into place. There is no doubt you are my bondmate. Did you not feel something similar?"

Thinking back on her strong reaction to him she nodded. "I did, but I thought it was just because you are ridiculously sexy."

Pride shown in his eyes and his grin was pure male arrogance. "I am glad you are attracted to me, because I think you are the most beautiful woman I have ever beheld."

She snorted. "You must have different standards of beauty on your planet than Earth."

"Thank the Lord of Life your Earth males are too stupid to see the bounty before them. They are spoiled by having so many females to choose from. Plus they are mentally crippled and cannot see your soul."

"Umm, I can't see your soul either."

"Yes, you can. Close your eyes, Casey."

She did as he asked then sighed when he began to slowly finger comb her hair. "Relax, let yourself feel me. Concentrate on my touch and your muscles easing, your heart slowing. Every inch of your body is softening, sinking into me. You have nothing to fear because I will never let anything happen to you. Breathe in my scent in slow, deep inhalations. Look within you to that place where love comes from."

Slowly she descended into his touch and tried to still her thoughts. After a few moments that warmth she'd experienced earlier with Lorn tickled at the edges of her senses. It seemed like the more she tried to focus on it the harder it was grasp. "I feel...something...it's faint...but nice. Warm, happy, pleased. I can't describe it, but it is a wonderful feeling."

"It will grow stronger as your trust in me grows. Earth females are special in that you have a natural impenetrable psychic shielding that keeps everyone out unless you care deeply for them. It makes you unique in all the universe."

Opening her eyes she found he'd moved closer. "That warmth, that's you?"

"Yes."

The realization he already loved her slammed into her and she took a deep breath. Holy shit. "Lorn, I don't...that is...I mean, I really like you but..."

"Do not worry, Casey. I have not proven myself to you yet, but I will." He hesitated, his gaze searching her face. "Which brings us to a situation that I am afraid will make you reject me."

Trying to steel herself for what he had to say next she took a deep breath and let it out. "Okay, hit me."

His surprise would have been comical if their conversation hadn't been so grim. "I would never harm a woman, Casey, ever."

"No, sorry, that's an expression that means I'm ready for the bad news."

His face softened slightly. "Understood. If you decide to bond with me we will go to Kadothia and you will never return to Earth."

"Never?" She blinked at him, trying to process what he'd said. "Like never ever?"

Reaching out, he cupped her cheek and ran his thumb over her lips, leaving a growing ache of desire with each stroke. "We could not risk the wormhole closing and leaving us stranded on Earth. My people, my galaxy, need every Warrior they can get, but more importantly they need every Matriarch, which if you chose to bond with me you will become."

The thought of never seeing her family again, never watching her nephews grow up, and leaving her friends behind made her heart ache. "Lorn...I don't think I can do that."

"I understand and you do not have to make your decision now. That is why we have the courting rights, so I can prove myself to you as a worthy mate." He cocked his head and licked his lower lip, making her yearn for his kiss. "I understand you would feel isolated from all those you love, and I wish I could bring them with us, but the Galactic Treaty forbids it. We cannot take people from their world in order to make our bride happy. Would it help if I told you your friends are also potential brides?"

"What?"

"The women who came with you to our base of operations with sweets. They have the potential to be bondmates to some of the Warriors there. My men are staying at that base because their hearts led them to that area to search for their bride. The Lord of Life was generous with the souls of your friends, they are good, strong women worthy of my men's love."

In a very selfish way it made her feel better to know her friends might be hopping on the same crazy train she was currently riding. "Who are they? Which ones?"

He smiled and shook his head. "That is between the Warrior and his bride. But if you decided to become my bondmate, and they bonded their Warriors, we could make sure that we lived near each other on Kadothia, or on the moon that is being converted to resemble your planet."

She blinked in shock. "What do you mean converted?"

"For each world that our brides are taken from we've replicated it on a smaller scale on one of our moons. Your planet is so tiny that the moon selected, now known as New Earth, is twice the size of Earth. We will take samples from your animals and plants and try to recreate them and their habitat. In a way you could think of it like your fable of Noah's Ark, except we aren't actually taking anything from your planet other than DNA samples. With the rate your people are destroying their environment and overpopulating the planet I would not be surprised if in a hundred years half of the samples we collect will be from life no longer found on Earth."

An ache started behind her eyes as her overloaded brain struggled to keep up with everything he was saying.

"You hurt," he said in a soft voice. "Why?"

She looked at him in surprise. "You can feel that?"

"Yes. Our souls have begun to bond." He smiled and ran his hand over her shoulder in a soothing touch that nonetheless made her long for him to caress her all over her body.

"Wow, that's kind of cool—creepy, but cool." She sighed and rubbed her temples. "I'm getting a headache from trying to understand everything. I mean it's a lot to take on at once."

He pulled her into his arms and she took in a deep breath of his crisp, clean scent. "Then let me help you stop thinking for a little bit and begin the courting."

Chapter Nine

Leaning closer, Lorn gently pressed her back until he was hovering over her. The need for him to take her, to soothe the desire for his touch had Casey reaching up and stroking the exposed skin of his chest, enjoying the slightly rough texture of his skin. His gaze softened and he brushed her hair back from her face. The heavy weight of his body pinned her to the bed and she loved it, loved how solid and strong he was.

"The first stage of courting is the tasting."

The deep rumble of his voice made her pussy clench and she became hyperaware of the robe rubbing against her erect, very sensitive nipples with every breath. "Tasting?"

"Yes." Keeping his movements deliberate and unhurried he leaned back enough to begin to tug at the sides of her robe, slowly exposing her body to him. "Though you are already beginning to carry my essence mixed with yours, I need to lick your body, to leave my scent on you. The need to mark you as mine claws at my self-control but I will not harm you, Casey. I promise."

"I know."

She smiled up at him, realizing the truth of his words. Lorn wouldn't hurt her. She didn't have to deal with the constant background thoughts of worrying about him cheating on her or leaving her. From what she knew of his culture once they bonded he would be loyal to her forever. That thought was a hard concept for her to grasp. Her older sister, Roxy, went through a nasty divorce after she found out her husband had gotten another woman pregnant while she was deployed with the Army in the Middle East. She had watched her strong sister try to recover from her dickhead husband's betrayal, and the realization that people lied about loving each other sucked. Casey would never have to worry about that kind of betrayal, but the cost might be too high to bear.

Those thoughts fled her mind as Lorn captured her gaze and leaned forward. The soft fall of his hair stroked over her skin as it tickled the side of her neck, sending chills through her. God, she loved his hair. Sinking her fingers into the long strands she massaged his scalp and delighted in the way he growled against her, almost like a purr. Starting at the top of her forehead he began to kiss and lick his way over her body, his slightly raspy tongue an unusual, very pleasant sensation. His touch was surprisingly gentle and she appreciated that even as she craved a harder caress. With his body mass and incredible strength he could crush her like one of her grandmother's porcelain teacups.

The delicious heat of his mouth reached her neck and she instinctively arched into his touch, baring her throat to him. He kissed and nuzzled her there, drawing her desire closer to the surface with each brush of his full lips. By the time he reached her breasts she was wiggling enough that he had to place one large hand on her belly to keep her still.

"Easy, *alyah*, you will not rush me in this. I have waited too long, dreamed about pleasuring you for hundreds of cycles. I will savor touching you, tasting you, owning your passion until you know that we are meant to be." He rubbed his smooth cheek over her breasts, his breath teasing her distended nipple. "These are so soft, so lush. Beautiful."

She cried out with the first lick against her swollen tip, the sensation overwhelming. After another experimental lick, he nipped first one nipple, then the other, in a teasing manner that threatened to tear her apart.

"Please, Lorn," she whispered in a husky voice.

"Please what, my bride?" He looked up and gave her a teasing smirk. "I'm not sure I know how to pleasure an Earth female."

Remembering the way he ruthlessly drove her to an orgasm she grabbed two fistfuls of his hair and tried to shove him back to her breast. "Suck them. Hard. Like before."

He gave her a pleased look and took her right nipple into his mouth, drawing hard on the sensitive nub and flicking the tip with his tongue. He toyed with her breasts, moving so he lay between her legs, trapping her in place while using his other hand to pinch and pull at the increasingly sensitive nipple. It soon became too much and she tried to jerk his head away but instead of moving he merely gentled his touch, using surprisingly delicate strokes with the pads of his fingers that made her hunger for him increase until her pussy throbbed to the beat of her heart.

At last he released her breasts from his torment, the mounds now swollen and topped with hot pink nipples.

"So pretty," he murmured before kissing the space between her breasts.

He licked his way down her ribs, tracing patterns with his tongue as she shivered beneath him. With each touch, her pussy contracted, spilling more of her arousal through the folds of her sex and down the crack of her ass. Unable to help herself, she rocked her hips against him, straining for more, needing relief from the terrible hunger tearing her apart from the inside out.

The width of his shoulders shoved her thighs apart and she gladly opened for him, arching against the silken sheets, still wearing the robe that was now spread open, revealing her body to his ravenous gaze. His eye color had reverted to neon blue and an almost constant growl echoed from his body into hers. Looking up at her, he spread open her sex with his thumbs and took a deep, audible breath.

If she wasn't so turned on she would have been embarrassed at his blatant scenting of her, but when he met her gaze again, he gave her a wicked smile that showed a flash of fang. "Delicious. And all these folds are so pretty, such a beautiful pussy. It will feel amazing to sheath myself with such softness. "

With that he lowered his mouth to her sex and gave her a long, hard lick from the entrance of her sex all the way to her clit.

He pulled back and blew a warm breath over her wet slit. "It is unbelievable how tender these little petals of flesh are, how sensitive. I love sucking them, licking them, taking them into my mouth so you make your pleasure pain sounds. But, my favorite part of your pussy has to be this little dark pink nub you call a clit. I love it, because it makes you climax, hard."

With that he began to suck at her pussy, playing with her outer and inner labia, making her cry out, and she grabbed his wrists, sinking her nails into his tough skin as she held on.

Pleasure detonated through her nervous system, throwing her out of her mind and into a realm of pure sensation. He didn't tease, didn't play around. His lips fastened right around her clit while he slid first one finger, then two into her pussy. She could only moan weakly, so overcome by him and caught up in what he was making her feel that her ability to do anything other than try to survive the onslaught of lust roaring through her was nearly impossible. Flicking his tongue quickly over the tip of her clit, he fucked her with his fingers, that hard, fast fucking he did so well, and she clutched at the bed as her body raced to orgasm.

Two more good sucks and she flew over the edge into a climax and screamed out his name. He kept eating her, releasing her clit and replacing his fingers with his very long, very thick tongue that he plunged into her rippling flesh. Shudders racked her as her body tried to keep up with his sensual demands until she was begging him for mercy. Finally, he eased his tongue out and even as overly sensitive as she was now, she felt her pussy contract around it and keep him inside.

He moved up next to her and held her while he stroked her skin, soothing her until her breathing returned to something resembling normal and the final shiver worked through her.

Turning in his arms, she stared up at him in awe. "That was amazing."

While he looked satisfied, his hunger stroked against her soul, seducing her into wanting more even as she reveled in what had to be the best afterglow ever.

His voice was rough with lust as he said, "Would you like to taste me?"

He laughed when she shoved him onto his back and straddled his waist with an eager smile. "I can't think of anything I want to do more than lick you, bite you, and eat you alive."

His massive erection pressed into her pussy and she ground herself against the cloth-covered length of him. Arousal sparked through her blood again, somehow deeper than it was before, more intense. In a way, it was almost as if her desire had doubled and gained a sharp edge she hadn't experienced before. Eager to feel his skin against her, she wrapped her arms around his neck and jerked him closer, making him growl and show another small flash of his fangs, which even when sheathed, were still impressive.

"You are so fucking hot."

With an arrogant smile he put his hands behind his head, opening himself to her inspection. The fullness of his lips called to her but she was pretty sure if she started kissing him she wouldn't stop. Running her fingertips down his body she decided to start with his thick neck. At the first stroke of her tongue he tensed beneath her.

"Lord of Life that feels amazing. Your mouth is so small and unbearably sweet."

Smiling, she kissed her way down his chest, sliding just a bit so she could reach him better. The angle pressed her engorged clit against him and she moaned, then gasped when that pleasurable sensation seemed to bounce back at her. Experimenting, she did it again and gulped.

"Why does it feel so good when I touch you? I mean like beyond usual good."

His voice came out strained. "I feel your pleasure and you are starting to feel mine. If we fully bond, and keep the connection between us wide open, you will feel my pleasure to the point where I could make you orgasm from across the room without you having to move a muscle."

"For real?"

"Yes." His biceps flexed as he lifted his head to look at her with such hunger that she had to bite back a moan. "Please, Casey, touch me. Let me show you the pleasure of my love."

His words echoed in her soul and she stared at him for long moments before reaching out and tenderly exploring his face with her fingertips, absorbing his deep pleasure at her touch. As she stroked her hand down his neck, across the rise of his pectoral, and over to his hard nipple the need flared to life, fed by his ravenous greed for her touch. God, he wanted her so much, maybe more than she wanted him and that was next to impossible. She gave in to a naughty urge and pinched his nipple, a gasp leaving her lips as his arousal filled her.

Eager to experience more she leaned down and inhaled his scent, then licked at his nipple, a zing of his arousal merging with her own desire and increasing the craving for his cock deep inside of her. Sucking on the hard disk she grinned as he bucked beneath her. After switching to the other he lifted her from his body.

"Hey, I wasn't done."

He cupped her face in his hands. "If you continue, I will spill my seed in my pants."

Feeling mischievous, aroused, and surprisingly playful despite the need burning through her she gently pulled out of his grasp. "I can help you with that."

Before he could protest she attacked the front closure of his pants, eager to see what he was packing.

He sat up, brushing her aside and quickly removed his pants, his long hair hiding his sex from her sight. When he lay back down she gasped.

"Holy...oh...*oh*..."

Leaning forward she lightly traced her fingers over his cock, which was similar to a human penis, but different. It was thicker and the head was noticeably bigger and flared out enough that she wondered how he would fit. Small ridges rose around an inch apart on all sides and she traced one, moaning as she felt his pleasure spill into her. His testicles looked similar to a human's, but they weren't loose, instead, they were tight and held closer to his body. Tracing one of the ridges she followed it to where it met his sac and delicately cupped the smooth skin. While he had a patch of platinum blond hair above his shaft, he had none on his testicles. The skin over them was incredibly soft, and she laughed when he twitched as she explored him.

"Do you find my body pleasing, bride?" he asked in a strained voice.

Not looking up from his erection, she nodded. "Very, very much."

A small amount of what looked like a shimmering pale lilac

precum had gathered at the tip of his cock. Curious, she leaned forward and took a lick, delighting in how delicious it was. The same taste she got while kissing Lorn was there, but intensified until it was like eating rich candy. Eager for more, she grasped him in her hand and brought his cock to her lips.

Lorn let out a growling roar as her mouth engulfed him, her jaw hurting slightly as she tried to open wide enough to take him. Deep-throating this beast would never happen, but she tried to make up for the lack of depth by using both hands to grip his shaft. The ache in her jaw increased but she couldn't stop, not when it felt so damn good to have an echo of his pleasure moving through her. Sucking him almost felt like someone was sucking on her clit and she spread her thighs, arching up to that invisible mouth that seemed to be tormenting her.

"Enough!" Lorn shouted. Moving quicker than should have been possible, he had her on her back with his heavy erection pressing against her slick entrance. His eyes were wild and his lips curled in a savage snarl to reveal his fangs as he growled out, "Give me permission, Casey. Let me have you. Please."

She wrapped her legs around his waist and her arms around his neck, opening herself to him in all ways. "Take me."

To her surprise, he leaned back so he was kneeling and gathered her up in his arms, easily holding her body suspended over his thighs. Their eyes met and her world exploded with pleasure as the fat head of his cock began to slowly work into her. He lowered her the tiniest bit at a time, her pussy burning as it tried to accommodate him. Gritting his teeth, looking unbelievably sexy, he adjusted his hold on her and began to press her down again, the head of his cock entering her with an audible pop. The sensation of him filling her was beyond good, beyond anything even as it stung. The ridges along the sides of his cock seemed to vibrate and she looked at him in shock as the sensation increased until it almost felt like he was fucking her with a very large version of her favorite vibrator.

His pleased, utterly male smile of satisfaction deepened as he continued to push into her. Unable to hold his gaze anymore she closed her eyes and let her head fall back, utterly absorbed with the delicious push and burn of his erection filling her. When he was halfway in he pulled almost all the way out until the bulbous crest stretched her before pushing back in.

"Oh, God," she moaned and dug her fingernails into his shoulders. "So good."

"The feel of your tight pussy gripping me, rippling around my pleasure ridges, it is the best thing I have ever experienced. You will kill me with pleasure, *alyah*."

She could only moan in agreement as her body struggled to take the final inches, sweat slicking their skin and her breath coming in short pants. At last he was all the way in and they both stilled. Warmth, bliss, and joy exploded within her, carrying her away in a tidal wave of sensations.

With a growl that was so deep it resonated in her bones, Lorn began to lift and thrust into her, making her toes curl as those amazing vibrating ridges dragged over the hyperactive nerve endings of her stretched pussy. She clung to him, not even needing the direct stimulation on her clit that she usually required in order to climax. Each hard thrust, each slow withdraw drew her release closer until she was trying to move against him, wiggling her hips as he moved her up and down with his hands on her hips.

"Casey, stop, I will not last."

Feeling savage, she bit his chest hard enough to feel his skin almost give way beneath her teeth before she released him and he growled. "Give it to me, Lorn. Come with me."

He held her close and rocked into her, gentling her against him as she struggled to go harder and faster. Then his cock seemed to swell inside of her and she stilled, crying out at the exquisite sensation of those vibrating ridges pressing deeper into her pussy, nearly killing her with an overwhelming sense of being filled, taken, and owned by the glorious male who now possessed her in every way possible.

With the first contraction of her orgasm, she screamed and bucked against him, only to feel the blinding pleasure increase exponentially when Lorn gave that roaring howl and began to pump his seed into her. It was hot, so hot, and filled her until she completely lost herself in him. His love thundered into her mind along with his seed in her body, and she clawed at his muscled back, overcome by the shudders racing through them both. He held her close, caressed her, and whispered to her how important she was to him, how he'd been waiting so long for her, that he'd dreamed of her before he even knew she existed and how much he adored her. Her lonely heart filled with his words like he filled her body, and she rubbed her face against his chest, fighting back tears as she recognized the truth of his words and knew Lorn was the man she'd been waiting for.

Her soul opened and she accepted the precious gift of his love.

She felt a riot of impressions and emotions, each filling an empty place inside of herself she didn't know she had, each soothing emotional pain that she wasn't aware she carried, cleansing her and making her stronger. He was so much older than she was, world-weary and jaded in a way she couldn't understand but nonetheless wanted to soothe. She'd tasted his soul and knew he was a good and honorable man and that he loved her with everything he had. No, love wasn't a strong enough word. She couldn't describe this feeling of belonging to each other, of finding an emotion so intense it tore apart any concept of romantic love she'd ever held.

He was hers and she was his.

After what felt like a long time the intense rush of emotions eased and she slowly came back to herself. Forcing her eyes open she found that Lorn had put them beneath the deliciously soft covers of his bed at some point, and that he was watching her with a heart wrenchingly gentle smile. His long hair hung loose about his shoulders and she loved the contrast of it against the deep tan of his skin.

Reaching up, she traced her fingertips over his face. "Hi."

He turned and kissed her fingers. "Hello, *alyah*."

The pride that teased at the edges of her mind made her smile. He was so utterly satisfied that if he was a cat he'd be purring right now. "That was...wow."

"I pleased you?"

His innocent look didn't fool her, not when she could feel his masculine satisfaction, and she lightly punched his solid chest. "You know you did."

His smile was so full of joy she couldn't help but smile back. "I am glad I pleased you, bride."

She sat up and pulled the covers around her, now sitting just slightly higher than his head. "Will it always be like that?"

"No. It gets better."

A shaky laugh mixed with a giggle bubbled up out of her chest. "I don't know if I could survive that."

He grinned and pulled her down for a long, slow, deep kiss that began to warm her again. "I would keep you properly fed and rested."

Snuggling into his arms she turned so her butt pressed against his erection. "What would I do on Kadothia? I mean, would I have like a job or something?"

"You would be the Matriarch of House Westfall."

"What does that mean?"

"While your planet is patriarchal for the most part, Kadothia is matriarchal. Every profession that is available to men is also available to women, except for that of a Warrior. You would be in charge of the estate, the household, and the men that you bond with, and your children, so I'm not sure if you would have the time to take on other duties."

"Wait, what do you mean the men I bond with? Bond like you and I are bonding?"

His expression closed down and she had the strangest feeling of separation from him even though they hadn't moved an inch. "It is my most fervent prayer you will consider taking another bondmate."

Hurt raced through her and she stared at him, a terrible sensation tightening her stomach as she searched his face for some indication he was joking. No, he was deadly serious. "I don't want to bond with anyone else. I only want you. You want to *share* me?"

Lorn nuzzled his face against her neck and she calmed somewhat, even though she was still super fucking pissed and unhappy. What the hell was it about his touch that soothed her against her will? Part of her wanted to shove him away and another part wanted to curl up and cry in the shelter of his arms.

"Remember our discussion about the Knights? At some point you would have to claim at least three men as your Knights, though I hope you will bond many more. You could easily bond over a hundred. There are not enough women on our planet, and without the partial bond we would lose them to the madness. I would lose my friends, the men I love like brothers, to the madness if you choose to not take them on. Even worse, without a partial bond they are easy prey to the Hive."

Anguish tore at her and her lower lip trembled as she blinked back tears of betrayal. "Hundreds of men? You want to share me with hundreds of men? How could you even suggest that? What kind of woman do you think I am?"

He made a frustrated noise. "This is very hard for me to explain due to our cultural differences. I do not see this as sharing you. I am in your soul, I am a part of you so I have no insecurity about your love for me just as you should have no doubt about my love for you. You do not understand what I am asking of you. Casey, you are their last hope. I know what a valuable gift you would be giving to these men. If the Matriarch of House Qaulin had not partially bonded me I would have been dead long ago."

Jealousy coiled in her stomach as she tried to make sense of what he was saying. First he wanted her to have sex with *hundreds* of men and now she had to deal with some other woman having a claim on his soul. "You're bonded to another woman? Are you fucking kidding me!"

"I am not kidding you and I am not partially bonded to her anymore." His amusement did nothing to help her jealous anger.

"My love for her is nothing like my love for you. It is…lesser. Like the love you would have for a respected friend. Plus, my bond with Matriarch Qaulin was not forged through sexual contact. That is a trait unique to Earth women."

She tried to wrap her mind around what he was saying and couldn't imagine feeling the connection she had with Lorn with anyone else. "Would I feel this passion I feel for you for them? Would I need to have sex with them to bond them?"

"Because of the nature of Earth female's shielding you would need to find physical pleasure with them at least once."

She stiffened and tears filled her eyes. Their relationship was doomed from the start. "I can't have sex with anyone else, Lorn. If I love a man I only want him. Please don't ask that of me."

He cupped her face and stroked her cheek with a tormented expression that matched how she felt at the moment. "Shhh, *alyah*, there are other ways to have pleasure than having a man plant his seed in you. And I would not subject you to hundreds of men against your will. Just because you can do something does not mean you have to, ever. Your happiness is more important to me than anything in the universe and I want you to never fear being honest with me. Just know that anyone I would bring to you for consideration will be a good friend of mine and a man worthy of you. Never doubt that."

She tried to move away from him but he wouldn't let her. His touch and scent seduced her even as she shoved at his restraining arm around her waist. "How could you even want to share me, Lorn? You wouldn't be jealous? How could you not be jealous? If you loved me you wouldn't be able to stand another man touching me. And I'm sure as fuck not letting another woman touch you."

"I do not want any other woman. You are my soul mate." He let out a frustrated breath when she snorted and rolled her eyes. "I *know* you, Casey. I am not limited to what I think of a situation like your Earth males. We are connected; I do not fear my place being taken in your life because no one *can* take my place. If you are willing, and I pray that you are, I will be your bondmate and your love; your pleasure already is my pleasure."

Her lower lip trembled as she tried to hold back her tears. "I don't understand this, Lorn. Relationships aren't like this on Earth."

"*Alyah*," he brought her resisting hand to his mouth and softly kissed her knuckles. "I am sorry I am explaining this so badly. Please try to keep an open mind and listen to me. Kadothia is not like Earth; Kadothian men are not like the men of Earth. While people on your planet have to hide who they love, or lie about it because your society does not approve, on Kadothia we embrace love in all its forms."

She was so confused, so tired, and she allowed Lorn to pull her back down so she was lying on her side, facing him. "I'm trying to understand, Lorn, I really am, but this is just all so...overwhelming and weird. I don't get how you won't be jealous because I'd cut your fucking dick off if you cheated on me."

A smile teased at the corners of his mouth and she glared at him. "Thank the Lord of Life Kadothian men do not cheat."

She sighed and rested her cheek on her hand. "So watching me with other guys would turn you on?"

A hint of hard male lust and frustration came through their bond. "I will admit it is very arousing for me to think of you finding pleasure with your Knights, but you will not love them like you love me because you are not their soul mate. And it would not be watching them with you that would be arousing. Well, I would enjoy watching you find your pleasure, you are beautiful when you orgasm, but remember, what you feel I feel. Your pleasure *is* my pleasure. That is one of the reasons marriages with one woman and multiple men work so well on my planet. There is no jealousy because there is no feeling of being left out. And if I ever brought a man to you as a potential husband, you must understand that I believe with all of my heart that you are meant for each other."

"You really want me to marry someone else?"

His expression closed down but not before she felt a mixture of longing and hurt so staggering it made her breath catch. "There is someone, very special to me, that I would like you to consider."

"Who?"

She found her curiosity was overwhelming her anger and fear as she tried to see the world through Lorn's eyes. He was right, she couldn't think of this from the point of view of Casey the college student. That life might be gone forever, and if she wanted what Lorn had to offer, she needed to try and listen to him without judgment. But it was so hard to keep an open mind when her inner critic was yelling at her for even considering such a whorish thing as fucking around on a man who might be her husband—even if he did want to set her up with other men.

What a mess.

A wave of fondness came from Lorn and she let herself sink into it, his love clearing her head and her heart. "He is my blood brother. A man I have known for hundreds of cycles and who has been my partner for almost as long. He is a good, honorable male who would love you with all of his heart."

"How can you say that? He doesn't even know me. I mean we could meet each other and it could be hate at first sight."

His soft chuckle irritated her and she clenched her jaw as he smiled at her. "You will not hate him. I believe it is impossible to hate Nast."

"That's his name? Nast?"

"Yes." Affection poured into her and she softened even though she didn't like how his love deflected her anger. Jealousy tried to rear its ugly head but this feeling of love was different than what he felt for her. Lorn reached out and took her hand, stroking her with his thumb as his gaze went distant. "Nast is the youngest son of a poor House that ruled one of the small agricultural districts of Kadothia. Despite being born into a lazy House with a Matriarch who always believed things should be handed to her, he worked his way up to become one of our greatest fighters and has a very generous heart. Of all the men in the universe he is the only one I would choose for you as a second husband, Casey. Feel the truth of my words."

His desperation pushed into her and she wanted to relent, to give him what he was asking for but she just couldn't. There was no way two men could share a woman and not get jealous. It just didn't happen and then she'd be stuck in some distant galaxy with a husband who hated her, or that she hated in return. Tears threatened to fall as she said, "Lorn...I don't think I can marry more than one man."

With a soft sigh he pulled her close, tucking her head beneath his chin so she could nuzzle her face against his throat. "Shhh, my bride. There is no rush. If it is meant to be it will happen, but I will not force it. You mean too much to me and your happiness always comes first. I hope that once our bond is complete you will understand what I'm trying to tell you, to share with you, but rest assured I would never, ever force you to love someone. Please believe me, Casey."

She mulled this over, trying to see it from his point of view even as she struggled with the knowledge that Lorn wanted to share her. "Are we bonded now?"

"Almost. There is a ceremony where we are blessed by the Lord of Life that is the final step." He drew in a deep breath, his hope moving through her like a warm breeze, calming her soul. "Are you saying you wish to honor me with a bond?"

Letting out a slow breath, she hesitated. "Can I think about it?"

Hurt flowed through their bond and she winced when he said, "You do not want me?"

"I mean this is more serious than marriage. I want you Lorn, with everything I have, but I also don't want to make this commitment on a whim. And everything you've told me tonight...it's a lot to take in. Can I please just have a little more time? I'm really, really tired and I just want to go to sleep."

For a long moment he was silent and she had trouble sensing him at all. She felt like she was alone in her body, as weird as that sounded. It disturbed her more than she would like to admit and she tried to reach out to him, to somehow follow the muted path of emotion, but she couldn't reach him. Panic gnawed at her and she tried harder, searching for him even though she had no idea how to do it.

Her voice came out high with stress as she said, "Lorn, why can't I feel you?"

"Easy, Casey. I am still here. I have shielded myself from you. Once you learn how the bond works you could easily rip my shields down, but for right now I ask that you respect my privacy."

The tears that had threatened earlier now fell freely at the loss of his touch inside her heart. "Why are you shielding yourself? Are you mad at me?"

"What? No, no, *alyah*, I am not mad at you. Not at all." He cupped her face with his hands, brushing away her tears. "I am shielding because I do not want to hurt you or influence your decision. I also want you to love me for who I am with no lies between us and I do not want you with me out of pity because my pain."

"You're hurting?"

He placed a gentle kiss on her temple. "I am okay, *alyah*. Please do not be upset. I am trying to protect you. It is difficult but I am doing everything to give you the space you need to decide what you want. I never want you feeling like you were manipulated into doing something because of my wishes and needs."

Pulling his arms closer around her she tried to close the emotional distance between them by having his body enfolding her as much as she could. "Can you lower them just a little bit, please?"

"Why?"

"Because...I miss you. I feel alone without you and I don't like it."

The smallest bit of Lorn returned to her heart and she let out a sigh that held so much relief it was almost comical. "Thank you."

He made a hand motion that lowered the lights until they were in absolute darkness. Then his arm moved again and the wall dissolved, revealing the glory of the universe to her. Awe filled her, trumping even the mess of emotions currently swirling around in her head. With his love and reassurance filling her, she was able to relax, and as her thoughts slowed, she found that the emotional pain had eased as well. Lorn's words kept running through her head and the more she thought about it the more he made sense; she had no doubt he was being truthful with her. While she could be totally wrong, she didn't think he could lie to her when they were connected like this. Besides, he could have easily not even talked about those things he had to know would upset her, but she had a feeling his sense of honor wouldn't allow it. He seemed to be doing everything he could to make sure she knew exactly who he was and what her life would be like if she married him.

Scary, but wonderful.

Far off in the distant reaches of space, an endless field of stars glimmered behind the curve of Jupiter and she marveled that she was here, seeing this, while being held by a man who was even more amazing than the view. The thought of returning to Earth didn't hold the appeal it did when she'd first arrived on the ship. Yes, she would miss her family terribly, but what Lorn offered her, the good she could do in that distant galaxy by protecting men like Lorn and the innocent people of all those planets against the Hive, weighed heavily on her mind. What would she do on Earth that would have such an impact on so many people? Her dreams of someday being a manager of a five-star hotel seemed petty compared to a future at Lorn's side. But the thought of her family never knowing what happened to her, always searching for an answer they would never find, tore at her heart. She spent a long, long time staring out into the Universe and wondering about her place in it.

Chapter Ten

Nast walked through the barracks housing the youngest of the new Warrior recruits and tried not to smile as the men fell all over themselves trying to come to attention during his unannounced inspection. They were on planet Obulous, a small planet that was entirely a temperate jungle. The people of Obulous were an aggressive society of tribes and the world was filled with hostile plants and animals, making it a perfect training ground for the recruits. At the other end of the room stood a tall woman with dark green skin and four arms dressed in shiny bronze armor, clearly an elder battle maiden of the Obulous society. Wrinkles creased her face but her body was still as strong as that of a young woman. The Obulons were a long-lived race and many, many cycles ago the elder battle maiden had been one of Nast's trainers when he was a recruit.

The woman, Dreda, gave him a small smirk as she watched the recruits scramble about, making sure their bunks were squared away, their gear properly stored, and their uniforms were in order.

He slowly strolled past the eight-person-high sleep pods going up the far side of the room and had to bite his inner cheek at the sheer panic his presence caused. Earlier in the day he'd sent in a group of native women to flirt and divert the men in order to see who was susceptible to being easily distracted when the men had been told to clean their weapons. The results were easy enough to figure out. Those who had spent their time responding to the flirting and adoring attention of the women had weapons that were still covered with the sticky mud of the training pits, while those that had either resisted the women's charms, or feared an ass chewing from Nast, had gear that was sparkling clean.

Warrior recruits wore grey uniforms to denote their status and the deep orange mud stood out against the armor and weapons.

Nast waited until he reached the center of the massive egg shaped chamber and slowly turned around.

At his side Vilpon, his second-in-command, made a disgusted noise and said in a low voice, "Pathetic. Less than half managed to get their gear clean, and all because of women with four breasts."

Cutting a glance in Dreda's direction, Nast softly replied, "Well, they *are* nice breasts."

Vilpon shook his head, his green Healer's armor gleaming

beneath the overhead lights. The other man had light brown hair streaked with black and a casual grace that went well with his lean, muscled body. Like Nast, he came from the Western Continent and the two men had spent a great deal of time together as recruits.

Giving Nast an amused look, Vilpon whispered, "Too bad the Obuloun women would never consider being pleasure servants."

Unable to help himself, Nast barked out a laugh. "Are you serious? You know rumor has it they castrate men who disappoint them in bed, right?"

Giving him a wolfish smile, Vilpon said, "Well then, I'd just have to make sure that never happened."

Before Nast could reply Dreda joined them with an amused smile. "You two are as bad as your recruits."

Instead of looking abashed at being caught, Vilpon gave Dreda a charming smile. "You can't blame a man for being entranced by your beauty."

Dreda rolled her eyes. "Are you gentlemen ready to put some fear into these soft little boys? My women could have slit the throats of over half of your recruits today."

Giving a disgusted sigh, Nast nodded. "For most of them this is their first time off-planet and away from their families, but that doesn't mean shit. Time to bring the pain. Vilpon, if you will."

All humor left Vilpon's face, and he turned to the now silent recruits. "All eyes forward, you pathetic bunch of *nimnam* larva."

Nast took a step forward and anger clenched his gut at the sight of so many recruits with fucked up gear. "All of you who have gear that is still dirty, put it on. NOW."

His voice rang through the giant room and men scrambled to do as he commanded. Once everyone who had dirty armor was geared up, he shook his head in disgust. "Pathetic. Absolutely pathetic. I cannot believe you let some tits distract you from your duty. This isn't Kadothia, gentlemen. Your Matriarch isn't going to be here to help you wipe your ass, and your gear is the only thing that is going to keep you alive. Because you don't love your weapons and your armor like you should, you are about to get well-acquainted with it. We're going to go on a nice run through the forest. A three-day run. By the time we're done running your pathetic hides, that armor is going to be fused to your body with your blood, sweat and tears."

Nast had to clench his teeth at the psychic wave of utter dismay coming from the troops, then nodded to Vilpon. The man in the green armor stepped forward and let his gaze roam over the lines of recruits. "All of you that have clean gear, congratulations. I'd love to say how proud of you I am and make you feel all warm and fuzzy inside, but that's not fucking true. You should have made sure every fucking man in your division was squaring his shit away. Every one. These men may one day save your miserable, useless asses. Your fellow recruits are your greatest weapon, your best armor, and in allowing them to fuck around and stare at titties instead of taking care of their shit you fucked up. So to make sure you understand that you are all one fucking unit, you're going to run with those pathetic wastes of air. And you will thank them when we're done."

Anger now mixed with the despair and when Dreda stepped forward in all her muscled glory and crossed her arms over her chest and waist, a collective inhalation of air swept through the barracks the subtle roar of an ocean wave, and with good reason. Dreda and her women were merciless with the recruits. The men of Kadothia were the only thing that stood between them and the Hive, and unlike these recruits, the Obuloun knew it and did their best to hone the recruits into the most deadly fighters possible. Dreda, in particular, was pitiless, but she was also kind and compassionate beneath her hard exterior. She wanted every man here to live and did everything she could to make that happen.

"Recruits," she said with a low purr in her voice that made Nast's balls draw up even tighter, "just to make things interesting, those pretty females that were in here earlier will be hunting you."

Vilpon coughed and Nast had a hell of a time keeping a straight face at the shock and misery showing clearly on some of the men's faces.

Moving slowly down the line of men scrambling into their armor, Dreda smiled, revealing sharp teeth. "But don't worry, we aren't hunting to kill, though you may wish we had. Instead we're going to make you respect your armor, love your armor, and care for your armor. If we catch you we're going to shove stinging thorns under the armor, which will make you very, very uncomfortable during your run. If we catch you more than once we'll be wrapping it around those big dicks you're all so fond of."

A pained noise came from the back of the room and Nast had to look away as Vilpon yelled, "I said, gear up!"

Nast looked out the large windows on the upper part of the room, examining the sky for any signs of rain. As he did so the building vibrated slightly and he exchanged a glance with Vilpon. "We getting a delivery today?"

Vilpon frowned and opened the communicator on his armor. "Lieutenant Vilpon to Receiving."

"How can I help you, Lieutenant?"

"That ship that just came in, what's it doing here?"

"Merchant ship named *Cantoilo's Pride*, Lieutenant. It's on the approved list and is one of our regular suppliers, but it came in early."

Pursing his lips, Vilpon nodded. "What's it doing landing at the Recruit quarters?"

"What? Lieutenant it shouldn't be landing there."

Nast and Vilpon exchanged a glance before Nast turned and yelled, "Battle ready! This is not a drill!"

Dreda sprinted for the doors closest to the landing pad and opened them. A moment later her short scream filled the air a moment before her head exploded in a burst of blood, bone, and brains. Rage filled Nast and he sprinted over to a weapon's locker while shouting, "Everyone out! Far door, go!"

From outside came the sounds of battle, the blast of guns and loud roars. Then came a bone-chilling snarl that made Nast's gut clench. Fuck. He knew that sound, knew the creature that made it, and knew what that meant. That roar belonged to a Chintar mercenary, the murderous race that were the personal bodyguards to the Hive.

Vilpon reached his side and they exchanged a look while Vilpon grabbed a blaster cannon. No words needed to be said, but Nast reached out and gave Vilpon's shoulder a squeeze. They both knew that the chances were pretty high that neither of them would make it out of this alive. There were too many recruits with bonds so weak they might as well have no mental shielding at all. While Nast doubted a full contingent of the Hive could make it this far into protected space, even one Hive member would slice through the recruits like a reaping blade at harvest time.

A low, rich hum began to fill the air and they both looked to the door where Dreda's corpse still lay propped up against the side, then to the other end of the room where the recruits were still streaming out of the building.

Opening his com link, Nast processed the information pouring into his mind and took a few precious moments to try and figure out what was going on outside. So far, only one Hive member had been spotted, but she was astride a Chintar mercenary and had managed to enslave over a dozen recruits, using them to kill their fellow Kadothians. The guns on base weren't responding, which meant someone had sabotaged them. Help was on the way, but the six fully bonded males on base had either been grievously wounded or killed.

For a moment, desolation filled Nast at the thought that he'd survived this long, only to die before he could meet his bondmate. An image of Casey flashed through his mind, one of many that Lorn had sent him earlier this morning, and his soul cried out for her. The only consolation he could take was that Lorn wouldn't be alone, but oh, how his heart ached for his blood brother. Even as Nast ran for the door leading out to the landing pad he sent up a silent prayer to the Lord of Life that Lorn managed to bond his *alyah* before he would learn of Nast's death.

"What the fuck are you doing?" Vilpon yelled out from behind him while Nast began to climb the rungs of the ladder leading to the row of bunks at the end of the room.

A hole had been blasted into the wall about six racks up, and through it Nast could see the battle going on outside. The animal side of his nature was snarling to be set loose, to let the madness overtake him and surge out into battle, to go berserk and slaughter anything that stood in his path; Nast barely managed to hold onto his sanity. The ground shook slightly and he had to raise his arm to shield his face from a spray of dirt as a sonic bomb exploded outside the recruit barracks.

As he'd guessed, the Chintar was making its way to the barracks with a Hive member sitting astride its massive shoulders. Easily five times the size of a Kadothian male, the Chintar had a massive body covered in heavy armor, turning the mercenary into a machine of destruction. Even though the mercenary was bleeding, it continued to lay waste to anything and anyone in its path, but Nast didn't pay the beast any attention. The true threat sat astride the mercenary, and she was one of the most powerful Hive members he'd ever encountered. Her flat-black armor, a mockery of the black armor of the Kadothian Warrior class, seemed to absorb the light around her. Like all Hive members there was nothing about her armor to distinguish her, but her psychic signature was terrible. Cold, calculating, and homicidally gleeful as she wallowed in the misery around her.

The waves of psychic pain radiating from her made Nast's whole body ache, but he tried to block it out as he hooked his foot through a rung in the ladder and carefully balanced his gun on his shoulder. Gathering himself, Nast carefully focused his sights on the harness securing the Hive member onto her mercenary. There was no way he could blast her off. A visible energy shield extended around her that would repel the plasma gun he held, but if he could get her off her mount then he had a better chance of slitting her throat. While a plasma gun couldn't penetrate her energy shield, his hand could if he moved slow enough to press through the shield.

Two quick shots severed the straps holding her harness in place. He didn't wait around to see her fall, instead, he leapt from his position, gritting his teeth against the jarring pain of his landing. The armor he wore was necessary, but fuck, it was heavy. As he sprinted to the exit, he found himself slipping closer to the madness. He struggled to remain objective, to view the battle before him in a rational manner rather than seeing it as a potential slaughter. Deep inside his mind a raging animal clawed at his self-control, urging him to leap into the fray and begin to slaughter the enemy.

A recruit lay nearby, groaning in agony as he lay dying. Half of his face was gone and death was imminent. Saying a quick prayer, Nast ended his suffering, costing himself precious seconds before he began to fight his way through the horde to where he'd last seen the Hive member. He knew she'd managed to survive the initial fall because recruits froze in place all around him. Some began to scream and shake, while others slowly raised their weapons and began to shoot their fellow Kadothians. A searing blast of energy caught him in his thigh and he struggled to keep moving forward, to reach the Hive member he could now clearly see.

Here and there partially bonded Kadothian men continued to fight and his heart ached as he had to watch his men shoot the recruits that had been compromised. The only mercy was that the Hive member was overtaxing herself by controlling so many recruits at once. For her this suffering had to be a constant, orgiastic feast to her senses, a massive dose of her narcotic of choice. The Chintar was preoccupied by a small group of Obuloun warriors, but they were struggling to avoid the compromised recruits and still take the hulking man-beast down.

A recruit slowly turned to Nast and raised his weapon, but before he could shoot, Nast snapped his neck. Just the night before, Nast had talked with that recruit about his family back home, helped him deal with his homesickness and talked about the glory of being a Warrior. Now, with the physical pain in his leg beginning to cripple him and the emotional pain of having to kill the recruit tearing at his sanity, Nast reached the Hive member.

Her back was turned to him, but he crouched down and slowed his movements. It took everything he had to drag his damaged leg along behind him and strengthen his mental shields enough for her not to notice him. If he had not been surrounded by so much agony she would have felt his presence instantly, but his suffering was nothing compared to the devastation she was causing all around her. He tried to not see what she was doing, to ignore the recruits clawing their eyes out, or torturing each other, but his sanity snapped.

With a low snarl the primitive animal within rose to the surface and nothing mattered except killing her. He leapt, landing on her shield hard enough to knock her down while he drew his knife from his boot. Slowly, ever so slowly, the hand holding the knife began to penetrate her shield, aiming for the base of her skull where it joined her neck. Another plasma discharge caught his shoulder, snapping the bone in the arm not holding his knife. He was almost there, almost close enough to cut, when she turned her terrible thoughts directly on him.

Malevolent, terrifying pain ricocheted through his mind as every terror he'd ever experienced, every fear he'd ever hidden away came crashing into his mind. He cried out in agony and tried to jerk his hand back, but the shield wouldn't let him move quickly. The madness screamed within him, meeting the cold evil of the Hive member with the heat of insanity. Roaring he jerked forward and the knife managed to penetrate the armor at the base of her skull.

His mind was released abruptly and he sagged, the blade pressing deeper and deeper as his weight fell onto it. A high pitched scream echoed through his mind and just as the blade severed her brainstem another plasma blast, this one from right next to him, caught him in the side, blowing him off of her, but it didn't matter. She was dead.

He struggled to stand, to roar out his victory, but his body was crippled. All he could do was writhe and gnash his teeth, the madness almost totally in control now. Red insanity veiled his vision and he snapped at the hand of a man reaching for him, mindless with the need to destroy. To kill.

Voices rang out around him and he howled in misery as someone pressed something cool to his neck before darkness overtook him.

Nast hunted through an unfamiliar forest with trees and vegetation that he'd never seen before. He sniffed at the air, pungent scents hitting his nose and growled softly. The madness had taken almost full control of his mind and the need to kill overwhelmed everything else, but he couldn't scent any prey. Lowering his nose to the ground, he inhaled deeply but could only smell dirt.

A small part of his mind wanted to dig his hands into the soil and pray, but that essential hint of humanity was growing weaker by the moment.

Off in the distance a sound reached him, a splashing noise.

Instantly, he was on his feet, dimly aware that he was naked, but that was fine. He didn't need weapons to kill. He was a weapon.

Sprinting through the forest he followed the faint noises until he reached the edge of a gently curving creek that flowed down the sheer face of a cliff into a pool of water below. At first he didn't see anything, then movement at the edge of the pool caught his hunter's eye. A low snarl worked from him as he prepared to leap into the pool and destroy his prey, but when the shapely form of a woman came up from beneath the water, slicking her hair back as she took a deep breath of air, he froze.

She was exquisite, both man and beast agreed on that.

Her long, dark hair floated on the water around her as she turned her face up to the sky and wiped at her eyes. The tips of her breasts broke the surface and hunger slammed into him at the sight of her pink nipples hardening in the cool air. He'd never seen skin as perfect as hers, a creamy color that contrasted nicely with her hair. The need to touch her, to smell her, overwhelmed the urge to kill and he dove into the water without thought.

It only took him a few strokes to reach her, and when he did he found her trying to scramble away from him, her fear scenting the air around her.

With a low growl he easily captured her around her waist and pulled her closer. At the sight of her beautiful *benali* eyes, a rich brown flecked with gold, something in his heart rejoiced. Then she screamed and tried to push him away, making the predator rise to the surface again, but instead of wanting to harm her, he wanted to soothe her. The animal didn't know how to do that, so it receded a bit and let more of his human side rise to the surface of his thoughts.

"Let me go!" she screamed and her voice brushed over him.

Instead of doing that, he pulled her closer until her breasts pressed against his chest even as she tried to shove away. He lowered his head to the side of her neck and bit her gently, growling out his warning. She shuddered against him and whimpered.

"Please don't hurt me."

Not releasing his hold on her, he ran his hands over the silk of her wet skin, stroking her and learning her body. Slowly her shivers ceased and when he licked at the flesh between his teeth she moaned softly. His mind turned from curious exploration to desire and he made a pleased noise as she tilted her head to the side, exposing her neck to him. The submissive gesture pleased his inner beast and he licked along the column of her throat, feeling the heat of her life against his tongue.

She turned her head and whispered against his lips, "Who are you?"

It took him a long time to remember, but finally a word came to him. "Nast."

"Your name is Nast?"

He nodded, brushing his mouth against her small one. She was tiny all over, yet incredibly lush and her scent was driving him crazy with lust, but her words made him think. "Your name?"

She wrapped her arms around his neck. "My name is Casey, and this is one of the best wet dreams I've ever had."

Her words confused him, but her actions didn't. She began to kiss him and he groaned into her mouth, enjoying the delicate stroke of her tongue against his. He sucked her tongue into his mouth and she groaned against his lips, putting her legs around his waist beneath the water. The tickle of her floating hair felt delicious against his skin, as did her hot core rubbing against his stomach. He shifted her slightly so the head of his cock pressed between the lips of her sex and they both gasped.

Something about this situation began to bother him, but before he could dwell on it, or even wonder about how he got here, Casey began to lick along his neck and place gentle, erotic bites along the column of his throat, teasing his animal.

He growled and she laughed softly against his skin, "I don't know if you're trying to frighten me with all that growling, but it's so not working. I find it so damn sexy."

Catching her bottom with both of his hands, he gave the abundant flesh a squeeze, delighting in how soft and deliciously rounded she was.

She made a little mewling noise and wiggled against him. "Fuck me."

The thought of plunging into her was wonderful, but as he began to remember more his mind urged him to pleasure her, to taste her, to feel her sex quiver against his tongue as she came.

Instead of slipping into her welcoming heat, he moved them back so they were near the edge of the pool. "Put your hands on the stones behind you."

She blinked at him, then allowed him to lower her back until she was floating on her back, supported by both his hands and her grip on the stones. Lifting her pelvis to the surface, he smiled at the sight of her swollen, pink flesh even as he wondered why it looked so different than he'd imagined. Instead of a smooth slit, she had petal-like folds above the entrance to her sheath and he lifted her further, studying her body.

Casey made a soft little moan. "Please, Nast, don't look at it. Lick it."

That made him laugh and with that laughter his madness fully receded, leaving his human mind back in charge of his body. "Oh, little *alyah*, I plan on doing more than that. I want to dine on you, eat you until you scream my name, and start all over again. I could feast on you for days and still be hungry."

She gave an involuntary arch of her hips. "Please."

Intrigued by the petals of her pussy, he gave them an experimental lick and groaned at the rich flavor of her. She tasted like sunshine, like the green scent of spring mixed with the sweetest of fruits and the salt of the earth. Delicious, utterly addictive and delicious.

Embolden by her responses, he set about learning the shape of her body, the different parts that made her moan and what made her scream. While she enjoyed him fucking her with his tongue, the loudest response he got was when he licked at the stiff little bundle of nerves at the top of her pussy. That little bump seemed to be extremely sensitive and she shivered as he pet it with his tongue.

Looking up at her, over the wet planes and rises of her body floating in the water, he nuzzled her with his mouth and said, "This small bump, what is it?"

Her passion glazed eyes barely focused on him. "What?"

He gave that little bundle a kiss and grinned as she shuddered. "That part of your sweet sex that I just kissed, what is it?"

"My clit?" He licked it and she moaned. "Fuck."

"Your clit. Hmmm."

When he hummed against it she cried out and her legs tried to tighten on his head. Liking that reaction, he took her soft, slick flesh into his mouth and hummed again, then licked her while he did it. Her hips bucked and the water splashed around them as her cries grew in volume. Soon she was writhing against his mouth and he sealed his lips over her entire pussy and growled, letting the vibration travel through his lips and tongue into her sex.

She froze, then screamed out her pleasure, calling out his name into the strange blue sky while he drank her abundant arousal down.

Suckling at her, he discovered that she became very sensitive after her release and he gentled his mouth. When he licked at her entrance he found that she hadn't sealed up tight. Thrusting his tongue into her, he groaned at the sensation of her velvet sex gripping him, but she didn't resist the intrusion. If anything, the thrusting of his tongue into her sheath made her moan in a way that made his cock ache. Curious, he pressed a finger into her and began to stroke her.

"Shit, Nast," she whispered and thrashed her head in the water. "Please, please fuck me. I need you inside of me."

He leaned down and placed a kiss on what she called her clit while continuing to penetrate her with his finger, adding another in an attempt to stretch her out. She was so tight inside he was afraid of hurting her. That was the last thing he would ever do because she was special. His mind tried to figure out why she was so special, but the more he thought about it the more the concept seemed to slip away. Her inner muscles clenched his fingers and he groaned, imagining what it would be like to have his dick inside of her when she did that.

A wind began to blow through the forest and unease prickled along his spine. He removed his fingers from Casey and gathered her into his arms and they both looked around them at the swaying trees. She clung to him and began to shiver as the cool air blew over them.

"Nast? What's going on?"

"I don't know, *alyah*."

"*Alyah*...that word sounds familiar." She looked up at him, a small frown marring her sweet face. "Why do I know that word?"

His head ached, hell his whole body began to ache and he struggled to think. "It means eternal beloved. You're my *alyah*, Casey, and I am your bondmate."

As soon as those words left his mouth his vision began to dim and he panicked, trying to hold onto this moment, to stay here, but something was dragging him away from his Casey.

Pain blackened his thoughts and for an eternity he writhed in torment before he finally managed to control his body. He opened his eyes and found that he was in a room, a room with grey walls that vibrated slightly. The lighting was dim and he blinked in confusion, his mouth unbearably dry and his body aching. Smells filled his nose as he took his next breath and slowly he identified the distinct scent of a med bay. He was in a med bay, and if his guess was right, on a ship.

A whooshing noise came from his left and he turned his head, watching as Vilpon came in, dressed in his dark green leathers. Behind him were two lower ranking healers and an unfamiliar Captain. All three men studied him with mournful looks.

Vilpon searched Nast's face and said in a low voice, "You almost can't even tell he's fallen to the madness."

Blinking, Nast said in a broken voice, "That's because I haven't."

One of the lower ranking healers was so shocked he dropped his tablet while the other two men stared at Nast.

Vilpon took a step forward, but the Captain grabbed his arm. "Wait. I've seen men still able to speak in the early stages, let me test him."

Nast tried to sit up, but found himself strapped to the table.

"What happened to me? Why do I hurt like I just got gored by a *pintarilin?*"

The Captain stared at him. "What's your name and your ancestry?"

Nast gave the information then glanced down at his bound body. "What the hell is going on?"

Letting out a loud whoop, Vilpon began to unstrap him. "We thought we lost you to the madness. What's the last thing you remember?"

He struggled to think, but his mind kept going back to a beautiful woman with gorgeous dark eyes calling out his name in passion. "Was I with a woman?"

The men laughed and Vilpon's assistant healers helped Nast sit up as Vilpon said, "Not quite."

The Captain continued to stare at Nast before he gave himself a visible shake. "You were on Obulous, training recruits."

Bits and pieces of memories came back to him, and as they began to form a timeline in his mind he looked at Vilpon. "The Hive."

"Yes."

Sorrow filled Nast and he took a deep breath, then slowly let it out. "How bad is it?"

Vilpon began to examine Nast. "It would have been a lot worse if you hadn't managed to kill the Hive member. Can you remember that?"

He shook his head. "Last thing I remember was shooting her off her Chintar. Then...nothing."

The three men exchanged a look before the Captain said, "You managed to kill her, but Nast, I swear I thought we lost you to the madness."

A sick feeling filled him and a fragmented memory of sitting on the Hive member's back and sinking his blade into her spine danced through his mind, but it was an odd, skewed thought. "What do you mean?"

Vilpon poked around at Nast's injured leg. "You were feral."

"What?" He shook his head. "But if I was lost to the madness I'd still be feral."

The Captain leaned against the wall, his gaze intent on Nast. "We can't figure it out either. If it was just Vilpon's word I would question his diagnosis, no offense Healer, but dozens of men were needed to secure you for transport and we had to knock you out to move you."

Vilpon replaced the healing wrap on Nast's leg with shaking hands. "I swear, Nast, I thought you were lost to us."

Laying back on the bed, Nast stared at the ceiling. "I don't understand."

"None of us do." The Captain gave him a small smile. "Well, at least I won't have to contact Commander Lorn and tell him his blood brother was lost to us."

At the thought of Lorn, the memory of the woman flitted through his mind again and he realized that he'd dreamed of Casey. The remnants of the dream were so insubstantial he couldn't remember them, but he slowly raised his hands to his face and took in a deep breath, then growled. Her smell was all over his hands, like he'd been rubbing her body in truth, and his cock got immediately hard.

Vilpon cleared his throat. "Well, at least we know that part of you still works."

Thrusting his hands out to his friend, Nast said, "Smell."

With a curious look Vilpon did, then gasped. "I smell her."

The Captain tilted his head, then stepped forward, reaching for Nast's hands before he hesitated. "May I?"

Nast wanted to tell him now, that his woman's scent was for him alone, but instead he nodded.

Touching Nast as little as possible, the Captain took a quick smell, then a deeper inhalation. His voice came out rough as he said, "By the Lord of Light she smells good."

"Mine," Nast growled.

Vilpon and the Captain exchanged a look before his friend shook his head slowly. "I've never heard of a true dream helping to stave off the madness. But with all the wild reports coming from the Reaping ship, I'm not surprised."

The Captain stared at Nast for a long time before a sliver of hope moved through his psychic shield. "Maybe it is worth the risk to seek an Earth bride."

Cupping his hands to his face, Nast took in another deep inhalation of her scent, then the Captain's words registered. "What do you mean worth the risk?"

Vilpon cleared his throat. "There are...rumors of lots of suicides happening on the Reaping ship."

"What?"

Turning, Vilpon looked to his assistants. "Out."

The healers nodded, but they each shot Nast a sympathetic look before they left the room.

He tried to sit up but Vilpon pressed him back down. "Easy, my friend. They are just rumors."

The Captain sighed and crossed his arms. "It's no secret your blood brother is there right now, so I'll be honest with you, Nast. I've heard that the Earth women are terrified of the Kadothian men. That only a small portion are actually accepting their bondmates, and those that do are not accepting a second husband."

"Shut the fuck up," Vilpon snarled.

The Captain shook his head. "No, he needs to hear this. If my blood brother was on that ship I'd want to know."

Despair dimmed the joy that had suffused Nast at the knowledge that he'd true dreamed of Casey. "How bad is it?"

The Captain exchanged a loaded glance with Vilpon before blowing out a harsh breath. "From what I've heard, bad."

"But that doesn't mean there isn't any hope," Vilpon added quickly.

Nast stared at the ceiling, trying to fight off the pain filling him. "I'd like to be alone."

Patting his uninjured shoulder, Vilpon said in a low voice, "Rest. You're going to want to be healed enough to travel when Lorn calls you to meet your *alyah*."

Nast didn't respond and soon the men left him alone, holding his hands to his face and breathing in the scent of the woman who'd stolen his heart in a dream.

Chapter Eleven

Casey woke with a long, deep stretch that seemed to make every joint in her body pop into place as satisfaction filled her with languor. The smooth fabric beneath her caressed her skin in decadent luxury, and she snuggled closer to the good-smelling, firm male shape next to her. Right away she knew it was Lorn because contentment flowed through her from their bond. That and his amazingly hard cock pressed up against her ass.

Turning over she brushed her hair back off her face and smiled at him. "Morning."

He watched her with slumberous eyes, a dark, sapphire blue color that stole her breath with their beauty. "Good morning, my bride."

She grinned, then smacked her lips. "Ummm, can you show me where the bathroom is and what I can use to brush my teeth?"

Chagrin tickled through their bond. "Forgive me. I was so eager for you that I forgot your comforts."

"Hey, it's okay. We had a pretty full day yesterday. It was yesterday, right? My sense of time is all screwed up."

He stood from the bed, his cock sticking out from his body, making her wish she didn't have to use the bathroom so bad. Instead of dressing himself he held out her peach robe and helped her slip into it. Before they left the room she brushed her fingers over the flowers again, delighting in the little glowing specs dancing through the air. Directly across the hall he showed her the bathroom and how to use everything. It wasn't much different from how things worked back on Earth, except for the body cleansing part. In order to conserve water she had to stand in a closed cubicle with her eyes and mouth closed, then lifted her arms and spread her legs as she was sprayed with ultra-fine powder, then blasted with warm air that blew all the powder off.

To her surprise, after the powder shower she was clean and her hair was shinier than she'd ever seen it before, like she'd had a treatment at a high-end spa.

Instead of her fuzzy robe Lorn had left her a gown that appeared to be made of some kind black silky material with long, fitted sleeves and an empire waist. It fit her perfectly and when she examined herself in the mirror she was rather pleased with how she looked.

Instead of a frizzy mess her hair hung in soft waves and the gown really brought out her figure. Lorn came up behind her and she couldn't help but grin at their image as he wrapped his arms around her. She barely came up to his chest and what a chest it was.

She smiled up at him in the mirror, scarcely able to believe she was really here, being held by the hottest man in the universe while he gazed at her as if she was the amazing thing. "I look like a munchkin standing next to you."

"What is a munchkin?"

"It's...it's a character from a book. It basically means that I'm so small and you're so big."

He ducked his hips a bit and rubbed his erection against her back. "Yes, I am."

She couldn't help but laugh at his leering expression. "Okay, obviously men being proud of their penises is a universal thing."

"But I have so much to be proud of," he replied as his hands wandered towards her breasts.

Gently smacking his hands away, she gave him a scolding look. "I'm hungry."

He sighed but released her with a longing expression. "I have a meal set out for you, *alyah*. I will cleanse then join you."

They exchanged places in the bathroom and she found Lorn had made her a breakfast of some kind of blue stuff that tasted like pancakes and looked like mashed potatoes along with slices of what she assumed was a fruit. She couldn't find anything to compare the taste to from her own world. It was kind of like a spicy peach dipped in honey, but not really. Thankfully her drink appeared to be plain water and she quickly drained the glass, not sure where to find more.

Nibbling on her breakfast, she looked around his living room area and went to one of the nearest paintings. It was framed in the same pale wood, or what she assumed was wood, as the end table near the couch. Wiggling her toes in the strangely plush carpet she studied the scene in the picture, wondering if it was an accurate depiction of Kadothia. The landscape appeared to be a view from a hilltop and the sky was a deep cobalt blue instead of the azure blue of Earth's sky and the clouds were more golden than white. The trees looked nearly the same except the bark ranged from stark white to cream and they were curvier, almost like they'd been trained into sweeping shapes that linked together to form a lattice work and their leaves ranged from the traditional green to brilliant yellows and blues. Off in the distance, tall spires of a fairytale-like city went high into the sky and as she looked closer she realized it had graceful characteristics of Rivendel, the mythical home of the elves from the *Lord of the Rings*. Beyond that enormous sandstone cliffs and spires reached up high enough to disappear into the clouds.

She became aware of Lorn before he touched her, his affection and arousal making her tingle. When he slipped his arms around her she fed him the last bite of her fruit, enjoying the way he licked the juice from her fingertips with his talented tongue. It reminded her of the masterful way he'd licked at her pussy and tingles raced through her, awakening the arousal that never seemed to sleep around him.

"Thanks for breakfast."

"It is my honor to prepare food for you, my bride." His voice had taken on that growling purr he had when he was aroused, but she tried to ignore it because she wanted some answers before she lost herself in him again.

Pointing to the picture she asked, "Is that real or from an artist's imagination?"

"Very real. That is the view from my home on Kadothia. From the back viewing deck of my bedroom to be exact." Hope mixed with anxiety flooded her from Lorn before she sensed him semi-closing the link. "It will be your home as well if you bond with me."

His strong arms tightened around her and she idly stroked his hand. "Is there someplace I can do some research? Like um, computers on my earth that I can do an Internet search on?"

"Why?"

"I want to figure some things out."

"There are, but I would rather answer your questions. You can ask me anything and I will tell you the truth."

"I know that." She sighed and turned so she could look up at him. His hair shone like spun silver falling over his shoulders and she blinked in surprise. "Your hair is silver?"

"Does it displease you? I had to wear a disguise while on Earth to blend into your population."

She laughed and ran her fingers through his long strands that now reminded her almost of Christmas tinsel. "No, it's beautiful, but honey, trust me when I say you didn't blend."

Frown lines deepened around his kissable lips. "I did everything required to merge seamlessly with your people. Were my clothes incorrect? Did something about my appearance give me away? If it did I need to know so I can share it with our Scouts."

Giggling she stroked his cheek, loving the velvety texture. "No, nothing like that. You're just so fucking hot. There's nothing you could have done to change that."

He smiled at her and male pride tickled at her mind. "I am pleased you find me appealing."

Taking a step back she examined him slowly from head to foot. His outfit consisted of a silky white shirt that hung loose on him, yet somehow managed to highlight his sculpted physique. A pair of black breeches encased his legs and what she thought of as his black shit kicker boots completed an outfit that was an odd mixture of pirate and rock star. The way his pants cupped the bulge of his erection made her mouth water.

When she met his gaze she grinned as she recognized the hungry gleam in his eyes. "I find you more than appealing. You're so hot you make my ovaries explode."

He gave her an alarmed look. "What?"

A giggle escaped at the sight of his wide eyes. "It means I can't look at you without becoming turned on, without wanting to do wicked things with you."

The predatory gleam in his eyes should have tipped her off, but she let out a startled scream as he scooped her up and tossed her gently on the couch. The odd material seemed to embrace her and she yelped when Lorn leapt like a cat and landed between her spread legs. Heat rushed through their bond and she moaned at the sensation, letting her head fall onto the back of the couch. God, the blast of desire was so intense, it was almost painful. She realized with a start she must also be feeling Lorn's need. It was so different from hers, more...aggressive...hungry. Lord of Life, he was so hungry for her.

"This is what you do to me, Casey. All it takes is one look into your amazing eyes, one scent of your delicious nectar and it is all I can do to keep from falling on you like I am in rut."

"What is rut?"

"It is the time, once a cycle, where a male Kadothian is fertile. Unlike your Earth men our sperm is inactive except for three days out of every cycle. During those three days I will want to couple with you over, and over again as the hormones will put me into a form of sexual frenzy."

She blinked up at him, trying to imagine Lorn in a sexual frenzy and rather liking the idea. "Will I get pregnant? I mean I'm on a birth control shot...shit, how am I supposed to get another one? Do you have some kind of birth control that would work on me?"

Hurt flashed through his eyes and their bond. "You do not wish to have my children?"

"No, not that's not it at all. I would just like to wait a bit, get to know you and stuff."

His tight lips softened and he nodded. "I agree. We have many, many cycles ahead of us for having children. Though I must confess the thought of you swollen with my seed fills me with pleasure."

It certainly did, she could feel that happiness mixed with a sexual need coming from him. With a soft smile she caressed his cheek, then his lips and her clit hardened as his desire stroked against her soul. Leaning forward, he captured her lips in a long, devastating kiss until she was moaning against him. When she reached between them and cupped his erection the blast of arousal from him would have knocked her off her feet if she wasn't already lying down.

The sensation eased enough so she could breathe and she gaped at him. "No wonder men want to have sex all the time. It's like a craving, an actual hurt."

Sliding his hands beneath the bottom edge of her gown, he slowly pressed it up her thighs, revealing her body bit by bit. "I do hurt for you, *alyah*, but never feel like you have to mate with me. Because of the lack of bondable women on my planet, we are taught how to relieve ourselves and we have pleasure servants to take care of us. I had two myself."

Shock raced through her and she stared at him before slapping his hands away from her. "What? You have some...some kind of woman to have sex with at home?"

His laughter enraged her and she tried to shove him off of her, but he easily pinned her to the couch with her robe hiked up around her thighs. "You have nothing to be jealous of. I dismissed them before I came to Earth. It is not like the relationships on your planet where there is affection involved; pleasure servants are...business? I cannot think of the right way to explain it."

Anger threatened to explode and she seethed. "So you have whores waiting at home for you?"

Now it was his turn to get angry. "That is a disrespectful word. Pleasure servants are women trained to relieve a male's need. It is nothing like I have with you but they are not morally poor women because of their profession."

"They have sex for money!"

"Yes, they do. And we pay them because they are highly trained to have sex with Kadothian males without becoming attached in a romantic way. Casey, if I were to have intercourse with a woman who was not a pleasure worker I would be morally corrupt. It would not be fair to her to let her form an attachment when I could *never* love her. There is only one woman in the universe I was meant to love and that is you. Unlike some Kadothian males, none of my pleasure servants lived with me, and like I said, I canceled their contracts before I left. Why are you angry? Should I be angry you had sexual relations with another man before I met you?"

Guilt panged through her, even though she knew it was stupid. "That's different."

"How so? Because you tried to forge a romantic relationship with these men? I never had any feelings of love for my pleasure workers. Those men failed to win your heart because you were meant to love me, just like any attempt at a relationship I might have made would have failed because I was born to love you."

At times like this she really wished she couldn't feel his honesty, his sincerity, because it was easier to be pissed about this than understanding almost against her will. "Never again. Do you understand me, Lorn? I know you want me to screw half of Kadothia but if I ever see another woman touch you I will kick her ass and kill you."

He grinned at her and she wanted to throttle him for his surge of pride. "But of course, my bride. If I ever need release that you are unwilling or unable to give me I will look to a pleasure 'bot."

"Pleasure 'bot?" Narrowing her eyes at him, she shoved his shoulders. "So you're going to have sex with a robot?"

His gaze went distant for a moment and she blinked hard as she watched his pupils expand and dilate quickly. "Not if I can help it. They are the equivalent of your earth sex toys. I would hope you would come to me before you used a dildo, but I would not be jealous of it."

"What did you just do? Your eyes went all weird."

"My pupils dilate as I accessed the Kadothian libraries."

"How?"

"I have crystal chips implanted in different portions of my brain. It not only helps to protect me from the Hive's mental abilities but gives me access to knowledge and helps my body to repair itself."

"Wow." She touched her temple. "Will I get those?"

"If you bond with me, yes. If you choose to return to Earth, no." He leaned closer and bent his head to lick at the shell of her ear, sending ripples of pleasure through her even as his determination filled her mind. "But I promise you, Casey, there isn't a man or machine on your world that can give you the love and pleasure I can."

Lorn drew in a deep breath of his bride's arousal, letting the physical proof of her need fill his senses. Though he was trying as hard as he could to keep his shields in place, the intensity of his emotions made it difficult when all he wanted to do was surrender himself to her. He needed her more than anything he'd ever desired, knew she was his perfect mate, yet he didn't know how to make her want to stay with him. He was asking her to choose between him and her family as well as her world and everything she'd ever known. He feared that he would lose. As if that wasn't hard enough he was also asking her to consider at least partially bonding another man, something that hurt her deeply for reasons he couldn't fully understand.

Near-panic filled him that if she left he would not only lose his soul mate, but Nast's potential *alyah* as well. There wasn't a doubt in his mind Casey had been made for both of them but he didn't dare mention Nast again, at least not right now. His bride was skittish as it was, and her refusal to believe it was possible to love more than one man worried him deeply, even as it filled him with sorrow for Casey. What kind of planet did she live on where they were taught they could only love one person? It hurt his heart to imagine what it must have been like to be trained from such a young age that any kind of love except for the kind approved by her society was evil and immoral. Casey had such a generous heart and he could only pray he could somehow make her see that love in all of its forms was a blessing and that there was no limit to how much love her heart could hold. She deserved the kind of pleasure that could only come from having more than one husband.

But first, he needed to get her to accept him as her bondmate.

All those thoughts fled from his mind as she pressed her lush breasts against his chest with a wanton little moan, her need spinning through their psychic bond like a firestorm of pleasure.

Her purr as he licked at the sensitive skin behind her ear and down along her neck made him want to shove himself between her legs, to fuck her until she admitted she was his.

"God, Lorn," she moaned out and thrust her breasts up against him. "You make me feel so good."

Eager to pleasure his little bride, he cupped her soft mounds in his hands, squeezing gently and loving the feel of her lush body. The Lord of Life had truly gifted the women of Earth with bodies built for a man's pleasure. Soft limbs to hold him, rounded thighs to wrap around his hips, and an endless supply of nectar for him to drink. His mouth watered but he held himself back, needing to build her arousal higher. Easing down his shields between them a bit more, he pushed his lust into her, groaning against her neck when she arched and cried out against him.

"Fuck me, Lorn, please!"

"Not yet, my bride."

"I can't take it!"

"Yes, you can." He gave her a sharp nip on the mound of her breast where the bondmark should appear once they were joined.

She fisted her hands in his hair and he lowered his head, sucking and nibbling at her breast through the black gown. The color set off her creamy skin and lightened her eyes to a stunning shade of golden brown. Her head was thrown back and his cock twitched at the sight of her neck exposed to him. Even if she didn't know it that was an act of submission to him, an acceptance of his dominance in the bedroom, it still drove him crazy. Matriarchs had so much responsibility that it was her husband's sacred duty to take over the pleasures of the bedroom and give his wife a release that would help ease the pressure on her. A duty he took very, very seriously.

Biting her hard nipples, he grinned at her efforts to tug his head from her breast, reading her through their bond, enjoying the hot surge of her arousal, he bit even harder until she stiffened beneath him and moaned long and loud. Hmmm, his *alyah* liked a bit of pain with her pleasure. Unable to resist he slipped his hand between her lush thighs and at the feel of her hot, wet pussy beneath his fingers it was his turn to groan against her breast. He'd never felt anything even close to the perfection of her body.

Finding that tight little nub of flesh unique to human women, he manipulated it by gently rubbing on it with his thumb. Most women of his galaxy gained pleasure from penetration, which he greatly enjoyed, but there was something to be said for being able to build Casey's desire while keeping his own somewhat in check. The ache in his testicles was beginning to border on pain, but he tried to ignore it as he continued to stroke her arousal higher.

She gripped his shoulders and sank her nails into the skin beneath the thin cloth, letting out a keening wail as she stiffened beneath him. Before she could find her release he withdrew his fingers and watched her, amused when she opened her eyes and gave him a look that promised his swift and violent death.

"Why did you stop?"

"I need to taste you."

Her protest faded as he pulled her hips out so her ass was on the very edge of the couch before throwing her legs over his shoulders. Starting with her inner thighs he licked up her abundant nectar, glorying in the taste. Her essence exploded on his tongue and he growled as he licked the crease where her plump thighs met her swollen sex. Leaning back he took a moment to examine the results of his efforts, enjoying the way her sex flushed a deep pink and her clit had pressed out from its soft hood as if begging for his kiss. She was so wet some of her honey had dripped down the crack of her buttocks.

He did not want to waste a drop of her desire so he started there, working his tongue between her rounded cheeks. She gave a startled squeak when he slipped his hands beneath her curvy ass and tilted her hips up so he could torment the nerve-laden area of her anus. He could feel her protest so before she could wiggle away he gently probed the entrance to her ass with his tongue and let her feel how much he enjoyed pleasuring every inch of her body. Her thighs fell open and she arched into his mouth.

"Oh, Lorn, fuck, that is so hot."

Growling as his cock swelled almost enough to extend the pleasure ridges, he feasted on her, licking up every bit of nectar her generous body offered him while he struggled to control himself. By the time he reached her clit and placed a gentle kiss on it she was writhing against him, pleading then yelling at him to make her come. Instead of giving in to her demands he placed small, feather light licks around that little nub until it swelled further and quivered beneath his lips. He rode the edge with her, opening the bond between them as wide as it could go and drowning in the fierce heat of her desire.

Before she could climax he drew away again and would have laughed at her heartfelt wail of despair if he wasn't hurting as bad as she was.

Moving back he ripped open his breeches and released his aching cock, gripping the shaft in an effort to keep from coming the moment the swollen crest touched her hot, slick entrance.

"Look at me," he said in a barely understandable growl.

She forced her eyes open with obvious effort and he began to push his way into her. She was so damned tight he feared he would hurt her, but women's bodies were built to stretch and accept their mate. Her plentiful liquid arousal coated him and it was his turn to struggle to look into her eyes. She reached out and pulled him to her, kissing him with surprising tenderness despite the wild need flowing through her. With a growl he sank further into her and stroked her tongue with his own, reveling in the unique taste that made her his.

Slowly pressing into her wet heat he broke their kiss and breathed hard against her lips as she trembled beneath him. Once he was fully seated in her body he stopped. "I love you, Casey. With everything that I am and everything that I have. I am yours and you are mine."

A massive surge of emotion blasted through their bond drawing their souls closer until they were almost fully merged and he began to move inside of her, feeling her love even if she didn't say it. There were no lies between them when they were joined like this, no fear or distrust. She was his and he was hers. They belonged together because they'd been created for each other. Her tight little pussy sucked at his cock and he had to grit his teeth as his pleasure ridges began to vibrate. Casey went crazy beneath him, thrusting her hips into his, clawing at his back through his shirt and screaming at him to fuck her harder, faster.

His control snapped and he gave her exactly what she wanted.

Together they fought and strained for their mutual orgasm, their lips meeting as they pressed together as close as they could get, their bodies trying to mimic their souls. Fire lit through his blood and Casey locked her legs around his hips, grinding herself against him while she panted his name. Ecstasy exploded through every inch of his body while she began to climax beneath him, crying out and shuddering while her soul enveloped him with the delicious warmth of her orgasm, triggering his own.

Unable to help himself, he roared out his pleasure, pressing himself up on his arms and arching his back, shoving himself as deep into her as he could. Through it all her tight sheath milked him, sucking at him and squeezing every drop of seed he had to offer. He gave her everything he had, straining to extend her pleasure until she was whimpering beneath him. The agonizing ecstasy eased at last and he collapsed on her, managing to keep most of his weight from crushing her.

She gasped beneath him, her heart racing as her body shivered and the mixture of their mutual release soaked his balls. Satisfaction filled him when he gently stroked her cheek and she nuzzled her face against his hand, kissing his knuckles with such gentleness that it broke his heart. After a lifetime of searching for her, of slowly losing his sense of compassion and empathy to the madness, he was overwhelmed by the things this tiny female made him feel. Trying to be gentle, he pulled out of her then staggered to the bathroom to get a cleansing cloth.

Returning quickly to her he found Casey sprawled out in the same position, the lilac tint of his seed dripping from her swollen sex. She barely stirred when he cleaned her and made a grumpy noise after he pulled her into his arms and reclined back on the couch with her draped over him. For a long time they lay like that, heart to heart while she gently stroked the portion of his chest exposed by his shirt. Closing down the link between them a little bit so his emotions wouldn't distract her, he kissed the top of her head.

"Sleep, *alyah*, nothing will harm you here. You are safe."

He felt a tiny bit of irritation from her, then she yawned and snuggled closer. "Okay, just a small nap."

Holding her as she relaxed against him he began to pray harder than he'd ever prayed before that she wouldn't leave him.

A sense of alarm woke Casey from her nap. She pushed up on the couch to a seated position and it took a few moments to orient herself. Looking around she found Lorn attaching some kind of crimson-lined black cape to his armored shoulders. Instead of his soft white shirt and black breeches he wore what she could only describe as some sort of military uniform complete with what appeared to be ribbons and medals over the breastplate and on his forearms. He'd pulled his hair back into a tight braid and his face was shut down into a cold mask of concern tinged with anger.

"Lorn?"

He glanced up while checking the fastenings containing various daggers strapped to his legs. "I must leave you for a little bit, Casey. There is someone I must meet."

Chilled at the mixture of anger, worry, and determination coming from their bond she sat up and tucked her hair behind her ear. "Are they a threat? Are you in danger?"

He gave her a grim smile. "No more than usual. Do not worry, Casey, I will deal with this and will be back as soon as I can."

That didn't reassure her at all and she stood before hesitantly approaching him. "Deal with what? Do you need me with you? I may not know how to fight but I'm sure I can point and shoot a gun."

Shaking his head, the anger faded a bit. "No, I am afraid you can't shoot my mother, though I am sure many would appreciate if you did."

"Your Mom is here?" She smoothed her hands over her dress and tried to finger comb her hair.

"I am sure she came to meet my bride, which I will try to prevent if at all possible."

"And you're not happy about us? You don't want me to meet her?" She wondered if he was embarrassed about her and didn't want his family to meet her.

"*Alyah*, I feel your pain and worry." He cupped her face with both hands and kissed her forehead. "It is not that I am ashamed of you. It is...my mother is a very high-ranking political figure and she did not attain that position by being sweet and charming. Can you understand that? While she loves me, she also loves power and would have preferred it if I bonded with a woman of her choosing. I want to have a talk with her before she meets you for the first time."

Worry filled her that his mother wouldn't like her and she cupped his face with her hands just as he held hers. "Lorn, I know it's crazy but I love you with all of my heart but I don't want to cause issues with your family."

He smiled at her and warmth tinged with reassurance filled her. "I know you love me; I can feel it, but it is nice to hear you say. There is no need for you to worry. My mother is just one of those women who...well, Lord of Life forgive me for criticizing her, she is sort of what you would call a bully. If she feels she can force you to do things her way she will. Not out of evil or malice but because she truly believes her way is the best way."

"Awesome," Casey muttered and forced Lorn to release her so she could give him a hug. "I've met women like that before. The only thing they respect is strength."

"Exactly. Do not take any feces from her because you do not have to."

That made her giggle. "You mean don't take any shit?"

"Yes." He pulled back and his pupil's expanded then contracted. "I must go. When I return, my parents will be with me."

She nervously twisted her hands. "Umm, should I like make cookies for them or something?"

Shaking his head with a smile he started for the door. "You are adorable beyond words. Know that I love you, Casey, and no matter your choice I will not let my mother hurt you. You are mine and I am yours. Never forget that."

He left before she could confess that she wanted to bond with him completely. She'd come to that decision while she was drifting off to sleep on his chest, wrapped up in his love. They'd have to talk about somehow letting her family know she was okay before she went through the wormhole with him, and about the possibility of bonding other men, but her decision was made.

With those heavy thoughts in mind she went to the bathroom and tried to do something with her hair so it wasn't just hanging around her shoulders in a crazy 'I just got really well fucked' mess. She had to smile at the sight of her lips still swollen and pink from Lorn's kisses. Looking at herself in the mirror dressed in the shimmery black gown she had a moment where she could hardly believe that this was real, that she was actually on a spaceship, on one of Jupiter's moons, about to commit herself to the most amazing man in the universe.

Her thoughts went to Lorn and she tried to reach out to him then felt the slightest hint of reassurance coming back through their bond and smiled. She had to giggle at the way her eyes lit up and how she practically radiated happiness. Was this wonderful feeling what true love was like? It was hard to imagine anything more sacred or magnificent.

The melodic trill of an unfamiliar chime broke through her besotted giggles and she quickly moved out into the hallway, unsure of what was going on. A moment later the doors leading to the apartment opened and a tall, mature, but still stunning blonde woman in a glittering white robe that extended up to her neck in an almost priest-like collar strode into the room. She quickly spotted Casey standing in the hallway and her lips turned down with obvious distaste. Casey knew right away this was Lorn's mother. He had her hair and glowing blue eyes along with a few facial features that marked them as obviously being related.

When Lorn didn't appear behind the woman, a hint of panic came through their bond, and Casey realized Lorn's mother had somehow managed to sidestep her son.

Strapping some steel to her spine Casey walked slowly into the room. "Hello. You must be Lorn's mother."

The slightest tightening around the woman's eyes betrayed her surprise and she continued to stare at Casey. Cocking her head to the side, Casey met her gaze head on. If this woman thought she was going to be intimidated by an icy look she had another think coming. While Lorn's mother was tall and imposing, she was just a woman. From the way Lorn described her Casey had been expecting some kind of evil witch from a fairytale.

Finally the woman let out a tense breath. "You have not bonded my son yet."

With Lorn's advice in mind Casey lifted her chin. "Oh, I'm sorry. Where are my manners? My name is Casey Westfall. And you are?"

The woman blinked and her shock was obvious. Drawing herself taller she looked down her nose at Casey. "I am Lady Elsin Adar, Matriarch of the House Adar and Lead Representative of the Northern Congress to the High Congress of Kadothia."

She looked at Casey as if expecting her to be awed, but if the Congress of Kadothia was anything like the Congress of the United States, she wasn't impressed. "How may I help you?"

Lady Elsin practically gritted her teeth, and Casey had a hard time holding back her laughter. Things were obviously not going the way this woman thought they would. "I came to see the barbarian bride that managed to connive her way into my son's heart. Do not think I am unaware of your schemes and your weakness."

Obviously Lady Elsin was trying to anger her but Casey wouldn't give her the pleasure. She couldn't argue with being physically weaker, the other woman had a good seven inches on her, but the other part irked her. "Schemes? What the hell kind of schemes would I have? He's the one who kidnapped me. I don't know what the world is like where you're from, but I love Lorn because he's a good man. Honest, kind, and honorable, not because I want something he has. He must get those traits from his father."

For a second she was pretty sure Lady Elsin was trying to kill her by glaring at her, but Casey merely quirked an eyebrow and crossed her arms. "Look, I don't know you and you don't know me. You've obviously come here with some preconceived, and wrong, notions, but you are Lorn's mother so I will allow that you have the right to be worried about the woman that he's marrying. Let me assure you I do love him and I want only the best for him."

Lady Elsin sneered. "But you will not take more than one husband, will you? Or allow his men to bond with you. I have heard about you Earth brides. You care for nothing but yourselves."

That threw her for a loop and she dropped her arms. "What?"

"You are selfish. Lorn loves his blood brother but you will not even consider him for a second husband, will you? Nast is a good, honorable man and I love him like a son, but instead of watching him finally have the happiness he deserves I will have to stand by, along with my son, as Nast slowly loses his mind to the madness. Eventually he will have to be put down like a rabid animal, all because you think loving two men is a sin. Like I said, selfish and ignorant."

"But...Lorn never told me Nast would die if I didn't bond him."

The tall woman gave Casey a look of such disgust that she flinched. "Of course he would not tell you. He loves you and would do nothing to hurt your feelings. He fears losing you if you feel forced to love another man because of your barbaric upbringing. Do you know how badly you will be hurting Lorn if you reject Nast? How much you will be putting my son's life in danger because you are rejecting *love* out of fear of the unknown? Out of stupidity? You might as well slit his throat now and save him the agony."

Casey struggled to keep up with the conversation. "Wait, do you mean Lorn could die? I don't understand."

Giving a bitter laugh Lady Elsin strolled over to a chair and took a seat like a queen on her throne. "Did Lorn not tell you about the infighting?"

For a moment she considered trying to hide her ignorance, but finally shook her head. "He might have mentioned something about it, but I thought the Hive was your enemy."

Her honesty appeared to calm Lady Elsin slightly and she took a deep breath before lifting her chin. "Let me be straightforward with you, Earth bride. I cannot read your emotions and that alarms me. If you were a normal bride I would know your love was true. Because of who Lorn is he is in constant danger not only from the Hive, but from those on Kadothia who would use his death as an excuse to weaken me. While it is true no open wars are fought, I can assure you there is a constant power struggle that is just as deadly, and I do everything in my power to keep them from starting a civil war." She leaned forward the slightest bit, holding Casey's gaze. "Without a strong, partially or fully bonded circle of men around you and Lorn, he will be vulnerable. Nast is a fearsome Warrior and I trust him above all others to keep my son alive and safe. He would be an excellent husband. Once your bond is complete I will no longer be able to protect Lorn as he will be yours and because of your fear and self-centeredness, you will not bond other Warriors strong enough to defend you both. You will leave him open to assassinations with no one to guard his back with the unquestionable loyalty and love of other bonded males. What will you do without a Healer you can trust implicitly, or a Negotiator to make sure you get dealt with fairly? I highly doubt either of you will survive more than a month."

Moving on unsteady feet Casey made her way to the couch where she'd recently made love to Lorn and sat on it with far less grace than Lady Elsin had displayed. "I didn't know."

"Now that you do, will you do what is necessary to protect my son?"

"I don't know." She repeated and looked down at her hands then back up. "Lorn said I can only bond through pleasure. Is it that way with you? I mean did you have to...be intimate with the men who you're partially bonded to?"

Lady Elsin studied her. "This distresses you. Why?"

Trying not to blush, Casey looked back at her hands. "Well, on Earth a woman who is intimate with a man other than her husband is considered a cheating bitch. It means she doesn't love him and she's a bad person."

"You said you do love my son, correct?"

"Yes."

"Then he knows that. I cannot imagine what it is like to live without the ability to read emotions, but Lorn will always know how you feel about him. Stop being such a child. Any bonding you do will be arousing for both you and Lorn." She shifted uncomfortably. "As

I am sure you are aware he will feel your pleasure and will enjoy it as well. You have everything to gain and nothing to lose by at least trying."

"I could lose Lorn."

Lady Elsin threw her hands up. "Have you not heard a word I said? Bonding multiple males is not shameful, or a sin, or whatever else your backwards planet has attributed to the idea of caring for more than one man. If you will not do it for my son, do it for all the Warriors who will have to face the Hive without your shielding. We can only bond so many men before our protection runs too thin to do any good. That means millions of mothers are facing their sons going off to almost certain death in their efforts to protect us all from the Hive. But, what is that in the face of your delicate sensibilities?"

Anger mixed with a heavy dose of guilt and made Casey defensive. "Look, this is hard for me, okay? I'm trying to adapt as best I can. I love Lorn but we're just learning about each other."

"Do not be so daft. You will be the other half of his soul and you will know him better than he knows himself." She made a sour look. "In some ways you already are."

"What?"

"I can no longer sense my son like I used to. Whatever natural shielding you carry that prevents my mind from reaching yours has extended to him. While I appreciate the tactical advantage it will give my son, I do not like not being able to fully read him." Lady Elsin's expression softened and she swallowed hard before saying in a low voice, "It is...distressing to me. For the first time since his birth I cannot feel him like I should."

Casey tried to see it from the other woman's point of view and nodded. "I understand, kind of."

The elegant woman tilted her head and her pupils did that weird flexing thing then she gave a small smile. "Lorn is almost here, and he is very angry with me, as are my husbands. Know this, Casey Westfall of Earth, you will not be proving your love by refusing to at least partially bond other men, to not even give Nast a chance to win your heart. Lorn would never force you because Kadothian men are devoted to their wives beyond anything you've experienced, but I'm asking you as a mother to her son's chosen bride—please try. Allow yourself to open fully to Lorn and you will feel that there is no jealousy. These men will not take his place in your life nor do they want to. Even Nast as a second husband would not weaken your bond with Lorn in any way. In fact, bonding Nast would strengthen your marriage immeasurably."

"I don't understand."

Lady Elsin sighed and rubbed her temples. "How do I explain love to someone so emotionally crippled? To the men you partially bond with you will be their Matriarch, not their wife, and your decision will not only possibly save Lorn's life, but yours as well because if either of you die the other will soon follow. And even if Lorn did bring a man for you to consider as a husband, do you really believe my son would ask you to bond with anyone unworthy? That he would ever share you with a man he didn't think would love you just as much? Think on it."

With that Lady Elsin stood and for the briefest moment Casey could see the other woman's internal conflict reflected on her face before her expression once again smoothed into a haughty, icy mask. A moment later the door slid open and Lorn burst through with three equally large older men on his heels. The man directly behind Lorn who looked the most like him moved towards Lady Elsin with a severely disapproving expression. All three men were huge. Two of them had hair in different shades of brown with dark tan skin while the third, who gripped Lady Elsin's arm, had silver hair like Lorn's. They wore armor similar to Lorn's but with far more decorations and in different colors. One navy blue, one green, and the man who looked like Lorn had black armor embellished with white.

Before they'd taken two steps Lady Elsin jerked her arm out of the man's grip and held up her hand. "Stop."

The older men did but Lorn kept approaching Casey. Before he could close the distance he let out an agonized scream and dropped to the floor, writhing in agony. Casey screamed as well as his pain came pouring through the bond, drowning her in agony mixed with his anger and self-loathing for failing her. Lorn managed to crawl to her side as she moaned in anguish, sure she was dying, wishing she was dying so this would end. As quickly as the pain came it vanished and she panted, her muscles still twitching and jerking.

Lorn gathered her against him, trying to soothe her as she cried with relief at the cessation of the agonizing torture. His voice came out in a broken rasp as he said, "Mother, how could you?"

Casey pushed at his chest, ready to slap the shit out of his mother when she realized the other woman was the cause of their pain. But when she looked up at Lorn's mother she found Lady Elsin had tears streaming down her face while her men supported her with equally distressed expressions. "She had to know, Lorn. Forgive me for hurting you both, but she had to know what could happen to you, to your men, if they do not have her protection."

Rage poured through Lorn and Casey struggled to clear her mind of his emotions. "Get out of here. I will no longer acknowledge you as my mother."

Lady Elsin's grief-stricken cry matched the emotional pain roaring through Lorn, and Casey fought to find a way to think past it all. She threw her arms around Lorn and held him close. "It's okay, Lorn, I'm all right. She's a fucking bitch but she's right, I had to know."

Lorn held her so hard she had trouble catching a breath. "Forgive me, *alyah*, she hurt you and I could not stop her. I have failed you."

With her heart breaking she clasped his face between her hands and forced him to look at her. Though tears filled his eyes and she could feel his soul crying out in misery, he refused to let one fall. "Is it true? What she just did to us...is what the unbonded men will feel if they're attacked by the Hive?"

He hesitated, then nodded. "It is similar."

"What he means," Lady Elsin whispered, "is that what he felt, what I felt and you felt, is maybe one-tenth the power of just one of the Hive would unleash on him and our men."

"Enough, Elsin," the man who looked the most like Lorn said in a firm voice. "Our son is a grown man. It is his choice and his bride's choice to make. You will not force their hand in this matter."

With that Lady Elsin crumbled entirely and began to sob. The man in the navy blue armor behind her scooped her into his arms and exchanged a look with the other two men. "We are very sorry about this, Lorn. We did not know she would lock us in our room and come here on her own. I promise you we did not come with the intent of harming you or your bride. Forgive us."

With that the two men in the green and navy blue armor went out the door with a crying Lady Elsin held between them. The man she was pretty sure was Lorn's father crouched next to them. "My name is Malin and I am Lorn's sire. Little bride, please forgive my wife. Yesterday we lost over two thousand men to the Hive when they attacked a barracks full of poorly bonded men."

Lorn tensed against her. "How did they manage that?"

"They hid in a supply ship run by a trusted merchant that went deep into the safe zone." His steady, dark gaze focused on Casey again. "My wife had the unenviable task of breaking the news to their families this morning and it hurt her deeply. Though it is completely foolish, she feels responsible for the death of every one of our men. That is no excuse for what she did to you, but I pray to the Lord of Life that my wife did not harm your love for our son." He sighed and rubbed his face hard before giving Lorn a look filled with such sorrow that her heart ached. "Nast was at the training center that was attacked."

Instant, overwhelming fear filled her causing her to tremble and cling to Lorn as he stared at his father. "Is he...?"

"No, he lives. He managed to rally his troops and they fought off the attack. Thankfully there were only two Hive members with the mercenaries."

Immense relief filled her and she realized Lorn loved Nast, really loved him. Jealousy panged through her and Lorn looked down with an agonized expression. "*Alyah*, please do not be upset about my feelings for my blood brother."

Things started to fall into place as she stared up at Lorn. "Are you...are you lovers?"

"Yes. We have been lovers for a long, long time." He glanced at his father then back at her, his bond between them shutting down tight. "Sire, may we please be alone?"

His father stood and gave Casey a hard look that made her flinch. "Even without being able to read your emotions I can see your fear and judgment, Earth bride. I am aware you consider two men loving each other to be wrong, but you do not understand. Nast is Lorn's blood brother, did he explain to you what that is? Or did you just immediately assume the worst? I believe I know which one. You do not deserve Nast or my son."

Lorn quickly stood and pulled her up with him so that he had her pressed to his body as anger filled him, mixing with his heartache and fear until Casey was close to tears. "Father-"

"Silence!" Lorn's father roared, and she let out a frightened yelp.

Lorn started to move, violence coming off of him in waves, but before he could go very far she clung to his neck and put her face in front of his. She couldn't let him try to disown both his parents in one day, especially when everything they'd said was true. She did assume the worst and she did unfairly judge both Lorn and his culture. And yes, she'd even been selfish about putting her feelings above his. She was woman enough to admit it and loved Lorn enough to try and understand. Her family would have done the same thing if they were in a similar situation. Though she couldn't imagine ever being in this kind of relationship on Earth. It shamed her to admit her fear of what people would think about her still influenced her despite her best attempts to not care.

"No! Lorn don't do it! Please, please don't fight with your father."

The connection between them closed down and he trembled against her hold. "He is hurting you."

"No, he's not." Lorn glared at her and she quickly added. "I mean he hurt my feelings, but not bad."

"He has no right to say those things to you. It is not his place to speak of Nast to you."

His shields cracked just the smallest bit and she found herself drowning in his pain. Hugging him close she buried her face against his neck and she whispered, "Shhh, my *alyah*, it's all right."

He gave a startled bark of laughter that made her pull back. "*Alyah* is considered a feminine word. It is like...like if we were on Earth and you called me your sugar baby girl."

His father coughed and she gave Lorn a relieved smile, happy to feel his sorrow and fear pulling back to a manageable level. "I kind of like that. Maybe I will start calling you my sugar baby boy."

Malin cleared his throat, "Casey..."

Lorn glared at his father. "Leave. You have said enough and done enough damage."

"No, wait. I want to hear him out. If I'm willing to listen then maybe he would be willing to explain to me what he is trying to say like a calm, rational adult instead of just yelling at me."

"You are correct, I was unnecessarily harsh with you." Closing his eyes Malin took a deep breath and slowly let it out. "Forgive me, bride of my son, but I find your fear to be offensive. The two other men in my own marriage are my blood brothers and I love them as much as I love my wife. To know your people would look down on us and condemn us for our love angers me greatly."

She went to move but Lorn held her tight with a frantic look. "It's okay. I just want to sit down for this conversation. You guys are so tall I get a crick in my neck looking up at you."

He reluctantly released her then joined her on the couch as soon as she sat, pulling her as close as physically possible. Malin was right, she was being judgmental but she couldn't comprehend how Lorn could love both Nast and her. "I'm listening. Please help me to understand."

"Before he is bonded, a Kadothian male leads a very lonely existence. Yes, we have the love of our friends and family, but can you imagine what it would be like to live thousands of your Earth years without someone to care for as your own? Someone you can return home to and would be there to hold at night as you slept? Someone you can find not only physical affection with, but can trust with all of your heart and soul? A Kadothian male cannot just take any woman into his home to fill that role. First, it would not be fair to that woman because he would never love her, and second, because our race is empathetic and we need the special bond with another of our race in order to truly love them."

She frowned. "But I'm not of your race."

"You are once my son kissed you and changed your physiology. In many ways you are no longer human, Casey. You won't age as you used to, instead, you will live as long as your bondmate lives once your bond is completed."

Lorn stroked her cheek with the back of his hand. "Don't be scared."

She went to deny it, then shook her head. "I'm not really scared, I mean I am but I'm more in shock than anything else. How long will I live?"

"At least another thousand cycles."

"How many earth years is that?"

"Around two thousand five hundred years."

"Holy shit..."

Lorn's father gave her a gentle smile much like his sons. "Now imagine spending all that time alone."

"That would be terrible."

"It would. Fortunately, Kadothian males have the ability to form blood bonds with each other. It only works with men we can someday share a wife with, but it is the closest thing to bonding we can achieve without her in our life. We keep each other sane while we wait for our *alyah* and we love each other in a way that is not wrong or a sin, and neither is it a threat to your love for Lorn." He looked frustrated and ran his hand through his hair. "This is so difficult to explain to someone who cannot sense others' emotions."

"I can feel Lorn's," she offered.

He gave her a relieved smile. "Thank the Lord of Life. I was wondering, but did not want to ask such a personal question. When the bond is fully open between you it will be impossible to lie to each other because you will know the truth in his heart. Lorn loves Nast because they have been keeping each other alive and strong while waiting for you."

She glanced at Lorn out of the corner of her eye. "Does...is Nast jealous of me?"

"Absolutely not," Lorn said quickly. "He insisted that if you refused to bond me because of him that he would remove himself from my life. But he wants you, Casey, desperately, just as I wanted you before I even saw you because we are meant to be together. However, if you cannot live with that I will still love you and accept your decision."

The burst of sorrow following his words had her closing her eyes and taking a deep breath before letting it out slowly and looking at his father. "Will this be easier to understand if I'm married to Lorn?"

"Yes," both men said at once.

His father shook his head with a small smile. "Becoming a bondmate is only slightly similar to your Earth marriage. It is not just an exchange of words and a promise. It is a true blending of souls. You will never again doubt Lorn's adoration for you in any way."

Turning, she studied Lorn, trying to really look at him with a clear mind. His blue eyes were filled with love and worry as she examined him, loving the way his full lips were framed by his high cheekbones and square jaw. The silver glints in his hair shimmered as he breathed and just looking at him made her all weak and hot inside. She would never find a more perfect husband, and if it was true that there was another man who would love her as much as he did, she would be foolish to dismiss it out of fear fueled by ignorance. While she couldn't imagine feeling for anyone the way she did for Lorn, she had to admit that before meeting him she had no idea what true love really was. And he did love her, with all his heart and soul. Just like she loved him.

More importantly, Lorn loved Nast, and she couldn't break up a relationship that had existed for hundreds of years without even meeting the other man. Everything she'd ever wanted in life lay within her reach if she just had the courage to take it. She thought about what it would be like to watch Lorn kiss another no doubt unfairly handsome Kadothian man and had to admit the idea wasn't as disturbing as she'd first thought. Especially if she was there while he did it and Nast was anywhere near as hot as every other Kadothian man she'd seen. A sudden, intense fantasy came to her of being pressed between two men, naked, surrounded by them and the focus of their passion. She cleared her throat and tried to get that naughty image out of her mind before looking at Malin again.

"Thank you for taking the time to explain it to me in a way I can understand." She took a deep breath and held tight to Lorn's hand, not daring to look at him as she asked, "Can you do me a favor?"

Before his father could respond Lorn said, "What do you need? You have but to ask and I will do all in my power to give it to you."

Lorn gently cupped her chin and tried to get her to look at him, but she shrugged away. She didn't need to read his emotions to know he was just about out of his mind with worry, but she hoped what she did next would help him to never doubt her again. If she looked at him she wouldn't be able to continue so she kept her gaze on his father.

Malin studied her for a moment, then nodded. "I will help you however I can, bride of my son."

Her words tumbled out in a rapid spill as her nerves got away from her. "How soon can you arrange a bonding ceremony?"

Shock poured through her from Lorn followed by elation and when both father and son did that roaring howl she clasped her hands over her ears and started to laugh, unable to contain the joy and love flowing from Lorn and mixing with her own. Somehow they would make this work and with Lorn's love to support her she would find the strength to do whatever was necessary to make him safe.

Chapter Twelve

Nast stood in line at the back of the transport ship that had just taken him and two dozen other Kadothian males through the wormhole. His right leg ached as it healed, and his skin still tingled and burned where he'd taken a laser shot to the shoulder, and his right hand shook slightly as the nerves rapidly regenerated thanks to Vilpon who'd managed to save his hand. Though now he was wondering why the other man even bothered.

Slowly, but surely, his emotions were draining away. The rage that was characteristic of the madness hadn't yet begun to fill the emotional void of his fading empathy and compassion, but he knew it wasn't far away. Right now his heart should be racing with the anticipation of seeing Lorn again, of seeing Casey for the first time, but instead he felt nothing but depression. The day prior, he'd witnessed the deaths of over a thousand of Kadothia's youngest and brightest warriors during a well-planned Hive attack deep in the safe zone, and those deaths haunted him. Men he'd trained, men who had looked up to him, men he failed to keep safe. Faces kept scrolling through his memories, the faces of the dying pleading with the Lord of Life to save them, the faces of the men who would no longer be coming home to their mothers, and the faces of those would never meet their *alyah*.

For a while there, he'd been sure he was going to die as well and he'd almost embraced that feeling, an insidious part of the madness insisting Lorn would be better off without him, that Casey would never accept someone as unworthy as Nast, but he'd managed to hold on. While he wanted to think it was his strength that gave him the will to survive, to heal, it was his true dream with Casey that had saved him. Nast refused to believe that the Lord of Life would send him that meeting with her soul when he needed it most if they were not meant to be. But the rumors swirling around about the frailty and weakness of the Earth brides was wearing away his hope. But he had the dream and Casey's scent to give him enough strength to hold on. His faint memory of that dream, of how good it felt to hold her, of her smile, kept him going when all he wanted to do was stop fighting.

He clung to that memory, praying it meant something even as he found it hard to care.

In the line ahead of him, Nast overheard two Scouts who were waiting for their turn to step through the scanners and decontamination unit as they whispered to each other.

"Did you hear about Kalit of House Menaw?"

"Yeah, poor guy. His bondmate attempted to kill herself after she partially bonded two other Warriors."

"Heard he tried to join her, but his blood brother reached them in time."

Both men sighed heavily, but the man on the right gave the one on the left a quick hug. "That won't happen to us."

The line moved forward and Nast wanted to yell at them that it could happen to them, to anyone, because death, disaster and torment were never more than a breath away, but he managed to hold his tongue. They must have sensed some of his emotions leaking through his shields because they both stiffened and turned back to look at him. As soon as they did and recognized who he was, they both turned quickly back around. No one wanted to anger the blood brother of Lady Elsin's oldest son.

After moving through the scanner Nast stood in the crowded terminal and his heart seized in his chest at the first faint trace of Lorn somewhere on the ship. His soul grabbed onto that sense of belonging, that sense of love and he took a deep breath for what felt like the first time since Lorn had left the Bel'Tan galaxy. Moving as quickly as he could to one of the information stations, he stared at what had to be an Earth female standing with a big Warrior in the navy blue armor of a Negotiator he assumed was her husband. She had lightly tanned skin and soft hazel green eyes with short brown hair that framed her petite features. A triple bondmark showed on her exposed cleavage and he couldn't help his rude examination of this Earth Matriarch who had taken three husbands.

Before her husband could speak, the Matriarch smiled up at him. "Greetings, Warrior. How may I help you?"

Nast stared at her husband, protocol demanding she state her name before he could talk directly to her. With a small smile the blue-eyed warrior leaned down to his bride and whispered, "You forgot to say your name, *alyah*."

She flushed a pretty pink. "Ahem, my name is Bonnie of House Turner. This is my third husband, Denod."

Charmed by this pretty female Nast smiled. "My name is Nast of House Enn. It is an honor to meet you, Matriarch of House Turner."

Her husband stiffened slightly and the woman narrowed her eyes at Nast with hostility now radiating from her tense posture. "Why is my husband fearful of you?"

While Nast couldn't feel her husband's emotions—he was so totally shielded that it was like the other man wasn't even there—he could easily read his embarrassment in his face. Trying to keep from laughing at the Matriarch unknowingly insulting her husband by exposing his anxiety, Nast struggled to keep his expression carefully blank. "I am sure it is not fear of me, Matriarch. He is probably afraid I'll manage to charm you away from him. I do have a way with the ladies."

That wasn't entirely true, but her husband relaxed and Bonnie went from defensive to exasperated as Nast gave her a wink and a charming smile. "Men. No matter what galaxy you're from you're all nothing but trouble."

Denod cleared his throat. "How may we assist you, Elder Master Sergeant?"

"I was wondering if the bonding ceremony between Lorn Adar and Casey Westfall has begun? I received word it would be happening today."

Denod looked down at his wife and said in a low voice, "Do you remember how to do this?"

She swallowed then nodded and closed her eyes. "Okay, I'm looking through the general database, then going to the ship...hold on, I think I'm on the wrong ship. Okay, right one now. Looking through the logs, narrowing it down to the names of Lorn and Casey along with bonding. Got it. No, it hasn't begun yet."

"Can you tell me where Lorn is, Matriarch?"

Her eyes closed again and her small face tensed. "Yeah, gimme a sec. Okay, he's on eight deck, sector sixty-five, room 266."

"Security protocol," her husband whispered.

"Oh, shit." Her eyes flashed open, wide with panic. "Fuck, that was restricted information."

"Do not worry, Elder Master Sergeant Nast has clearance. I would not have allowed you to make a mistake that would have led to a reprimand."

To Nast's surprise Bonnie grabbed her husband in a hug and buried her face against his chest. "I'll never get this right."

"You are doing fine." Denod briefly caressed her back before pulling away and tilting his head in Nast's direction. "Permissions."

Once again she flushed then straightened her shoulders. "If you will give me one moment I'll make sure you can get through the security points."

"Thank you, Matriarch."

A trace of humor went through Nast and he almost let out a sigh of relief as some of his normal emotions began to return. He didn't know if it was because he was once again near Lorn, or if it was being near Casey, but either way he was grateful that he wouldn't have to go to his blood brother feeling emotionally dead. This was a time for celebration, not worry, and Lorn would have worried about him.

He clung to that thread of humor and it grew as the bonded couple before him engaged in a battle of whispers while Denod walked his frustrated wife through how to access her crystal implants in order to give Nast the permissions he needed to move through the ship. She would hiss back that the Kadothian system was overly complicated, that she'd managed to run a Fortune 500 company—whatever that was—as an administrative assistant that had been better managed than the 'hot mess' she was trying to deal with now.

A few moments later she turned back to Nast with an overly bright smile. "There, done. I hope you enjoy the bonding ceremony."

"I will. Thank you for your help, Matriarch." He gave her a low bow and when he straightened her smile was now genuine.

"You are most welcome, Elder...um...."

"Just call me Nast, Matriarch. And thank you again. Now, if you will excuse me, I need to try to make it to the ceremony in time."

Denod bowed in return, the thanks for Nast's patience plain on his face. "Safe travels."

Lifting his hand, Nast slowly made his way through the terminal, easily spotting the Earth brides and Matriarchs as he crossed through the ship. Not only were they mostly physically smaller than females of the Bel'Tan galaxy, they were also more expressive. They wore their emotions on their faces, in their movements, and Nast realized a smart Warrior didn't need to have a bond with them to see what they were feeling. No doubt their bondmates would train them on how to hide their emotions and thoughts better, but he enjoyed being able to see this unguarded side of the females who would help rule his planet.

Laughter filled the air of the terminal, both male and female, and more than that there was a great deal of hope coming from the unbonded Kadothian males he passed. From the rumors swirling around the Bel'Tan galaxy he'd expected to find a ship full of broken men and crying women, but instead he found strong little females who obviously loved their men. Everywhere he looked he'd catch the women giving their males small touches, little looks and kisses that showed their love just as strong as if he could read their emotions. It shocked him even more to see how many multiple couples there were, Matriarchs walking and holding hands with both of her bondmates or just as often, arguing with them while the Kadothian men looked equal parts frustrated, amused, irritated, and in love.

He couldn't help but choke back a laugh at the utterly confused expression on many of the men being scolded by their wives and his laughter escaped as he imagined Lorn in their position. His blood brother was so high-ranking, so smooth and cultured that he was rarely flustered by anyone or anything, but if Casey was like the Earth women he'd seen so far they didn't hold back their opinion on things. The closer he got to where Lorn was getting ready for his bonding ceremony the more he wondered why such a dire picture was being painted of Earth women back in the Bel'Tan galaxy. These women weren't the shrinking, scared, hysterical, and stupid women he'd been led to believe they were.

Something about the rumors versus the reality bothered him, but before he could question it further he came to the room where Lorn was getting ready. Two of his fathers stood guard outside and they both let out a shout of greeting when they saw him. Malin, Lorn's sire, strode forward and caught Nast in a hard embrace.

"We did not know if you were going to make it. Thank the Lord of Life you did. Lorn will be very glad to have you here."

Tegowl, a Healer, thumped Malin on the shoulder. "He is still regenerating, you idiot. Let him go before you mess up his shoulder."

Nast tried to hold back a wheeze when Malin abruptly released him. "I was not going to let a little wound keep me from being here today."

Both men examined him from head to foot and he had to fight the urge to fidget beneath their experienced gaze. Malin grunted and took a step back. "Lorn is inside. We did not tell him you were coming like you asked."

Tegowl, always the most observant of Lorn's fathers and the best at reading emotions, cocked his head to the side. "You are worried."

For a moment he considered lying to the other men, but both were apt to beat his ass for the insult, bonding ceremony or not. "I have been concerned about Casey's willingness to consider another bondmate. There are rumors floating among the Bel'Tan galaxy that the Earth females are rejecting most of the Kadothian males at an alarming rate. That the ship is besieged with suicide attempts because the females are too weak to even consider bonding more than one man. That they are selfish and will make poor Matriarchs."

Malin shook his head. "We had heard those rumors as well and I am ashamed to admit we assumed they were true. Lady Elsin came here believing the whispers and she found out the hard way Casey is not at all how she thought she would be. Lorn's bride may look non-threatening, but she is fierce."

"Very fierce. I do not think I have ever seen a woman stand up to Elsin like Lorn's bride did, not even Lady Yanush." Laughing, Tegowl leaned against the doorway. "Casey is very young, but also a very strong female, as are most of the Earth women we have encountered. We have found the key to their acceptance of another bondmate in addition to their first husband is communication. These females like to think for themselves, and for the most part, they have been receptive to the truth. Of course there were a few that refused to accept multiple bondings, but they did not break their bonds with their husbands."

Nast frowned. "I do not understand. On the way here the transport was filled with tales of men and Earth brides breaking bonds, or killing themselves, or refusing to touch their bondmates. Why would such lies be spread about them?"

Lowering his voice, Malin stepped forward and pressed his wrist, the tiny hiss of a communications blocker filling the air around them with barely audible electrical static. "These Earth women are powerful, perhaps the most powerful females we have ever encountered. Some of them have displayed an ability to kill and maim across great distances, without even seeing their opponents."

"What?" Nast sucked in a deep breath. "How is that even possible?"

"We have no idea, but it has been done. Others have the ability to mind speak from across the galaxy and yet others can invade their bondmates' dreams and speak to them as if they were standing before them in the flesh. There are even rumors that some of the brides can communicate with animals. It seems a full bonding awakens some sleeping part of their mind that controls their psychic powers, but it's utterly random how they manifest. The Earth natives are like nothing we have ever encountered, but because of their shielding we have no idea how they are doing what they do, and neither do they. There is hope they may be the weapon we need to finally stop the Hive's advance."

Shocked, Nast put out a hand to steady himself on the wall. "You are talking about putting our Matriarchs into battle? Have you lost your mind?"

Tegowl stepped closer. "Lower your voice. There are elements of the Kadothian ruling class that do not like what they view as a challenge to their power. Houses are moving to try and secure an Earth female for their own, to get their men through the wormhole without the permission of the High Congress. Or to eliminate the Earth Matriarchs as a threat all together. There have been attempts on the Earth Matriarchs that have already returned to Kadothia.

Two days ago, we caught a shuttle loaded with Earth females headed for the slave markets of Daouloon. All the women were rescued, and a few even found their bondmates, but most had their memory wiped before being returned to the surface."

Tegowl added, "There is a rumor going around that the current ruling class want the Earth Matriarchs banned from holding high political positions until they've been assimilated. Meaning they fear the entire power base of Kadothia is about to shift, and there are some that would rather it remain as it is and will do anything to make that happen."

"I will slay anyone who seeks to harm Casey," Nast said in a harsh whisper as rage flooded him, mixing with his shock.

"Easy," Tegowl crooned and a wave of relaxing energy came from the Healer. "This is not the time of the place for this discussion. All you need to focus on right now is to being there for Lorn on his bonding day."

Feeling like an ass for harboring such anger, Nast tried to let it go. Bringing negative emotions to a bonding ceremony was bad luck of the worst kind. "Yes, you are correct. Tell me one thing, please. Do you think Casey will consider me for a second husband?"

Malin smiled, then gave him a gentle shove to the door. "Go, talk with my son and help him get ready. Though he will not admit it, he is very nervous."

"Go, with our blessings," Tegowl added. "The Lord of Life meant for you to be together, trust in His love."

Nast nodded then took a deep breath and when the door opened he walked into the spacious room where Lorn was getting ready for his bonding ceremony. It struck him almost like a physical blow to feel the block against his mental connection with Lorn. He instinctively tried to get a read on his blood brother's emotions and came up against an impossibly strong shield with only the tiniest of cracks remaining. While he knew of the strength of the Earth women's shields in theory, to actually feel it from his blood brother left him shaken.

Dressed in his black dress armor embellished with his awards and accolades, Lorn was everything good and strong, a Kadothian man in his prime and Nast swallowed hard as he fought the urge to take the other man in his arms.

Before he could take another step Lorn turned and the wide smile on his face and the way his eyes lit up gave Nast hope. "You are here! I prayed you would make it out of medical in time."

"You think I would let a little thing like some broken bones stop me?"

He walked forward, the brace holding his thigh bone together giving him the support he needed while the injury repaired itself. In two days he would be as good as new, but for right now he was as weak as a newborn babe as his body regenerated, but he wouldn't have missed this for anything. Lorn strode across the room to him and embraced him tightly, each breathing the other in, and Nast smiled at the profound relief that made it past Lorn's bride's shields. The feeling of loving and being loved filled him, helping him ground himself and find his own inner strength.

"I heard about the attack," Lorn said against his neck. "Thank the Lord of Life you survived."

Nast closed his eyes and took another deep breath of Lorn's scent, now deliciously mixed with Casey's. He wanted to ask where she was, if he could see her, but he kept those selfish thoughts locked away. Today wasn't about him, it was about Lorn and his bride, but oh how he craved just a moment in her presence.

They pulled apart and Lorn studied his face with a sorrowful expression. "I can hardly feel you."

"No dark thoughts, blood brother. Not today." He cupped Lorn's cheek and wanted to kiss him as they always did when they returned to each other, but he hesitated. Lorn was no longer his to touch.

Smiling, Lorn leaned forward and placed a careful, soft kiss on his lips. Nast could taste Casey on the other man's skin and he couldn't help licking against the seam of Lorn's mouth to taste her. Lorn obligingly parted his lips and Nast was soon drowning in their combined essence, his desire roaring to life as the primitive part of his mind demanded he find the woman that carried this tempting flavor, now.

With his heart thundering in his chest he broke away from Lorn and took an unsteady step back. "I am sorry. I should not have done that."

Lorn sighed and shook his head. "Nast, it is all right."

"No, it is not. You are about to bond Casey and I have no right touching you without her permission." Panic seized him at the thought of never meeting the woman the Lord of Life had created for him to share with Lorn, but he ruthlessly pushed it back. "I will not risk her turning you away, not now."

Lorn closed the distance between them and placed his hands on Nast's shoulders. "Casey and I had a long talk, well as long as we could have when she demanded that we bond as soon as possible. She does not understand our ways, but she is willing to try. After the bonding ceremony, and after what she calls our honeymoon, she wants to meet you and two other men that I want her to partially bond with."

Elation filled Nast but he tried to hold it back. If it didn't mean what he thought it did he was afraid it would crush his heart. "Does she...is she willing to consider me as more than a partial bond? As a husband?"

"She is, but you need to know you will have a hard road to win her love. Casey has a generous heart, but loving you will go against everything she was raised to believe. I have no doubt she will eventually see we belong together, but you must go slow with her. It will be torture for you not to go after her with everything you have, but believe me when I say she is worth the wait."

Nast closed his eyes, afraid if he looked at Lorn any longer the tears that were trying to escape would fall free. He never cried—it was simply something a Warrior did not do, an unacceptable weakness—but damned if he didn't struggle with the stinging pain of tears threatening to break free. It wasn't sorrow, but a relief so profound he had no words to describe it. All hope was not lost. Casey would not banish him or worse, leave Lorn like those other Earth brides had left their potential bondmates when faced with the reality of Kadothian life.

"What is she like?" he whispered as he kept his eyes closed and struggled with himself.

"She is kind, compassionate, and has a good sense of humor. Though this is all new and no doubt frightening, she has faced it with the courage of a Warrior. And smart, so smart. Her thirst for knowledge will make her a formidable Matriarch."

"Do you..." he took a deep breath as his voice faltered, "do you think she will like me?"

"No, Nast, she will love you with everything she is and everything she has because that is who she is. She will fill every empty space in your soul, surround your with warmth until you will question how you ever lived without her." Lorn's soft exhale stirred the hair against his neck and he rested his head on his blood brother's shoulder. "She is not like other Earth women who let fear rule them, Nast. She will not run from me just because she does not understand. I can feel your worry and it is unfounded. Have faith our love was meant to be because it is."

When he opened his eyes again he found Lorn giving him an understanding look that made those fucking tears want to fall. He cleared his throat and gave Lorn a gentle shove. "Come on, you have a bonding ceremony to attend."

Laughing, Lorn grabbed his cloak and tossed it to Nast. "Help me put this thing on."

Nast shook out the crimson-lined, black silk cloak and grinned. "How are you holding up?"

"Nervous as a virgin before the first ritual of pleasure."

"Can you feel Casey? How is she?"

Lorn's gaze went distant for a moment and Nast envied him his ability to talk to their *alyah*. He was going to do everything he could to make sure she knew how good things would be between them once they were together. Even if Lorn had never been born Nast would have loved her because he was made to love her and she was made to love him. The relief continued to spread through him, chasing back the deadening of emotions that was the hallmark of the madness. On the trip out here he'd felt as if he was trapped in a block of ice, only anger and fear giving him any sense of living. With all of his might he had hung on, promising himself he would see Lorn one more time before he turned himself in to be taken to one of the prison moons.

Nast had been so sure, so positive that Casey would reject him after listening to all the tales of rejected Kadothian men that he wasn't sure how to even deal with the onslaught of emotions bombarding him. He was still trying to wrap his head around the concept of not losing himself to the madness while he attached the cloak to the hidden fastenings on Lorn's armor. Once it was secured he give Lorn a firm thump on his shoulders and smiled at him, savoring the pride and happiness for his friend now filling his barren soul.

A trickle of lust came from Lorn and his friend turned to him with a wide smile. "Casey has her shields down and I can feel her soul. She is happy—apprehensive but very, very happy."

Malin stepped into the room and smiled. "Warriors, if you will, it is time for the bonding ceremony to begin."

Grabbing Nast in a fierce hug Lorn whispered against his neck, "Soon it will be your turn."

"Lord of Life willing, my blood brother, Lord of Life willing."

Chapter Thirteen

Jaz gave Casey a huge smile in the vast set of mirrors, the soft golden tones of the sumptuous dressing room complimenting her dark skin. "Okay, so it may not be the big white dress that you always dreamed of, but you gotta admit, it's pretty awesome." Unable to speak for fear of tearing up and ruining her makeup, though she was pretty sure nothing could make the alien cosmetics smear, Casey took a hesitant step toward the full length mirror and let out a soft sigh. "I wish my mom was here."

As she gazed into the mirror she could scarcely recognize herself. She looked like a princess out of some fantasy movie. Turning in the flattering lighting surrounding the enormous angled mirrors she tipped her head slightly and watched the fire of the gems in her dark hair flair to life. Jaz had done her makeup so well that her skin looked flawless and her deep brown eyes had been rimmed with black liner so they appeared even bigger than usual. Add to that the crimson red lipstick and she actually felt confident enough to walk out in front of a huge crowd for her bonding ceremony. It certainly helped she was barely aware of her surroundings now, choosing instead to keep her bond open and basking in Lorn's love. Her heart was overflowing with his affection and she knew he felt hers in return because an occasional burst of male pride would come from him followed by lust. She had no idea what he was doing right now, but he was overjoyed about something.

Turning in the mirror, she examined herself critically, wanting Lorn to be proud of her. The gown itself was a pretty standard A-line design made of a shimmering crimson material. The neck plunged far enough that she was afraid her nipples might show if she sneezed, but she had to admit the hidden supports constructed within the gown gave her pretty rocking cleavage.

According to Jaz, once the ceremony was completed some kind of mark would appear on her lower chest above her heart and over the top of her breast. It wasn't a tattoo, it was more like a magical mark that would brand her. Casey had laughed at first, but then had to admit it was kind of cool that when the Kadothian's God, the Lord of Life, blessed a union something actually happened. For Jaz her mark was elegant black scrollwork in a circular pattern that went over her left and right breast because she had two husbands, but she said each woman was different. Some women had five husbands yet had only a small mark between their breasts, while others only had two yet ended up with a massive design spreading from shoulder to shoulder. If Casey ever decided to take another husband, something she was still trying to come to terms with, that mark would be added to at her second bonding ceremony.

While the dress was almost plain, the feathered cloak fastened to the shoulders of the gown was spectacular. A cape of the most amazing mass of carefully layered feathers in shades of red, orange, gold and browns, flowed out behind her in a burning waterfall of exquisite design. It extended a full five feet and some of the feathers were as long as her arm. They gleamed with every breath she took and looked almost like fire, as if they were made from the feathers of the mythical Phoenix.

Blinking back tears, Jaz gave her a hug. "Honey, I totally understand about wishing your mom could be here. I almost called the whole thing off when I found out my family couldn't attend, but then I realized that at the end of the day the only thing that really mattered was me and my men. Hell, people run off and elope all the time back on Earth, then move far away from the families. And didn't the Good Book say something about cleaving unto your husband?"

Smoothing her hand over an ultra-soft, deep gold and burnt orange-tipped feather Casey sighed. "Believe me, I would go through Hell if I knew Lorn was waiting for me at the other side; it's just hard. When I was a little girl I always imagined my wedding with my dad walking me down the aisle and my mom crying in the front row while my bridesmaids checked out which groomsman they'd flirt with at the reception. I wanted to get married at the Detroit Zoo like one of my aunts and my girlfriends and I spent a lot of time talking about what our weddings would be like. Never thought it would be on a spaceship."

"Well, it may not be like you imagined, but sometimes reality is even more amazing." Jaz fussed with Casey's hair, swept up in a riot of curls and secured with those beautiful red jewels.

"True."

Casey almost bit her lower lip before catching herself. "Jaz, can I ask you a personal question?"

"Sure."

"When...when you were first with both of your husbands did it...did they...that is on your honeymoon....did they do...stuff? Together?"

Jaz gave her a grin filled with pure sin in the mirror. "Did they get it on?"

Heat raced through her and she tried to ignore the bright flush turning her image almost as red as her dress. "Yeah."

"They did."

"Did you get jealous?"

"For about half of a second. Before we all were together, like *together* together, I'd already had sex with my second husband. They were afraid of telling me that they loved each other, but I knew. How could I not? I felt their love as clearly as I felt my own and when you're surrounded by the love of not just one amazing man, but two, it's the best thing ever. Then to add their feelings for each other on top of that and I swear I'm the happiest woman in the universe."

Unnecessarily smoothing her dress, Casey let out a slow breath. "I just don't understand how Lorn could share me without getting jealous. I know he says he won't get pissed, but it just doesn't make sense."

"That's because you've only grown up around insecure men." Jaz stroked her cleavage where her bondmark gleamed against her dark skin. "You need to stop thinking about Kadothian men like Earth men. They may look similar, but the way they feel and think is entirely different. Trust me when I say there is nothing in the world more erotic to Lorn than the thought of you being with Nast."

"You know Nast?"

"Yep."

Trying to appear composed, but wanting to put Jaz in a chokehold until she told Casey what she wanted to know, she went over to the small table holding a beautiful crystal pitcher and poured herself a drink of some kind of juice that burst over her tongue in an explosion of amazing flavors. "How do you know him?"

"My husbands served under him. I've never actually met him but there is a picture of him with my husbands at some kind of military awards ceremony."

Casey turned and gave a smirking Jaz a narrow eyed look. "Details woman, I want details!"

"Well, he is incredibly handsome, but I haven't met a single Kadothian man who isn't. I will say he has some of the prettiest hair I've ever seen, blond with streaks of pure burning red that my husbands assure me is natural. Hmm, what else? He's something of a legend among his troops and some of the stories they told me about the battles he was in sound like fables, but my husbands swear they are true. Oh, and evidently Nast was born into what passes for poverty on their planet to a family of traitors."

"What?"

"Yeah, his mother tried to assassinate Lorn's mother." She frowned. "Maybe I shouldn't be telling you this."

"No, please, I need to know. Was Nast involved?"

"Not at all. Nast and Lorn have been blood brothers for a long time and are totally devoted to each other just like my husbands are. It was Nast who took the laser blast meant for Lorn's mother."

"Wow."

"I know. So yeah, my husbands kind of worship him. You know how my guys are Healers, right?"

Casey nodded, remembering a conversation she had with Lorn about the different armor colors. "Yes. They're high ranking because they have silver etching on their armor. Lorn's started to explain the Kadothian military to me."

"Right. Well they say Nast and Lorn are two of the best men they've ever served under. That they would be dead a thousand times over if not for your bondmates. I mean your bondmate and your potential bondmate."

After taking a sip of her juice Casey moved back to the mirror. Looking herself in the eye she said, "What if I can't love him, Jaz?"

"You're worrying too much." Jaz gave her a quick hug, careful not to mess up her outfit. "Sometimes you just have to have faith. I know it's especially hard for us because we come from a place where people lie to each other all the time and the only happily ever after comes from fairy tales, but we're not on Earth anymore. We have the incredible luck, or as I believe, the divine blessing of having the chance to not only find personal happiness, but to make a difference in trillions of people's lives."

"Trillions?"

"The Bel'Tan galaxy is pretty big." She grinned. "Hell, Kadothia is twice the size of our sun."

"Wow."

"I know." Jaz's dark eyes sparkled. "Imagine the kind of adventures we'll have exploring their world, the things we'll experience. And the best part is we'll have those experiences with our soul mates. It doesn't get much better than that. Sure as shit beats the hell out of working at a shitty fast food restaurant while saving up for college."

Thinking back to her last night as a cashier at the grocery store Casey couldn't help but laugh. "I hear that."

Casey caught movement out of the corner of her eye and to her surprise she saw Lady Elsin standing stiffly in the doorway.

"May I come in?"

Resentment at Lady Elsin for hurting Lorn still burned in Casey's gut. "Depends. Are you here to try to stop the wedding?"

Jaz elbowed her and whispered, "Casey, don't piss her off, she's like a queen around here."

Casey ignored her and watched Lady Elsin approach slowly, her gaze going over the elaborate bridal gown. "Did you know my son killed the *calnix* with only his knives for the feathers of your bridal cloak? It is a fearsome beast native to the northern continent of Kadothia that is usually hunted by at least dozen of our Warriors, but Lorn managed to slay it alone. When he came home that day with the spoils from the battle, I knew whoever his bride was, she would be getting an exceptional husband. I was very proud of him. Did he also tell you I was the one who made your cloak?"

Startled, Jaz and Casey exchanged a glance before she returned her attention to Lorn's mother. "No, I didn't know about the feathers, nor did he tell me you made the cloak."

"I did. I wanted Lorn to have the very best gifts for his bride so she would know she was so very much wanted by my son. He's dreamed about you for a long time." Her gaze grew distant as she looked at the elaborate mass of feathers with open fondness. "This cloak is just part of the long series of trials Kadothian men must go through to prove themselves worthy of a bride. We are the most precious thing in the universe to them, though it goes both ways. They are my most valued gift as well. I love my husbands and my sons more than my own life."

Casey had to blink back tears as she got what she was pretty sure was a rare glimpse of Lorn's mother. Everyone seemed to live in fear of her, and with good reason. But seeing Lady Elsin like this, with her expression softened and her eyes filled with warmth, made Casey's heart ease a bit. While the other woman was still a bitch, she loved Lorn with all her heart and that was a bond between them.

Lady Elsin went to touch the cloak, then stopped. "Forgive me. I forget I cannot feel your emotions nor you mine. It is very difficult to communicate with you. I cannot imagine what it is like to live in a world without feeling others emotions. It must be very lonely."

Casey turned so the cloak more fully faced the other woman. "Touch away. I guess I never missed it because I never had it. But you need to know the love I feel for Lorn is as real as what I feel for my family. Maybe we don't need to sense others emotion because we know it's true. I know my family loves me. I know Lorn loves me. In my mind they are equal. Besides, I'm not alone anymore. Lorn...he's....he's...my everything."

"I believe you." Tilting her head in Casey's direction, Lady Elsin then began to softly stroke the cloak. "I remember when Lorn went out on his quest to attain these feathers. I wanted to strangle him for picking one of our most vicious beasts to hunt, but he would not be dissuaded. He wanted his future bride to have only the best. Even then he knew you were waiting for him. After he attained enough points to qualify for the Reaping I prayed he would find his bride, but he never did. We hoped that maybe it was Nast that was meant to find their bride first, but it was the same with him. Billions of women would have given their soul to bond with them, yet none of them mattered." She met Casey's gaze head on. "They were waiting for you."

Flustered, Casey smoothed the dress again. "I don't..."

Lady Elsin's voice snapped like a whip. "Do not dismiss the truth. I do not know about the religions of your world, but when a Kadothian man takes a bride it is because your souls are meant to be together. It has been ordained since the beginning of time by the Creator of us all and is our most sacred belief."

Casey swallowed hard and turned back to the mirror, pretending to check her flawless makeup. "How can you be so sure?"

Moving up behind her, Lady Elsin tucked a stray curl of Casey's hair back in place. "When I was in my son's mind I could read your soul, Casey. You belong to Lorn and he belongs to you. I am sorry I doubted you and I pray the Lord of Life, and you, will forgive me for my arrogance and lack of faith."

She didn't know if it was the wedding, or the stress, or just that she needed Lady Elsin's approval more than she knew, because she started to cry. Jaz shushed her and handed her a tissue while Lady Elsin looked faintly horrified. "Did I say something to hurt you?"

"What? No, no. It's just...well it's been a long couple of days for me."

A slight smile curved the other woman's lips and she reached into a pocket of her white robe. "I was wondering if I might give you a bonding gift?"

"Oh, you don't have to give me anything, really."

Lady Elsin pulled out a teardrop necklace made of shimmering brown stones strung on a gleaming golden chain. "My son is quite taken by your *bezel* eyes. The rich color is considered a mark of great beauty among the people of the Northern Kadothian continent, and much sought after by our men. I would like you to have this *bezel* necklace to honor your beauty. It has been in my family for generations, passed from mother to daughter as part of our dowry, but part of the sacrifice I made in bonding with my husbands is that I will never have a daughter. I would like for you to have it."

She had to bite her lip to keep from tearing up again. "Thank you, it's beautiful. Do you mind putting it on me?"

Once the necklace was in place she stroked her fingers over the stones and gasped softly as they threw off tiny amber and gold sparks. "Wow."

Lady Elsin tilted her head and Casey watched her eyes do that weird dilation thing Lorn's did when he was listening to something only he could hear. "My son is worried I am trying to talk you out of the bonding ceremony. I need to get out there before he decides to come look for you. Whenever you are ready, Lorn is waiting and he loves you very much."

With that Lady Elsin left and Jaz moved up behind her, smoothing out her train. "And I thought my mothers-in-law were scary."

Stroking the necklace Casey smiled. "Oh, she's not that bad."

Jaz snorted then grinned. "Really?"

"Really." She swallowed hard then glanced at the door leading to where the bonding ceremony would take place. "So I just walk out there and go to Lorn's side?"

A mysterious smiled danced over Jaz's full lips and she nodded. "Something like that."

"What are you not telling me?"

"You'll see. I promise, it's nothing bad."

Jaz opened the door leading to a hallway Casey hadn't been in before. "Just remember to breathe."

Casey stepped out into the hall and turned to the right, the sound of people talking guiding her. She gasped when she caught her first sight of the massive room where the bonding ceremony would take place. An enormous curved chamber with rows of stadium style seats, all filled, stretched out before her. The back wall was totally transparent, showing a spectacular view of Jupiter. On either side of the doorway, forming an aisle, had to be at least a hundred men dressed in different colored armor snapping to attention as one. They then drew their plasma swords and formed an arch for her to walk through with an impressive clang of steel that reminded her of a military wedding on Earth.

At the very end of the row of Warriors, standing before the vast window, was Lorn dressed in gleaming black armor wearing a black cape with crimson lining the inside that matched her dress. His adoration and pride coursed through her, forcing her to try and keep from sprinting to him. The moment she walked beneath the first sword pink and white flowers began to fall from above. Whenever they touched a solid surface they threw off a tiny shower of golden sparkles, bathing her with light as she made her way to Lorn. The audience was so quiet that all she could hear was her own breathing and the sigh of the petals falling over the men standing on either side. They were all handsome, but none could compare to Lorn.

As she made her way through the raised swords something tickled at her senses, a distraction that demanded her attention from somewhere to her right. It called to her, made her want to search out the source of the disturbance, to find that elusive touch that was stroking at her mind. She paused to look, but then she focused on Lorn and nothing else mattered. The world fell away around her so that by the time she reached Lorn, he was the only thing in her universe. He held out his hand and when they touched, she swore sparks flew between them. His gaze landed on the necklace and a sense of relief came through their bond, mixing with his love. She tried to push her feelings to him, to let him know without words how much she adored him and that everything was okay.

An elderly woman in pale gold robes stepped up onto the small platform and smiled at them, peace rolling off of her in almost visible waves. Remembering the next step of the ceremony, Casey knelt with Lorn and placed her palms flat against his. She knew she was smaller than he was, but it wasn't until she looked at his hands dwarfing hers that she realized she must look like a doll next to him. Yet as large as he was she never once feared he would harm her. Well, except for when she thought he might be holding up the grocery store, but even then she'd somehow known her life was forever changed the moment their eyes met.

The officiant began to sing a lilting chant the translation crystal behind her ear couldn't decipher, but it didn't matter. Looking into Lorn's glowing blue eyes she smiled as energy began to flare between them and sparks of the purest white, like the burning embers of the sparklers she'd played with as a child on warm Fourth of July nights, dripped down from where their hands met. A tingling started between them and she drew in a deep breath, her gaze never leaving Lorn's while a cool breeze seemed to move across her soul. Lorn had told her it was the purifying touch of the Lord of Life but she'd never actually expected to feel it.

A sense of the divine swept through her and she surrendered willingly to it. Love, in all of its forms, filled her until she thought her heart might burst, then it did indeed feel as if her soul exploded. Instead of being frightened or in pain she found her spirit mixing and blending with Lorn's soul, bits and pieces of his memories filling her until she felt as if she'd lived parts of his life. He'd waited so long for her, had prayed with all of his might to find her, suffered through so much to keep his galaxy safe, and the Lord of Life had rewarded his efforts.

Moving as one they stood with their hands almost fused together by the sparks that now enveloped them with a white glow.

The elderly priestess said in a voice that rang through the hall with an echo of bells, "And the Lord of Life proclaimed there is no beginning or end to love, that it shall be eternal in the hearts of those worthy of His greatest gift."

A tingling sensation raced up Casey's arms and seemed to settle just above her heart. When she looked down she gasped at the sight of Lorn's mark forming on the upper mound of her left breast. It looked almost as if someone was drawing on her chest as the lines spread out and twisted together, forming delicate scrolling knotwork that extended over her left breast towards her heart and ended with an almost floral pattern. She looked up at Lorn and smiled as she sank into his love, losing herself in him.

He swept her into his arms as cheers rang out around them, but none of that mattered. The only thing she wanted was to be alone with him as quickly as possible, to have him inside of her so their bodies could lock together to match their souls. He was her bondmate and she was the luckiest woman in the Universe.

Chapter Fourteen

Three days later, Casey and Lorn finally emerged from what she considered their honeymoon for the first time since she'd gone to medical and been inoculated and basically upgraded enough to survive life in the Bel'Tan galaxy. They were about to make their first public appearance together on the ship and she was more than a bit nervous. Way more.

Fiddling with the silken bell sleeves of her black gown, she checked her appearance again. "Are you sure I'm wearing this right?"

He smiled down at her then bent to kiss the side of her neck. "You look good enough to eat."

His arousal tickled at her senses, but she'd gained enough control of their bond by now to partially close down her side enough so that only intense emotions would get through. She could still feel him, but she wasn't swamped by his emotions. In private it was wonderful to immerse herself in him fully, but outside of the bedroom, she had a much harder time focusing on anything but Lorn if their bond was fully opened. It just felt so damn good to lose herself in him that it was addicting. But she needed all her wits about her right now, and then some. They were going to meet some of his friends today and she wanted to make a good first impression.

After all, Lorn was hoping she would partially bond them.

Even more nerve wracking, Nast would be there as well. To her surprise she hadn't needed Lorn to tell her Nast was on the ship. She'd been able to smell the other man on Lorn and had found out Nast had attended their bonding ceremony. Even more startling was the fact that she felt him there. He'd been that elusive touch that had called to her even as she was in the middle of her own wedding. Now she was going to meet the man she'd never seen, but had dreamed about last night with such intensity she swore she woke up with his kiss still burning her lips. It had been one hot, dirty dream that had her waking Lorn up by riding his cock and seeking a relief to the fire the dream had started in her blood.

Anxiety raced through her and she took a deep breath. Lady Elsin's bonding gift glittered around her neck, reminding her of the importance of building up her House. After all, she was now the Matriarch of House Westfall and she needed gather her 'Knights', as Lorn liked to call them, around her. He'd summoned two of his best friends, men he'd fought with but were too young or didn't have enough points to seek brides of their own and they were waiting for them on another part of the ship. Last night he'd told her about each man so she felt like she knew them in a way, even if they were strangers. Some of the stories had made her laugh but others had made her weep because she was feeling what Lorn felt when he told those stories and not all of them were happy.

He'd suffered and triumphed with these men, building a bond in battle and in times of peace that couldn't be denied. Because Lorn loved them in an odd way she did as well even though she'd never met them. It was kind of like the way she loved her best friends, but a little more intense. Lorn made no effort to hide the fact he found the idea of these men bonding with her to be highly arousing.

Highly arousing.

And when he talked about Nast being with her, his horniness shot off the charts to the point where he'd had to stop and fuck her into a screaming orgasm before he could continue. Not that she minded that one bit. If half of what Lorn had told her about Nast was true he was a remarkable man by anyone's standards and Lorn loved him deeply. She waited to feel jealous of their love, had expected resentment, but it was impossible for her to be jealous of something that really did not affect Lorn's feelings for her. During their discussions he kept his side of the bond wide open, letting her experience every nuance of his emotions. Whenever he talked about Nast she'd experienced her husband's love for him like it was her own, a rather peculiar sensation, but not bad.

Lorn had charmed her with stories of growing up with Nast, making it hard to reconcile the mighty Warrior Jaz told her about with the man who'd cleared a spot of land by hand so that she might have a garden where she could go if she needed some time by herself. She had to admit she was more than a little curious to see if Nast lived up to her husband's expectations. Hell, if she was being honest with herself she was more than curious, she was eager in a way she didn't quite understand but didn't fight. It sure beat the hell out of being scared.

"Ready, *alyah*?"

Blowing out a long breath she nodded. "Let's go."

He laughed and held her hand as they left their apartment. "You look as if you are going off to battle. Relax, Casey. I promise you will enjoy this almost as much as I will."

"Right."

Lifting her in his arms he brought her up so she was eye level with him. "You do not have to do this, *alyah*."

"I want to do this. You know I do."

"I also feel your apprehension. If it is too soon please tell me. I would rather wait until you are ready than to push you into doing something you do not want."

She gripped two fistfuls of his hair and brought their faces together until they were forehead to forehead. "Listen to me, husband, I want to do this, and not just for you. Shit, look, I...I dreamed of Nast last night. At least I think I did. Does he have light green eyes and a scar on his neck going from his ear to his collarbone? Does he have a ticklish spot on his shoulder where if you bite him there it makes him shiver? And does he like to sing to you while he holds you?"

"For you he would sing. It is the tradition for the men of his region to sing love songs, but only for their *alyah*." Joy surged through him and he hugged her so hard she had to thump him to ease up. "You true dreamed of him."

Slipping out of his arms she scowled at him as she tried to fix her dress. "What does that mean?"

"It means your souls found each other. The Lord of Life will sometimes show you your bondmate before you meet so you know it is meant to be."

"Wow...really?"

"Yes, really. I dreamed of you while I was still on Kadothia. It was such a strong dream that I still carried the scent of you on my hands when I woke."

"That's crazy. Why didn't I dream of you?"

"It is usually one partner that dreams of the other. I sometimes wonder if we true dream and neither of us remember it." He shrugged. "I have no idea why, the priests and philosophers have their theories. I just accept it as the will of the Lord of Life. My personal belief is he sends the dream to the person who needs it the most. Before I found you I was terrified, Casey, by the thought that I was not meant to find my bondmate in this lifetime."

A hint of his fear stroked her and she grabbed his hand, tugging him down until he knelt before her. "What is it you always tell me? That the Lord of Life is love? Well if anyone is worthy of my love it's you, Lorn. You are everything I've ever wanted in a husband."

He smiled at her and gently kissed the swell of her breast where his mark stood out against her pale skin. "You are my greatest joy."

Closing her eyes for a moment she let Lorn's love wash over her and sent hers back to him before gently closing their bond. "Are you ready?"

"Ready to watch you have orgasm after orgasm? Of course."

"Pervert."

She rolled her eyes at him but his teasing did help a bit. Then they left the living quarters and came to one of the main social areas of the ship and she forgot about everything but the amazing sight before her. An open area about the size of two football fields stretched out six floors below her where all manners of stalls and tents had been set up in the space.

"What is that?"

"We have a fully operational public market available for our brides. It helps to show the wares of the planet and gives the bondmates an excuse to spoil their wives." He gently tugged her arm. "Come on, *alyah*, if you like, we can go there later. I would love to take you to a restaurant where they serve food from the part of Kadothia where our home is. We grow the most perfect *sanga* fruit in all the galaxy and it is made into an exceptional wine."

Reluctantly, she let him pull her away, fascinated by not only the items displayed below but by the people browsing the wares. It was easy for her to spot the Earth women among the crowd; they were much smaller than everyone else, and they were everywhere. Each one was smiling, touching and holding their bondmates, obviously in love. Seeing so many women from her planet did her heart good and helped ease some of her homesickness.

Lorn led her further through the immense ship and the reception they received startled her. Every Kadothian man they passed would salute her by touching the space over his heart with his fingertips and a small bow of their head. Lorn had told her no response was expected from her, but she couldn't help but smile in return and that led to more than one bewildered man. After her smile caused a Scout they passed to walk into the wall she stopped Lorn so she could tug him down and whisper in his ear.

"Why are they so shocked when I smile at them?"

"You are a high-ranking Matriarch. It would be like...like a princess on your planet smiling at janitor."

"That's weird."

He grinned and tugged her along. "Come, your Knights await."

The urge to stick her tongue out at him was strong, but with the way people were studying them she resisted.

They reached a closed door and Lorn gave her hand a squeeze. "Lower your shields a bit, Casey. It will be easier for you. Remember, to them you are a princess and they are but lowly servants. Even Nast. Maybe especially Nast."

She did as he asked and his emotions flowed through her, a mixture of anticipation, worry, and love. A moment later he pressed his palm next to the door and a chime sounded before it slid open. Her heart threatened to beat right out of her chest as she entered the room and faced the three men her husband wanted her to have carnal relations with.

The apartment was similar to the one she shared with Lorn, but there was no artwork on the bare walls and it had an empty feeling. The men all stood as one, two Warriors in black and one Healer in green, each more than handsome in their own way and from their expressions, nervous as hell.

Well, except for the one in the middle.

Nast.

God, he looked just liked he had in her dreams and...hungry. No, ravenous, like he was a starving man and she was an all you can eat buffet. Her body gave a surge of arousal as she met his green-eyed gaze and embarrassment had her looking away while her nipples stiffened with desire. It didn't help, because the image of Nast's beautiful green eyes and chiseled features were etched forever into her mind, blending with her dreams and making her ache for his touch.

Worse yet, she could *feel* him and it was all she could do to stay in place and not throw herself at him so he would pick her up, hold her to that amazingly hard body and give her the gentleness he hid from the rest of the universe. The intense reaction of both her body and mind scared her. She didn't feel this way about strangers, hell she didn't feel this way about anyone but Lorn, yet there was no denying her soul deep need for this stranger with his silken red and gold hair. Her heart raced and she reached out to Lorn, letting out a shuddering sigh when his love embraced her and chased away the fear.

Lorn looked down at her and gave her a smile filled with gentle understanding. He bent and whispered into her ear, "Be easy, *alyah*, what has upset you so?"

She tugged him down until she could whisper as soft as she could directly into his ear, "I can feel Nast. I can feel how much he needs me. His hunger...God I've never felt anything like that. How can he live with such hunger without going mad?"

He turned his head to speak into her ear so his lips grazed her skin. "Do not be afraid, he will not push you into doing anything."

"I'm not afraid of Nast. I'm afraid of how much I want him, of how much I want to fill the emptiness in his soul, of how desperate I am for his touch. This is insane." Happiness combined with desire flowed through their bond and she huffed out a breath. "Don't get all excited. I haven't promised to do anything."

"But you want to," Lorn said with laughter in his voice. She tried to jerk away but he looped an arm around her waist, holding her close. "Be calm, Casey. We will take this slow and easy. Let me introduce you to the men. Perhaps it will ease your anxiety if you know them."

Her husband released her and stepped forward then clasped the shoulder of the man on the left. "My Matriarch, may I present Onyo of the House Casil."

Grateful he hadn't started with Nast, she focused on the young Warrior and tried to ignore the increasing clamor of her heart for Nast. With long black hair and golden skin, Onyo had surprisingly full lips any woman would kill for. His eyes were a pretty light green and when he stepped forward and knelt before her, she found that he smelled like a pleasant mixture of spices. Even on his knees he was almost as tall as she was so when she moved to give him the ritual kisses of welcome, the first being on his forehead, his face was almost buried in her breasts, exposed to show her bondmark. Leaning forward, close enough now that his lips barely grazed her cleavage, she bestowed the welcoming kiss on his forehead, then on each of his soft eyelids, an act of supreme trust on his part meant to honor her.

A blast of male heat came from Lorn and she shot him a dirty look while he had the balls to try and appear innocent. When Onyo stood again his gaze held a definite sensual tone and she inwardly sighed. While Kadothian men had sex with women, they were usually brothel workers who knew not to get attached. To have a Matriarch touch them in such an intimate fashion was one of the most erotic moments of their lives. To these men she was the epitome of sexy, which was very, very weird.

Lorn moved onto the next man. "My Matriarch, may I present Nast of House Enn."

Almost unwillingly her gaze went to the man who meant so much to her husband, and if she was being honest, to her as well. As soon as he filled her sight, a warmth surged through her that made her pant softly while her body went into sexual overdrive. She fought the sensation, and she might have been able to handle her own desires, but with Lorn practically screaming his need at her she was helpless to do anything more than remain upright.

There was a definite swagger in Nast's stride as he moved to kneel before her. With his exotic deep red-streaked blond hair he was undeniably handsome. Add the sea green tilted eyes and he rivaled Lorn for the Sex-on-a-Stick title. There was something about him, some intangible energy that seemed to draw her. She wanted to reach out and run her fingers through his fabulous hair, to kiss the scar that ran from his ear to his collarbone. For some reason Nast seemed more...real than the other men. She knew he was older and it showed in the way he carefully assessed her. While the younger men might look at her with something bordering on awe, he looked at her like a grown man confident in himself and in what he wanted.

And Nast wanted her with a passion so great she struggled to understand it.

Taking a deep breath she stepped forward and stiffened when he boldly nuzzled her breasts. Acting on instinct, she grabbed his ear and jerked his attention to her. "Behave."

The other men laughed while Nast gave her a roguish grin. Oh, he was trouble. "Forgive me, Matriarch, it has been a long time since I've been presented with such bounty. You smell like the sweetest summer sunshine, all warmth and life. So sweet that your body melting on my tongue would taste like candy and I have a very big sweet tooth."

All she could do was blink at him while Lorn's arousal added to her own burn until she ached and the swollen folds of her pussy flooded with her juices to the point where her inner thighs grew slick. Nast flared his nostrils and audibly inhaled, then gave her a slow, dirty smile. He lowered his head again and her nipples grew hard and aching from more of Lorn's hot male desire pouring through their link. Well, that and her own sudden urge to let Nast do whatever the hell he wanted to her. There was no denying how much she wanted him, not when she stood here glassy-eyed with desire. When she leaned forward to kiss his forehead, Nast's breath was hot on her skin, stroking her own excitement until she shuddered at the slightest brush of his lips over her cleavage when she kissed his eyelids. She didn't move away immediately; instead, she fairly shook with the need to touch him. Her skin grew excruciatingly sensitive and she whimpered.

Nast whispered against her breasts, "Easy, little Matriarch. I will take care of you."

When Nast stood again he paused for a moment to look down on her, his gaze promising a long, hard fuck if she'd give him the chance. Then his desire pulled back and the loneliness, the desperation filling him tickled at her senses and she stood on her tiptoes and reached up, brushing a stray strand of his hair back from his face.

"But who will take care of you?"

The mixture of emotions coming from Lorn was so strong she had to partially close their link down so she could focus on Nast.

Their gaze held and he was the first to look away, to close his eyes and blow out a harsh breath. "Do not worry about me. I am a Warrior. I will survive."

"But surviving isn't the same thing as living, is it, Nast?"

Before she could understand her own motivations she did what she would do for any friend who was hurting, she gave him a hug.

He stiffened against her then wrapped his arms around her like she was made of glass. With a barely audible groan he ran his fingers through her hair, causing pleasant little tingles from her scalp to move down her body. "So beautiful, such a generous heart."

They remained like that for a little while longer, Nast running his fingers through her hair while she listened to the steady beat of his heart. She barely came up to his chest but as with Lorn, she didn't fear Nast. He would die to protect her and she knew it. He began to caress the sensitive side of her neck with his rough fingertips and she bit her lower lip as her body flared to life beneath his knowing caress, the energy between them changing as well until her pussy began to swell and soften again. Embarrassed by reacting like this in front of the other men, especially Lorn, she broke their hug and stepped back.

His nostrils flared and a slow, pleased smile curved his lips. "You honor me, Matriarch."

She had a sneaking suspicion what he was so happy about. No doubt he could smell her arousal just like Lorn could. Giving her that heavy-lidded look that made her want to jump him again, he went back to his place between the two younger men. Lorn was practically panting on the other side of the room and she sent a bolt of disapproval through their bond that didn't faze him in the least.

Giving up on her horn dog of a husband, she focused her attention on the man whose shoulder he now clasped. "My Matriarch, may I present Chel of House Lamont."

The man in the green armor approached her and while he was nervous, there was also an air of serenity to him. His hair was a rich chestnut brown and his skin was paler than the other men, closer to her own coloring. He had brown eyes like she did, but his also had flecks of amber and gold in them. Very pretty eyes framed by long dark lashes and well arched brows.

When he knelt before her she caught the scent of herbs and she leaned closer, intrigued by the elusive aroma. Being near Chel was like a cool, calming balm after the rough fire of Nast's desire. While she loved to burn, it was also nice to just enjoy and relax.

He chuckled against her chest, his words vibrating against her skin. "Matriarch, I'm trying very hard to behave as you demand, but it is rather difficult when you press such generous softness against me. I do have a weakness for breasts and yours are magnificent."

Flushing, she ignored the other men's soft laughter and focused on Chel. He looked up at her and winked, deepening her blush until she was sure her entire body was bright red. Lowering his head, he closed his eyes and awaited her touch. Cursing the fact these men were all chest level to her on their knees she leaned forward and shivered as his face pressed between her breasts, her stiff nipples pleading with her to let him move his head just the slightest bit to the right so his generous mouth could give her the attention her body craved. A fire burned through her now that made her eager for the feel of Chel's skin against her own and her resistance against their overwhelming desire weakened further.

She pressed her lips to his forehead, then over each eyelid, trembling as her movements rubbed his lips over the now swollen mounds of her breasts. It certainly wasn't helping her self-control that Lorn ached with lust right now, feeding her own arousal until she was ready to lift her skirts and bend over for the promise of blissful relief. Stepping back with a shaky breath she watched Chel slowly stand, his gaze devouring her body until he reached her face. He gave her a look that was more of a sensual promise than Nast's sexual threat and Onyo's raw hunger.

The ability to speak fled her so she was thankful when Lorn came to her side. His gaze went to her stiff nipples pressing against the thin fabric of her gown and he let out a small growl that the other men echoed. Then, in a bold move that shocked her, he cupped her right breast and rubbed his thumb over it, sending a cascade of pleasurable sparks streaming through her body and settling in her clit. With all the sex they'd had there was no way she should feel as needy as she did now, but she did. She wanted him, bad, and if she was being honest with herself she wanted the other men as well.

But especially Nast.

God help her but she was beginning to think Lorn was right. Nast did belong with them but she wasn't sure if she was ready to admit it to herself yet, let alone her husband. Still, her desire for the other man went beyond just lust. She wanted to soothe his fears, to comfort him and make sure that he knew how much he was wanted, how much he mattered to her. The logical part of her brain argued she was delusional, but in her heart she knew there was something special about Nast, something that set him apart from every man in the universe except for Lorn. While she understood there was a bond between her husband and Nast, she didn't expect to feel that connection between them, as if she had a tiny flash of insight into the handsome Warrior, and that glimpse into Nast's heart showed her how desperate he was for her, how much he needed her in ways even Lorn didn't. Lorn loved her with everything he had, of that she had no doubt, but Nast was far more vulnerable than her husband and she feared hurting the other man, but she just wasn't ready to leap into his arms.

At least not yet, despite her libido's fervent protests.

"*Alyah*, you are thinking too much. Come with me," Lorn murmured and led her into another room of the apartment. When her gaze landed on a bed big enough to throw an orgy on she balked.

"Lorn..."

"Shhh, Casey, there is nothing to fear here. Only pleasure." He cupped her face with his hands. "Let us worship you."

Her half-hearted protest died in her throat as Lorn kissed her, drowning her in his raw need. His tongue stroked against hers, coaxing forth a reaction that sent a hard burn simmering in her lower belly. Taking his time he stroked the fires in her blood higher until she was frantic for more.

Breaking the kiss he stared into her eyes. "Do you wish for any of the men to join us?"

She licked her lips and hesitated, trying to think not only of who she desired, but who would help to keep her husband safe. All three men would bring different skills to her household and all three would be loyal. More importantly, she would be able to keep them safe. Her mind kept returning to Nast, insisting she wanted him above the others, but he scared her. The things she felt for the handsome Warrior were shockingly similar to what she felt for Lorn when they first met and she wasn't sure if she could handle two husbands when she was just beginning to learn how to be a wife to Lorn. "All of them. But I only want you inside of me, please."

Lorn's joy and relief overcame his lust, but not for long. He shouted for the other men and soon she found herself surrounded on all sides by eager male hands. Lorn never stopped touching her, so as panic began to set in at being intimately caressed by so many strangers, he was her anchor, an endless source of unquestioning love and hard desire.

Then he stepped back and sat on the edge of the bed, pulling off his boots as Nast and Chel joined him, leaving her alone with Onyo. The dark haired man gave her a smile that was almost shy as he bent down to brush his lips over hers. It was a pleasant kiss and she could almost taste his inexperience with women and apprehension of displeasing her. With a start she realized she was feeling his emotions and the need to comfort him blended in with his gentle desire.

She laced her arms around his neck and tugged him closer, tracing his lips with her tongue, urging him to open to her kiss. With a low groan he did and at the first stroke of her tongue against his he let out a long, deep growl. His relief tickled at her and she lowered her shields further, reaching for him. Not breaking their kiss he stripped out of his armored top then easily lifted her so her dress hiked up as she wrapped her legs around his hips.

Remembering back to a time when the farthest she would go with a boy was kiss him, she lost herself in Onyo's eager touch, threading her hands through his silky black hair and sighing against his mouth. Despite his age this was his first time in many ways. He gave her lower lip an experimental nip with his fang and she moaned loudly.

He pulled back immediately and gave her a worried look. "Did I hurt you?"

"No," Lorn said from behind Onyo's back. "Earth women make noises like that when they're aroused. It means you did something that pleased them."

Onyo's gaze gleamed as he focused on her mouth. "Then let me make sure she makes more of them."

He returned to kissing her, now licking at her lips and exploring her mouth with an eagerness she found very arousing. Soon she was rubbing against him, scoring his back with her fingernails as her need built. Onyo gripped her bottom and rocked her against his hard abdominals. Shock mixed with her pleasure as she realized she might climax from just grinding against him.

Turning, he walked back to the bed and sat down on the edge with her on his lap, never breaking their kiss. This put his hard shaft, still trapped behind his pants, right against her slit and she moaned again. Heat spun through her blood and she cried out when Onyo began to thrust against her. A hint of his hard, male lust mixed with the passion coming from Lorn and she threw her head back, unable to think of anything beyond her aching need to climax.

Lorn's voice tickled over her senses as he said, "That's it, *alyah*, give us your pleasure. You are so beautiful in your passion."

Riding Onyo's lap as if she was riding his cock she thrust her hips against the other man, screaming out as he stiffened beneath her. The sensation of Onyo hovering on the edge of his own orgasm hit her just right and she cried out, loving the way his cock vibrated against her pussy through his pants as she ground her aching sex against him. His howling roar mixed with her cries of passion and she hugged him close, giving him the affection his soul was starved for. He wrapped his arms around her and squeezed her tight, his love pouring into her. It was a different kind of love, an affection that wasn't as much romantic as it was...belonging.

He gave her one last kiss and slid her off his lap and into Chel's arms.

Dazed with pleasure she barely noticed Onyo speaking with Lorn in a low voice before leaving the room. Chel's gaze was locked on her breasts and she noticed for the first time he'd already removed his green armor top, but like Onyo, he kept his breeches on. Licking his lips he held her back with one hand while teasing down the front of her robe enough so just the first pink hint of her nipples showed above the fabric. Despite her orgasm she found her arousal building at an alarming rate and knew it was coming from Lorn. He was so pleased with her, so happy she'd given Onyo the gift of a partial bond.

When she glanced over at him she found Lorn completely nude and sprawled out at the head of the bed along with Nast who'd taken off his shirt but still wore his pants. A smattering of light red and blond hair covered Nast's broad chest and she licked her lips at the thought of biting his firm pectoral muscle. Lorn stroked his impressive erection as he watched her and she was about to demand he join them when Chel licked along her breast.

His tongue was rougher than both Lorn and Onyo's and she wondered why right before he freed her left nipple and sucked it into his mouth.

Hard.

A shudder wracked her as he laved the tip of her breast, sucking and biting at that nub until she was panting and crying out against him, begging him not to stop. With a pleased growl he switched to her other breast, using his free hand to stroke the overly sensitive tip of the nipple he'd just released. At the pinch of a fang she stiffened, then moaned. Biting harder, he scored her with his fangs and she shamelessly thrust her breast into his mouth, needing more.

The warm, intense edge of his desire brushed against her soul and she eagerly reached for him, needing the connection between them as he drove her wild with his talented mouth. It was his turn to snarl as that elusive connection between them was made and she thrust her passion at him. His loneliness, his relief at her acceptance of him, raced through her heart and she buried her hands into his hair, pulling him closer.

"I'm here," she whispered. "It's okay."

He froze against her breast then lifted his head and met her gaze with such passion mixed with adoration that it almost threw her into her own orgasm. "My Matriarch."

She smiled and shifted her hips, rubbing against his trapped erection. "Give me your pleasure."

For a moment his eyes cleared and he grinned at her before returning to his gaze to her breasts. "Look how pretty they are, all creamy with such pink nipples. So hard for me. I could lick these berries forever and never tire of your taste."

The men behind him groaned and she could no longer think when his mouth fastened onto her breast again, flicking that devil-blessed rough tongue of his over the painfully hard tip. He gripped her hips with his free hand and helped her grind her pussy against his shaft, the drag of the thick crest of his erection over her swollen clit driving her wild. Soon he had to abandon her nipple and rested his head against her chest, his ear over her heart as they both strained for their release.

Lorn chose that moment send a burst of arousal through their bond and she jerked against Chel, screaming as his cock began to vibrate beneath her. She could sense his shock at the feeling of her beginning to orgasm, followed by a strong surge of male lust that mixed with her own, driving her wild in his arms. Ecstasy tore her apart as he continued to grind against her even as he climaxed, his howling roar muffled against her chest and sending more vibrations through her body until she could barely breathe.

At last he gentled beneath her, his breath hot on her skin and his adoration for her mixing with Lorn's love.

With unsteady hands he moved her off of his lap and onto the bed, leaving her in a blissed-out sensual coma of satisfaction against the smooth sheets. The men's voices were meaningless as she stretched and let out a sound that was almost like a purr. When big, unfamiliar hands stroked along her thighs all she could do was smile.

"Look at me, little Matriarch, and know who is touching you," Nast demanded in a rough voice.

Forcing her eyes to at least partially open she took in the masculine beauty that was Nast. With his long hair falling over his sculpted shoulders and his lips lifted from his teeth in a sensual snarl, he seemed to hit all the right buttons of her desire. Lorn moved behind her and cushioned her head on his lap, his erection pressed against her cheek. He stroked her hair while Nast began to slowly undress her and when she closed her eyes at the sensation of the air hitting her wet pussy, Nast gave her inner thigh a sharp pinch that sent pleasure and pain mixing through her already overheated body.

"Look at me, Casey," he growled out in a feral tone.

Lorn gripped her hair and forced her to watch Nast while his wild arousal stroked her soul. Evidently Nast touching her turned Lorn on more than the other men had because his cock against the side of her face was hard enough to pound nails and his need was relentless. "Give him what he wants, *alyah*. He has been waiting a long, long time for you."

Nast chose that moment to place his mouth over her entire sex and suck. With a scream she arched into his touch and clawed at the sheets, trying to deal with the overwhelming sensations that threatened to drive her crazy. She desperately reached out to Lorn both mentally and physically, only to find his lust even fiercer than hers. A sob of pleasure escaped from her as she struggled to deal with an emotional onslaught of desire thick enough to drown in.

Nast eased back a bit and held her sex open with his thumbs, examining her as he gently blew on her pussy. "She has such a beautiful pussy, all these soft folds of skin for me to play with. And such abundant nectar, so sweet. I could eat you for days. You have no idea how much I want you, how badly I need to feel you climax against my lips."

"Oh, God," she whimpered as the tip of his tongue breached her sheath.

"Suckle gently on her clit, the hard little bump at the top of her slit. She loves that. Use a little bit of fang and tease her. Make her beg."

Casey wanted to glare at Lorn for telling Nast how to drive her crazy but when the other man did as her husband asked all she could do was grip the sheets again and try to keep her mind from being torn apart. A brush of a strong male presence touched her soul and she hesitated to answer his call, frightened by the enormity of his need. Lorn stroked her sweaty brow with a gentle touch so at odds with his best friend's almost animalistic licks at her swollen sex.

"Do not be scared, Casey. It is all right. Let him join our love, please. I am begging you to accept his gift."

The ability to think was beyond her, but Lorn's plea touched her heart. Even though she was scared by the intensity of Nast's call to her soul she opened herself to him, trusting Lorn to keep her safe. Instead of rushing into her as she feared, Nast's energy slowly eased through her like a warm rush of water that washed away the fright trying to raise her shields. He didn't plunder her mind or overtake her soul, though he could. His spirit was incredibly strong. Instead he seamlessly merged with her and with Lorn. The potential for a more complete bonding was there, but Nast held himself back, and in doing so, allowed her to relax.

She sat up further, Lorn shifting so she could lie back against him and watch Nast eat her pussy like it was his most favorite meal in the entire universe. His green-eyed gaze met hers and she smiled at him, feeling his soul and knowing he was hers. Not the same as Lorn, not yet, but someday he would be. Reaching out she gripped his hair and pressed him to her sex, rocking her pussy against his lips.

"Stick your tongue out." She was shocked that the husky murmur came from her but she knew what he wanted and what she needed.

Gripping his hair tighter, enough to hurt, she rocked her clit over his raspy tongue, shuddering as his lust overtook her own and buried her in a burning need so fierce she came almost instantly. He snarled and latched his mouth around her slit again, swirling his tongue through her labia before thrusting it into her sheath as he greedily ate the juice spilling from her body. To her surprise he didn't join her in her climax, closing the bond between them and fighting it even as he strove to drive her higher. She screamed and Lorn had to hold her hands pinned to the side of his hips as she tried to claw at something, anything to hold onto while Nast continued to feast on her overly sensitive sex.

At last he gentled his mouth and softly nuzzled her, something resembling a growling purr vibrating against her and making her moan weakly.

The men chuckled and when he finally lifted his mouth from between her thighs his lips and chin glistened with her release.

"Come here," she whispered and tugged his face to hers.

With soft licks she cleaned the earthy taste of herself from his mouth and he shuddered with each stroke of her tongue, his tormented arousal giving her a wicked sense of power. It was her body, her touch, her soul that was driving him crazy. He had so much self-control, but he wouldn't be able to resist her teasing for long. When their lips met in a kiss he ate at her mouth just like he'd eaten at her pussy and she moaned against his tongue.

Nast released her from his kiss just as Lorn pulled her into his arms then placed her on her hands and knees in a lightning fast move that left her head spinning.

Positioning his cock at her entrance, Lorn slowly eased in so the fat head was stretching her sheath, making her cry out. He leaned over and fed her a little more of his cock. "Will you honor him by taking his seed in your mouth, *alyah*?"

She glanced over her shoulder and found Nast already naked. His erection was a fierce, dark amethyst with beads of lilac precum dripping from the tip. She could feel his need, his emotional craving to join them, but he wouldn't move without her permission. Their gazes met and she had a hard time keeping her eyes open as Lorn continued to press into her, filling both her mind and body.

"Come to me, Nast, let me take care of you," she murmured in a voice gone rough from screaming.

In an instant he was before her. Instead of reaching for her head he clasped his hands behind his back and knelt near her face, his throbbing erection inches from her lips. She reached out and traced her fingers along his length, playing with the pleasure ridges in a way she knew drove Lorn crazy. It seemed to be the same with Nast because he gave a fierce growl and more precum spilled from him. Catching the wetness with her finger she smeared it over the engorged head of his shaft before licking it off with delicate swipes of her tongue. He had a slightly richer taste than Lorn, still delicious, but different.

"Lord of Life," Nast groaned out.

"I know," Lorn replied in a strained voice. "She makes you want to spill yourself the moment she touches you with her hot little mouth."

Giving Nast a heated look, reveling in her sensual power as a woman, she began to lick along his shaft, gripping him with one hand while Lorn picked up his pace, sliding in and out of her body and making her buck back against him, eager for her husband to spill himself in her. With their combined passion creating a bonfire of need within her she sucked hard on Nast, tonguing him and scraping his crest with her teeth before rubbing her hand up and down his shaft in a twisting motion that had him snarling.

Unable to focus anymore she reached up and grabbed his hands, placing them on her head.

Lorn gave her a harsh thrust that moved her mouth further down Nast's shaft. "She wants you to use her mouth, to fuck yourself with it so she can come. The act of swallowing our seed arouses her fiercely."

She moaned in agreement as Nast tightened his hold on her hair, delicious tingles of pain racing from her scalp and somehow turning into ecstasy.

Then the men really began to work her.

Moving in perfect rhythm, they fucked her with animalistic abandon, each thrusting then dragging back out, throwing her into her climax so fast it caught her by surprise. They stilled and barely moved as she contracted and jerked between them, pinned into place by the cock in her mouth and in her pussy, eaten alive by their desire and their hard determination not to go over with her.

Before her sex had even stopped quivering they picked up the pace again, opening the bond they'd closed between her and them when she'd climaxed. Their need, masculine and fierce, reduced her to nothing but sensation as she strove to bring them to completion. So good, this moment with them had to be as close to divine ecstasy as a mortal could get. Lorn sank his fingers into her hips and performed a rotating motion that hit some spot deep inside her body and made her see stars. Nast stroked her cheeks as he slid in and out of her eager mouth, pausing to let her suck on the tip.

"That is it, Casey, drink me down. You are perfect, Lord of Life you are perfect." He shuddered hard and Lorn ground himself into her.

Her moans were muffled by Nast's thick head stretching her mouth and she drew in a deep breath through her nose before taking him as far as she could, then swallowing so her throat sucked at the tip. He shouted then roared as the first hot blast of his seed filled her. She swallowed frantically, having to pull away and let his cum paint her lips as she tensed, Lorn's orgasm triggering her own.

For a brief moment there were no walls between them and their souls entwined in a pleasure greater than anything their bodies could endure. She was distantly aware of the rough melody of Lorn and Nast's roaring howls mixing with her own screams but the only thing she could really feel was paradise. Satisfaction, love, security, and a profound sense of adoration blanketed her even as she collapsed against the bed, with Nast's twitching cock in her loose grip and Lorn barely moving enough not to crush her as he fell against her.

Exhaustion overcame her and she could barely breathe let alone move as the men hauled her between them. They were so big, so solid that she felt tiny between them, yet protected.

Cherished. Adored. Worshipped.

She had no idea how long she slept, only that she gradually became aware of her body again and the sensation of hands caressing her. The touch was sensual, but not demanding. More like whoever touched her simply enjoyed the feeling of her skin. She opened her eyes and found both Lorn and Nast watching her with identical, pleased smiles.

The memory of what they'd done together made her flush with embarrassment and she wanted to pull a pillow over her face. Instead she curled into Lorn's chest and buried her heated cheeks against him. Hurt radiated from Nast and she realized he thought she was rejecting him. Reaching back, she hauled his arm around her so he was pressed against her back, his erection nestled between her buttocks.

"Why do you hide from us, *alyah*?" Lorn asked in a concerned voice.

She closed down the connection between them enough so she could still feel the men but also have a sense of privacy. "I can't believe I just did that with both of you. And Onyo...and Chel...oh God."

"Are you regretting it?" Nast asked in a coldly neutral voice.

Shaking her head, she turned again so it was Nast she was looking at. "I don't know you. And on my world a woman who sleeps with two men is considered morally corrupt. Let alone a woman who has orgasms with two other men in front of her husband."

Lorn laughed then Nast began to chuckle. "What a horrible world to live in where females would deny themselves the pleasure we just had."

She stared up at them, irritated they were making light of it, but enough of their amusement seeped through that her embarrassed anger faded a bit. "Well, when you put it that way it sounds silly."

Cuddling her close, Lorn kissed the top of her head. "They do not believe a woman can love more than one man."

Nast stared at Lorn in shock. "What?"

"It is true. They were raised to believe that love is limited, that you can only feel it for one person."

"That is...that is just idiotic."

"I agree."

She shoved at both of them. "Get off me."

Nast grinned and snatched her up, rolling over so she was draped on his chest. "Little bride, I understand you feel conflicted. But know this, Lorn and I have discussed it while you slept and we are in complete agreement. I'm declaring my intent to become your second husband."

"What?"

Lorn lay next to Nast and tugged her over so she was draped atop both of them. "We will not rush you as we have the rest of our lives to convince you we belong together, but you need to know it is my deepest wish for us to be family."

With a soft sigh, Nast smoothed her hair off the side of her face. "You have no idea how hard it was not to leap from the stands and claim you when I first saw you in your bonding gown. So beautiful, the most stunning woman I have ever seen," Nast said in a rumbling growl with his cock beginning to thicken against her hip. "Casey, if I had found you first I would have somehow found a way to bring Lorn into your life. I understand you do not feel the same for me as you do for Lorn and I respect that, but please give me a chance to prove myself to you. I promise you will be happy with me as a husband." His lips turned into a slight smile. "I am willing to lick that delicious little pussy of yours, drink down your sweet nectar, and give you orgasm after orgasm until you agree. I will live with your soft thighs wrapped around my shoulders and my face. I will only stop pleasuring you so that I may sleep against your lush breasts, suckling at your pretty nipples until you come one more time before drifting off."

Despite her best shielding efforts lust poured into her from both men and she frowned at them, fighting a smile at the same time. "That is so not fair."

Lorn chuckled and reached to touch her again, but this time she let him. Instantly she felt his love and even though she didn't understand it, his total acceptance of Nast. "I learned one Earth saying while I was there that I happen to agree with."

Unable to resist touching him, touching both of them, she stroked her hands on their chest and they gave an almost identical rumbling growl. "And what's that?"

"All is fair in love and war."

Shaking her head, she couldn't hold back her smile this time. "You're such a dork."

Lorn and Nast exchanged a puzzled look, their silver and red streaked blond hair blending together where it spread around them.

"Does a dork mean a man of great sexual powers? If so, than I am indeed a dork."

That made her giggle and both men began to tickle her gently with the tips of their fingers, causing chills to skitter across her skin. "Stop that. I need to talk to you."

With a heavy sigh they didn't remove their hands, but stilled their touch.

She looked between them, studying their faces as she tried to put her chaotic thoughts into words. "What happens next? I mean, where do we go from here?"

Lorn and Nast exchanged a glance then, her husband smiled. "We take you home."

Chapter Fifteen

Casey sat in the seat of what Lorn had called a planetary shuttle, basically a small spaceship big enough to carry six people, and tried to keep her fear of the unknown under control. They'd made the jump through the wormhole and were now on their way to Kadothia and her new home. Lorn was in the cabin sending some messages to the staff of his home in Kadothia while she and Nast sat in the small passenger compartment. To say she was suffering a case of nerves was a huge understatement.

The small room she sat in was comfortable containing a smoothly contoured couch and four chairs with a complicated restraint system on the other side of the room from her. It was a plain space with soft cream walls and some strange controls by the door leading to the control room where Lorn currently was, leaving her alone with Nast. The main source of her unease.

It wasn't because he scared her, but rather because her draw to him was so strong that she was having a hard time dealing with it. This was the first time she'd been alone with the other man, and without Lorn here as a buffer between them she wasn't quite sure how to act around Nast. Fighting the need to fully bond him was becoming increasingly hard and she felt like two people. One wanted to bring Nast into their lives as her second husband while the other was scared shitless of the rapid changes she'd gone through and wanted to cling to her old life with its restrictive rules only because it was familiar.

It didn't help that the hard knowledge she would never see her family again, never taste her Mom's cookies, never see Roxy marry a good man who deserved her, or watch her nieces or nephews grow up, was tearing through her. She was terribly homesick but at the same time she didn't want Lorn or Nast to feel like she was sad because she was with them because that wasn't true. They were the best things in her life, the anchors she could hold onto.

Nast looked up from a tablet he'd been working on with a concerned expression on his handsome face. Today his hair was back in a tight braid, as was Lorn's, and she'd learned Warriors only let their hair down when they were in a safe place like the Reaping ship or Earth. Otherwise it could be used as a weapon against them. He was dressed in what she'd come to think of as his and Lorn's everyday armor, a thick pair of black pants made from what looked like leather combined with a black shirt that clung to his body like it was painted on from his thick neck to his solid wrist. With his hair pulled back his sharp features were more severe and she tried to overlay the image of Nast sprawled naked beneath her in bed like a big lazy cat with the predator who now looked back at her.

His green eyes softened until they were the color of a new leaf in spring. "Casey, what is wrong?"

"Nothing." Her lower lip quivered and she looked away, trying to shield the hot mess of her emotions from him.

A moment later he joined her on the couch. "Look at me, little bride."

With a gentle touch he turned her face to his and made a rough sound of distress as he examined her tear filled eyes. "Why are you so sad? Did we do something to hurt you?"

"No, no." She closed her eyes and her tears fell. "It's just...I miss my family."

"Oh, *alyah.*" He gathered her unresisting body into his arms, surrounding her with his warmth. "I am sorry. With everything that is going on I forgot you would miss your family. Forgive me for not caring for you as I should, my bride."

She cuddled into him, breathing his earthy scent into her lungs. Much like Lorn's touch, Nast's gentle rubbing of her back helped chase back some of her sorrow as though his caress was a narcotic. "It's okay."

"No it is not." He let out a soft sigh and rubbed his lips against her head. "You are giving up everything you know to be with us and I do not know how to thank you for your sacrifice. I do not want you ever to have a moment of sadness yet your heart is hurting because you have to leave behind everything you know for us."

His understanding made her cry harder and he held her close, whispering soft words of affection while she clung to him. Lorn brushed against her mind and she opened herself fully to both men, allowing their reassurance and love to bolster her. Nast shifted so her head was cushioned against the crook of his arm.

"Tell me about your family on Earth."

She gave a watery laugh. "What do you want to know?"

"Everything."

She thought about it, then began to tell him about her loving but crazy mother who had more hobbies than she had time to do them and an attention span that lasted for all of an hour. Their basement was full of half-finished projects ranging from a latch hook Christmas tree skirt to a kiln her mother had bought, as yet unused, at a going-out-of-business sale at a pottery company. Then she talked about her father and how overprotective he was which led to her telling Nast about the time she maced Lorn.

He roared with laughter at that and she couldn't help but giggle with him. "You attacked him?"

"I didn't know it was Lorn," she protested and sat up straighter on his lap. "I mean he didn't, like, announce himself or anything."

"He probably forgot you could not sense him." Nast chuckled again. "I would have given my right leg to have seen that."

With the amusement softening his face Casey marveled at how handsome he was. She lightly traced her fingertips over his forehead, then over the hard sweep of his cheekbones to the curve of his square jaw. His eyes half closed and a rumbling growl came from deep in his chest. Moving unhurriedly, taking her time, she had to admit it was nice to be able to take things slowly with Nast. With Lorn their relationship had happened so fast she could scarcely wrap her mind around it. While it has been glorious in every way, there was a different kind of pleasure that came from savoring each step. Looking away from his tempting lips she let her fingers trail over the scar beneath his ear and followed the thick line to where it disappeared beneath his shirt.

"How did this happen?"

He stiffened against her and anguish came through their bond along with concern from Lorn. Wanting to take away Nast's pain from her question she leaned up and gently kissed his lips, stroking against their smooth surface while she felt him struggle against whatever dark memories that scar held. He kissed her back, softly and with a reverence she felt unworthy of.

Pulling back slightly she rubbed her nose against his. "It's okay, you don't need to talk about it. I'm sorry I asked."

He turned his head slightly and brushed his lips against hers. "No, little bride, it is all right. I just have not spoken to anyone but Lorn about that day, and he was there so he understands. I do not...I hesitate to expose you to such tragedy, especially when you have your own sorrow to bear."

Oddly enough her homesickness faded as she focused on Nast, needing to somehow make him feel better because when he hurt, she hurt for him. "If you want to talk about it I'll listen, okay? But if you don't that's fine as well."

"I think I need to tell you so you will understand me better. I know I am a stranger to you, Casey, but in my world the people a man knows he can trust absolutely are his bondmates. Even though we are not fully bonded, I need you to know I trust you, so I will share my story with you, but I warn you, it is not a pleasant one." He gave a rough laugh that made her heart hurt. "Not many of my stories are."

She moved so she could straddle his lap, then laid her head against his chest, wrapping her arms around him as much as she could. When it came to talking about bad things that had happened in the past she knew from experience it was easier sometimes if the person didn't have to look at you. Back on Earth her friend Paige had suffered through horrible abuse from her asshole father after her mother died. It was only after he put her in the hospital when she was fifteen that she finally told the truth about the nightmare she'd been living and hiding from the rest of the world.

Casey had been there when Paige talked to the social worker, along with Dawn and Kimber and their mothers. Together they'd comforted Paige while she'd stared at the ceiling and talked about the beatings, being locked in the basement, not eating for days, and how her father had switched from alcohol to crystal meth. He'd been in a drug-fueled rage when he took a baseball bat to his only daughter, breaking not only Paige's body but also her spirit. Despite all the terrible things he'd done to her in the past, up until the day he broke both her legs, her cheekbone, and a few of her ribs with his bat she'd held out hope that if she was good enough, if she tried hard enough he would love her more than the drugs. Now it was practically impossible for Paige to trust any male over the age of fourteen and Casey could understand why.

Shaking off those terrible memories she focused on the present, listening to the accelerated beat of Nast's heart as they flew through space to her new home.

"Two hundred and five cycles ago, around five hundred Earth years, I was part of an advance party specially trained for infiltration into enemy territory. In this case into one of the outer planets where the Hive was harvesting people."

"Harvesting people?"

"Their planet is run on slave power. They kidnap people from other planets, those too weak or not technologically advanced enough to defend themselves, and bring them to the Hive planet of Xithar. We received word one of their mercenary ships was spotted around Cuthos, a peaceful planet that was mostly an agrarian culture and supplied our army with food in exchange for protection. Cuthos was deep enough in Kadothian-held territory that they should have been safe, but most of the population was naturally pacifistic and they did not have the defenses their neighboring planets held. This made them a tempting target to the Hive."

She watched his face as he talked, the bond between them closed down on his side so only a hint of his sorrow came through, but it was enough to make her throat close up with unshed tears.

"Our main forces were drawn to another part of the galaxy where a bitter fight was being waged, but when the desperate call for help reached us Commander Trenzent, one of our highest-ranking military officers, selected an elite company of Warriors to go and fight off the Hive with an army from a nearby planet not far behind us. While the members of the Hive will fight, they prefer to stay out of direct conflict and use their mercenaries if they can, men and women so morally corrupt they can be bought to do just about anything."

He took a deep breath and his heart continued to slam hard enough that she swore she could feel it against her cheek. "We walked into an utter slaughter. Hundreds of thousands of men, women, and children dead or begging for death, their minds broken by the nightmares they had witnessed. Tortured for their pain in the most depraved manner possible, even the children...Lord of Life, the children... Entire village populations were missing, no doubt taken back to the Hive's home base. After sweeping the planet we found the mercenaries laying siege to a naturally fortified underground city sunk deep into a mountain with only one entrance in and out. It was the Cuthosians' last stand and they were not going to last much longer. We could not wait for backup, not if we were going to save those people."

She stared up at him, enthralled by his tale yet sensing that the worst was yet to come. "What happened?"

"Help was not far behind us, Commander Trenzent had sent out an emergency signal that would alert all friendly forces in the area, but we did not have time to wait for them. It was a suicide mission— we all knew it—but none of us could have lived with ourselves if the Hive managed to gain access to that mountain." A hard shudder worked through him. "Commander Trenzent is a brilliant Warrior and he devised a series of strikes that greatly weakened the enemy, but it only slowed them the smallest bit. Help began to arrive and the battle raged for days. We had not slept more than an hour as we fought and we were exhausted, but we continued to battle through a never-ending stream of enemies. I am not sure how it happened, but we ended up cut off from our forces and surrounded by a group of at least two hundred mercenaries led by a half dozen members of the Hive."

Fright, rage, and disgust surged through her link to Nast, but she didn't dare close her side down, struggling against his emotions to send her own reassurance and love. It must have helped because he softened slightly against her.

"Did you know the Hive live below ground in darkness? That their eyes have adjusted to see without light? When above ground they wear a mask that protects their eyes and turns them into faceless creatures from a nightmare, incredibly strong women who all look the same and almost move the same. We were dead—there was no doubt about it—and we all knew our sworn duty was to kill ourselves before they could take us, but we were determined to slay as many of them as we could."

"Why would you kill yourself?"

His breathing increased until he was panting beneath her. "Because they took special pleasure from torturing Kadothian males and forcing them to breed. Only once a year do Kadothian males have viable sperm and they are kept alive until their fertile period is reached, though a male's mind had broken well before that, throwing him into the madness. Matings between a Hive female and a Kadothian male produce stronger than normal Hive females so we had to do everything we could make sure it does not happen."

"Oh, God."

"I was ready to move onto my next life, Casey, I swear I was, but before we could attack Commander Trenzent threw aside his weapon and stepped onto the field of battle alone. He bargained his life for ours."

"What do you mean?"

"He would surrender to them, knowing what would happen to him, if they agreed to spare our lives. We tried to protest, but he ordered us to stand down. Commander Trenzent is sterile so he knew he could trade his life for ours and not weaken our cause. The Hive accepted his offer and...and..." his voice broke and she silently cried for him, shedding the tears she knew he wouldn't. "We managed to rescue him before they could leave the planet but in the few hours they had him they had tortured him. Removed pieces of his body while keeping him alive. All they needed was his torso for breeding purposes back on their home planet. I can only thank the Lord of Life they did not have any of their torture masters with them."

Her stomach lurched as she could all too easily imagine what had happened to the man. "Did he survive?"

A sudden surge of hard male pride burst from Nast. "He did. They may have taken parts of his body, but they did not break him. I have no idea how he managed to stay strong but he did. To this day he still fights the Hive but he kept the portions of his body that had been replaced with cyborg parts in their mechanical state as a reminder to everyone who sees him of the very real threat of the Hive. Some elements of our society have grown complacent living in peace and safety on Kadothia. It is as if to them the fighting that happens so far away is not real, merely a scary story to ensure the Kadothian males continue to rule the planet." He gave a mirthless laugh. "Commander Trenzent's body makes them uncomfortable because they cannot ignore the proof of the Hive's evil."

She rubbed her face against his chest, wiping her tears against the fabric of his shirt before she looked up at him. "Is that why you keep your scar?"

"Yes. Every Warrior who was there that day forbade the Healers from healing our most visible wounds fully so they would scar. We will never forget the sacrifice the Commander made for us."

"He sounds like an amazing man."

"He is." Nast gave her a sad smile. "Do you think an Earth woman could look past his mechanical parts? Could she possibly love him even though he is no longer what you consider physically appealing?"

"Is he searching for a bride?"

"Yes. But...I fear for his chances. He has not been around women or civilization in a long time. And he scares people."

She pasted on a big smile even as she tried to imagine a woman's reaction to a man who was partially a machine try to seduce them. "Oh, I'm sure he'll find his bride if she's meant to be. I mean, the Lord of Life wouldn't hook him up with someone who wasn't meant for him, right?"

He gave her a disbelieving look then shook his head with a small smile. "If you are going to tell lies to make me feel better, close your side of the bond down first."

"Oh...damn." She lowered her head and peeked through her lashes at him, giving him the look that always made Lorn growl, needing to distract Nast from his painful past. "Forgot about that. I was wondering about something."

His nostril's flared and the green of his eyes darkened to emerald. "And what would that be?"

"What it will feel like when you make love to me." She gave him another flirtatious look from beneath her lashes and enjoyed his desire burning away the sorrow.

Shifting beneath her, his erection pressed between her thighs. Lorn had relented and found some panties for her, but both he and Nast believed it was unnatural to cover herself like that. She was pretty sure it was just because they wanted as little clothing between her and them as possible. A decadent frisson of excitement raced through her as she met Nast's gaze and licked her lower lip, teasing him.

"You are nothing but trouble when you look at me like that, *alyah*."

Amusement mixed with lust completely replaced the anger and pain in Nast and she almost sighed with relief. Knowing someone hurt and feeling empathy for them was one thing, but to actually experience their pain put a whole new spin on how she saw the world. In some ways Nast was more fragile than Lorn. She had a feeling Nast didn't have a lot of happiness in his life and from what she knew of his past she was surprised he had survived with his innate goodness intact.

While he might not have had much to be happy about in his past, he did now and she was going to make sure the rest of this trip was one he would remember fondly. Lorn had tipped her off that Nast enjoyed a bit of roughness with his sex, that he liked to play dominance and submission games. While she'd let a past boyfriend tie her up she'd never gone as far as for-real BDSM, but she had to admit the idea of letting Nast loose to do whatever he wanted to her was more than appealing. He was so hungry for her—and she had to admit she wanted him as well—but she also wanted to draw their desire out. For some reason teasing Nast really turned her on. Some kinky part of her psyche really liked the idea of driving this controlled man so wild that he would snap beneath the sexual tension.

A small shudder went through the ship and she looked up with alarm. "What was that?"

"We've entered the atmosphere of Kadothia. Only a few more minutes until we arrive at your new home."

Their breath mingled as she leaned forward and brushed her lips over Nast's firm mouth. "Nast?"

"Yes, Casey?"

His voice came out rough and strained, turning her on even more.

"When we get to *our* home, I have a proposal for you."

Even if she hadn't been partially bonded to him she would have felt his pleasure. "What is that?"

Feeling incredibly wanton she rocked her pussy over his hard cock, a soft moan escaping when he tilted his hips so he ground into her clit. "Oh God."

"Casey, talk to me," he chided in a soft voice all while continuing to slide her pussy over his leather-covered dick.

"I can't, feels too good."

"Yes, you can." He moved one hand up and gripped her hair in a painful hold that only made her moan harder. "Mmm, you like some spice with your pleasure, don't you?"

"She does," Lorn said from somewhere behind her.

Embarrassment and a trace of guilt made her try to pull away, but Lorn moved behind her and braced her back, holding her on Nast's lap. "No, Casey, do not move. I want to feel you enjoying Nast."

Cupping her chin, Nast tilted her face up so she had to look at him. "Are you embarrassed to touch me?"

"No," she said right away. "It's just...having my husband walk in on me straddling another man is difficult to get used to."

"Do not worry, *alyah*," Lorn crooned, "I was aware the whole time. I felt what you felt, and it was hard to keep command of my voice and expression during my meeting with the head chef and grounds keeper of our home knowing that you were back here giving my blood brother pleasure. Not because I was jealous or angry, but because you were going to make me spill in my pants."

The men chuckled while she flushed then Nast returned his grip to her hair. "Now, what was it you wanted to do when we get home? And do not lie to us, we will know and you will be punished."

The hot flare of desire from both of them made her raise her eyebrows. "Punished how?"

Nast flashed his fangs at her and she shuddered. "Curious, little bride?"

"Very," Lorn answered for her as he stroked her shoulders.

"Mmm, interesting. Now Casey, tell me what you want."

"I would...well I'd like to watch you kiss each other." The last words came out in an embarrassed whisper.

"Just kiss?" Lorn said with an amused smile.

She frowned at him, not liking how both men seemed to be laughing at her. "I'm sorry, but on Earth it's kind of a big deal to ask my husband to kiss another man."

"Shhh, Casey" Nast said in a soothing voice. "We would be honored to fulfill any desire you might have, and I will confess that kissing Lorn would be no hardship. Let us take care of you; be honest with us about your needs, and I promise you the rewards will be beyond anything you've ever imagined."

Figuring this was a win-win situation she gave a wanton moan when Nast gripped one nipple between his fingers while Lorn tormented the other. Soon she was squirming between them, crying out as they twisted and pinched her sensitive nubs and making her desperate for a cock inside of her. Then they both stopped, leaving her straining and panting.

"Noooo....Why did you stop? Keep going...please."

Lorn lifted her from Nast's lap and gave her a toe-curling kiss before setting her on her feet. "I know you are shy about your desires in public. We have arrived on Kadothia and I thought you might want to meet your new household without scenting like sex. You will still smell of arousal because of your sweet, wet pussy but that is considered a good and normal way for a Matriarch that has just been bonded to smell."

"Everyone can smell my pussy? Seriously? Shit, shoot me now."

Laughing, Lorn tapped her nose gently with his finger. "It is not a bad thing, Casey. You are a Matriarch on Kadothia. The rules of your restrictive society no longer apply.

"Thank the Lord of Life," Nast added as he stood next to Lorn and looked down at her, reminding her how tiny she was compared to them. "Sex is not taboo in our culture, but a natural part of living."

Part of her wanted to reach out and grab their cocks and make them fuck her, but she was grateful for their sensitivity to her needs. "Thank you."

They each took one of her hands and smiled down at her. Nast leaned down and gave her a quick, heated kiss before standing again. "Come on, Matriarch of House Westfall, it is time for you to meet your people."

Chapter Sixteen

C asey pressed her hands against her eyes and took a deep breath, totally overwhelmed by the house...no, mansion...no, palace she now evidently owned. She'd spent the last three hours being shown around the massive residence that boasted four floors, three kitchens, and well over one hundred bedrooms. And that was just the inside of the place. She still had to tour the village attached to the manor as well as the fields and orchards that supported them. Then there was the fishing village farther down the river, beyond that some outlying villages that raised animals, and beyond that the people who chose to live in isolation and safety on her land. They were all under the protection of House Westfall. Shit. In a way she felt like she was back in the middle ages on Earth and suddenly found herself as part of a royal family.

She'd been shocked to see women among the servants, but Lorn and Nast explained to her that many people came to Kadothia seeking work or asylum. The planet was so massive that without the immigrants it would be a desolate place. She was still trying to wrap her mind around the concept that Kadothia was twenty-eight times as big Earth. On the ride to the home from the space port in a weird egg-shaped vehicle that floated off the ground, she caught glimpses of children playing in the village as they drove through it and had feebly waved back at the cheering reception she'd gotten everywhere they went. Lorn and Nast had found her bemusement funny, but she wasn't sure how to process all of this.

The duties she would eventually take on were staggering and she would spend a portion of each day with her different advisors going over the estate and learning how it was run. She was the head of House Westfall now. How could she be expected to govern these people and tell them how to live their lives when she couldn't even handle her own? Overwhelmed didn't even begin to describe her state of mind at the moment.

As a result she shut down her end of the bond between the men with the excuse she needed to concentrate on her surroundings. Lorn and Nast had been understanding and solicitous as always, but she'd also noticed how reserved they were with the people who worked for them, or served them, or whatever. She'd felt like a child next to them as their experience and maturity gave them a social grace she totally lacked. More than one servant had gasped in shock and nearly fainted when she smiled at them or held out her hand for a handshake out of habit.

The more stressed out she'd become, the more Nast and Lorn hovered over her to the point where she closed her shields so only the tiniest hint of their presence remained in her soul. She knew it hurt their feelings, but she didn't want them to think she was unhappy because of them. They'd obviously gone out of their way to make her feel comfortable, as had the servants and the members of the household, but everyone looked at her with something bordering on awe and she just didn't know how to deal with it. The men had wanted to come with her but she'd asked them for some time alone to rest and they reluctantly agreed.

Now she was hiding in one of the bathrooms in the family wing of the manor while Nast and Lorn attended to some business in the stables, though she had no idea what the heck the stables actually housed. All she knew was that the building was really, really tall, at least four stories, and she was more than a little apprehensive at the roars and chirps coming from inside. The men offered her a tour but she pleaded exhaustion. Lorn had given her a concerned look but let her go with a brief kiss before she was escorted to the family wing by one of her guards. She could tell Nast wanted a kiss as well but she didn't feel comfortable with everyone watching them. They'd been followed around by a dozen people during her tour and the way they all watched her like she was some kind of celebrity only added to her discomfort.

As she looked around the opulent bathing room with its enormous tub made out of some kind of sparkling gold crystal and the creamy fur rug that cushioned her feet she ruefully shook her head. Why couldn't she have fallen in love with a normal guy? She had to laugh at herself at that thought. No matter how stressful this was she had the best man...no, men in the universe to help her learn how to do her job. She knew if she let Lorn and Nast know how she was feeling they would help her with anything she wanted, and she was going to talk to them, but first she wanted to take a nap. Catching a few Z's always helped to clear her mind, and she was hoping that when she woke up things would be a little less scary.

Exhaustion pulled at her and she splashed her face with water from the sink as soon as she figured out how to turn it on. As she dried her face she stared at the door, not wanting to deal with anyone, just wanting to try to find the over-the-top bedroom she'd been shown earlier. She was pretty sure it was on this floor. If she was lucky she could just slip out without anyone seeing her. Lorn had said only a few trusted servants were allowed in this area of the manor and that for the most part it would usually just be her, Lorn, and Nast. The family wing was relatively isolated from the rest of the house and she was never more thankful for having a little privacy than right now.

After opening the door to the hallway with its creamy walls and pale stone floors she let out a silent sigh of relief that she appeared to be alone. Hanging a left she passed a familiar painting of Lorn's mother and fathers, grinning to herself that she must be freaked out if she found the sight of Lorn's mother reassuring.

A matronly woman wearing the deep purple uniform of a house servant came around the corner and smiled at her. "Matriarch, can I help you?"

"Yes. Could you please tell me where my bedroom is?"

The woman nodded, and something hard and cold flashed through her blue eyes that almost looked malicious, but it was gone so quickly Casey was sure she was imagining things.

"Your room is three doors down on the left."

"Thank you."

"You are most welcome, Matriarch."

Once again, that flash of hardness went through the other woman's eyes, but Casey was so damn tired she didn't care. Following the woman's directions, she came to an ornately carved pale wood door that she remembered from her brief tour of the family portion of the residence. She was relieved she'd managed to find her room, and she placed her hand on the sensor next to the door and walked into her bedroom when it slid open, then came to a complete halt.

There, on the enormous bed, were two beautiful nude women with light blonde hair, on their knees with their faces pressed to the bedding and their asses in the air with their pussies totally exposed to her view. She blinked in confusion at the shape of their sex, just the barest hint of an outer labia then nothing but a slit.

"Greetings, Master Nast," one of the women purred and arched her back in an obscene matter that gave Casey a view of the other woman's pussy she bet even the woman's gynecologist hadn't seen.

"I've missed you Master Lorn," the other one said in an equally sultry voice. "I can't wait for you to both take me at once. I love you so much and hate it when you are gone. I know how much you love me and I could not wait for your return. We have waited for you, just like we promised we would. We love you so much."

"*What the fuck?*" she said in a shocked whisper.

The two women, exquisite blondes who looked enough alike to be sisters, turned as one and gave her a puzzled look.

"You are not my beloved Master Nast," the one on the right said, her ass still high in the air.

"You are not Master Lorn," intoned the other as she gave Casey a puzzled look. "Where are our Masters?"

She stared at them, her heart breaking. "Your what?"

"Our wonderful Masters," the one on the left said. "We are instructed to present ourselves upon their return so that we may pleasure them. Have our Masters been delayed?"

"Who are you?"

The blonde on the right gave her a sultry look. "I am Master Lorn's pride and joy. He loves me and I love him."

"And I am Master Nast's beloved," the other blonde said with a bright smile. "Who are you? Where are our Masters?"

Pain and betrayal roared through her and she stepped out the door without making a sound, running down the hall and lifting her stupid robe so she didn't fall. She was so stupid! Nast and Lorn had those two women—they must be the pleasure servants Lorn was talking about—waiting for them in bed while they were busy seducing her back on the ship. All that bullshit about her being the only one for them, the one woman in the universe and all that, had been complete bullshit and she'd fallen for it.

"Matriarch?" a woman's voice reached her. She turned and saw the same hard-eyed servant from earlier watching her. "Are you all right?"

She swallowed hard, willing back the tears. "Who are those women in my bedroom?"

"Master Lorn and Master Nast's pleasure servants? They were waiting for the Masters to return. Do you wish them moved to another room to wait? Master Lorn and Master Nast asked that they wait for them in their chambers as they always do." The woman moved closer. "They are always eager to return to their women."

"What?"

"Oh, that is right, you are from Earth. Surely the Masters told you that on Kadothia the men love their pleasure servants. They are the men's pride and joy while their wife is their duty." She tilted her head and narrowed her eyes. "Does that upset you? Why? You must know that they brought you here to run the house for the Masters so they could spend their days loving their pleasure servants. Did not anyone explain that to you? Of course you may have as many pleasure servants as you want as well." She paused. "Poor thing, you seem so upset. Come with me and we will get you something to eat and drink that I am sure will make you feel better."

The woman reached out to touch Casey and she backed away, her emotional pain roaring through her. "Leave me alone!"

With a slight frown the woman glanced around, then stepped closer. "Just come with me, Matriarch. Do not make a scene and further embarrass yourself."

"I don't want to come with you, just...just go tell Lorn and Nast that they can go fuck themselves." When the woman grasped her upper arm in a harsh grip Casey jerked away, then shoved the other woman hard enough so she stumbled then landed on her ass with a harsh cry. "I said leave me alone!"

Her breath came out in a harsh sob and she ran down the hallway, ignoring the woman's shouts that she stop and sprinting as fast as she could away from the servant. Her heart insisted the woman was lying, but her mind showed her the proof over and over again of the two naked blonde women.

Oh, god she was such an idiot.

The men tried to reach her through their bond, she could feel their panic, but she shut it down as tight as she could, tighter than she was even aware was possible. Running through the family quarters of the manor she went past dozens of rooms until she found a set of stairs that led to the main floor. The sound of footsteps and whispers seemed to follow her so she hid in what looked like a library of sorts until she was sure the coast was clear, then ran again. She tried one door after another until she finally found one that led outside. There was no fucking way she was staying here with the men and their whores. The women had been so beautiful, so perfect, that Casey knew she could never compete with them. And they loved Lorn and Nast. Those lying bastards said they would never allow another woman to love them. If they lied about that then they could have lied about everything. Hell, they probably manipulated her emotions with their psychic powers, making her believe them.

Tears streamed down her face but she checked around before darting out into what looked like a field of trees. The sun was setting over the horizon and she quickly made her way through the trunks, keeping an eye open for anyone while trying to stifle her sobs. For a time she thought someone might be following her again, but when she ducked beneath a thicket and hid the footsteps went in a different direction. The last thing she wanted right now was to see anyone who might take her back to those cheating bastards.

Moving out of the thicket she ran until her legs hurt, until her lungs burned and she wanted to throw up from the pain, both physical and emotional. Despair set in as she staggered out of the other end of the orchard and came to a wide, vast river that churned with gold toned white caps. A warm breeze blew off the water, drying the tears on her cheeks. Knowing she couldn't swim across it, and terrified as to what could lurk beneath the water, she made her way to an outcropping of water smoothed dark boulders and climbed onto them, wedging herself into a gap between the stones before she finally broke down and cried.

Her heart ached like a physical wound and she'd never wanted so desperately to go home in her entire life. Right now, she should be in her small house, safe in her bed, on her safe planet, with men who might cheat on her but at least she'd be able to leave. Her friends would be coming to her rescue and they'd eat fattening desserts while getting drunk and lamenting about what losers guys were. Instead she was all alone in the dark, on an alien planet where she knew no one and nothing.

Wrapping her arms around herself she tried to gain comfort as her sobs tapered off to those heaving breaths she hated so much. The night air had chilled and she really hoped she wouldn't freeze to death out here, though that would be preferable to having to face Lorn and Nast. Hell, they were probably fucking their whores right now, sure she was asleep in bed waiting for them.

Fucking bastards.

What really pissed her off was she had believed them. She had trusted Lorn with all of her heart and was beginning to trust Nast as well. They'd tricked her somehow into believing their feelings were real when they'd probably just been using her to get their bond. It probably hadn't been hard at all to manipulate her, after all they knew all about bonding while she just had to trust what they said. No doubt they'd been laughing behind her back at how easily she'd fallen for their lies. God, she was so fucking stupid and naïve. Anything that seemed too good to be true had to be a lie, yet she'd been so desperate for the kind of love they claimed to have for her that she'd just fallen for their bullshit long enough for Lorn to bond her.

Well, they could have their whores and their bond, but she was leaving. Somehow she was going to find a way off this planet and back to her world. Maybe if she found a way to contact Lorn's mother she'd help her leave. Casey would just explain the situation and let the other woman know Lorn could keep his bond, but Casey would be gone and out of their lives. He and Nast could fuck those whores, in what was supposed to be *her* bed, until their dicks fell off.

Lying assholes.

Every once in a while some hint of their fear would break through her shields but she'd ruthlessly push it away until she was alone with her heartache. The sound of claws skittering over stone reached her above the roar of the river and she froze, backing further into her hiding space. Trying to breathe as little as possible, she heard that skittering noise again followed by a strange harsh coughing sound, then a whistle.

She looked around for something to use as a weapon but only came up with a few loose stones. Clutching them in her fist, she screamed and hurled them at the dark shape that suddenly darted in front of her hole. The round shape made a pained noise and jumped away, letting out another high-pitched whistle. A few moments later an unfamiliar man's voice reached her ears and she debated between yelling for help and keeping silent. The decision was made for her as a bright light was thrust into her hiding spot, blinding her as she held up her hands to shield herself.

A man's rough voice filled with confusion said, "What in the name of the Lord of Life?"

The brightness receded and she cautiously lowered her hands from her face, squinting at the sight of an older man dressed in a loose fitting light brown pair of pants and a shirt secured with a black belt. Attached to the belt was what looked like a gun of some sort along with a long sheathed knife. Unlike the Kadothian men she'd seen so far his hair was cut short and instead of the sculpted facial features like Lorn and Nast, he had a rounded chin and small, kind eyes. He was easily double her size and she frantically tried to remember what she learned in the women's self-defense class her dad had made her take.

"Who are you?" she asked, but remained pressed back into the corner.

He stared at her in amazement and a moment later a ball of black fur with emerald green highlights and six fuzzy legs trundled up to his side, making that soft whistle again. She screamed and crouched into a defensive ball.

The creature whistled shrilly until the man said, "Bofus, hush."

"What is that," she asked, peering through her fingers at the fuzzy thing.

"Matriarch, you know not what a *zendor* is?"

She gave a laugh that sounded more than a little hysterical. "I'm not from around here."

"You must be one of those Earth Matriarchs. Are you injured?"

She cautiously stood and brushed off her black robes. "No, I'm okay. My name is Casey Westfall. Who are you?"

He dropped to his knees while the ball of fur scampered around him. "Forgive me, Matriarch of House Westfall, I did not mean to offend you."

"What? No, um, my name is Casey Westfall and I'm not a Matriarch."

He looked up at her with a clearly disbelieving expression and said in a slow voice as if he were speaking to someone who might be mentally challenged, "My Lady, you wear the bondmark and robes of a Matriarch."

"Yeah, well I'm getting rid of that as soon as I can. Look, can you tell me how to get to Lady Elsin?"

Now he stood fully and looked almost panicked. "Of course."

"Oh, good." She moved out of her little hole and tried to assume an expression of confidence while brushing off her clothes. Her father had often told her that even if she didn't know what she was doing, if she at least looked like it most people wouldn't know the difference. "If you would show me the way I would be grateful."

"Matriarch, where is your bondmate? Why are you out here alone?"

Anger sizzled along her nerves and she forced herself not to lower her shields in the slightest. "I'm sorry, but that is between Lady Elsin and myself."

That seemed to ease his anxiety and he gave her a rough smile. "Of course, begging your pardon, Matriarch."

The ball of fur approached her and she swallowed hard. "Is it dangerous?"

"Bofus?" He looked down at the ball of fluff then back at her. "To you? Not at all. He helps me hunt for shellfish. Got a good nose on him he does, can find anything he has a scent lock on. Hold out your hand. I'm sure he'll find you're no threat."

She stared at the furball and tried to detect any kind of face...or anything. It rubbed against her skirts and let loose a soft trilling whistle that was rather pleasant to hear. "Can I touch him?"

"Matriarch, I don't want you getting your hands dirty. He likes to roll around in the sands."

She looked down at her dirt-covered hands from scrambling for rocks and back up at him with a wry grin. "Maybe you should worry about me getting you dirty."

He stared at her for a moment, then smiled with a low chuckle. "Now I know you're an Earth Matriarch. I'm sure Bofus would enjoy your touch."

Kneeling she held out her hand and from somewhere in all that fur came a snuffling sound followed by a hot puff of air. Its fur was incredibly soft and she pressed her hand a good four inches in before she felt a round and warm body. It skin was slightly bumpy and as she dug into its fur to gently stroke the animal it emitted a lovely whistled tune. Turning rapidly it shook and shivered, making excited little whistles. She laughed and gave it a good rub before standing. The creature's obvious affection helped clear her mind a bit and she stared up into the sky, astounded by the sight of what had to be hundreds of moons. Somewhere up there they had a moon that was being converted to resemble Earth. If they wouldn't let her go home maybe they would let her stay there.

A few seconds later two more fuzz balls came scampering out of the darkness, one black with red-tipped fur and the other a pale grey with green-tipped fur.

She giggled, delighted as Bofus ran over to them, whistling and chirping while they talked back to him.

"There're more of them?"

Cint nodded and whistled a complex tune. The other two fur balls moved off into the darkness beyond the lantern. "Aye. Those two are Bofus' brother and sister. There are a few more out there but you won't see them. The main pack moves ahead of us to make sure the trails is clear."

"Clear of what?"

He glanced at her, then looked away and pursed his lips. "Nothing for you to worry about, Matriarch. Just night creatures."

The tone of voice he used reminded her of her father's when he didn't want to discuss something with her, but she let it go. "Excuse me...what is your name?"

"Cint, Matriarch."

"Cint, do you think you could help me get to Lady Elsin? I'm afraid I don't have any money but I can give you this." She pulled the silver barrette out of her hair Lorn had given her early this morning and tried to still the pang of hurt at the reminder of his smile, his touch, his warmth.

God, she was pathetic.

"I cannot take that." He shook his head and stepped back with a small frown. "My Lady, why don't you ask your bondmate to take you? Does he know you're here? He must be worried."

Not wanting to say Lorn's name for fear that this man might know him, she shook her head. "No. I'm never speaking to him again."

"I see. May I ask why?"

"I'd rather not discuss it." Tears threatened again so she lifted her chin and fought them back. "Can you just take me to Lady Elsin please?"

Giving her a shrewd look he nodded. "Of course. Follow me."

As they made their way down the shore she smiled in delight at the different kinds of tiny glowing fish swimming at the edges of the river. They seemed attracted to the light of the man's lantern, and followed them along the edges of the fast moving water. The fluff ball stood between them and the water, keeping pace with Cint and occasionally running a circle around them while whistling. "Those fish are so pretty."

"I thought so as well when I first came here."

He held his lantern closer to the water and she swore she saw something massive moving beneath the fast flowing water further out into the river but the brief gleam of scales was there and gone and before she could really make sense of it.

"Where are you from?"

A sad look overcame his face looked into the sky, nodding his head to the right. "My world fell to the Hive and I took refuge on Kadothia hundreds of cycles ago when I was a young man with my wife. Lord of Life guide her on her journey to the next life."

"Is she...did she pass?"

"Long ago, though it seems like yesterday." He gave her a small smile. "While my people don't bond like yours, I still loved her with all of my heart and that's the truth."

"I believe you." Depression made her shoulders slump as they walked further down the shore, the fur ball bounding ahead of them then racing back. "People on Earth don't bond either."

"Really?"

"Yeah. We don't have all that mind reading stuff like the people of your galaxy do."

"Not all of us have the psychic gifts. Take myself. I can't read your mind or move objects with my thoughts. The gifts of my people run more along the lines of being able to communicate with animals."

Intrigued she looked over at Bofus then back to Cint. "You can talk to them?"

"Not like you and I are talking, animals think different than people, but we understand each other. More like images and emotions."

"That is so awesome. I wish I could do that. I don't have any powers or anything like that."

He glanced down at her chest and for a moment she thought he was staring at her breasts, but then he looked back up at her face. "But you managed to bond a Warrior, right?"

Her lower lip quivered as she glanced down at her bondmark, the contrasting memories of her bonding ceremony and seeing the whores on her bed blending together. "I wish I hadn't."

"Why?" His voice hardened. "Is he cruel to you? I've never heard of it happening but who knows how things may differ with Earth brides."

"No." Tears threatened and she swallowed hard. "I don't want to talk about it."

"Does he love you?"

"He said he did, but he lied."

"Why do you say that?"

Anger heated her blood and she clung to it, preferring her resentment over sorrow. "He promised me he would be faithful to me, that he wouldn't have any other women. Him and his blood brother."

"How did they betray you?"

"I just arrived on your planet today and I found two whores waiting for them in our bed."

He frowned and looked out in the distance as the came to a narrow pale wood bridge arching over a small creek that fed into the river. "Do you mean pleasure servants?"

"Yes," she seethed.

"But all Warriors have them."

"Why the hell would their wives allow that?"

He flushed bright red and cleared his throat a couple of times. "Because of the discomfort."

"The what?"

"You know...the swelling."

"I have no idea what you're talking about."

He stopped and stared at her. "The swelling of your woman parts after you're intimate with your husband. Where you seal tight to hold onto his seed."

"Um, what?"

He rubbed his face with his hand and started to walk again. "I'm too old for this."

"Wait, I really don't know what you're talking about."

"Forgive me for being blunt, Matriarch, but do the women of your world not swell shut after you've made love? Does the entrance to your body not close off after a man spills his seed in you?"

She was so shocked she almost walked into a tree as they exited the other side of the bridge. "No."

"You mean you don't swell? You can service your husband more than once in half a day's time?"

"Well, yes. Do you mean that Kadothian women can't?"

He laughed. "No. No women in the Bel'Tan galaxy can. Kadothian males are a highly sexual race. They need to release on a regular basis or they will get overly aggressive and become a danger. Those who can afford pleasure servants have them, those that don't...I'm sure you can figure that out."

She crossed her arms and ducked beneath a dripping strand of what looked like glowing pink moss. "Well on my planet only a man who has no respect or love for his wife has sex with another woman."

"Did your bondmate know this?"

"Yes, and he promised me he'd gotten rid of his pleasure servants before he ever came to Earth. I know Nas...the other man didn't, but there's no way he couldn't have known how I would react." She took in a hitched breath at the memory of how good she'd felt with Nast, how connected to him all while he'd had two whores waiting for him when he got home. Fuck them both for manipulating her like this. "Well he can forget ever bonding with me. In fact if I never see either of them again it will be too soon."

"Seeing those women hurt you?"

"They were in my bed!" she practically shouted and the fur ball made a startled whistle. "Sorry, fuzzy wuzzy, didn't mean to freak you out."

She bent and held out her hand to the fur ball. "Can I carry Bofus?"

"I wouldn't suggest it. He'll shed all over your robe."

With a snort she lifted the warm and cuddly creature close and continued to follow them man. "Wouldn't you be upset if your wife had two men waiting for you in your bed on the first night in your new home?"

He gave her a considering look and nodded. "I would."

She buried her face in the creature's fur, soothed by its soft whistles of pleasure. "I left my world for him, left my family and friends, everything I know because I thought he loved me."

"Do you love him?"

Her lower lip trembled and she shook her head. "Not anymore."

He made a noncommittal noise and soon they approached the small village she had seen earlier. The streets were paved in some kind of dark brown stone and there were huge circular planters filled with what looked like stunning flowers in front of every store. Bright curtains hung in all the windows of pale cream buildings, and the streetlights illuminated a busy street filled with people and more of those egg-shaped vehicles. Here, on the outskirts, she caught glimpses of families going about their lives inside of their homes through their windows and the ache in her heart deepened. She wanted that, a simple life with a husband who loved her with all her heart.

"Is there any way to break a bond?"

Cint jerked to a stop and stared at her. "Why would you want to do that?"

"Maybe if I broke our bond they'd let me return home and Lor...that bastard could find another woman who'd put up with his cheating ass."

Slowly shaking his head, Cint took a step closer, then ducked down, making sure she was looking up at him in the eye before he spoke. "If you break your bond you will kill your husband, Matriarch."

"What?"

"His soul is tied to yours now. Without you to anchor him he will quickly fall to his beast."

"And he would die?"

"He would be sent to one of the feral moons where he would live among others like him, animals in the shape of men that have no one to turn their blood lust on but each other."

The thought of that happening to Lorn horrified her, even if he was a cheating bastard he didn't deserve that fate. "Can't he bond someone else?"

Cint began to walk again, leading her around the edge of the village. "No, Matriarch, you are his soul mate."

Oh, how she wanted to believe that. "If I was his soul mate he wouldn't have lied to me."

"Did you ask him about the women?"

She chewed her lower lip and switched the fuzzy-wuzzy to her other arm. "No, I mean, what was there to ask? They were naked in his bed, saying they loved him and he loved them. You can't get clearer than that."

He didn't say anything more and when they reached a small two-story building with a blue tile roof, the creature in her arms wiggled out with an excited whistle. From the darkness more fuzz balls swarmed around them until she couldn't help but laugh at the way they bounced up at her, each trying to gain her attention. Cint let out a piercing whistle and the creatures ran off to a small building to left of the main house with only Bofus remaining with them.

"Come inside and I'll get you something to eat and drink. Then we can contact Lady Elsin and arrange for transportation to her home."

Despite its rustic exterior, the inside of the home was as clean and modern as Lorn's manor. Anguish flooded her again at the thought of Nast pressed between those two women, or Lorn and Nast taking one of them together. She could all too easily imagine having to feel them having sex with those women through their bond and the thought made her want to puke. Thankfully, she couldn't sense either of them right now and that was just how she liked it. She was going to totally ignore the fact that even imagining them touching those women made it feel like a knife was being twisted in her heart and salt rubbed into the wound. Cint led her to a worn green chair made of some kind of material that reminded her of cotton, but was much softer. She gratefully curled up in it and was thankful for once that everything on this planet was made for larger people.

A few minutes later, Cint returned with a dark red mug full of some kind of steaming liquid and a plate of some squiggly green things that reminded her of oblong blobs of Jello. She took the mug and eyed the plate with a dubious smile. "Thank you."

He looked at her expectantly and she took a sip of the drink, surprised to find it tasted like a combination of butterscotch and honey mixed with cream. Taking another big drink she sighed as it warmed her from the inside out. Looking around the room she spotted a picture of a younger Cint with his arm around a pretty blonde woman with a joyful smile.

"Your wife?"

The corners of his lips lifted as he glanced at the picture. "Beautiful, wasn't she?"

"Very."

Draining the rest of the drink she hesitated before poking at the green stuff with her finger, not wanting to be rude but at the same time not wanting to eat anything that moved. "What is this?"

"*Kichi* eggs. They are very good."

Her stomach clenched and she worked off a tiny piece before placing it in her mouth, ready to swallow it as quickly as possible, but to her surprise she found it was delicious, a savory flavor that made her hungry for more. Cint smiled and took a seat in the chair across from her, whistling for Bofus who obediently hopped onto his lap. He stroked the animal and watched her as she finished her meal then settled back into the chair with a sigh, feeling very relaxed.

Too relaxed.

Way too relaxed.

Her eyelids became heavy and she fought the lassitude that tried to take her over. "What did you do to me?"

"It's for your own good, Matriarch."

She tried to shove herself up from the chair, intent on running, but she did no more than slump forward the slightest bit before falling back again. "Killing me, why?"

Shock filled his weathered face. "No, just something to help you calm."

Forcing the words around her numb lips was difficult but she managed, trying with all her might to fight off the sleepiness. "Why?"

"Master Lorn Adar, sorry Master Lorn Westfall and Master Nast Enn are good men. They deserve to at least give you an explanation." He must have seen her confused expression because he smiled. "I saw you arriving with them today, Matriarch. I owe Master Lorn and Master Nast for all the years that I've been safely able to raise my family here, and like I said, they are good men who love you, no matter what else you were led to believe. It's a miracle you weren't killed by one of the predators who roam the river at night. When it was discovered you were missing, your bondmate and his blood brother contacted me and asked me to aid in the search. I was given a piece of your clothing holding your scent so Bofus and his pack could find you."

"No." Tears spilled down her cheeks and he made a pained noise.

"Please don't cry." His face hardened. "You are very lucky we found you when we did. If one of the nocturnal river predators had reached you first..." He closed his eyes and let out a slow breath while Bofus gave a mournful whistle. "Thank the Lord of Life we found you first."

A choked sob managed to make it past her numb lips and Cint gave her a pained look.

"You are mistaken in your belief about the Masters betraying you. Those men couldn't deceive you even if they wanted. You are their *alyah* and I know you don't understand it, but I've been around Kadothian men for most of my adult life and they would never knowingly harm their bondmate. Your pain *is* their pain. If you leave them they will die of broken hearts or kill themselves rather than face a life without you." His expression firmed and he blew out a harsh breath. "Master Lorn and Master Nast have protected our village for hundreds of cycles. They gave me a safe place to live with my family and have worked hard to make our home an oasis of peace in our very violent galaxy. I've seen the Hive, watched it slowly devour my home world and I know the danger Master Lorn and Master Nast face every time they've gone to battle. They are good men and you must give them a chance to explain themselves. Running off like that was not only foolish, it was childish as well. Begging your pardon for any offense, Matriarch."

Darkness began to dance around the edges of her vision and she gave up fighting, gave up everything. Her shields fell and as soon as they did Lorn and Nast's terror roared through her, making her jerk before their fear turned to a relief so profound she whimpered. Her last thought was that she had to get away before they broke her so badly she never recovered.

Chapter Seventeen

Lorn stared at the still-sleeping form of his wife, tied to their marriage bed by long and sturdy velvet ropes ending with fur lined cuffs. She looked so fragile as she slumbered with her pink lips slightly parted and her dark hair spread around her pale face. A burst of dread moved through him again at the thought of how easily she could have been killed and how well she'd completely closed the bond between them. If not for the faintest trace of her presence he would have thought her dead.

After her initial surge of intense emotional pain, and her subsequent closing of the bond between them, both he and Nast had been frantic to get to her, only to find out that Casey had somehow vanished. When their guards found indications that someone had managed to slip into the manor he'd been filled with alarm they'd kidnapped his wife. Though it was considered taboo to harm a Matriarch, there were those who were willing to do anything in the name of money and power. Thankfully they'd found a faint trace of Casey's scent trail that went into the orchards while the unfamiliar scents branched off towards the village. The fruit of the orchard provided a natural cover for her scent and only a fool would run for the river at night. It was probably her ignorance of the dangers of the river that saved her, though his stomach threatened to empty every time he thought of all the terrible things that could have happened to her. No one went near the river without being heavily armed at night.

On the other side of the bed Nast had an equally brooding expression and even though wariness tried to drag them both into sleep they continued to watch over her. When Cint contacted them and said he'd found their Matriarch, Lorn had almost passed out with relief. Then when he and Nast learned why Casey had fled them he wanted to spank her creamy ass until it was bright red. He probably still would and give Nast the opportunity to get in a few spanks of his own. While a Kadothian male would never abuse his wife, he was allowed to dispense some domestic discipline when his Matriarch put herself in danger for foolish reasons.

And Casey's reasons were about as foolish as they could get. When they'd found the women waiting for them in their bedroom he'd quickly figured out what had happened, and how Casey had been set up by someone who obviously knew the weakness of the

Earth female's jealousy. If Casey had only come to them all of this could have been avoided and they might have been able to catch the infiltrators in their home. Shame filled him that anyone had managed to breech their security, mixing with anger that anyone would dare to harm Casey. While he'd known there was a great deal of political upset at the discovery of the ability of Earth females to bond, he hadn't thought things would get so bloody so quick.

She stirred on the bed, a slight whimper coming from her that hurt his heart before she slipped back into sleep. This could never happen again. If she ran from them whenever she felt threatened she'd be as good as dead. Her lack of trust in them hurt the most of all and he tried to keep his own wounded feelings from turning to anger. She should wake soon and when she did they had a lesson for her that she wouldn't forget. Spread on the wall above and behind the bed, illuminated by spotlights, Casey's bridal cloak gleamed like orange, red, and gold fire as the feathers moved in the light breeze stirring through the room. Lorn stared at that cloak, a symbol of his devotion to his wife before he even found her, and calmed himself.

Nast leaned forward, wearing only his loose grey lounging pants. His blood brother had been sure Casey had fled them because of something he did and the other man's misplaced guilt had only added to Lorn's determination to make Casey see the truth. The lights had been lowered to a dim glow and night still reigned outside while groups of guards patrolled the manor, searching for any more potential security breaches.

Lorn had been angry at himself for growing complacent in the peacefulness of their home. No one had really challenged them for the land he and Nast held and Lorn had to admit it never occurred to him someone would try to hurt Casey so soon. He'd been so concerned about his wife and her comforts that he'd thought more like a besotted husband than a Warrior. The household had settled down after she returned, everyone equally exhausted after searching for their missing Matriarch. She'd not only hurt Lorn and Nast, she'd wounded her people's feelings as well, and she would have to atone for it or lose their loyalty.

"I can't believe Cint let her carry Bofus," Nast muttered for at least the twentieth time.

The thought of his wife carrying a *zendor* pack leader, one of the deadliest creatures on Kadothia, made Lorn slightly ill. "I want to kill Cint for endangering her as well, but Bofus accepted her as one of his pack and he would never hurt her, nor would his packmates."

"Still," Nast shuddered, "if that creature had deployed his spikes he could have pierced through her delicate skin and turned her into a pile of meat before she had time to scream."

Lorn swallowed hard, memories of watching a pack of *zendors* dispatch predators like a ball of whirling razor sharp blades made his stomach cramp. "But they did not and they kept her safe. Even a river *skagalion* wouldn't take on a pack of *zendors*, thank the Lord of Life"

Nast let out a weary sigh. "Think she's going to want one of her own?"

"I would not be adverse to it. A pack of *zendors* would make anyone think twice about approaching our *alyah*."

They exchanged an equally wary look and for the first time since Casey had run from them Lorn smiled. "Let us just hope she does not send them after us when she's angry."

On the bed Casey mumbled something and tried to roll over, but the restraints kept her on her back. After another jerk at her bonds she frowned, stretched out her legs and yawned. They'd kept her in her gown for the time being, not wanting her to mistake their intentions for tying her to the bed. Oh, they anticipated taking full advantage of her restrained state later, but right now they would explain to her how wrong she'd been and she'd be forced to listen to them.

Yawning again she opened her eyes with a frown and pulled at her arms, finding she had enough slack to touch herself but not enough to move more than a few inches on either side. Both he and Nast were quiet while they watched as she opened her eyes and stared at the high ceiling with its massive skylight showing the night sky above. She blinked once, twice, and the confusion left her expression, quickly replaced by anger.

"What the fuck..." she said in a harsh voice.

Lorn immediately picked up the bottle of water next to him and went to Casey, bracing her head so she could drink.

"Get your fucking hands off..."

He rudely shoved the straw in her mouth. "Drink or choke."

She took two long pulls before jerking her head away. "I'm going to choke you unless you untie me right now!"

After setting the bottle on the table next to the bed he stood at the edge and looked down at her, all too aware of her rage burning through their bond, but behind it her anguish. "Enough, Casey. You will listen to me or I will gag you."

"You cheating, asshole, fucking..."

Her angry tirade was cut off by Nast placing his hand over her mouth, effectively shutting her up. "*Alyah*, you will listen to us or I swear by the Lord of Life I will spank you until you cannot sit comfortably for days."

Oh, that pissed her off.

She thrashed and kicked, whipped her head back and forth and appeared to try to bite Nast but he couldn't be moved. Finally she stilled and tears slid down her cheeks as she gave his blood brother a glare that was supposed to be angry but ended up looking heartbroken instead. He eased his hand away then brushed back a tear that had slid down one of her full cheeks.

Lorn's heart ached as he watched the two people he loved most in the world in pain. "We did not betray you, Casey, and it hurts us deeply you would think that."

"Yeah, right," she said in bitter voice. "I saw those women, Nast. They said you were their Master. And your servant clued me into how things work."

He stilled and exchanged a glance with Nast before returning his attention to Casey. "This is very important, *alyah*, I need you to try and remember everything you can about who you talked to and what they said. What did the servant look like?"

She described the woman then her voice trembled as she said, "I remember everything the servant said. How you only married me to handle the estate and that Kadothian men really love their pleasure servants and how you loved those women in our fucking bed!"

Nast leaned closer, "We need to know more about that servant. What did she look like?"

"Fuck you! I don't give a fuck about that woman, you cheating asshole!" she screamed in his face, then began to sob.

Knowing they weren't going to get anywhere with her until the damage done to their relationship was repaired, Lorn sighed and held up a hand to Nast. "Hold on. Casey, we are their Masters."

She looked at him with such a broken expression that Nast quickly said, "You have this wrong. It is not what you think."

"Then what is it?" she asked in a whisper.

"Ula, Tula, come."

From across the room a hidden panel opened and the two pleasure 'bots obediently approached them, their gel filled breasts barely moving with each step. Pure hatred filled Casey and before she could go off again he stepped forward and slipped his fingers between the synthetic skin and the hair behind Tula's left ear then gently peeled it back, revealing the mechanics of his pleasure 'bot. He stepped back and gave his wife a hard look.

"I told you I owned two pleasure 'bots."

"But...but..." she seemed to deflate in front of his eyes, then paled until he was afraid she might pass out. "Oh my God, I'm such a bitch. But why would that woman tell me they were your pleasure servants? Not robots?"

Nast moved forward and replaced the pleasure 'bot's skin. "Ula, Tula, go back to your pod."

"Yes, Master," the pleasure 'bots said as one with identical sultry smiles and quickly left the room.

"You were deceived by someone wishing to hurt you. The pleasure 'bots' programming was tampered with. They were programed by someone who knew of Earth women's jealousy issues to say exactly what would hurt you most. What would make you run."

Confusion filled her and her jaw went slack before she swallowed hard. "You mean I was set up?"

"Yes."

"But, why?"

Nast moved her hair off her face with a gentle touch. "Politics—dirty, backstabbing, fucking terrible politics. I am so sorry we allowed this to happen to you."

Once again Casey's generous nature rose to the surface and she held Nast's hand. "It's not your fault."

"We will discuss that later. Right now we have more important things to talk about."

Silence filled the room as Nast and Lorn watched their *alyah*, each wanting to comfort her but needing this lesson to sink in. She could not run off every time she was offended or hurt. If she'd simply trusted them enough to explain none of this would have happened. They'd been warned about Earth brides' jealousy but even Lorn had underestimated how strong it was.

She looked from him to Nast and back again. "I'm so, so sorry. Please untie me, I won't run. I didn't know they were just robots."

Shaking his head, Nast took a seat on the edge of the bed and moved until he was stretched out next to her, but far enough away so she couldn't touch him. "What you did today was beyond foolish, Casey. You could have died because of your jealousy and lack of trust. Do you have any idea of the creatures that roam these lands at night? Not to mention our enemies who were tracking you."

Her already large eyes grew wider. "Enemies? What enemies were tracking me?"

"That servant was not part of our household. We think the only reason you managed to escape them was that you don't know the area or the house and took an unexpected exit through an empty portion of the servant's quarters. There were men stationed at the two entrances nearest to our bedroom. They tried to track you, but

225

because of your natural shielding they could not get a lock on you. You were very, very lucky." He closed his eyes and blew out a harsh breath. "You have no idea how terrified I was that you had been kidnapped. Do you not understand, Casey? You mean everything to us, everything."

"Oh, Nast," she whispered. Her lower lip trembled and she nodded. "I'm sorry, I really am."

Anger made Lorn's words come out harsher than he intended. "Yet you so easily believed the worst of us. Your lack of faith hurt us deeply."

"Please forgive me. I never meant to hurt you and I'm so sorry." Her eyes swam with more tears and she rubbed her cheek against the sleeve of her gown. "You have to understand, I didn't grow up in a place like this, with all this crazy drama."

Lorn couldn't help but grin. "Crazy drama?"

"Well what the hell would you call sabotaged sex robots and kidnappers? I mean really." She huffed and jerked at her restraints. "And tying me up? I'm not going to run away, Lorn. Believe me, I've learned my lesson and I'm not mad at you anymore, so can you untie me now?"

With a gentle smile he cupped her cheek, his big hand enveloping half her face. "I know you are not mad at us, because I can feel it, Casey. Just as you would have been able to feel the truth of our words if you had allowed yourself to do so. We are not like your Earth men, we cannot and will not lie to you."

Unable to resist comforting her, Lorn slid closer. The bed was big enough they could have easily fit another four people on it, and he planned to make use of that space. "Casey, I fear your jealousy. It causes you to act irrationally, to let distrust and anger rule you when I know you have a generous, kind soul. We have decided we will show you why you have nothing to be jealous of, that even if Nast and I are together it will always involve you, even if you are not touching either of us."

"But I will not touch your husband without your permission," Nast murmured as he stroked Casey's soft cheek.

She gave Nast a searching look, then slowly nodded. "I want to trust you, Nast, I really do, but I don't understand how to get over my fear of a relationship with three people ending up in disaster. I can't wrap my mind around the idea that no one will get jealous or have their feelings hurt. Help me understand, please. Show me. I want you to touch Lorn, and if I'm being honest with myself, which I'm really trying to be, I find the idea of watching you with my husband hot."

Lorn didn't even try to hide the hard rush of lust that filled him at the thought of making love to Nast with their *alyah* watching. His wife had no idea what she was in for, but he couldn't wait to show her the reason why none of them would ever feel jealous. But first they had to get her to relax and lower her shields all the way so she could fully immerse herself in the moment.

Looking up at Lorn, Nast smiled and a delicious wave of arousal came from Casey. "Let us get her comfortable."

Together they helped Casey move up and she jerked at her restraints. "Come on, guys, untie me."

"No," Lorn said and rubbed his lips over the swell of her breast with the bondmark. "You have no self-control when it comes to pleasure, *alyah*, and while I love it, we get to torture you a little for scaring us."

She huffed at them, but a smile played at the corners of her pink, kissable mouth. As if reading his mind Nast leaned over and gave her a soft, tender kiss that left her pleasure-dazed when he pulled back. Having been on the receiving end of one of Nast's devastatingly gentle kisses Lorn could sympathize with her stunned look. Grabbing the bodice of her robe he swiftly tore it in two while Nast grabbed the sleeve of her robe and ripped it. Together they shredded her clothing from her in violent moves that had her wet and panting by the time she was naked with her robe lying in ruins around her pale body.

Lord of Life, she was beautiful.

Nast gripped his forearm and pulled them down the bed so they were just beyond her tiny feet. With a low growl he held his blood brother to him, enjoying the familiar perfection of the other man's body. They'd been together so long they knew each other's pleasures intimately and Lorn put that knowledge to good use, gripping the back of Nast's neck and drawing him in for a punishing kiss. Fire streaked through their bond from Casey and he silently rejoiced she wasn't upset about their touching.

Pleasure built hot and fierce in his blood and he slipped his hand beneath the loose band of Nast's pants, curving his palm around the other man's hard cock, milking some of that precum which Casey seemed to like so much. Lifting his fingers, now coated with lilac precum, Lorn held his hand to Nast and together they began to lick his fingers clean, their tongues twining and their growls blending together.

Having Casey here watching them had to be one of the most erotic acts of Lorn's life.

"Holy shit, that's hot," their little bride whimpered from where she was propped up at the head of the bed. "I'm going to come from just watching you kiss."

Satisfaction flowed through Nast, matching Lorn's pride in pleasing their woman. And she was their woman; it was as plain as the moons in the sky, as true as his love. They were meant to be together and his wife was finally beginning to accept that. The more the men kissed the more her soul opened to Nast until it almost felt as if the other man was already bonded to them. Lorn rejoiced in the sensation of finally almost being completely linked to his blood brother like he'd yearned to be all these years.

Nast grabbed Lorn's ass and pressed their still covered cocks together as they kissed, grinding against each other while Casey began to moan softly.

"I can feel you," she marveled. "Both of you. Like you're touching me."

Pressing his lips up against Lorn's ear, Nast whispered, "I want you to take me, then I want Casey."

The thought of Nast moving over Casey, covering her small frame with his as he worked his cock into her had Lorn close to spilling in his pants. He pulled back with a ragged gasp, straining for control that was quickly stripped away by the sight of Casey rubbing her legs together and squeezing her lush thighs trying to ease the ache of her very wet sex.

"What a pretty pussy," Nast murmured. "I cannot wait to get my tongue into it."

"Please," Casey begged as she strained against her bonds. "Eat me, lick me, make me come, Nast, please."

"Oh, I will *alyah*, after I take care of your husband."

Both men stiffened as Casey's lust overwhelmed them. It was so strong Lorn had to close his bond the slightest bit before his wife took away all his control. A fine tremor ran through Nast and the need to fuck his blood brother filled Lorn with a vengeance.

"Hands and knees," Lorn said in a voice barely above an inhuman growl.

Nast, of course, resisted and the men wrestled on the bed. Soon Lorn had Nast pinned and moved enough so Casey could watch him spit down the crack of his blood brother's ass.

"You're so fucking dirty," she whispered. "I love it."

He gave her a feral grin, flashing his fangs before planting a hand on Nast's lower back and dipping his head down to kiss along the hard curve of the other man's buttock. Nast arched with a low moan and Lorn quickly rewarded him by teasing the sensitive rim of his anus, pausing to wet two of his fingers before he slid them into the welcoming heat of his future husband's body. The feeling of that tight, firm entrance clasping around his fingers was enough to have Lorn finger-fucking the other man fast and hard, eager to open his body enough to accept him.

"Take me," Nast groaned and got onto his hands and knees, the heavy muscles of his back and shoulders flexing as he looked over at Casey.

She stared back at Nast with a dazed expression and love wove into her lust, throwing them all higher until Lorn was fumbling with the drawstring of his pants before shoving them down enough to free his aching cock. Lorn groaned with the sensation of the cool air on his oversensitive flesh, a sound quickly echoed by his wife and lover. Spreading open the crack of Nast's ass with one hand, he spit into his other hand and smeared the lubrication over his cock. Once he was positioned at the entrance to his blood brother's body he looked over at Casey and began to sink in.

With wide eyes she watched avidly at where the men's bodies joined and spread her legs. The sight of her flushed, wet sex made his mouth water and Nast growled like a beast beneath him. She was so aroused her sex contracted as she unconsciously raised her hips as if she was the one receiving his cock, and in a way she was. As connected to them as she was now she was feeling an edge of the sensations filling both men. The burn of being stretched along with the hard pleasure of pushing a cock into willing, hot flesh. It was so good he had to close his eyes as he eased into his lover until their balls brushed each other.

A hard shudder worked through Nast and he whispered, "Have to close myself off. Need to last. Need to come in her."

Lorn completely understood and while he mourned the loss of Nast's emotions it allowed him to concentrate fully on Casey. He let out a snarl as she silently urged him to move with a jerk of her hips. All finesse left him as he drowned in their mutual need, her desires building his own until he felt almost like he was in rut, eager to fuck until he couldn't fuck anymore. Moving with harsh thrusts of his hips he pounded into Nast, certain of his blood brother's ability to take him. Nast responded by squeezing with his inner muscles, gripping Lorn's shaft as tight as a fist. His heart filled with love and he opened his eyes again, looking to Casey, needing to see her pleasure.

She was watching him and wiggling on the bed, her magnificent breasts topped with hard little nipples trembling with her shaky breaths. When their eyes met her love overwhelmed him and he threw his head back, feeling overwhelmed from the pleasure blasting through him. Nast fucked him back, meeting his thrusts until the sound of their flesh slapping together mingled with the low growls spilling from them both. His climax threatened and he fought it, working to prolong this intense pleasure.

"Please, Lorn," Casey screamed. "Please come. Oh God, I can't stand it."

With a roar spilling out of him he did as his wife begged, the first hard blast of his semen coinciding with a shockwave through his bond with his *alyah*, followed by the warm pleasure of her own orgasm. Her moans drove him crazy as he continued to press himself into Nast, leaning forward so he could hug the other man, to tell him without words how much he loved him, how much he loved them both. When his orgasm stilled at last he pulled gently out of his lover and gave his ass a smack before rolling off the bed on unsteady feet.

By the time he made it back with the cleansing cloth Nast had moved so he lay on his stomach at Casey's feet, gently suckling her toes one by one while she moaned for him. Her body was flushed with arousal and she'd created a wet spot on the bed with her climax. She barely stirred as Lorn cleaned Nast before placing a gentle kiss on each of the dimples at the top of the other man's ass.

"Nast, I can't feel you," she whispered in a husky voice. "Please open to me. I miss you."

It warmed Lorn's heart to hear his wife say that and he collapsed next to her, content and utterly drained. Soon his desire would build but first it was time for Nast to teach their woman a lesson.

"She is all yours," he said in a low voice as he reclined back on the pillows, getting ready for what would be a visual and emotional feast fit for the Lord of Life Himself.

Chapter Eighteen

Nast nibbled on Casey's tiny toes, loving how small and feminine they were. She'd painted them with some kind of pink polish a few shades lighter than her rose red pussy. The scent of her nectar called to him but he resisted the lure of her hot, tight sex. They needed to get a few things straight first.

He leaned over her to untie her wrists, enjoying the way she immediately wrapped herself around him and showered every inch of his skin she could reach with kisses. She was such an affectionate little female and he enjoyed that about her. He loved everything about her except her destructive jealousy. Which made the lesson he was about to impart necessary, but he'd be lying if he didn't admit the thought of punishing his bride appealed to him.

Immensely.

He unwound her arms from around his neck and took her hand. "Come with me."

Giving him a confused look she did as he asked but he didn't dare lower his shields yet. His self-control was hanging by a thread as it was and he needed to have a clear mind. Casey was a smart woman, but very young. He'd have to be gentle but firm with her.

Once they reached the edge of the bed he had her stand before he sat on the edge with his feet bracing on the floor. Before she could guess what he was about to do, he pulled her over his lap with her plump ass wiggling in the air. The press of her breasts against his leg, the sensation of her soft body trying to squirm out of his grip, made him growl with need.

"What the hell are you doing?" she yelled as she tried to push off his legs.

"You will be still. You will take your punishment, and you will think about why you deserve this."

She froze, then tried to push off of him but there was no way she could escape his superior strength. "Don't you fucking *dare* spank me!"

In response he brought his large hand down on her ass with a satisfying crack, then slid his fingers over to her pussy, stroking the slick entrance.

"Get the fuck off of me," she yelled.

Her anger pushed at his shields and he grinned at her mental strength, proud of how formidable his little bride was. "You will

231

never run from us again, Casey. Ever."

"Fuck you!"

He looked up and met Lorn's amused gaze before the other man nodded. Settling her into the position he wanted, he placed his forearm over her back and pressed down, pinning her. Then he began to spank her in earnest, not hard enough to do real damage, but firm enough to sting. With each slap her ass bloomed white, then red as her blood rushed to the surface. He started on her left buttock, then switched to the right. She howled, spit, and cursed as he continued to spank her, becoming progressively wilder until she'd insulted not only him, but his mother and just about every relative he'd ever had. After the fifteenth slap he leaned back to admire his work, loving the hot, red flush covering her plump buttocks.

Tears wet his thigh and she was no longer struggling as hard, instead, she clung to him. Slipping his fingers between her legs, he found her pussy even hotter than her ass and his cock surged against her body while Lorn groaned from the bed. With a slow breath he lowered his shields, testing her emotional state while letting his love flow through along with his desire. She went limp against him and began to cry in earnest while he stroked the slit of her soft little sex.

"That is a good girl. You know you were wrong, Casey, and you have to be punished for endangering yourself, but you are doing so well. Only a little more, *alyah*."

She sobbed and clung to him, her trust mixing with her love and embarrassment. Confusion lingered beneath the hot swirl of her emotions and he began to rub her stiff clit with his thumb. Desire overwhelmed everything else in her mind as he kept one hand playing with her dripping wet pussy and began to spank her with the other. Soon she was moaning and sobbing, her mind totally focused on her body while he built the fires in her higher. Not all women responded to a mix of pain with their pleasure, but his bride did and he loved being able to give this to her. The confusion melted away until only trust and need remained, her legs spreading and her back arching as she offered herself to him.

The last few spanks he gave her were hard enough to bruise and he wanted that, wanted her ass to be tender when she sat so she would remember this lesson, so she would never endanger herself like that again. When they discovered she'd fled he was devastated, and when he and Lorn hadn't been able to reach her and learned she might have been taken against her will, his world crumbled. He could see why men killed themselves after being rejected by their bondmate because if it hadn't been for Lorn telling him Casey was still alive he would have wanted to go to sleep and never wake up.

A trace of that icy fear lanced through his veins as he hauled her off his lap and drew her between his thighs, helping her stand on wobbly legs and making her look at him. Her face was wet and blotchy with her tears and her hair was a tangled mess, but he'd never found her more beautiful and he shoved that intense feeling at her through their bond.

"You will never run from us again, Casey. Do you hear me? Never."

She threw her arms around his neck, wetting his shoulder with her tears. "I'm so sorry, Nast. I didn't think, I just reacted and I hurt you so much. I'm so sorry."

His heart broke and he held her close, taking in deep breaths of her scent, reassuring himself she was alive and safe, loving her with every ounce of his battered soul. Their bond strengthened and she began to place delicate kisses along his neck, working her way to his mouth. Once their lips met they both sighed in a mixture of need and relief that pushed the last bit of doubt from his soul.

"Take me, Nast," she whispered against his lips. "Take me, bond with me, love me. Love us."

He didn't realize Lorn was behind them until she said that but soon his friend was sitting with his hips and chest cradling Nast. "Take her, my blood brother. Make love to our wife."

Unable to think past the emotions destroying his soul and remaking it into something stronger, something better, he helped Casey straddle his lap. She slid her fingers through his hair and urged his head up. When his gaze met her dark, reddened eyes his breath caught in his throat at the fierce desire mixed with love flowing through their bond.

"Look at me, Nast, know who is taking you."

She gave him a saucy little smile as she threw his words back at him, but it allowed him to pull back and refocus on her, on the gift she was giving him. Placing his hands onto her ample hips he lifted her while she reached between them and placed his cock at her entrance. Letting it go once he was snugly tucked against her, she then cupped his face with her small hands and softly kissed him as he lowered her onto his cock.

As the first inch of his shaft stretched her he moaned into her mouth, her sheath convulsing tight enough that he was afraid he was going to hurt her. She pressed down and the mushroom shaped head pushed into her softness. He felt like he'd come home. Wrapping his arms around her slight form he marveled at the tenderness flowing from her, a soothing balm to his heart that only raised his desire higher. He loved her, so very much, and after all of his fears of not only losing Lorn but her as well he could scarcely believe it was real.

"It's real," she whispered against his lips.

"You heard me?" He held her still, only halfway in the soft clutch of her pussy.

"Yes." She rubbed her tiny nose against his.

Lorn swept his hair to the side and kissed along Nast's neck, adding a bit of fang that made his balls draw up tight.

Nast returned to kissing Casey, all rational thought leaving him as she enveloped him all the way to his balls. Seated fully on his lap she sighed into his mouth and he couldn't help but smile at the contentment radiating from her. But he didn't want her content, he wanted her begging for release.

With that thought in mind he gripped her buttocks, still hot from his spanking, and gave a gentle squeeze that made her yelp, then groan as he tilted her hips so her clit pressed against his pelvis. Her lush breasts crushed to his chest and he set a languid rhythm, each stroke into her welcoming heat better than the last. Lorn's fierce male lust mixed with Casey's softer, but just as intense need, until Nast felt more connected to them than himself. Soon she shifted so she had more control of her movements and began to ride him, her head tossed back and her long dark hair tickling his thighs as she moved.

Lorn ground his cock against Nast's back and he gave himself over to them, letting Lorn hold him while Casey worked her little pussy along his aching shaft until his pleasure ridges began to fill and vibrate. She immediately stiffened and he barely had time to shut down his side of the link before she and Lorn began to come. Just the sight of her coming apart on his cock almost sent him over the edge, but he held on. He wanted to fuck her hard and fierce, not climax yet, so he bit his tongue until it bled and held back even though he felt like he was one stroke away from going over.

Nast clenched his hands into fists as his blood brother roared and the heat of Lorn's seed pulsed against his back. Unable to hold on one second longer he flipped Casey over onto her back while remaining inside of her and slipped his hand beneath her ass, lifting her to him as he pounded into her. She cried out and scored his back with her fingernails and he opened his side of the bond again, shoving his need and ferocious desire into her mind just as he was shoving his cock into her hot, swollen pussy.

The contractions from her orgasm seemed to go on forever and she became violent beneath him, biting him, scratching him, wrapping her legs around his waist and trying to shove her hips against his. He kissed her and shared the taste of his blood, loving how she moaned and sucked on his tongue. With a final plunge he tore his mouth from hers as he roared out his orgasm. Casey screamed and arched her back so harshly he distantly feared she'd injure herself so he lay atop her and held her close while he continued to fill her with his seed, his heart racing and his soul rejoicing in her total acceptance of him.

She loved him as much as he loved her, as much as she loved Lorn, and it made her extraordinarily happy.

For a long, long time he remained inside of her, not moving even as his cock eventually softened. Lorn lay next to Casey and gently stroked both of them, his love and approval adding another layer to the joy flowing through Nast.

He did it. He survived battles, his own doubt, and a universe out to kill him and won the heart of his bride. There were no words for his satisfaction, his absolute relief and joy so he shared his emotions with his soon-to-be bondmates and drifted to sleep, knowing Lorn would keep them all safe.

****

Casey slipped her arms around Lorn's thick neck and gave him a kiss as she surveyed the small breakfast table set up on the balcony of their personal apartments. Her body ached like she'd just run a marathon but her heart and her soul felt somehow renewed. The strength of her love for her men was still staggering when she concentrated on it, but she was no longer scared of her feelings. There was no reason to be because their love for her and for each other was just as intense.

Nast smiled at her from across the table and she blew him a kiss before settling into her chair. To her delight she'd found clothes in her closet other than black gowns and Lorn had explained that while she wore the gowns for official or formal functions, at her home she was allowed to dress for her comfort. Now she wore a pair of pale green silky pants and a loose shirt that had a high collar with cleavage cut out to display her bondmark. They'd even included bras and panties for her, even though both men grumbled as she put them on. Tracing the design of her bondmark with her finger, she looked up at Nast with a smile.

"So, when do you want to get bonded?"

Both of her men were looking incredibly edible as they relaxed at the table in their black pants with no shirts on. From their vantage point they had a view of the orchard and the river beyond along with an amazing city full of spires and flying specks in the distance in the early morning light. Lorn had explained the city in the distance was Vastal, the northern capital where his extended family lived. They would go visit his parents later today so she could meet one of Lorn's younger brothers who was home on leave from the military. The other two were on distant planets, fighting the Hive and their mercenaries.

Reaching across the table, Nast picked her hand up and kissed her fingertips before releasing her. "As soon as possible?"

She giggled and took a seat between the two men, luxuriating in their adoration. "Sounds good to me."

The men took turns feeding her by hand and by the time they were finished all three were ready to head back to bed. Before they could a chime sounded from the bedroom door and Lorn stood, stretching out in a mouthwatering display of rippling muscles while he smiled at them. "I will answer it. You should show our *alyah* the pleasures of the soaking tub."

Nast picked her up and held her against his chest, dipping his head to inhale her scent while she wrapped her legs around him as much as she could. He gripped her bottom and she winced. Right away his touch gentled as hurt flavored his emotions. "I am sorry, little bride. I did not mean to bruise you so much."

She nuzzled her nose against his, letting him know with both her body and heart that she wasn't angry at him. Well, not totally angry. "If you ever try to spank me like that again I'll have Lorn help me tie you down so I can spank you."

His startled laugh made her grin and he slipped her a little lower before adjusting his shaft with one hand so it slid between the lips of her sex. "Hmmm, I might have to spank you tonight in that case."

She arched a brow at him. "You like the idea of being spanked?"

"Not so much spanking, but I enjoy rough sex. I like having to fight for dominance. It is a Kadothian male thing. While I am afraid I would break you, I would enjoy you trying to help Lorn pin me. Very much."

The heat of his arousal certainly backed that statement up and she moaned softly while he rocked against her. "I swear you're turning me into a nymphomaniac."

"What is that?"

"It's a word used on Earth for a condition where someone constantly wants to have sex."

The sexy flash of his fangs as he smiled only added to her growing need for him. "That sounds like a good problem to have."

She giggled and he turned to carry her back to the bedroom when they both caught a hint of Lorn's distress before he closed their bond down. Nast quickly slid her down his body and they both took off in the direction Lorn had gone. When they entered the bedroom they found Lorn standing with a Warrior who looked vaguely familiar. He had dark blond hair streaked with rich brown pulled back into a tight braid and very nice lips along with a killer pair of pale green eyes. Before she could say anything the man dropped to his knees and bowed his head.

"Greetings, Matriarch of House Westfall. Forgive my intrusion but I have a boon to beg of you."

Lorn was seriously pissed but he didn't say anything. Nast stood directly behind her and she was reminded once again how much smaller than her men she was as the man kneeling before her looked up again. She gave Lorn a questioning glance but he'd shut his bond down tight.

"Please call me Cas-er-Matriarch Westfall. Um, rise Warrior. What's your name?"

"My name is Cormac, Matriarch, I met you briefly back on Earth. I picked Lorn up from your home."

"Oh!" She smiled at him and gave him a quick hug, moving back when he stiffened against her. "So nice to see you again."

He shot Lorn a worried look but her husband sighed. "She likes to hug people she knows."

"What do you want?" Nast said in a low, growling voice thick with warning.

Cormac took a deep breath then let it out slowly. "Matriarch Westfall..."

"Please, call me Casey."

He licked his lips in a nervous gesture, then nodded. "Casey, I have an enormous boon to ask of you."

"What is it?"

Going to his knees again he looked up at her with such a beseeching expression that she felt sorry for him. "I am begging you to please return to Earth, just for a short time."

Startled, she jumped when Nast wrapped his arms around her and held her tight to his body. "No."

She elbowed him in the ribs but he ignored her until she sent a blast of her disapproval through their bond then he flinched. "Ouch. That hurt."

"Don't answer for me," she frowned up at him. "We need to at least hear him out."

"No we do not," Lorn muttered but she ignored him.

"Why do you need me to go back?"

"The Lord of Life had blessed your home region with a great many women who have the potential to be brides. Your disappearance has made it very, very hard to court them. They fear Lorn has kidnapped you, or killed you, and view any men associated with Lorn with great suspicion. It is very frustrating to see your bondmate standing before you, but being unable to court her because she thinks our men killed Casey."

"What?" Casey yelled and kicked back at Nast as he tried to hold her again.

"Forgive me for angering you, Matriarch, but our men are getting desperate and that desperation is pushing those struggling with their inner beast closer to losing themselves to the madness. I beg you to come back just for a few days, long enough to give some kind of excuse for your disappearance and soothe the females. Without a doubt I will suffer your husbands' wrath for this, but it is worth it if I can have a chance to get a kiss."

The thought of seeing her family again elated her but on the heels of her joy came her men's pain. Absently, she wondered who Cormac believed his bondmate was. She looked up at Lorn and studied him, trying to figure out why the thought of her going back to Earth made him...scared. Examining Nast's emotions she felt the same thing and it dawned on her that they worried she would leave them.

"Can I have a moment alone with my husbands, please?" Cormac looked at her breast, then up at Nast with a puzzled look. "No, he's not my husband yet but he will be as soon as we can find a High Priestess to bond us."

"Of course, Matriarch."

He quickly left the room and she tried to wiggle out of Nast's grip but he refused to let her go. "Oh would you two relax? Nothing, and I mean nothing, could take me away from you. Okay?"

"What if your family disapproves of us," Lorn asked in a low voice, his expression and mental touch so filled with despair that she wanted to choke him. "What if you find the thought of leaving them again too painful and want to stay on Earth?"

"Nothing. Not my family, not my friends, not even God or the Lord of Life could take me from you or you from me. You are my world, my loves, my joy and my soul. Both of you. I could no more leave you than I could cut my heart from chest."

Nast loosened his hold and she reached out to Lorn, drawing them both to her until she was buried between two mountains of male muscle. "What if they try to take you from us?"

"Then you don't let them, but it won't come to that. You can have me beamed up right?"

"Beamed up?" Nast asked as he leaned down then lifted her so she was held between them.

"You know, whatever that thing is they did to bring Lorn and I to the ship."

Lorn's low laugh vibrated against her back and his relief eased the strain on her heart. "Fast track. Yes, we could fast track you from anywhere in your world."

"See? No big deal. We go back to Earth, I let everyone know that I'm okay, tell them we ran off to Vegas to get married or whatever, everyone will calm down, and your men can court their brides. Hell, I'll even help your men seduce my friends, and not just because I'd like to have them here with me, because there is nothing better than being loved by a Kadothian man; if they are meant to be with one of your men then I have to help make that happen. The Lord of Life doesn't make bad matches, right?"

Lorn rubbed his cheek against her head. "Forgive us for doubting you, Casey."

Nast gave her a gentle kiss before exchanging another kiss with Lorn. "I will miss you."

She grabbed Nast's chin and forced him to look at her. "You're coming with us."

"But your people will shun you if you have more than one husband. I do not want you shamed."

"I don't give a fuck what they think. If they can't accept our love that's their problem."

"What about your family?" Lorn asked in a soft voice. "I do not want you to fight with them."

Apprehension filled her but she brushed it off. "They'll have to deal with it too. My sister will be jealous as hell, my brother might want to kick your asses, but my parents will see how good it is between us. Please, Lorn, I want to be able to say goodbye to my family. Please let me go home so I can give them closure. I don't want them to suffer for the rest of their lives, thinking something terrible happened to me."

"How will you explain your absence?"

"I'll think of something." She leaned against Lorn and absently stroked Nast's chest, liking being held between them like this. "Can we give them like a coded message or something that will activate when the wormhole closes? A device that will let them know I'm all right?"

The men exchanged a glance and Nast nodded. "A

communication crystal could be left with them. Perhaps something that could be worn as a piece of jewelry by your mother."

She let out a sigh of relief, her heart filled with love for her men. "Thank you. I also had another idea I've been thinking about. Something that might help other brides."

"What is it?" Lorn asked in a soft voice that sent desire through her and she realized both men were starting to feel frisky.

Rolling her eyes she shook her head. "Hear me out first, okay? You were right about it being silly to think having more than one person to love is evil, and I agree it is totally stupid, but most Earth women won't. While I don't approve of your mother's teaching methods, she was effective in showing me why bonding more than one male isn't only necessary, but the right thing to do."

Nast began to stroke her right buttock while Lorn stroked her left, distracting her. "Stop that or I'll make you get dressed and sit across the room from me so you'll listen."

They gave her disgruntled looks that almost made them appear childish and she shook her head. "Anyway, I was thinking, you know how Jaz is part of a welcoming committee? Maybe I could run a class with a few of the other Earth women who have bonded more than one man on why it's not only necessary, but also why it's not wrong. Yeah, we could bring your mom in to zap everyone's man, but that may hurt more couples than it helps. Not every woman will understand, and some women will flat out refuse no matter what I say, but at least I can try to get through to them. Because everyone deserves a chance to have the kind of love we have. It is the most amazing thing I've ever felt and I want to do all I can to help your men find their bondmates."

Their happiness and pride surrounded her, leaving her in a pleased little puddle of joy on their chests as she melted beneath their combined adoration.

Lorn brought her fingers to his lips and kissed them as he spoke, "This is the way it is supposed to be, Casey. To share our love with each other. The Lord of Life did not create us with a limited amount, he gave us as much love as he has, enough for the whole universe."

"Now," Nast said in a rumbling purr, "let us show you how much we love you."

"Wait," she said as she tried to fight off the growing need to have them inside of her. "Cormac."

Lorn stepped away and Nast continued to hold her while placing hungry kisses along her neck that made her shiver. A second later Lorn opened the door and said, "We'll be ready to leave in two hours."

"Three," Nast said in a low voice before returning to tormenting her with pleasure that stole her mind and her heart.

"Make it four," Lorn growled before he shut the door and returned to their side where he belonged.

Chapter Nineteen

asey took a deep breath and let out slowly, the hum of the busy fast track port on the Reaping ship washing over her. Just hours ago, she'd bonded Nast fully and she was still adjusting to the sensation of having him fully merged with her soul and Lorn's. Her beautiful new bonding cloak, this one made of a shimmering turquoise green lizard skin, was safely stored in their room on the ship, and her body still hummed with the hard loving Nast had given her while Lorn watched. In a perfect world, she'd still be in bed with her men, drowning in their love, but they needed to get to Earth ASAP.

Her heart raced as she thought about the news articles Cormac had shown her, pleas from her parents all over the local papers and the Internet for anyone with information on Casey's whereabouts, or Lorn's, to come forward. The image of her family holding a candlelight vigil still haunted her, and she had to battle her impatience to return to home so she could put her friends and family out of their misery. Her friends had all been claimed by different Kadothian Warriors but so far, none had managed to secure a kiss. No wonder, considering her friends were pretty sure Lorn had kidnapped her.

The group of Kadothian men ahead of them dissolved before her eyes as they were fast tracked to Earth and Lorn looked down at her with a smile. "Ready?"

He'd put on his Earth disguise again, though she persuaded him to color his hair a more traditional dark blond rather than the almost pure white he sported the first time she met him. Dressed in a pair of worn jeans and a tight, dark grey t-shirt he was still the hottest man she'd ever seen. Then she looked over at Nast and had to amend that thought as she took in his more rugged good looks. This would be his first trip to Earth, and despite the dire nature of their journey, she was still excited to show him her planet. Like Lorn, Nast wore a pair of jeans that clung to his thick, muscled legs and did wonderful things for his rounded ass. He'd gone for a light brown hair color and had pulled his hair back in a low-slung ponytail while Lorn had braided his.

Either way, they were both beyond delicious and she wanted to eat them alive.

"Casey," Lorn said in a teasing tone. "While your desire for us is more than welcome, we would rather not meet your family without our cocks hard."

"Oh, shit." She flushed and glanced down at her own outfit of jeans and a t-shirt, wishing she could see the new bondmark swirling over the center of her chest and dipping between her cleavage in a tendril of delicate scrolls. "Sorry about that."

Nast laughed and swept her up into his arms, placing a sound kiss on her lips. "Have I told you how much I love you, wife?"

She kissed him back, then leaned away and grinned. "You might have a time or two."

"Casey!" They looked over to find Jaz and her husbands making their way through the crowd to them.

"Hey, Jaz." Nast put her down so she could approach the other woman. "We're about to head back to Earth, what's up?"

The other woman gave her a brief hug and smiled. "Congratulations on bonding your second husband. Cormac told me you were going to say goodbye to your parents. Your husbands had these made for you."

She handed Casey a small green box. Giving the other woman a curious look, Casey opened it and found a lovely, huge solitaire diamond ring and three gold wedding bands. There was also a pretty crystal charm on a gold chain. She recognized right away what the rings were for, but didn't know the significance of the necklace. "Wedding rings! Thank you so much for thinking of that, but what's the necklace?"

"Your husbands had this made for your mother. When the Reaping ship departs it will send a beacon back to earth and it will emit a high-pitched ringing noise. Once someone touches it a recording will play of your bonding ceremony to Lorn and Nast, then it will give an explanation of where you went, all in this super awesome 3D holograph thing." She smiled and gave Casey another hug. "Thank you for thinking of this. The other brides are having some made for their families as well, that is, those that have families to worry about, and we hope this will help them accept our disappearances."

The Warrior running the transport said in a loud voice, "Captain Lorn Westfall, we have your coordinates ready."

The long line of people waiting to return to Earth stretched out behind them and Casey flushed, quickly slipping on her rings then handing the men theirs. "Put it on the third finger of your left hand. On Earth it means you're married."

Jaz blew them a kiss and moved off the platform. "Good luck!"

"Thanks," Casey replied in a faint voice, her earlier apprehension about being dissolved at a molecular level then put back together returning again.

"Eyes closed," Lorn whispered.

"Ri..." Before she could finish the word a weird tingle went through her and she had a disconcerting moment of everything going black, then a twist in her stomach and she stumbled back as the scents of coffee, breakfast, men, and fresh cut grass filled her nose.

She opened her eyes and found herself in the familiar backyard of Lorn's house with the birds singing and a picture-perfect summer morning blue sky stretching out overhead. She turned her face to the sun and let out a shuddering sigh, filled with immense relief tinged with regret. Then Nast and Lorn took her hands, their worry pressing into her, and her regret faded. She smiled and turned to Nast.

"Welcome to Earth."

He looked around with wide eyes, examining everything with open curiosity. "It is beautiful."

She took in another deep breath and something deep inside of her relaxed at the smell of home. "Thank you."

A nearby man cleared his throat and they turned to find at least two dozen Kadothian men watching them. "Welcome, Matriarch of House Westfall."

Cormac made his way through the crowd, the relief on his handsome face so evident she had to hold back a laugh. "Thank the Lord of Life you made it."

Nast let out a little growl, "I just bonded with my Matriarch, and I am not at all happy to be here instead of my wedding bed."

The men made sympathetic noises while others called out their congratulations. Cormac held up his hand and the fell into silence. "I truly apologize, but I must admit I am very happy to see you. My *alyah* will not let me anywhere near her; she distrusts me completely and has pulled a weapon on me three times. I am praying your appearance will calm her."

Lorn let out a low sigh. "Let us go meet your parents and soothe their fears."

Twenty minutes later, Nast helped Casey down from the luxury SUV that Cormac procured for them. On the way over, she'd called her parents from a cellphone another Kadothian man had given her to use. They'd been hysterical, and by the time she calmed them enough to listen they were pulling up to the front of her childhood home.

The well-kept Craftsman style two story house was festooned with pink and grey ribbons, her favorite colors, and a missing poster had been nailed to the telephone pole next to the driveway. Even with all that had happened to her she found herself nervous as shit at the thought of telling her parents she'd married two men. If it wasn't for the constant reassurance from Lorn and Nast flowing through their bond she would have been a shaking mess.

Roxy burst through the front door, her dark eyes filling with tears as she screamed her name. "Casey!"

Roxy sprinted across the lawn with her long black hair flying behind her as tears streamed down her face. Guilt pierced Casey's soul as Roxy totally ignored Nast and Lorn and grabbed Casey into a fierce hug. "Where have you been? Are you all right? I was so worried about you! Oh, thank God you're all right!"

Casey swallowed hard and hugged Roxy back. "What are you doing here? I thought you were still deployed over in Spain?"

Laughing, and crying, Roxy pulled back and her gaze darted behind Casey's shoulder then back again. "You disappear for two weeks and you're wondering what I'm doing here? Where the fuck have you been?"

"Casey," came her mother's voice and soon she found herself embraced by her entire family, each of them berating her for taking off and telling her how much they loved her, and how much they missed her.

Breaking from the mob of her relatives she wiped at her cheeks and quickly stepped back, grabbing her husbands' hands. "Mom, Dad, I'd like you to meet my husbands, Lorn and Nast."

Absolute silence filled the air as her family stared at her like she'd just announced she was a fairy.

Her mother was the first to break the silence. "What?"

Clearing her throat, she nodded at the house. "Can we do this inside? Alone?"

Blinking at her, Casey's dad nodded. He seemed to have aged since she last saw him, stress deepening the lines around his tired eyes and it looked like there was more silver in his hair almost overnight. "Yes, inside..." He cleared his throat. "As you can all see Casey is all right...and married...so if you could give us some privacy to talk with our daughter we would appreciate it."

Tugging Lorn and Nast after her she quickly made her way inside, nostalgia piercing her heart as she looked around the living room of the place she'd grown up, trying to memorize everyone and everything. She took a seat on the wide floral couch beneath the bay window and pulled Nast and Lorn down next to her before looking up at her family. They all stared at her and her husbands with expressions ranging from amused to pissed.

Her sister Roxy was the one who looked the most angry. Her parents just appeared relieved and confused while her mom's lips kept trying to twitch into a smile. Casey didn't see her older brother and his family, or Paige, but she didn't have the time to wait for them. She only had a few hours to spend on Earth before they had to return to the Reaping ship, and she needed to talk with her family, and reassure her friends that she was okay.

"Casey," her mother said in a soft voice, her brown eyes filling with tears, "where have you been? Who are these men? Why didn't you call us?"

"Well, Mom, I've been in Las Vegas with Lorn and Nast."

Roxy took an aggressive step forward, her hands curled into fists at her side. "Why the hell were you in Vegas? And who exactly are Lorn and Nast? And don't give me that bullshit that they're European models. Mom and dad may believe it, but I don't. I've been over there. Models don't fight like that."

Panic set in and Casey blurted out the first thing she could think of. "That wasn't fighting, that was part of an act they're going to perform in Las Vegas. They're strippers."

Lorn and Nast turned to her, and though they kept their expressions calm, shock radiated through their bond.

"Strippers?" her mother said in a faint voice while her father glared at her husbands.

"Well, kind of. More like dancers, but not the skanky kind. They're putting a show together for one of the big hotels in Las Vegas. One of those high-end shows like the Cirque de Solei. But with hot guys, for a reality TV show."

Amusement now rolled from her husbands and she had to grit her teeth to keep from elbowing them.

Lorn leaned forward and smiled at her mother, who actually blushed. "It is an honor to meet you, Mr. and Mrs. Westfall. I apologize for keeping Casey from contacting you, but it is part of the terms of our contract."

Once again it was Roxy who went on the attack. "What the fuck are you talking about?"

"Language," Casey's father said in a low voice. "But my daughter has a point, what *are* you talking about?"

"This is classified information," Lorn said in a low voice and leaned forward. "We are part of a reality television show and cannot divulge any information that may tell you who the winner of the contest may be."

Casey tried to keep the smile on her face as she glanced at Lorn. "Yes, a reality show."

"What kind of show?" Roxy asked, still suspicious but at least her fists had unclenched.

While Casey doubted her sister could actually hurt Lorn or Nast, Roxy had spent the last five years in the Army doing special ops stuff and could kick some serious ass.

Lorn smiled at her sister, once again laying on enough charm to make the other woman blush. "I cannot go into the specifics, but the men staying in our house are contestants, trying to win a spot in our new production in Las Vegas. Because of the secretive nature of the show we are not permitted to go into detail, but please be assured that the men at our home are good people who have gone through thorough background checks. But like us, they are not permitted to speak about the contest without facing enormous fines."

Her mother, a reality TV show junkie, visibly thawed and smiled at Lorn. "How exciting!"

Nast rubbed his thumb over Casey's hand. "That is why the men were evasive about where Casey was."

"Yes," Lorn continued smoothly, "the producers believed that the drama involving Casey's disappearance with Nast and myself would make for good entertainment. We had no idea how bad things had gotten here. As soon as we found out we brought Casey home so you could see she is alive and well."

Her father gave Nast a narrow eyed look. "And what about marrying Casey? Is that even real or more entertainment?"

After giving Casey a soft smile that made her mother sigh, Nast turned back to her father. "No, our love for Casey is very real."

"Both of you?" Roxy shook her head. "Is that even legal? I mean I know the world's gotten a little more liberal after 'The Event', but seriously? Two men?"

"Both of us," Lorn said, meeting her sister's disbelieving stare head on. "And she loves us as well. It is nothing to be ashamed of."

Casey gave Nast's hand a squeeze, his anger giving her the strength to face her parents. "It's true, Mom and Dad. While it may not be conventional, Lorn and Nast are my husbands. We love each other and we are a family."

"Holy shit," Roxy whispered, then snickered, then began to laugh outright. "Holy fucking shit."

"Roxy, language," her Dad said in a faint voice as he stared at Casey. "Both of them?"

"Yes, Dad. I know you may not approve, and I'm sorry, but I love them."

"But Casey, you barely know these men," her mother said while shooting her sister a glare that only made Roxy laugh harder.

Nast looked at Roxy, now slumped against the wall and howling with laughter. "Why do you find our marriage amusing?"

The hard edge of Nast's voice sobered Roxy a bit and she wiped the tears from her eyes. "No offense meant, but of all the things I thought had happened to Casey, running off to Vegas and marrying two strippers wasn't even on my radar." She abruptly sobered and stood up straight again. "Look, I don't care if Casey married ten guys as long as they treat her right. Hell, I'm living proof that even the most traditional of marriages fail so if you can make this work, more power to you. But I want you to know that if you hurt my sister I'll hunt you down and cut your dicks off."

"Roxy," her father said with a groan while burying his face in his hands.

Her sister gave Lorn and Nast a feral smile that was a challenging baring of her teeth. "I can do it, too. I'm part of a trial special ops program with the Army and I know ways to kill you in the middle of a crowded room without ever touching you."

To her surprise Lorn gave Roxy a wide smile. "Your sister is lucky to have such a brave warrior to care for her."

Roxy blinked while Casey's mother stood and smoothed her palms down her pants. She came over first to Lorn, then to Nast and gave them each a hug and a kiss on the cheek. "Welcome to the family."

When her mother went to hug Casey she stood and found herself clinging to her Mom, taking in a deep breath of her familiar perfume while fighting back tears. "Thanks, Mom."

Her mother hugged her back equally fierce. "I was so worried about you."

Stepping back, Casey dug around in her pocket and pulled out the crystal charm necklace. "It's uh, tradition in Lorn and Nast's country to give the mother of the bride a gift. We picked this out for you and I hope you'll wear it to remember me when I'm gone."

"Gone?" her father said and his gaze darted to Lorn and Nast before returning to her. "But you just got here."

It took a great deal of effort not to break down into tears, but Lorn and Nast sent her their strength and she clung to it. "We have to head back to Vegas. I'm part of the reality show now and while they gave us enough time to come here so I can talk with you, we have to head back so they can continue filming. I wish we didn't, but this show involves hundreds of people and they need to get back to work. The show is losing money waiting for us to return."

Her mom grabbed her in a hug again. "But you just got here!"

"I know, and I'm really sorry, but we can't stay. We're flying back to Vegas today on a private jet they chartered for us."

Her dad joined them and together they hugged Casey. "Are you sure you can't stay? Just for a little bit? Your brother and his family will be here soon."

"I'm sorry, Dad, I just can't. You have no idea how hard it was to bend the rules enough so I could come back and see you." She hugged them both tight. "And once I'm back in Vegas you probably won't hear from me for a bit, confidentiality clause and all of that. I'm going to stop by my house and get some things, then we have to leave."

Roxy tugged her away from her parents and grabbed her in a bone-crushing hug. Growing up Roxy had always been chubby, but the Army had given her sister an impressive set of cut muscles and her hug was strong enough to make Casey wheeze. "The minute, the absolute minute the show is wrapped up I want you to call me, got it? I'm on leave right now so I'll be staying with mom and dad for another three weeks before I have to head back. If your show wraps up before then maybe I can come visit you in Vegas and you can hook me up with one of those hotties. I could use some nice, guilt-free rebound sex."

With a laugh, Casey hugged her back while her father made a groaning noise and shook his head. "I'll see what I can do. You know you could always go visit them on your own. I'm sure they'd be more than happy to hang out with you if you get bored."

Something flashed through her sister's eyes and she blushed. "Um, maybe. I didn't really get off on the right foot with them."

Casey's mother snorted. "That's putting it mildly. She went searching for you at the old Johnson's farm."

"What did you do, Roxy?" Her sister had a temper and Casey cringed at the thought of a pissed off Roxy confronting the Kadothian men.

"Nothing." Her sister went red from her neck up to her hairline.

"Roxy..."

"Let's just say if they have that house wired with cameras I'm sure I gave them some great footage. Those guys are too hot for their own good."

Casey's father and mother moved over to Lorn and Nast, giving them the 'you better be good to my little girl' lecture.

Tilting her head, Casey examined her sister, a suspicion forming. "Anyone you find particularly hot? I can put in a good word for you."

"No." Even without being able to reader her sister's emotions

Casey could easily see the lie.

"Oh, you think one of them is sexy. Which one is he, Roxy? You can tell me. I won't say anything."

Roxy rolled her eyes. "Thanks, but I don't need my baby sister trying to hook me up with a couple strippers."

"A couple? Meaning more than one?" Hope filled Casey but she tried to keep it under control.

"I'm not saying another word." A melancholy look came over Roxy, sadness filling her brown eyes so like Casey's. "Besides, I'm not up for any kind of anything with a guy right now, let alone two amazingly hot strippers."

"Roxy, you can't let that cheating dickhead ruin the rest of your life." Casey pulled Roxy into a hug and whispered in her ear, "He wasn't the man you were supposed to marry anyway. I just know it. Look, you're going to be stuck here for the next three weeks, why not give the stripper hotties a chance to show you a good time?"

"Okay, my life has officially gotten too weird for words when my baby sister, who just married two of the yummiest guys on Earth, is giving me relationship advice. Do...do you happen to know anything about Cormac and Rastar?"

Trying to keep her excitement under control, Casey had to resist jumping up and down and clapping her hands together. Though she hated knowing that her parents might be losing two daughters, her sister deserved her Prince Charming, or in this case, Charmings. Having Roxy on Kadothia with her would make her new life so much better.

"I haven't met Rastar, but Cormac seems really nice." She remembered the armor he wore, showing he was a high-ranking officer, which according to Lorn meant he was well established with enough money to provide his Matriarch with whatever she wished. "I know that he's well off."

"If he's rich, why is he a stripper, or dancer, or whatever? I knew he was too hot to be real."

Casey tried to do damage control. "No, no. Cormac isn't a dancer. He's a martial artist. He helps train the dancers. He and Rastar. Really nice guys and if they like you, I say go for it."

"Just go for it?" Roxy asked with a husky laugh and a distant look in her eyes. "I must be out of my damn mind for even considering this."

"Look, I know it sounds crazy, maybe even feels crazy, but Roxy, I'm so very, very happy with them. Honestly. I'm so in love with my husbands that it's disgusting. There is nothing I would love more than to see you together with men like Cormac and Rastar. I mean, come on, how often do you have a chance to make the beast with two backs with two super hot and amazing men?"

"Pervert." With a laugh, Roxy pulled back but Casey didn't miss the gleam of tears in Roxy's eyes. "Your husbands look like they're ready to leave."

Casey glanced behind her and sighed. "Yeah, we gotta take off and catch our fas-er-flight out."

It took them another ten minutes of hugging and saying goodbye before Casey finally got out the front door with Lorn and Nast, then back into the SUV. To her surprise, Nast climbed into the back seat with her and pulled her close, cuddling her and stroking her until she let the tears go that she'd been holding inside. He smelled so good, felt so good, and her aching heart drank up the love he freely offered her.

Nast made a pained sound, "I am so sorry you must leave them behind, Casey. They love you very much. It hurts me that you must choose between them and us. I wish it were not so."

"I'm going to miss them," she whispered against his chest and snuggled closer. "But I don't regret my decision. I mean it, Nast, you and Lorn are my life, my everything. I can live without my family but I can't live without you."

"Oh, *alyah*," Nast said with a low groan and held her tight. "We love you so much and I promise we will do everything we can to make you happy."

"It's okay, really it is. I mean, yeah, I'm bummed out that I'll never get to see them again, but being able to say goodbye, to know that I'm leaving something behind that will help them deal with my leaving, it's the greatest gift you could have given me."

"I wish we could have stayed longer, Casey," Lorn said in a low voice from the front seat.

"Yeah, me too, but we can't leave your, I mean, our people on Kadothia alone. Someone tried to set me up and I'm afraid they might strike out against the villagers while we're gone. While my heart hurts and this sucks, I need to think about our people and how to give them the best life possible." She took a deep breath and sat up a bit. "After our honeymoon I want you to start looking for men for me to partially bond. You're right, we need loyal people around us. Obviously someone let that woman who tampered with your pleasure 'bots in, or for all we know, it was someone already working at the manor that did it. Either way someone is trying to hurt you and there is no way in hell I'm allowing that to happen."

Pride flooded into her from her men and Nast cupped her face with one hand. "I still cannot believe how lucky we are to have found you."

She softened into his touch and leaned her face against his calloused palm. "I'm the lucky one. I have two of the handsomest, bravest, most honorable men in the universe as my husbands. What more could a girl ask for?"

He grinned at her, then swopped in for a quick, hot kiss that left her panties damp. "I cannot wait to get you back to the ship so we can show you just how pleasurable having two husbands can be."

A little shiver raced down her spine and she looked to the front seat. "Hey Lorn? Drive faster."

Chapter Twenty

C asey's lips were swollen and sensitive by the time they made it back to her little home. Nast had kissed her over and over again while stroking her body, raising her arousal until Lorn had to tell them to stop so he didn't end up running off the road. As they pulled up to her house she gave the small, shabby place a good look, memorizing the details and trying to freeze this moment in her mind. When they parked, Nast practically dragged Casey out of the car and she allowed him to, laughing as he sped up the steps with her in his arms. They had an hour left down here before they were due back and Casey had wanted to share that time alone with her husbands.

Lorn followed closely behind and pointed the way to Casey's bedroom. They'd agreed earlier today that they had to have sex in Casey's room at least once, something about it being a Kadothian good luck tradition. She didn't know if that was true, but there was no way she was going to turn down a hot, hard fuck. Especially with the honeymoon surprise she and Lorn had for Nast. It was something he'd jokingly requested at one point and the naughty image had stuck with her, inspiring a number of steamy daydreams.

The moment they entered her room she gently pushed out of Nast's arms and stepped back, giving her new husband a sultry smile as she said, "Take your clothes off."

There was no doubt at the command, the dominance in her voice and Nast growled softly, just like she knew he would. Her defiance aroused him and she bit her lip as his arousal burned her. "Make me."

Casey was actually quite proud that she shielded herself well enough to not tip Nast off when Lorn slipped a pair of feather light, but extremely strong cuffs around Nast's wrists. For a moment the red haired man stared at her, then he flashed his fangs while flexing his arms. "It will take more than this to keep me from you, little Casey."

"Oh, I know." She grinned and took a step forward, lowering the strap of her dress over her shoulder and bearing the portion of her breast with his new bondmark on it. Just like Lorn had said, Nast's gaze went right to that mark and a savage satisfaction filled him, echoing in her soul and making her breath catch. "But even if I tied you up with a strand of my hair you wouldn't hurt me. I trust you

Nast, with everything that I have and everything that I cherish."

He stopped struggling, his muscles twitching with the urge to move, to break his bonds, but he fought it. She could feel his internal battle and found herself growing restless, like his agitation was infecting her. It must have done something to Lorn as well because he suddenly ripped open Nast's pants and fisted his solid cock. He placed his lips against Nast's cheek as he growled, "I, however, will hurt you and you will love it."

Nast snarled and she dropped to her knees, grasping his dick and flicking her tongue up and down the pleasure ridges of his shaft. The tension drained out of his big body and he sagged back into Lorn, a rich sound of pleasure coming from deep inside of him. "Oh, *alyah*, you have such a tiny, soft, wet mouth."

Her nipples were sensitive enough that when Lorn knelt behind her and cupped her breasts, she moaned against Nast's shaft. Feeling incredibly naughty, she leaned back and offered the head of Nast's cock to Lorn, beyond excited by the thought of watching Lorn suck Nast's dick. Licking his lips and reading her out of control desire, Lorn gave her a wink before easing forward and slowly wrapping his lips around the thick, flared crest. He slowly slid down, taking more of Nast into his mouth and throat than she could, before pulling back at an equally torturous pace. After repeating this motion three times he pulled back and released one of her breasts, using his free hand to hold Nast's erection so she could suck on it.

They traded back and forth, each of them drunk on each other's arousal. Casey was squirming in place by this point while she licked Nast's balls and Lorn jacked him off. Nast was trying his damndest to resist them, but Casey needed to come—bad—so she licked her finger and wiggled it between Nast's buttocks, playing with the tight entrance to his body. With a rough howl Nast came the moment she breached his ring of muscle, his body clenching on her finger while she continued to suck on his testicles. The echo of his orgasm slammed into her and she cried out, her body undulating with each hard muscle contraction as waves of pleasure swept through her.

Lorn held back, licking up Nast's seed where it had spilled on his hand. Her body ached even more to be filled after the glow of her release faded, her need growing stronger than before. Lorn cut Nast free, briefly steadying his new husband, before lifting Casey to her feet as if she weighed no more than a feather pillow. Her breath caught at the glint of his fangs, and when he leaned down and bit her neck hard enough to break the skin, all she could do was shudder.

"Sweet and coppery," he whispered against her skin. "The taste of your blood is an aphrodisiac to me."

"Please," she whispered, but Lorn ignored her before quickly stripping her clothes from her body.

Once she was naked the men closed in on her, their hands stroking her breasts, her arms, her belly, and even her inner thighs and ass, but not her pussy. She moaned and wiggled between them, sucking on whoever was offering her their mouth at the moment, touching as much of their physical perfection as she could. Their arousal blended together until it was like a wave of energy moving through them, the ebb and flow both bliss and torture. Her poor pussy was swollen with desire, and she really wished someone would give her some attention down there.

As if reading her mind, Lorn lay back on the bed and held his hand out. "Put me inside of you, my Matriarch."

Her legs could barely hold her as all of the blood in her body seemed to rush to her sex and nipples. Nast had to help her mount Lorn, holding her husband's cock in order to slide her down on it. He easily held her weight with one arm, teasing both her and Lorn by barely allowing any penetration. She was about ready to scratch his eyes out when he finally stopped his torment and let her sink blissfully down onto Lorn.

A twinge of pain went through her, blending with the pleasure as she took her handsome blond husband all the way to the base of his dick. He filled her completely and, when Nast began to play with her rear entrance, she gulped. Oh no. They wouldn't both want her...at the same time would they? Sure they'd hinted about it before, but it had to be physically impossible.

She tensed up and Nast murmured, "Why are you afraid?"

"You're too big," she blurted. "No way I can take both of you."

"Yes, you can," Nast purred. "I'm rubbing a special gel into your sweet pink bottom right now that will allow you to stretch without pain or tearing. I will not say there will be no pain, but the pleasure will be great."

Her reply was lost as her new husband eased one finger into her, then another, stroking her body in a way that felt at once weird and good. The more she relaxed, the better it felt, until she was trying to push back as he attempted to fit three fingers in her. The sensation of pain began to creep in and she screwed her eyes shut, trying to get her body to accept the intrusion.

Lorn made a soft, humming sound and began to gently lick her nipples, his cock throbbing inside of her while his desire flowed through her, chasing the pain away and giving her only pleasure. With a soft sigh her body relaxed and allowed Nast to fill and stretch her, moving his fingers around and pressing a slick gel deep inside of her. She could feel it when Nast would stroke Lorn's cock through the thin barrier between her pussy and ass, and the delicious arousal that came with his touch had her trying to move. She needed them to fuck her, to take her, to fill her with their scent and seed. She wanted them to own her in the most primitive way possible.

Nast's fingers left her and she made a disappointed noise that quickly turned to a moan of pleasure as Lorn began to move in her. The hard nub of her clit pressed against his well muscled abdomen and she rocked into him, wanting this feeling of belonging, of being loved, of being cherished and worshiped to never stop. When Nast's bare body pressed up behind her she arched her back and whispered, "Please, Nast, take me."

"Easy, *alyah*, even with the gel we must go slow."

He wasn't lying.

The moment the fat head of his cock pressed against her small rear entrance she tensed and both men groaned.

"Don't fight him," Lorn whispered. "Let him in. When you fight him you are provoking his lust."

She went limp against Lorn, allowing him to sweep her hair to the side and caress her back while Nast held her buttocks open and pressed his rock solid erection against her bottom. A small shriek escaped as he began to press in, but he wasn't letting her squirm away, and neither was Lorn. They held her pinned between them while she was being slowly impaled, pain shooting through only to be met by the roaring arousal from Nast as he took her back there, and from Lorn as he filled her pussy. She was stuffed full of dick, nothing but a doll between them as they totally possessed her.

Once both men were fully in she twitched and they all groaned, her slightest move sending off a chain reaction of pleasure. Turning her head, she began to nibble on Lorn's nipple, giving him little stinging bites while shifting her hips slowly, getting used to them being inside of her. Each man hovered on the edge of orgasm, her submission driving them wild. She abandoned Lorn's nipple and met his lips for a soft, amazingly decadent kiss while Nast slowly began to slide in and out of her.

In this position, she didn't have to do anything, just allow them to move her as they wished, to use her body, to do anything they wanted with it. The freedom of surrendering to them was staggering, and the strength of their emotions overwhelmed her until she realized she was crying. It wasn't long before Nast was fucking her harder, tearing screams from her and grunts from Lorn. Each thrust pushed them closer to the edge until Casey finally broke, crying out against Lorn's neck while Nast ground into her as deep as he could get, hurting her yet making it all better at the same moment. Her orgasm went incandescent, colors flashing before her eyes as her soul rang with happiness, Lorn and Nast's spirits blending with hers and reassuring her on every level that she was loved.

They had been lying there for what could have been an hour or ten minutes, naked and cuddling together, kissing each other and sighing with happiness, when the front door slammed open and a familiar voice screamed, "Casey!"

Alarm came from her husbands but the only emotion she felt was embarrassment at the sound of Paige's voice coming closer. She tried to draw the sheet over them, but it was trapped beneath the men. Before they could move Paige threw the door open.

"Where the hell have you..."

Staring at them with huge eyes, Paige's mouth opened and closed a couple times as Casey tried to cover herself and the men lounged indolently giving Paige a show Casey was sure her friend would never forget. When Paige made no move to say anything or even blink, she cleared her throat, "Mind turning around so my husbands and I can get dressed?"

"Husbands?" Paige whispered, her face going pale.

A man's gravelly voice came from the vicinity of the front door, "Paige? Where are you? Are you hurt? I feel so much distress from you."

Lorn and Nast suddenly scrambled for their clothing, exchanging a glance and saying at the same time, "Commander Trenzent."

Paige jumped as if goosed, and a moment later, a huge, older Kadothian man with scars on his face moved up behind Paige before stepping around front and kneeling in front of Casey's friend. He had short-cropped black hair threaded with silver and a very big, very solid body that made it look like he would crush Paige if he touched her. The scary man slowly raised his hand and touched two of his fingers to Paige's cheek, drawing her shocked gaze to him.

"*Alyah*, I told you they needed privacy."

With a quiver in her voice Paige said, "I'm sorry...I was worried about you."

Still nude, Casey clutched at her sheet, finally covering herself. "Well, as you can see I'm okay. I already went to see my parents and I didn't think I needed to lock the door."

Paige blinked rapidly, her blue eyes slightly red rimmed. "I'm sorry, Casey. I was so worried about you."

Feeling like a bitch for not considering how upset Paige must have been over Casey's disappearance, she gave Paige a warm smile.

"I'm so sorry for worrying you, sweetheart. But I promise you I'm extremely satisfied and happy."

Paige blushed and ducked her head a bit, turning her face toward the man who was still caressing her cheek. It astonished Casey to see Paige turn to the stranger for comfort, but she recognized the look of utter worship on the man's face. If they weren't bondmates Casey would eat her shoe. She only wondered if this man had a blood brother and what he was like. Of all the Kadothian men that Paige could have ended up with, Casey was surprised that it ended up being the battered war hero. Her friend was so soft, so gentle, so peaceful that she had a hard time imagining her married to a man who spent most of his life submerged in violence.

Paige dragged her eyes away from the man kneeling before her with a worried expression, she looked at Casey with a faint hint of pink on her cheeks. "He said you were fine, and I wanted to trust him, but I had to know. I'm so sorry, Tren, I had to know."

Ignoring everyone but the blushing girl standing before him, Trenzent said in a rumbling voice, "You owe me for doubting me, Paige. You promised you would not do it again."

Turning her attention back to the big, scarred man, Paige tilted her head to the side in a gesture Casey would have almost thought of as flirtatious. Her friend looked through lowered lashes at the man stroking his fingers down her throat. "I suppose you want to collect your prize now."

Even Casey could see the instant tension filling Commander Trenzent as he seemed to go into predator mode. "I do, but not here."

He stood and scooped Paige up into his arms. Instead of screaming and freaking out, Paige merely smiled at him and wrapped her arms around his neck. "This doesn't mean I'm going to kiss you."

"We will see about that," Commander Trenzent murmured as he carried Paige away from them, leaving behind a stunned audience.

Finally gathering a breath, Casey said, "Was that the scary guy with the metal face? The one who saved your life, Nast?"

"Yep," Lorn said and visibly shook himself. "I can't believe Commander Trenzent's bondmate is that sweet, shy little female. If he breathes on her wrong he will break her"

"Oh, I don't know," Casey murmured. "Paige is a lot stronger than she looks."

Tucking her hair back behind her ear, Lorn smiled at her. "Most women are."

Nast began to laugh softly. "May the Lord of Life bless him with a long and happy union. He's deserves it."

Jumping onto the bed with Casey, Lorn gave her a very thorough kiss. "Come, my wife. We must leave and spend a day on the Reaping ship updating the Scouts on the change in our cover story before returning to Kadothia."

Excitement filled her, and when Nast joined them on the bed, she smiled at them both. "Thank you."

"For what?" Nast asked in surprise.

"For loving me, for saving me, for giving me more than I ever thought was possible."

"Thank you," Lorn whispered while he kissed her neck. "For loving us, for saving us, for giving us more than we ever thought was possible. Our *alyah*."

"Our *alyah*," Nast repeated in a reverent tone.

Giving herself over to her husbands, Casey closed her eyes and lost herself in the touch of her eternal beloveds.

The End

Coming Next in the Bondmates Universe:

Paige or Roxy? You decide. Tell Ann in a review and see who find their HEA next!

A Thank you from Fated Desires

Thank you so much for reading **Casey's Warriors**! Ann Mayburn sure knows how to write sexy, sci fi menage. We do hope if you liked this, that you would please leave a review from where you purchased this or on another platform. Not only does a review spread the word to other readers, they let us know if you'd like to see more stories like this from us. Ann loves to hear from readers and talks to them when she can. You can reach her through her website and through her Facebook and Twitter accounts. You guys are the reason we get to do what we do and we thank you.

If you are looking for more stories like these, you don't have to wait much longer! She will write book two soon and in your review if you tell us which heroine—Paige or Roxy—you'd like to read next, that will get the ball rolling! Ann is cooking up new works in this series and a few others. Also, we have a few new authors coming that will be sure to whet your appetite.

If you'd like to know more about Fated Desires, check out our website or email us at admin@FatedDesires.com.

You can always find out more about the upcoming titles from Fated Desires by signing up for our MAILING LIST.

Also, join our Fated Desires Book Club to interact with our authors.

About the Author

With over thirty published books, Ann is Queen of the Castle to her wonderful husband and three sons in the mountains of West Virginia. In her past lives she's been an Import Broker, a Communications Specialist, a US Navy Civilian Contractor, a Bartender/Waitress, and an actor at the Michigan Renaissance Festival. She also spent a summer touring with the Grateful Dead-though she will deny to her children that it ever happened.

From a young age she's been fascinated by myths and fairytales, and the romance that was often the center of the story. As Ann grew older and her hormones kicked in, she discovered trashy romance novels. Great at first, but she soon grew tired of the endless stories with a big wonderful emotional buildup to really short and crappy sex. Never a big fan of purple prose, throbbing spears of fleshy pleasure and wet honey pots make her giggle, she sought out books that gave the sex scenes in the story just as much detail and plot as everything else-without using cringe worthy euphemisms. This led her to the wonderful world of Erotic Romance, and she's never looked back.

Now Ann spends her days trying to tune out cartoons playing in the background to get into her 'sexy space' and has accepted that her Muse has a severe case of ADD.

Ann loves to talk with her fans, as long as they realize she's weird and that sarcasm doesn't translate well via text.

Also from this Author

Now Available

Submissive's Wish
Ivan's Captive Submissive
Dimitri's Forbidden Submissive

The Chosen
Cursed
Blessed
Dreamer

Bondmates
Casey's Warriors

Coming Soon

Iron Horse MC
Exquisite Trouble

Bondmates
TBA

Other Titles
The Dark Fates Anthology

Did you enjoy this selection? Why not try another romance from Fated Desires?

From Ann Mayburn's series The Chosen

DREAMER

Chapter One

Waiting to be greeted and admitted by a Novice, Shan Harrison shuffled in line at the Temple of Aphrodite in downtown Washington, D.C. Daisy, her best friend, was completing her training as a Priestess and had asked Shan to come visit. She'd rather have spent the day in her studio working on a new jewelry commission, but Daisy had sounded desperate on the phone.

A girl standing in line behind Shan whispered to her friend in a snarky tone, "Is she wearing her Halloween costume? Did I miss the email we were supposed to wear costumes today?"

Her friend told her to shut up, and Shan pretended not to notice. It seemed like because she was a short Asian girl people expected her to dress up in pastel froofy dresses and giggle a lot. The fact that she loved gothic clothes and elaborate makeup just didn't mesh with preconceived notions, so people stared. She had long ago perfected her sneer of disdain and a list of cutting remarks that embarrassed even the most ignorant people, but she just ignored the crowd while she stood in line. The last thing she wanted to do was piss off Aphrodite and have her sex life cursed any more than it already was.

Maybe she had gone a bit overboard with her 1940s pinup girl look today, but she had just broken up with the latest in a string of controlling asshole boyfriends and needed the pick-me-up she got from looking nice. Or at least she thought she looked nice. Her ex-would hate her outfit and makeup. At first he'd seemed to like her style, but slowly he'd begun to manipulate her into dressing how he wanted. When she resisted, they had horrible fights, but when she gave in, he was so nice to her that it was hard to remember what a douche he could be. In an effort to please him, she had pretended to be someone she wasn't. The final straw came when he demanded she remove the blue streaks in her long black hair and get a French manicure before he would introduce her to his parents. After that she'd finally dumped him and a day or two of crying later she realized she was a lot happier without him.

To celebrate her independence, she had dressed to please herself, picking out a vintage Dior black polka dot dress with a full skirt and shiny black patent leather belt. Thigh-high black patent leather boots disappeared beneath the knee-length hem of the skirt. In an extra little bit of *"fuck you"* to her ex, she had added a cobalt blue patent leather choker that matched the streaks in her waist-length black hair. She'd also gone heavy on her eye makeup, accenting her exotic eyes with dark eyeliner and wearing bright red lipstick.

The crowd murmured as the line moved forward. Aphrodite's Temple was always a popular stop in the Greek Temple District. Everyone wanted to have a good love life, and gods knew she could use the help. Her choice in men seemed to be going from bad to worse. The elderly man in front of her received his blessing to enter the temple, and the Novice guarding the entrance turned to her with a smile.

"Good afternoon, Shan," the bronze-haired novice said in a pleasant voice. Her white tunic emphasized her breasts and a wide leather belt around her waist made the tunic flare around her hips in a pleasing manner. Shan was amused to see the tips of the novice's pink sneakers peeking out from beneath the robe.

"Hi, Alyssa. I'm here to see Daisy."

"She's waiting for you in the Reflection Room." Alyssa gently took her hand, turning her wrist and admiring the skull and crossbones charm bracelet. "Did you make this?"

Shan grinned. "Yep. On Saturday I'll be selling my jewelry at the Egyptian Temple Bazaar. If you want, I can bring one with me."

Someone behind them cleared their throat, and Alyssa blushed. "Thanks." Closing her eyes, she took Shan's hand, put it over her chest, and said the ritual words. "Welcome to the Temple of Aphrodite. Enter with an open heart."

Shan shivered as the incantation worked its magic and allowed her to step through the heavy wards that guarded the inner sanctuary of the temple.

Her boot heels clicked on the cream marble floors as she walked the familiar path to the Reflection Room. Daisy's mother was the High Priestess of the temple and Shan had spent a great deal of time here while she was growing up. While she wasn't drawn to Aphrodite's worship, the temple still filled her with a mellow peace. It was impossible to be surrounded by this much divine energy and not absorb some into your soul.

The doors leading to the Reflection Room opened with a smooth hiss, and she couldn't help but smile at the sight on the other side—Daisy reclined on a mound of oversized pillows at the other end of the room like an ancient Greek sculpture come to life. A long and shallow pool of clear blue water shimmered in the sunlight coming through the clear glass ceiling. Potted plants grew thick and lush between alabaster statues of couples in erotic poses.

Shan shut the door behind her and hurried across the room. Despite her tough and put-together exterior, her heart was easily wounded and her latest ex had left his mark. She needed the unconditional love of her best friend, and a good bitch-fest about what a loser he was and how better off she was without him. A conversation they seemed to be having with disturbing regularity. She pushed these thoughts out of her mind and forced a smile as she reached the spread of pillows.

"Hello, sweetheart." Daisy rose and pulled her into a hug. Tall and thin, Daisy would have fit on the cover of any fashion magazine if it wasn't for her long blonde dreadlocks and the sparkling diamond of her beauty mark piercing above her upper lip. She wore a white robe that hung off one slender tattooed shoulder, secured with a simple bronze pin. When Daisy achieved full status as a Priestess, she would get to wear a silver seashell broach in the pin's place. "You look amazing. Love those boots, very fierce."

Shan kissed her cheek, careful not to smear lipstick on her friend. "Hey, sugar. What's so important that you had me drag myself out of bed before noon?" As an artist, Shan had the luxury of making her own work hours. Not that her life was easy. She pushed herself hard and rarely took a day off.

Shan took a seat on a fuchsia pillow across from Daisy then let out a long sigh as the peace of the temple sank into her soul. She had always loved this room. Outside, it was the middle of October and the leaves were changing. In this magical space, summer reigned eternal.

Taking a deep breath, Daisy looked her in the eyes and squared her shoulders. "I'm staging an intervention before you commit emotional and sexual suicide."

It took a few seconds for her words to get through to Shan's stunned brain. "You're what?"

Smoothing her hands on her robe, Daisy took on the serene look that Shan thought of as her "Priestess face". As a favorite of her goddess, Daisy had a deeper connection to Aphrodite than the average worshiper, and the goddess often used the stunning blonde to bring love to those who needed it most. "Aphrodite wants me to help you find yourself." Daisy's blue eyes sparkled as she added,

"And I want you to stop dating arrogant, narcissistic, controlling, self-centered, overbear—"

Shan put her hand over Daisy's mouth. Great, she'd been hoping for Aphrodite's help, but this was a little much. Her parents' warning about being careful what you prayed for made her grimace. "I know I've made some bad relationship choices, but—"

Daisy removed Shan's hand and smiled gently. Something other than Daisy, *more* than Daisy, looked out from her bright blue eyes as she said in an unexpectedly lyrical voice, "Shan, stop lying to yourself. Embrace who you are, and wonderful things will happen."

Divine energy moved through the air like a perfumed breeze, and Shan hugged her knees to her chest. "I know who I am."

Daisy considered her. "Would you like to know what I see when I look at you, Shan?"

"No." She hadn't seen this coming and felt trapped. One of the last things she wanted to do was piss off a goddess, bad things always happened when someone did that. The sound of Daisy's chuckle raised the hair on her arms. It caressed over her body and sped her heartbeat. Power, as rich and warm as melted butter, rolled over her.

"I see a woman who craves dominance but is afraid to surrender herself to a worthy master. I see a woman who fights who she is and mistakes submission for weakness. I see a woman who deserves the love she needs but is afraid to ask for it. What you need to ask yourself is; How do I want to live my life? What's important to me? Who loves me? Is it some man you hide the dark side of your passion with? Or will you admit to yourself that you like spice with your sex, it's no big deal, and you'll be with some hung like a bull man, blissfully happy in the kind of relationship that will always challenge her with someone she trusts with everything she has."

Shan's breath left her body in a rush, and a tear trailed down her cheek as her hidden needs were brought into the light by the gentle touch of a Goddess. Denying her dark needs, those forbidden and perverted desires she hated herself for craving, was less than useless. Good girls didn't want their boyfriends to hit them. Nice girls didn't masturbate to BDSM erotica. Her parents had raised her to be a strong woman, to take pride in who she was, and to never, ever, let a man abuse her in any way

As these thoughts raced through her mind, Daisy watched her without judgment, only compassion so immense Shan had trouble meeting her gaze. She lay open, exposed to the core, before a hint of the divine.

"There is no shame in your desires. It is who you are."

"I don't want to be like this," Shan said angrily and dashed away her tears. "I wish I could make love like normal people, but I can't orgasm without pain"—her voice dropped to a whisper as she confessed her darkest secret—"without being owned. It's like I was born to be a victim."

Daisy smiled and patted her hand. That touch soothed Shan and chased back the shame with understanding and endless love. The touch of someone communing with a goddess was a small reflection of being in the presence of the divine, and Shan's heart lightened, some of the sorrow from her breakup easing, leaving her feeling remarkably clear headed. "You're only a victim if you allow yourself to be. You can be strong and fierce to the outside world, but submissive and cherished in the security of your relationship. Submissive doesn't mean weak."

Shan clenched her hands into fists as she struggled to keep her frustration under control. "I've tried that! I'm so sick of either being with a nice guy and faking orgasms because I'm afraid to let him know what I need or putting up with an asshole because he gives me what I want." Her anger drained away as Aphrodite's power soothed her and she took a deep, shivery breath as she struggled to control her rage. She'd always had a bit of a temper and it got worse when she was stressed. If thinking about her love life wasn't stressful, she didn't know what was.

"Look, the pretending? It never works. Any guy who gives me what I require in the bedroom tries to run my life or turns out to be an abusive douche bag."

"That's because you choose unworthy men." Shan couldn't argue with that, so she kept her mouth shut and watched the sun shimmer off the water. "You need to find the right Dominant. One who will love your fierce spirit and cherish it instead of trying to break you."

Shan crossed her arms and looked back to Daisy. "Yeah, 'cause guys like that exist outside of books." She flushed and closed her eyes, taking a deep breath. "I'm sorry, that was rude of me. I really do want your help. It's just...hard."

"I understand more than you know, Shan." Daisy ran her knuckles over Shan's cheek and gave her a gentle smile that warmed Shan from the top of her head to the tips of her toes. "You don't have to do this alone. Let me help."

She would have to be a fool to turn down an offer like that, even if asking for help from anyone made her feel weak. "I'll do my best."

A bit of Daisy surfaced through the sparkling energy in her eyes. It was odd, like watching an ocean of power drain from her pretty blue eyes until only Daisy's joyful spirit shone through. "Besides, I'm tired of having to sit through endless rounds of drinking wine and watching '80s movies every time you break up."

"You love *Pretty in Pink!*"

"I loved it the first five times I watched it. Not the twenty times after that."

Sighing, Shan played with her hair. "It's a classic." Daisy raised an eyebrow and waited for Shan to stop avoiding the issue. "So how do I find the right Mas—guy?"

An odd sense of the pressure in the air lessening around her made her body feel lighter somehow and the power that had filled the room slowly drained away like water pouring from a glass. Shan couldn't help but let a small sigh of relief escape. While having the attention of a goddess was wonderful, it was also terrifying. One wrong word and Aphrodite could have smite her, though considering how bad her love life was, she couldn't imagine it getting much worse. Knock on wood and all of that.

"I'm going to help you find a Top," Daisy said in a peppy voice that broke Shan out of her morose daydreaming like a slap in the face.

"You're what?"

"I'm going to help you get comfortable with your submissive side." Daisy practically vibrated with excitement. "I'm not naturally dominant enough to be a true Mistress, but I can teach you about BDSM and help you until you find the right Dominant. I'll give you what you need in order to relax and take your time finding the perfect Dom, inside and outside of the bedroom." Daisy grabbed her hands and gave her puppy dog eyes. "Please, Shan. I've been researching it, and I apprenticed with a fantastic Mistress."

Shan jerked her hands away and said through clenched teeth, "How long have you been planning this?"

Daisy avoided her eyes and looked at the wall behind Shan while toying with the clasp on her gown. "My mother—"

"You told your mother about this! Your mom knows I want to be spanked while I have sex?" Shan buried her face in her hands. "How the hell am I supposed to ever look at Nina again knowing that she thinks I'm a pervert?"

Daisy snorted. "Shan, I hate to break this to you, but my mom is the High Priestess of a Sex Goddess. Being a submissive doesn't even come close to being perverted. Besides, it's not like we discussed your crappy sex life in detail." She ignored Shan's glare and gave her a hopeful smile. "You're...you're my, ah, final test for making full Priestess."

Shan narrowed her eyes and crossed her arms again. "I'm your what?"

Daisy held her hands out in a pleading gesture. "Well, I'm supposed to help you find love. Erin... you remember Erin, right? You met her at the harvest party my mom threw last month, beautiful blonde with the body of a porn star and the face of an angel? Anyway, Erin said if I can't help my best friend find love then I need to spend more time learning how to recognize love in all of its forms, to help those who have a hard time seeing it. If I fail at this, it'll be another ten years before I can try again. I don't want to push you—you're like my sister, and I love you to death—but I really *really* think I can help you."

The uncertainty in Daisy's hopeful voice broke down Shan's last barrier. If it had been just about her, she could try to get out of this. But it was about Daisy now, and she couldn't crush her friend's dreams because of her own fears. She'd been raised with Daisy and they were as close as sisters. Crap, she had to do this for her friend. Bring on the embarrassment of Daisy's matchmaking.

"Fine," Shan snapped and sat up straight. "How do we begin?"

Daisy grabbed her in a hug and gave her a big loud kiss on the cheek. "Excellent! Oh, you won't regret this, Shan. I have it all worked out, and I've set up the perfect place to begin your training and get you used to the BDSM community. It's called the Steel Chalice, and it's an elite BDSM club."

"What?" Shan said in a faint voice. She'd imagined some kind of blind date or maybe a shopping trip to a fetish store first, not an elite BDSM club, whatever the hell that was.

Daisy snickered. "For you, it's best that I take you to a safe place where you can see the different styles of the D/s relationship. You need to see some established relationships and experienced Dominants. I thought about watching some BDSM porn with you, the instructional kind, but that just seemed kinda...weird. I think we'd both end up making fun of the movie, and that wouldn't help you at all."

"I don't know...that's a little scary." She hated admitting her fear, her weakness, but this was Daisy. She hadn't judged Shan when she went through her unfortunate Hello Kitty phase, and she wouldn't judge her now. "And I don't know how I feel about random strangers knowing about my...needs. I mean I'm a private person about my love life, I don't like to even kiss a guy in public let alone let them do stuff to me in a freaking club. And what if they see me on the street and recognize me? That would be too weird."

Crossing her legs, Daisy leaned closer. "I've thought of that too, well, not grocery store molestation, but protecting your identity. I got these awesome masks for us to wear. They're leather and custom-made. A lot of people in the club wear masks and all kinds of awesome outfits. Some even make their own, real pieces of art."

A flicker of real interest surfaced. "What color are the masks?" She had an extensive collection of leather and latex dresses, not to mention a drawer full of corsets that she wore to the clubs. Mentally flipping through her clothing, she tried to decide what to wear.

Daisy tossed one of her dreadlocks over her shoulder. "Shan, you're going to love this place. No one will judge you for your needs, and you will adore all the effort people put into creating a scene. It's really almost like a theater performance...with orgasms."

Excitement, worry, and anticipation flooded her body with a heady mixture of adrenaline. She took a deep breath and prayed that she was making the right choice.

****

Devon King crossed his heavily muscled arms over his black-leather-clad chest and examined the submissives offering themselves for the evening. Men and women wearing everything from suits with strategically cut out breast and crotch panels to nothing but skin covered in glittering body paint huddled together like a bunch of nervous rabbits. There were mostly women standing around, but also few unattached male submissives who darted glances at the section of the club where the single Doms tended to hold court.

Behind the unattached subs, a club Sentinel carefully kept watch over the main floor. Part of the appeal of this private club was the knowledge that safe, sane, and consensual was strictly enforced. It didn't hurt that most of the Doms were part of various Temple Guards, trained for battle and possessing the instinct to protect. From his seat on the black leather couch, he counted at least two dozen male and female guards roaming the room.

Toward the back of the small group of men and women, a stunning brunette caught his eye then sank to her knees with a pleading look. Thin, dressed in a see-through cream sheath, she arched her back and mouthed the word, "please." Biting back a sigh, he shook his head and purposefully looked away from her, signaling his disinterest in dominating her tonight.

Her name was Maria, and he had played with her once, weeks ago, and now she seemed fixated on him. Gods knew why. He wouldn't hurt and debase her like she wanted, and her attempts to top from the bottom totally turned him off. With a bitter twist of his

270

mouth, he remembered the way she had lied about what she wanted and tried to goad him into really beating her. So much of the D/s relationship was built on trust, even during the casual encounters at the club. No matter how beautiful and willing, her dishonesty was a total turn-off and he kept his distance from her.

His best friend, Malik, adjusted the leather mask he was wearing and equally ignored Maria and her silent pleading. Unlike Devon's solid black mask, Malik's had traces of gold that gleamed against his dark brown skin. Big and solid, the men filled the couch they shared. Though the club was crowded, no one sat near them, and a circle of masterless submissives whispered and admired them from across the room.

"I thought Maria got kicked out for causing that fight between Master Greg and Master Dane," Malik muttered as he scanned the crowd.

"Ben let her back in. From what he said, she recently got away from a fucked-up Master who put her in the hospital. Said her head is all messed up and she needs the good influence and safety of the club before she goes out and finds another abusive asshole. You know Ben. Show him a wounded sub, and he wants to make it all better."

Malik grunted a laugh and shook his head. "That girl is nothing but trouble. I've watched her play the baby Doms, bending them around her little finger and making them jump through hoops."

Shrugging, Devon minutely relaxed as he watched Maria pair off with an older sadist and head for the playroom downstairs. Despite the small amount of pity he felt for her, he was glad she wouldn't be following him around tonight. Something burned in his blood, and he felt an eager sense of anticipation he hadn't experienced in years. Almost as though he was waiting for something wonderful to happen. Snorting at his own foolishness, he cracked his knuckles for the third time in less than ten minutes.

Malik carefully scanned the floor. "What are you in the mood for tonight?"

Shrugging his broad shoulders, Devon ran a hand over his tight brush cut. He tried to keep his words light, but his tension crept through. "Something soft."

Malik grinned, his teeth a flash of white in the subdued lighting of the Steel Chalice. "The need is riding you hard tonight, isn't it?"

Instead of answering, Devon nodded. His gaze locked on a full-figured submissive with short red hair and skin as pale as cream. Her nice full hips would be a pleasure to grip. She noticed him watching her and dropped her gaze to the ground, toying with the ends of her fringed black dress.

"Being the Chosen of a War God isn't easy," Devon admitted and continued to watch the submissive. He drank in the hesitant way she edged across the floor toward him, the fear and anticipation coming off her in waves.

"Especially when you're already an arrogant prick." Malik turned his attention to the submissive who paused at the end of the stairs that led to where they were sitting. His voice dropped an octave. "The need to dominate, to own and possess, can become overwhelming."

Making up her mind, the submissive went to her knees and began to crawl up the steps toward them. Both men took a deep breath of her scent and sighed in disappointment.

"Human." Devon breathed out. "A little gold mist in her aura. I'm going to guess she's a Priestess of Zeus."

Malik leaned forward, his attention on the doorway. "What I wouldn't give to find an unattached submissive Chosen." He rolled his shoulders beneath his black leather shirt and cracked his neck. "All the good ones are taken. What I wouldn't give to find a single, hot submissive Chosen tonight. I need to let out some tension with a woman who can take it."

Guess I'm not the only one being ridden hard by the need tonight, Devon thought in amusement as he watched his friend. Malik was a Chosen of the Nubian War God, Apedemak, and he was the Captain of the Nubian Temple Guard like Devon was Captain of the Egyptian Temple Guard. They had been friends for over twenty years and were like brothers. "I know," Devon murmured in a cold voice and tried to push back the dull pain created by Malik's words.

Malik glanced back at him with an apologetic twist to his lips. "Sorry, Devon. I didn't mean—"

"It's okay." Devon glanced at him. "My mother knew the price she would pay when she married my mortal father." Even though his mother, a Chosen of Isis, was thirty years older than his father, she looked like a woman in her prime while his father's fragile mortal body was showing the wear and tear of his ninety-two years.

Watching her suffer through his father's slow slide into death had made Devon determined to take another Chosen as his mate. Too bad only about two percent of the world's population had what it took to be a Chosen, and of that two percent, only a fraction were actually picked by a god or goddess as their personal hand on Earth. Oh, and he couldn't be with another war diety Chosen. That relationship would be doomed from the start, two people determined to win. No, he needed someone belonging to a softer, gentler god or goddess. And, he had to like them. He really didn't like many people. That cut down his odds of finding a Chosen who could soothe his need to dominate and crave his rough brand of pleasure down to one-in-a-million odds.

"Do you want to share her?" Devon asked in a voice too low for the human to hear. She stopped three paces before them and knelt. Thighs spread, head held high with her eyes lowered to the ground, she knew what she was doing. Devon felt a slight twinge of disappointment. While he enjoyed the pleasures of a well-trained slave, he preferred to do the training himself. There was nothing like helping a woman discover the overwhelming satisfaction of true submission for the first time.

Standing with a long stretch, Malik grinned at Devon. "No, you and I are both too close to the edge. Our territorial instincts would get triggered, and we'd end up fighting and getting kicked out of the club." Unhooking the flogger from his belt, he twirled it in the air. "I'm going to see what lovelies are offering themselves on the lower level. I'm in the mood for a pain slut tonight."

The noise of the club faded into the background as Devon slowly rose into the hyper-reality of his Top space. Every nuance, every detail of the lovely sub before him became magnified. His world focused on the woman before him and how far he could push her for their mutual pleasure.

"Come," he said and watched the beat of her pulse increase beneath the pale skin of her neck.

She crawled toward him and looked up for permission with her lips hovering over his black motorcycle boot. Judging her need and desires, he nodded and felt the flow of energy from her as she kissed his boot. Though the soft press of her lips should not have registered through the heavy leather, in his magically heightened state, he could feel the warm press of her human aura against him. The favor of her god added a little extra zing to her energy but nothing like the psychic punch of another Chosen. What he wouldn't give to feel that connection just once. He'd heard that when two Chosen had sex their auras merged, and it was amazing.

Closing his eyes, he forced his wandering mind to focus only on the woman before him. She deserved his total attention, and he needed her total submission. When she pulled away, a trail of her tangerine aura trailed from her lips to his boot.

As his attention narrowed, he scanned the club one more time out of habit. With his focus narrowed entirely on the woman kneeling before him the building could blow up, and it wouldn't have broken his concentration. It was a dangerous state for both him and the object of his desire, so he valued the safety and security of the Steel Chalice.

The building was magically warded and guarded so the servants of Creation could seek their release here without having to fear an attack by the agents of Destruction. And, right now, he needed that release like he required air. The last few weeks had been filled with one emergency after another and he hadn't had the chance to take some time for himself. Now he was restless with the craving to lose himself in a submissive's pleasure.

"What do you need?" he asked, needing to set up the ground rules for their scene.

"I desire heavy bondage and light whipping." Her tone was matter of fact, and he appreciated that she knew what she wanted. He wasn't in the mood for playing twenty questions to drag the answers he needed out of a sub.

"What is off-limits?"

"No excessive humiliation. No blood, burning, or wet play. No marks that can be seen in public."

Leaning toward her, he watched her aura reach out to him, straining to bring him closer. "What's your name?" he asked in a soft whisper.

"Kelly." Her voice lowered to match his, easily giving herself to his control as her pale blue eyes flickered from his lips to his chest and down to his pelvis before flying back up to his face.

"Do you want to play with me, Kelly?" She was so soft and feminine and he loved full-figured women.

"Yes, sir." The surrender and anticipation in those two words stiffened his cock.

"Your safe word is 'ice.' Once you use it, all play will stop, and we will be done. If you think something may be on the edge of what you can handle, say 'cold', and we may or may not discuss it."

"My safe word is 'ice.' Thank you, sir." Her nipples hardened to peaks, and her hips shifted as she clenched her thighs together.

Standing, he tried to shrug off a twinge of disappointment. He felt as though

6792629R00163

Printed in Great Britain
by Amazon.co.uk, Ltd.,
Marston Gate.